Praise for *The Most Famous Girl in the World*

"Reading *The Most Famous Girl in the World* is like riding a roller coaster through the dark. Iman Hariri-Kia takes readers on a thrilling, fast-paced adventure, where you know the twists are coming but you're not sure when they'll happen or what they'll entail. Iman's sophomore novel is incredibly fun and deliciously chaotic. I loved it and couldn't put it down!"

—Carley Fortune, #1 *New York Times* bestselling author of *Every Summer After* and *Meet Me at the Lake*

"No one's voice sparkles with camp and au courant humor like Iman Hariri-Kia's. Combined with this gasp-inducing, galloping plot centering on female celebrity obsession, Hariri-Kia has penned a thrilling romp you'll down in just a couple of scrumptious sittings."

—Amanda Montell, author of *The Age of Magical Overthinking* and *Cultish*

"Clever, cutting, and completely unputdownable. *The Most Famous Girl in the World* is awash with humor, authenticity, and a dash of heat—all with a unique edge. Hariri-Kia's voice is the sharpest [illegible]

[illegible] *USA Today* bestselling [illegible]or of *Done and Dusted*

"With her distinctive voice, Iman Hariri-Kia has forged a zany, explosive romp skewering our cultural obsession with celebrities, influencers, and scammers. It's a fun and fast-paced read with two memorable antiheroines."

—Caitlin Barasch,
author of *A Novel Obsession*

"If you found yourself all the way down the Anna Delvey rabbit hole like I did, then *The Most Famous Girl in the World* is the perfect book for you. There's such a relatable bite to Iman Hariri-Kia's voice, a surprising vulnerability in her guarded characters, and a clever construction to this game of cat and mouse that will leave you guessing. I was completely immersed in the world of this book!"

—Alicia Thompson, *USA Today* bestselling
author of *Love in the Time of Serial Killers*

"In *The Most Famous Girl in the World*, Iman Hariri-Kia has crafted a thrilling, laugh-out-loud triumph. Hariri-Kia's central mystery is masterfully twisty, and its charismatic enemies-to-lovers romance is sweepingly sexy, but where this novel shines brightest is in its biting voice, narrated by the singular, sarcastic, and sensational heroine Rose Aslani. I was hooked from the first page of this whip-smart and fast-paced exploration of the stories we tell—about those we admire, those we loathe, and those who dare to hold a mirror back up to ourselves. This is a novel I couldn't put down. Hariri-Kia has cemented herself as an auto-buy author for me, and after that last chapter...I need a sequel!"

—Becky Chalsen,
author of *Kismet*

"A nonstop-entertaining romp that cheekily skewers internet culture's mindless glorification of convicts-turned-influencers, *The Most Famous Girl in the World* sparkles with wit, camp, thrills, and romance. Written in an addictively fun voice brimming with authenticity, I had a criminally good time reading this book."

—Nicolas DiDomizio,
author of *Nearlywed*

"A hilarious, self-aware, page-turner of a novel that expertly combines playful satire with a thoughtful rumination on societal obsession with celebrities. Rose is a gloriously unhinged heroine, and it's devilishly entertaining to watch her try to expose the world's latest celebrity obsession for who she really is—no matter what the cost."

—Shauna Robinson, author of
The Banned Bookshop of Maggie Banks

"A gripping satire of our society's obsession with fame."

—KJ Micciche,
author of *The Book Proposal*

"On the surface, *The Most Famous Girl in the World* is a highly thrilling, propulsive cat-and-mouse-style mystery. But at its core, it's a devilishly funny journey through the Scammer Industrial Complex—written with the authority, chronic online-ness, and IYKYK knowledge that only digital media veteran, and keen social observer, Iman Hariri-Kia can provide."

—Samantha Leach,
author of *The Elissas*

"In *The Most Famous Girl in the World*, Iman Hariri-Kia creates a story so addicting yet so unexpected, readers won't be able to put it down. You will oscillate from laughing out loud to hanging on the edge of every word and will wish for more of Hariri-Kia's dynamic storytelling when you reach the final page. From the first page, Hariri-Kia's sophomore novel enthralled me with her nuanced, complex characters and page-turning action. *The Most Famous Girl in the World* should serve as a masterclass on captivating world-building, clever plot points, and whip-smart humor."

—Eli Rallo, author of
I Didn't Know I Needed This

"Outrageously fun but also sharp and clear-eyed, *The Most Famous Girl in the World* is the perfect novel for our scammer-obsessed age. Iman Hariri-Kia has given readers an unapologetic satire filled with surprising humor and heart."

—Laura Hankin, author of
The Daydreams and *One-Star Romance*

"Whip-smart and laugh-out-loud funny, *The Most Famous Girl in the World* had me flying through its pages for so many reasons. This genre-bending novel will make you swoon, cackle, and gasp all at once, blending sweet (and silly!) romantic moments with razor-sharp social commentary and thriller-worthy twists. If you've ever found yourself eyeballs-deep down a rabbit hole about modern scammer culture (and let's be honest, who among us hasn't?), this is the book for you. I inhaled it."

—Genevieve Wheeler,
author of *Adelaide*

"Precise and sharp as hell, Iman Hariri-Kia's voice is a blast to read. *The Most Famous Girl in the World* commanded my attention from the first page and never loosened up its grip. Hot, funny, and satirical, I couldn't ask for more from this singular story."

—Tarah DeWitt, author of
Funny Feelings and *Savor It*

"Addictive and hilarious, *The Most Famous Girl in the World* holds up a mirror to our own questionable obsessions and asks us if we can ever really know who we're giving a platform to. Also, really really hot sex. Follow, like, fuck, subscribe."

—Haley Jakobson, author of *Old Enough*,
a *New York Times* Editor's Choice

The MOST FAMOUS GIRL in the WORLD

The MOST FAMOUS GIRL in the WORLD

IMAN HARIRI-KIA

Cover design by Emily Mahon
Cover image © CSA Images/Getty Images
Internal design by Laura Boren/Sourcebooks
Internal illustrations by Diane Cunningham/Sourcebooks

Published by Sourcebooks Landmark, an imprint of Sourcebooks
P.O. Box 4410, Naperville, Illinois 60567-4410
(630) 961-3900
sourcebooks.com

Cataloging-in-Publication Data is on file with the Library of Congress.

Printed and bound in Canada.
MBP 10 9 8 7 6 5 4 3 2 1

For Willa and Mel.
Behind every Strong Female
Protagonist™ is a group chat.
I'm so lucky you're mine.

And for my grandmother.
This one is longer and has more bad
words. I miss you. I'm sorry.

Content Warning

The Most Famous Girl in the World is an ode to modern celebrity culture, mass conspiracy, bandwagon-jumping, and our ability to see the best in the worst people—and vice versa. In order to examine these complex topics, this novel includes mentions of substance use disorder, mental illness, and suicidal ideation. I worked with sensitivity readers and copy editors in order to ensure that these subjects were attended to with the utmost care. It is my hope that between the lines of levity, the questions at the heart of this text will be treated with nuance and introspection. Thank you, as always, for being here.

"I don't believe in the glorification of murder, but
I do believe in the empowerment of women."

—LADY GAGA

Author's Note

Everything inside these pages is utterly, irrevocably,
and without a shadow of a doubt, 100 percent true.
Trust me. I was there.
Although, between you and me,
I might have had a drink.
Or five.

—ROSE ASLANI

Chapter One

When I learn that Poppy Hastings (née Watts) is being released from prison, I'm in the middle of getting my asshole waxed. I know, I know—that sounds like something a person would make up for the sake of telling a good story, but in this case, it's actually what happened.

You see, sometimes the truth is stranger than fiction. And reality really can write itself better than any great American novel.

That's one of the reasons I became a journalist in the first place.

Eighteen months have dragged by since Poppy was locked up at Albion Correctional Facility in upstate New York, a mere six-hour drive from the city. (You *could* say it's been eighteen months since I helped put her there. But that's neither here nor there.)

She was convicted by a unanimous jury and sentenced to five years, which I had expected to move as slowly as an East Coast winter. But the snow melted, Punxsutawney Phil saw his stupid shadow, and now spring has fucking sprung—three and half years too early.

My group chat blows up first, just like it always does. Multiple texts from my work friends turned real, best, should-we-take-a-blood-oath friends set my screen on fire. Steph (short for Estefania, but don't you dare call her that) and Fern have heard the news, and now the texts come flooding in like intrusive thoughts.

Omg. They're letting her out.

They're actually letting Poppy out early.

Rose. Are you there? This is not a drill.

911. Poppy Hastings is being released from prison.

Stop messing with me, I write back. I just went off Zoloft, you heartless wench.

I roll my eyes.

Just last week, Fern tried to convince me that she was getting back with an ex who used to *exclusively* sport fingerless gloves, just to see me sweat. It's this harmless little thing we do, my friends and I. We call it pranking. Others call it lying.

It's a game, but one we play only with each other.

Then I get the Apple News alert.

A notification pops onto my screen from *The New York Dweller*, the parent publication I work for, and I swear to god, the remaining hairs in my anus stand up fucking straight. I physically recoil as I process what I'm reading.

"Stop moving," my aesthetician, Sherry, commands.

She's standing behind my wide-spread legs, peering into

the crevice between my butt cheeks, attempting to continue the wax. Not that anyone other than Sherry will be staring down into the depths of my asshole any time soon. Ever since Zain left, the only thing in my apartment that's gotten even remotely close to fingered is Roommate's god-awful violin. I don't even know why I keep waxing. Probably because hair sprouts from every orifice of my body like I'm a walking, talking botanical garden. Or maybe because I'm a sadist. Sick in the head.

Perhaps a bit of both.

Most likely, I'm just trying to feel something—anything—other than chronic anger.

"Fuck," I say to Sherry. She gives me a scolding look of death. "I'm sorry."

She's a Slovenian woman in her late fifties with broad shoulders, bright red cheeks, and a thick, syrupy accent. When Sherry asks you to do something, you do it. I both admire and fear the living daylights out of that woman.

"No cursing." Sherry frowns like her job depends on it.

"Shit, okay," I say. "Oh no, I did it again. Fuck!"

Yeah. Sherry doesn't like me very much.

POPPY HASTINGS IS BEING RELEASED FROM PRISON.

The headline plays on a loop in my head. It reverberates between my eardrums as I leave my appointment and begin the five-minute trek back to my apartment. I attempt to nudge away the words swimming around my frontal cortex the way I would evade an older relative trying to kiss me on the cheek.

But they just bounce back with a grin, eager to tease and taunt me. My body is still stinging from the wax, so I place my phone in my pocket as I walk—a big journalist no-no. Heaven forbid I miss a breaking news notification. It's no use, though. Even without the push notifications, Poppy's name still gyrates around in my head. Goddammit.

Poppy.

Poppy Hastings.

Poppy Hastings is being released.

This is not happening to me.

I breathe in through my nose, out through my mouth, then try to remain present by focusing entirely on my surroundings.

A smoke shop with the door cracked open; a bodega cat without a collar peering in up and down the street with suspicion.

A mom-and-pop restaurant—simply called Fried Chicken—that sells only fried chicken.

A band of white boys dressed in tiny caps and cuffed jeans, parodying around as locals while their parents pay the rent on their newly renovated one-bedroom flexes.

Gentrification began flirting with Clinton Hill about two years before I moved here, which probably means I'm part of the problem. But I still like to shift the blame elsewhere. Partly because I'm the daughter of Iranian immigrants and was basically raised with a chip on my shoulder. And partly because I'm on the Gen Z–Millennial cusp. Pointing fingers and pouting are our favorite hobbies.

When I was a child, my classmates' parents were hesitant to set their kids up on playdates with me. I don't remember this, but my mother mentioned it once offhand, and it stuck with me in the way that small moments sometimes do when you're little and still making sense of the world. I don't know why I'm sharing this with you. You're not my therapist. (That's Julee. And she fired me last month. Did you know therapists could fire their clients? I sure didn't.)

I'm also pretty much always a tiny bit broke. As a journalist, even a "successful" one—an illusion, by the way—you grow accustomed to being underpaid. You're taught to be grateful for opportunities, to kiss the feet of those who came before you just for inviting you into the room. To wipe the asses of giant corporations as the board of trustees grows richer and your bank account begins to leak.

I'm a cynic.

Not that I can think of anything less original than being cynical in Brooklyn.

My apartment is a fifth-floor walk-up in a tentatively beautiful rent-controlled old brownstone that hasn't been renovated in at least a half a century. My street is quiet, like a suburban cul-de-sac without all the friendly faces. But I do prefer my neighborhood, at the very least, to Gramercy, where I commute every day for work. Across the bridge, the noise is incessant, the air polluted, and casual, god-awful acquaintances lurk around every corner. Given the choice of being anonymous in Brooklyn or visible in Manhattan, *always* pick the former.

Especially if it's all you can afford.

The radiator whistles its usual greeting as I walk through the front door. I immediately turn it off and open a window, allowing that April breeze to smack some sense into me.

"Hello?"

My voice reverberates through the small space, echoing back to me.

Roommate is sprawled out on our crusty green love seat, her boyfriend perched between her legs on the floor, eating ramen.

Oh, and they're both butt-ass naked.

Sigh.

Roommate is Romanian. (I think? She has a heavy accent.) The two met while microdosing mushrooms at a guided sound bath last year and have been attached at the pierced navel ever since. Based on their attire—or lack thereof—I can tell they weren't expecting me back so soon. When I'm home, they usually spend the majority of their time locked in their room, playing a Bartók violin concerto (badly) and crocheting pants.

The apartment belonged to me first. Roommate moved in after Zain moved out.

I was desperate; she was homeless. It was a match made in literal hell.

When I was still living in Ohio, I found an ad for this place on Craigslist. This was before I met Steph and Fern. I knew virtually no one in New York. Well, except for a few kids from J-school. But I had enough sense to know that I'd be better off licking a subway seat than inhabiting five hundred square feet with them. By the time I finally saw the place in person, I was screwed. The apartment looked much larger and much better maintained in the pictures.

It was, to be blunt, a shithole.

The bathtub had a red grime snaking its way up the drain; all of the last tenant's dishes were piled up in the sink, waiting to be hand-washed; the largest window faced a brick wall, blocking out most of the daylight. But I'd already signed the lease and couldn't afford to live in some four-story palace in Park Slope or whatever the fuck. At least the place has its charms. Prehistoric crown moldings on the ceiling that I was too oblivious to appreciate until Zain pointed them out. The scuffs that decorate the hardwood floor in meaningful, albeit vague, patterns. A disco ball that lives on a small Lucite coffee table, which Roommate stole at a rave in Bushwick from a girl who "smelled like fish."

I never moved out. Roommate moved in.

So here we are. Coexisting.

"I thought we talked about nudity in the common areas."

Roommate vaguely looks up, boredom in her eyes, and gives me a nod of acknowledgment. I toss her a blanket from the bin by the door, and she drapes it over her torso like a shawl.

Well, I tried.

I kick off my New Balances—which remind me of my elderly grandfather, but everyone at work insists they're cool, and I know fuck all about being cool—and lie down on the floor. My mind is still racing, and rest feels urgent. The wood is cool against my cheek, if a little sticky.

"What's wrong with her?" Boyfriend whispers a little too loudly.

"Who knows?" Roommate doesn't bother lowering her voice. Instead she throws a noodle at me, watching me flinch. "What's wrong with you?"

I haven't checked my phone in about twenty minutes, but I feel it buzzing against my abdomen. This means one of two things: Steph and Fern think I've jumped in front of the G train, or I've missed another breaking news alert.

Probably both.

Right now, I couldn't care less. Next to today's top headline, everything else feels meaningless.

"Poppy Hastings is being released from prison," I announce.

"Ah." Roommate makes a knowing hissing sound. "You're having breakdown."

"Looks like it."

She stands up, grabbing her keys and coat.

"You stay. I buy vodka."

She's not a *bad* roommate.

And it doesn't take a genius to see that I'm stewing in a mess of my own making.

Because in many ways, I created Poppy Hastings, and she created me.

Chapter Two

Before Poppy, I was just an associate reporter at the Shred, the digital arm of the newspaper *The New York Dweller.* (We're mostly known for our quippy headlines, which are meant to incite visceral reactions. You know, like the little internet terrorists we are.) It was a job I had basically landed out of luck. Back when I'd been a lowly freelancer, a practically unemployed graduate from The Ohio State University, a few essays I'd published on Medium had gone semiviral. They were all about growing up first-generation Iranian and therefore didn't count as real writing. Exploitation of one's identity, I've come to realize, is truly the cheapest form of clickbait. But what can I say? The industry is addicted to trauma porn, and the next thing I knew, I'd tricked the Shred into giving me an interview. I had manipulated everyone into believing I was legit enough to be a real journalist.

A true villain origin story.

But entry-level writing wasn't all it was cracked up to be. The job was essentially to pen speculative garbage about internet memes, whatever news Twitter deemed important, and pointless celebrity feuds—and all for minimum wage. I intensely resented being the greenest employee on staff. At meetings, I was given the least amount of time possible to pitch my ideas. Editors assigned me the stories that nobody else wanted to write. I was the Breaking News Bitch: always on call, social life nonexistent. And while I enjoyed any excuse to get out of date night with Zain, the topics I covered ranged from vapid to mundane. By the end, I knew so much about astrological compatibility that I repulsed myself. I spent my evenings fantasizing about reporting features, touching myself to thoughts of investigative journalism instead of ethical porn.

Then one morning, some higher power or simulation nerd sent me my golden ticket.

There it was: just sitting, unassuming, in my inbox.

An anonymous tip had come in overnight from an encrypted email. The source had written only one sentence, but the message was addressed directly to me.

Not the Shred.

Not my editor.

Me.

Poppy Hastings isn't who she says she is.

Until that very moment, I had never heard of Poppy Hastings. My life had been gloriously Poppy-free. But I got to googling. It didn't take long for photos to start popping up in all the society pages, from Getty Images to Patrick McMullan.

Slowly, I began to piece her together.

She was an English socialite who lived in New York City with houses in the South of France, the Hamptons, and fuck knows where else. Poppy was presumably from old money, and she was involved with a plethora of charitable organizations. From the looks of it, she never missed a benefit. There were photos of her cutting the ribbon to a new Mount Sinai hospital wing on the arm of the ambassador to Kuwait, others of her laughing at the Gabrielle's Angel Foundation's masked gala, clinking glasses with the CEO of Unicycle, a flashy exercise start-up. But her role at each event was opaque or never mentioned. Poppy herself was the face of coded luxury. She managed to fly somewhat under the radar, which isn't rare for people with large sums of money. When you have so much wealth that you no longer feel the weight of your riches, talking about your socioeconomic status is considered déclassé.

Nevertheless, she appeared to be rubbing her elbows raw with some of the richest and most powerful people in the world.

But what on earth was their connection?

According to my research, Poppy had been silently working the circuit for almost a decade. But before her debut, there was zero record of her existence. Unlike her lack of philanthropic credibility, this made no sense. Someone who presumably had ties to British aristocracy would surely have her French-tipped little fingerprints all over an age-old lineage's archives—or at the very least have left a record of where she attended private school. But Poppy appeared to have popped out of her mother's vagine as a fully formed woman in her late twenties with a bottomless bank account and a tight-lipped smile.

That deliciously smug, silently judging, tight-lipped smile.

My anonymous source was right.

Something wasn't adding up.

So I took a risk. I hadn't yet brought up my little research project to my editor at the Shred, mostly because I knew that she'd a) tell me to stop wasting my time or b) give the story to a more senior reporter. This was my big break, and I couldn't allow myself to get scooped by the culture-vultures. No, it was time to stop playing by the book.

I was ready to get my hands dirty.

Using my *NYD* email address, I began reaching out to some of the people Poppy had been photographed with, asking for a comment on a fake upcoming article. A nobody in the journo world, I fully expected never to hear back from any of them. And for the most part, I was right; many of the players I contacted never responded. Others agreed to speak with me only off the record or solely on background. A few declined my request but referred me to friends of friends—and that was how I landed my first jackpot interview.

I quickly learned that the circles of the 1 percent are minuscule; as soon as one influential source agreed to speak with me, the rest followed suit. And they weren't just willing to talk.

They were anxious to find out what I knew.

I soon learned that no one really had a comprehensive idea of who Poppy Hastings was, where she came from, or what she did for a living. One of my sources believed her to be a distant relative of the queen; another had heard through the grapevine that her family had invented transition lenses. Not one seemed able to recall how they'd met her, either; she always just appeared to be *waiting* wherever the rest of the horde went. Poppy attended every gallery opening, evening at the opera, and high-profile tennis match with some dashing and atrociously wealthy suitor who waited on her hand and foot.

The way her peers described her, Poppy Hastings wasn't just beautiful—she was iridescent. Witty, outrageously fun, and free-spirited, Poppy was that woman in the circuit who was always suggesting her comrades kick the party up a notch. The fundraiser for children with cleft palates in the Galápagos sure was lovely, but know what would be even lovelier? Flying to the island itself and conducting an expedition—for research, of course. Did the chocolate fountain at the fete make you shit yourself with nostalgia for the Trevi? Then why not jet off to Rome at sunrise? There were few plans you couldn't change, planes you couldn't charter, for the right opportunity or impulsive excursion. Poppy Hastings was known for three things: her infectious spontaneity, the row of gold-plated teeth she supposedly had lodged in the back of her mouth, and helping her dear friends invest in high-risk, high-reward opportunities.

The kinds that didn't get listed in the yellow pages, if you know what I mean.

But none of her investments ever came to fruition. Not that many people cared, or even realized the money was missing until they sat down to talk to me. When you're that well off, who notices a measly million here or there?

And that's precisely what Poppy was counting on.

After almost two years (639 days, but who's counting?) of pre-reporting, dead ends, no-show interviews, creepy internet meet-ups with foot fetishists, and failed attempts to piece the puzzle together, plus one blackout bus ride to Saratoga Springs, all the while quietly doing my actual job with my head held down, I finally stepped back.

And I saw the full picture, the real Poppy Hastings in all her grandeur and glory.

The woman was just another high-end scam artist.

Born in Hastings, England, one of the poorest areas in all of Britain, Poppy Watts had been orphaned at the age of five.

She'd stayed at an institution for another five years, then been adopted at the age of ten. After her adoption, she'd disappeared for another decade, then reemerged in London's high society at the ripe old age of twenty, draped in designer threads, sporting tastefully enhanced tits, and clutching the fattest Rolodex in town. I couldn't figure out where she'd gone or how she'd come into so much money, but she'd spent the next seven years quietly subsidizing her lifestyle by creating fleeting friendships and convincing her fair-weather companions to invest in non-existent business ventures, then pocketing the cash.

A girl boss if I ever saw one.

But how did Poppy Hastings get away with running what was essentially a one-woman MLM?

Here's the brilliant part: by hiding in plain sight.

Most grifters identify their mark, make their play, then move on before anyone is the wiser. Not Poppy. She never ran from her victims; she bought them another round. How could a woman so charming, so charitable, so motherfucking *rich*, have no real money of her own? Poppy knew no one would wonder long enough to actually out her. She was using their own egocentrism against them, banking on the fact that they were mostly thinking about themselves.

And they always, always were.

At this point, I knew what I had was big, and I was ready to bring it to my editor, Cat. Here's what you need to know about Cat: when she meets you, she will immediately assume that you're an idiot. It's on *you* to convince her otherwise. I had yet to break through Cat's impenetrable veneer but was determined to gain her respect.

As I ran through my outline, my findings, I watched her lips twitch upward slightly into a smile, and the vein in her forehead popped. She was pissed, sure. But she was also impressed. She instructed me never to do anything so stupid without her permission ever again and also to start writing as soon as humanly possible.

Feeling proud for the first time since joining the Shred, I happily obliged.

I typed furiously on my *NYD* loaner laptop. The words couldn't escape my fingers fast enough. Instead of fantasizing about having my way with feature writing, I was finally fucking it. I was about to make my first real wave as a journalist.

And then Brad Zarbos was found murdered in his goose-feather bed.

Chapter Three

Here's the first rule of conspiracy: Cable news can give you the headlines, but the truth is hidden somewhere in between the lines.

Twitter. Reddit. Tumblr. Twitch. The deep, dark web.

The news may belong to the people who report it, but theorists?

They live in the shadows.

Still, as a journalist, cable is nonnegotiable. When I was first starting out, I ate peanut butter and jelly sandwiches for days on end, savoring each bite of crust as if it were fucking caviar. But I *did* find the money (by going into debt) for network television, and I'll tell you why. As a reporter, I like to have the news on in the background 24-7. And then there are live events like sports games, awards shows, even the Olympics. The shit you have to stop, drop, and cover. But food with nutritional value? Now, *that* can be overlooked.

Settling onto the love seat—the one still stained with Roommate's bodily fluids—I crack open a lukewarm Heineken using a pair of Tweezerman scissors, then pick up the remote and cautiously turn on the TV.

It only takes a minute of channel surfing to find it: live footage of news anchors camped outside of Albion Correctional Facility, microphones at the ready, waiting for Poppy to be released. I suck in my cheeks and take a strained sip from my beer, choking on the carbonation. One of the broadcasters announces that Poppy is being let out early for good behavior—not, as I've been quietly speculating, because she's been pardoned by the president (a rumor that has been circulating for quite some time).

Good behavior.

What a joke.

She probably did what she does best: charmed the guards with lingering flirtation and the forbidden promise of bottomless pools of cold hard cash. Before they knew it, the staff was a bunch of turncoats.

I bet she manipulated her way out of Albion just like she manipulated Brad Zarbos.

Roommate throws the door open and rushes in, spewing curses I can't decipher. She's carrying a bottle of cheap vodka under one arm and what appears to be a stuffed caterpillar under the other. I assume the latter is for her. She heads straight for the cabinets and rummages through what's left of our clean glasses, which isn't much, finally settling on a brown WORLD'S BEST DAD mug. She fills the mug with enough distilled rubbing alcohol to kill a small cat and hands it to me. Then she plops down on the floor cradling the bottle, taking a big swig as if it's water.

"Drink," she commands, her tattooed eyebrows dancing in a way that makes her look like a cartoon villain.

I shudder, then oblige.

The liquid feels smooth until it burns my throat, and I

gag at the flavor. Roommate's eyes are glued to me. Once I've successfully swallowed, I go in for seconds. She nods, satisfied, then sets her sights on the TV.

"You're going to stay and watch?"

I'm surprised. Roommate doesn't usually take a huge interest in the news. She prefers Animal Planet, especially the segments on bee pollination.

Fucking weirdo.

She just shrugs and takes another sip from the bottle.

I settle back into my misery.

Buzz.

BUZZ.

I look up, annoyed, seeking out the source of the incessant vibrating sound humming in my ear, only to discover that it's Roommate's phone. Her face is hidden behind her screen as she texts furiously with characters I can't make sense of. Her phone is quite literally ringing off the hook.

Hm.

Maybe Boyfriend messaged her from the other room that he found another position in the Kama Sutra that he wants to try. That or he's actually worried about my well-being. His concern would explain why Roommate is suddenly dead set on babysitting me. And why she keeps glancing between her notifications and the TV.

I raise my mug to my lips, only to feel the ceramic clang against my teeth, almost chipping one.

It's empty.

Already.

A wave of nausea hits me, and I shake my head ever so slightly, trying to convince myself not to fucking panic.

Shit.

I haven't been this out of sorts since...well. Since the incident.

The last time Poppy Hastings ruined my entire fucking life.

Come on, Rose. You're better than this. Remember your breathing exercises. In for four. Hold for seven. Out for eight. What was it your therapist always used to say? Accountability is not just about what you do, but also what you don't do?

Actually, screw that bitch. She dumped me!

Instead of pouring another drink, I reach for my bottle of Adderall, the last prescription Julee wrote me before giving me the *it's not me, it's you* speech. The little miracle pill snags in the back of my throat, bringing on a bout of clarity.

I look down at the mug of diluted nail polish remover in my hand and the pills on the table and feel my breath shorten.

This can't happen again. I won't let it.

Poppy's presence can't trigger this kind of cataclysmic reaction in my bloodstream. I refuse to fall apart. The parental blocks Steph and Fern placed on my Google Chrome account will keep me from arguing with Reddit trolls. My Headspace notifications will keep me alert and present in the moment. Plus, I have people in my life now. Like Roommate. Who apparently gives enough of a fuck to sit with me and stake out Poppy Hastings's penitentiary walk of shame.

I turn my attention back to the TV.

The crowd outside of Albion begins to clear.

I finish my beer and turn up the volume.

And Poppy Hastings appears like an apparition.

Her blond hair has turned dishwater brown, her golden highlights grown out past her shoulders. There's a brand-new scar above her left eyelid and a suspicious bruise on her chin. At the sound of her name, she breaks out into a toothy grin, revealing three gold caps lodged in the back of her mouth.

"Ms. Hastings, what will you do now?"

"Actually, dear, I'm newly out of a job."

The press laughs in unison.

"Anyone hiring?"

More laughter.

"Poppy, are you planning on dating again?"

"The only man I have room for in my life is my parole officer." Her eyes dance across the horde. "And honey, he's not even worth half a mil!"

The reporter chortles into her tape recorder.

I've had a year and a half to put this all behind me. After Zain left, I forced myself to stop wallowing. I meditated, manifested, and even attempted to seduce a shaman in Hoboken named Shiv, who claimed to be a new-age prophet. I went out dancing with Steph and Fern and allowed myself to get blackout drunk, stumble home, and gorge on Chinese food until I threw up in Roommate's bed and blamed it on the dog. (We don't have a dog.)

Little by little, I started getting better.

I was so close to leaving Poppy Hastings in my past.

Now she's back to taunting me in the present.

"Poppy, is it true that your life rights are the hottest four-way auction in Hollywood right now?"

I vaguely recognize the reporter from *The New York Dweller* newsroom.

He's one of ours. Traitor.

But Poppy looks past him and directly into the camera lens.

"Now, where did you get that tasty bit of information?"

A familiar chill runs down my spine.

She throws her head back as laughs, exactly as Brad Zarbos described.

Chapter Four

Brad fucking Zarbos.

At thirty-seven years old, Brad Zarbos was already worth several billion dollars. He was the founder of Rainforest, a start-up turned conglomerate that functioned mainly as a wholesale site for small businesses that handled overnight shipping and returns. On paper, Zarbos was a wunderkind—one of the most cutthroat entrepreneurs in his age-group and the latest success story hot off the presses of Silicon Valley. He had everything you could ever want: a chesty wife with a trust fund, a virtually nonexistent tax bracket, and all of his hair. But he was also a professional nerd, the kind of man you could tell had been stuffed in a locker one too many times in high school, to the point that it had begun to cut off the flow of oxygen to his brain.

Above all else, Brad Zarbos was known to get off on being right.

And the man was rarely wrong.

Brad Zarbos and I secretly met face-to-face a month into my pre-reporting. He was my first source, a friend of a friend who was willing to speak with me on the record, albeit anonymously. He hadn't reached out to me directly. A contact of his had arranged a meeting at a remote diner off I-95 called the Mansion at seven a.m. sharp.

I liked him immediately.

As it turned out, Brad Zarbos could speak with authority on any given topic. The efficiency of a nationally run monorail system. March Madness brackets and hedging bets. He even had an informed opinion on who would win the latest season of *The Bachelorette*. When he spoke, he spoke with ease, cocking one eyebrow. After we settled into our conversational groove and ordered another pot of French roast, I brought up Poppy Hastings.

The second her name escaped my lips, Zarbos lost his composure. A smirk remained on his face, but the corner of his lips twitched. His posture stiffened.

"Ah, Ms. Hastings." He struggled to steady the tremor in his voice. "We met in 2015 for the first time. We attend the same parties, know the same people. She's...easy to talk to."

"What do you mean, easy?"

"Well, you know. Easy." He looked up at the ceiling. "A lot of people in my line of work, they size each other up right off the bat. Only chat up folks who they think will benefit them somehow in the long run. But when Pop speaks to you, she looks right through you, into your soul. It's her gift, really. She makes you feel like you're the only person in the room who matters. And she has this incredible laugh. She throws her head back, and the most amazing sound comes out. That laugh could bring a smile to anyone's face."

Pop.

He had called her Pop.

My gut told me, even then, that Brad Zarbos and Poppy Hastings were more than two old friends who knew the same people.

"She's never tried to pressure me into anything. She's kind. Selfless, even. Just last month, she helped me bid on a 1950 Cheval-Blanc. She knows I'm an avid collector and was able to get me in at the very last moment. I know she pulled a lot of strings to make that happen. All because she knew what it would mean to me. She's thoughtful."

What a schmuck.

"And do you remember how you paid for that bottle, Mr. Zarbos?"

"It's Brad." He sounded out every letter. "And I believe I wrote her a check."

"Have you received that bottle yet, Brad?"

Zarbos's forehead creased. "No, I can't say I have."

I could tell he was offended by what I was implying.

I looked up at him then with pity.

Not because he was a baby billionaire but because he was an unhappily married man, clearly lovestruck by a grifter, a woman who went out of her way to source his favorite wine and cackled every time he cracked a joke.

Had they ever acted on their flirtation? It was unclear. But Poppy had clearly played one of the most powerful men in America like a finely tuned fiddle.

She was a wolf in sheep's clothing, circling the herd with stars in her eyes.

I was in an all-hands staff meeting when the Shred's news editor announced that Zarbos had been found facedown in his Calabasas home, his skin blue as the Pacific, his eyes wide open like an American Girl doll. The coroner's report came in overnight, revealing that the man had been suffocated with his own down pillows, taking his very last breath in the silk sheets of his own king bed.

It was all so beautifully tragic—poetic, even.

At the end of the day, Zarbos's own prosperity was used to drain the life out of him.

The police ruled his case a homicide, which drove the media into a frenzy. His wife was the primary suspect, of course. But there was just one problem: She had been out of the country, sunbathing in Cabo with her Kappa Kappa Gamma sisters. So the investigation widened. Our team was on high alert. Associates were told to prep the story in case it broke overnight. Even though I was in the newsroom, sitting in on those meetings, no one on staff bothered to ask me who I thought the killer was, which was ironic.

Because I knew.

Deep down, I was certain that Brad Zarbos had been murdered by Poppy Hastings.

But it was just a conspiracy theory, a feeling deep down in my gut. Plus, my hands were tied. I couldn't reveal Zarbos as a source. I had promised the man anonymity, and I wasn't about to betray his position postmortem.

I was riddled with guilt and unsure who to tell or what to do next. Should I go to the police? Hire a private investigator? Defer to my editor in chief? There was no way around it: I was in way, way over my head. I mean, I suspected a dead man of having an affair so secret that nobody could corroborate it but me.

I began obsessing. Acting volatile. Fern and Steph even told me they were worried about me, and I reacted by shutting them out. I was determined to do right by Zarbos. I was going to find proof that Poppy Hastings wasn't just a white-collar criminal.

She was a cold-blooded killer.

Then, out of nowhere, two Russian mobsters were arrested and charged with Zarbos's death.

They were running an illegal gambling and prostitution ring right out of Brighton Beach, but their names were unfamiliar to me. Both men had criminal records—for battery and assault, for possession of a deadly weapon, for more crimes I dare not repeat. Per the police report, which I scoured after the arrest, Zarbos had a gambling problem. He owed the Russian Mafia half his fortune. They had come to collect, and when he hadn't paid up, they'd decided to cash in on his life.

The Russians had the means. They had the motive.

All the pieces fell into place.

Well, all but one.

Steph and Fern expected me to be happy about this new development.

They caught the guys!

It wasn't Poppy.

You can let it go now.

And I tried my hardest to listen. I really did. My facial muscles ached from fake smiling. But something still felt off. I didn't want to upset my friends further, so I kept investigating Poppy's connection to Brad Zarbos in private. I worked at night after I got home from the office, researching manically until the sun rose. I assured myself that I'd find something, anything, to tie the two of them together. I'd feel better when my article came out and Poppy was finally exposed. Then everyone—my friends, my family, the editorial team, the internet—would see her as I did.

Not as a "delightful creature," but as a delinquent.

And she'd be held accountable.

Punished.

But then the worst thing imaginable happened.

I got scooped—by the FBI.

On October 17, 2022, Poppy Hastings was arrested for embezzlement and fraud.

When I first found out, I couldn't breathe. It felt like someone had stolen my voice just as I'd opened my mouth to sing. I didn't even *know* that the FBI had been investigating her. I had naively believed that I'd be able to break the story in my own time, to control the narrative. But the red carpet had been pulled out from beneath me, and there was no going back.

A few hours after Poppy's arrest, Cat forced me to prematurely publish my story. She demanded that I use the arrest as a news peg before the trial stole what was left of our thunder.

But it wasn't ready. No, I wasn't ready.

I hadn't been able to identify a concrete link between Poppy and Brad or any sort of signal that the Russians had been set up. That it was all connected somehow. And I owed it to Brad to see that through. To expose her—not just for fraud, but for murder.

But none of that mattered.

The story flew off my screen and into the ether, and I lost what little control I had left.

And it blew up overnight.

That article I'd written about Poppy set me on fire. I was forged but also burned in the process.

"The Most Famous Girl In The World!" became the number-one story—not just site-wide, but *NYD*-wide—for six months straight. My name and Poppy's name trended on Twitter. My inbox overflowed with hate mail, interview requests, and follow-up questions.

I had done it. I was officially a prestigious journalist.

My professional life was transforming before my very eyes.

And I wanted to scream into the fucking void.

Why? Because the moment I clicked publish on that story, it wasn't just my life that changed forever. Poppy's did, too.

Yep, that's right.

In my attempt to expose her, I had accidentally done something much, much worse.

I had turned Poppy Hastings into a star.

Poppy Hastings was an overnight sensation. Readers adored her outlandish demeanor and quick witticisms. Her origin story resonated with them; they even went so far as to praise her for taking from the rich and giving to...well, herself. The media positioned her as a Robin Hood–esque vigilante in red lipstick with a black card and the self-serving attitude of a reality star. The internet crowned her a scammer queen, a girl boss, a she-ro, making memes plastered with her face and selling merch. A petition began circulating for her release, garnering more than a million signatures before she had even been sentenced. Her fans, who called themselves Poppers (fml), wrote pages of fanfic and devoted Instagram stan accounts to tracking her every move. Barstool even reached out to her attorney and inquired whether she'd consider hosting a podcast from prison.

Confirmed psychopath.

Secret killer.

And people couldn't care less.

It didn't matter what she had done. It didn't matter what she was capable of doing.

Poppy Hastings wasn't just infamous but *famous*.

My article hadn't painted her as a felon; I had accidentally turned her into an influencer.

The day of her televised trial, Poppy Hastings opted to wear a hot-pink pantsuit. She paused during her testimony to wink at the cameras, and I felt something inside me snap.

I'd created a monster.

The Shred rewarded me with a promotion accompanied by a generous raise. But I felt nothing. My editor expected me to write another hit, but instead of buckling down, I choked. None of my pieces performed well because, quite frankly, I didn't care to put in the work. I was so angry.

Angry at the FBI for making its arrest.

Angry at myself for being unable to catch a killer.

Angry at my audience for seeing humanity in horror.

But mostly, I was angry at Poppy.

For existing. For being born.

And so, in the aftermath, at the height of my career?

I had a complete fucking meltdown.

When she finally got carted off to Albion, my loved ones exhaled a sigh of relief. But I grew even more neurotically obsessed—with Poppy's guilt, with Poppy's fame, with *Poppy*. At first, I chose to fill the gaping void in my life with bitterness and booze, but that quickly devolved into prescription drugs—Adderall to keep me awake, and Zoloft to help me sleep. I missed Steph's birthday because I was so far down a Reddit snark rabbit hole that I lost track of the time—no, the days. Showering felt like too much effort, so I stopped altogether. I couldn't be bothered to eat anything that took more than five minutes to prepare. I sat in bed for months, withering away, searching for the title of my article on Twitter, then refreshing so I could hate-read the threads.

Back then, everyone who cared for me grew sick of me, including Zain. The final straw was the night he took me out to dinner at a swanky Chinese restaurant on the Upper East Side and pulled a ring out of his pocket. I looked at that black velvet box and blurted out, "Look, can we not do this right now?"

He dumped me before our entrées were served.

In many ways, he was the perfect Middle Eastern boy. But I was never the perfect Middle Eastern girl. My parents made sure of that. When they'd immigrated to the United States from Iran in the 80s, escaping the revolution under the cover of night, they'd committed to assimilation. I never learned Farsi and have no memory of hearing it around the house. My family did not celebrate Nowruz, treating Independence Day as a religious holiday instead. My mother didn't even give me a traditional Iranian name like Roya or Rostam.

No, instead they settled on Rose, which I find oddly fitting.

Prickly.

It was strange and disorienting growing up with a foot in each world.

My sourdough-skinned peers could tell I wasn't actually a blue-blooded American. My skin was brown, and my arms were hairy, and my parents talked funny when they came to pick me up in their Kia Rio.

The other Iranian kids didn't quite recognize me as their

own, either. I was too westernized to understand their jokes, to fully feel the weight of their dysphoria.

Since I couldn't be an active participant in either world, I grew into a silent observer.

And I began to write everything down.

14.6K^ Brad Zarbos Found Dead in Bed

TRENDING NEWS

Okay who do y'all think murdered tech tycoon brad zarbos??? I know the feds think his bitch wife did it but I think the obvious answer is a competitor? MAYBE the founder of Papaya Products? Pls let me know what you think bc it's keeping me up at night

3.1K comments **Share >** **Save *** ****2 people typing...**

MyMumps46

I was wondering the same thing. Do you guys think the government could be behind this??? Maybe even the president? Maybe Zarbos used his new tech to gain some sort of enemy secret and was blackmailing him...

^Vote **^ Reply** **~ Share** *****

TheZodiacKillerWasInnocent

BROOOOO I think you might be on to something. The prez is too broke a bitch to pull that off tho. I bet you Zarbos was cornering celebs. That or wall streeters. Someone with deep pockets who could pay him off. And when he didn't go silently into the night...BANG BANG!!!!

^Vote **^ Reply** **~ Share** ***

GodsFavorite69

You are all a bunch of idiots. Close, but not close enough. The illuminati obviously killed Zarbos. Washington. Hollywood. They're all in on it. Prob used his blood for some kind of ritual sacrifice.

^Vote **^ Reply** **~ Share** ***

MyMumps46

Yooo this is fucking crazy but I don't doubt it. Did you see Zarbos was cozying up to scammer queen Poppy Hastings??? I kind of love her ngl but it's the company you keep am I right??? My dude probably had it coming.

^Vote **^ Reply** **~ Share** ***

GodsFavorite69

100000%. Did u see that journalist who exposed her had some kind of nervous breakdown? Crazy bitch lmao

^Vote **^ Reply** **~ Share** ***

Chapter Five

I detest Monday mornings with a fiery passion.

Huddled outside the lobby of 513 Park Avenue South, I chug what remains of my coffee, grunting as the scalding liquid burns my tongue to a crisp, then toss it in the trash.

I'm twenty minutes late to work and have already blamed my absence on train traffic, but the beverage in my hand would be a dead giveaway. When I first started my job, running late felt like a recess game. Once I realized that the Shred's nine a.m. start time was a mere suggestion, I began testing the limits of how tardy I could be without being reprimanded by HR. Five minutes turned into ten turned into fifteen.

By twenty, I stopped playing altogether.

Not that anyone cares when I arrive. After my meltdown last year, my team is usually relieved when I decide to grace the office with my presence at all.

Now my delayed arrival can be chalked up to apathy.

The New York Dweller shares a building with ten other companies, including but not limited to a toothpaste start-up, a doggy daycare, and a venture capital firm. Our office is located on the top three floors of the west wing of the building with the Shred occupying the middle one. The setup feels more like a coworking space than a place of business. The office is open concept, so all the employees, regardless of status, sit elbow-to-elbow, typing away on their MacBook Airs. It's meant to be egalitarian, but in actuality it feels invasive, like anyone could be looking over your shoulder at any time. A Millennial pink surveillance state. The lack of privacy is startling.

But that's the whole point, isn't it?

Here's the second rule of conspiracy: There are no secrets.

Ever.

I inch toward my desk, which is conveniently nestled between the water fountain and the gender-inclusive bathrooms. Dark sunglasses and a worn-out Yankees cap (Zain's, misplaced during the split) cover my under-eye circles and bloodshot eyes, the telltale signs of my Poppy-induced hangover.

My stomach lurches, and I taste acidic bile rising up my throat.

I'm about to book it to the toilet when I overhear a couple of interns whispering loudly to each other. Their beady little eyes keep darting in my direction, then down at the floor, then back up at me. I narrow mine. One of the twerps immediately looks away, but the other holds my gaze steadily. Annoyed, I break eye contact first. It's abundantly clear that they're gossiping about me, so I pretend to stop and fill my water bottle so I can do the mature thing and eavesdrop.

The blonde speaks up first. "That's Rose Aslani." Her choppy hair is pinned back with colorful clips.

"Who?" This one's got a septum piercing. "I've never heard of her."

"The reporter who wrote the Poppy Hastings story, idiot!"

"No way! I love Poppy."

"Same, she's *such* an icon."

"A scammer queen!"

"Skinny legend!"

"But I've never heard of a Rose Aslani."

"That's because she apparently had a total meltdown after Poppy's arrest. She was, like, obsessed with her or something."

"That's so depressing."

"Oh, shit!"

I yelp, startling both girls.

I was so laser focused on their conversation that my water bottle overflowed and started spilling all over my pants and the floor. My jeans now sport a dark wet spot around the crotch.

Fan-fucking-tastic.

One of the interns runs into the bathroom and grabs me a couple of paper towels. The other helps me dry myself off. If I weren't so dead inside, I'd find the spectacle humiliating. Instead, I'm mildly amused by their tiny hands politely patting at my faux urine stain, clawing around my crotch.

I focus all my attention on *not* puking on them.

"Thanks, ladies," I say when they're all done.

Then I throw my shoulders back and saunter the rest of the way to my desk.

"What a freak," I hear one mutter behind me.

Oh, girl. If you only knew.

I open my laptop and review the assignments I have to complete before this afternoon's lineup meeting. There's an explainer on depression rooms (fitting, as I have one), a satirical brief comparing climate change to trying on prom dresses in the Macy's changing room (a stretch), and one entertainment angle detailing a certain male celebrity's penchant for collecting bobbleheads that look like his exes (highbrow despicable).

After organizing my calendar, I kill time mindlessly scrolling on Twitter, looking for controversy to feed the masses for breakfast.

But the second I see Poppy's face pop up on my timeline, I ex out of the window.

I briefly consider quitting the internet altogether, then decide against it. How else will I afford to live in my tiny box or wax my asshole?

I'm still very much in public, so I shut my eyes and take a couple of deep breaths, attempting to fight being triggered by Poppy. I knew this would happen; I should have prepared. I'm a reporter. I report the news. Poppy is news. But I thought I'd have more time to adjust.

It's been less than twenty-four hours, and Poppy Hastings is already making my life a living hell.

This is going to be a *massive* problem.

Around noon, I can no longer take the tension in my temples or the thumping in my chest, so I walk up the stairs to the top floor to meet Steph and Fern. We like to convene in the kitchen each day for Keurig coffee and small talk. Fern is already waiting, leaning back against the sink while she scrolls furiously on her phone. She's dressed in a plaid mini tennis skirt, exposing a risqué amount of her dark toned thighs for the workplace, an oversize leather blazer, and platform boots strapped around her legs like ankle weights. Last month, Fern shaved down her signature locs using her own Gillette Venus simply because she was bored and needed a change. Her deadpan delivery makes her sarcastic sense of humor seem earnest unless you know her personally, which is why she's the perfect person to run the Shred's social media team.

Fern likes what she likes and doesn't care if you think it's lame, which really makes her the coolest of us all.

I grab a paper mug and K-Cup from the cupboard. "Where's Steph?"

"She got fired," Fern says without looking up from her phone.

Classic prank.

"Sorry I'm late!" Steph runs into the kitchen, clutching her laptop close to her chest, looking around anxiously to make sure no one's giving us any weird looks. "You guys, we have to stop meeting in the kitchen like this. I swear to god, Deb thinks I'm, like, napping in the supply closet or something."

Deb is Steph's supervisor. She leads the Shred's analytics department, where Steph works as an engineer. She's a numbers prodigy with an embarrassing lack of reading comprehension skills who somehow ended up assisting an editorial team, which I personally think is hilarious. But her ex–horse girl guilt means that she's always a little bit paranoid that she's going to be wrung out for fraternizing too much with the middle floor when she *should* be looking at KPIs or making a spreadsheet or whatever people in analytics do. At five feet tall, she's known for scurrying around the *NYD* headquarters to some meeting or presentation, muttering dirty words under her breath in Spanish.

I love her to fucking pieces.

"I hear you've been fired," I tease.

Her tiny face immediately turns tomato red.

"What? Where did you hear that? Who told you that?"

"Calm down." I giggle. "Fern was just playing. Isn't that right, Fernie?"

At her least favorite nickname, Fern finally glances up from scheduling posts on her phone. She narrows her heavily lined eyes, gracing us with her undivided attention.

"Please, keep calling me that. Seriously, don't stop. I love sounding like a queer Muppet and will definitely *not* murder you in cold blood."

God, I hate everyone but my friends.

I met Fern and Steph my first week at the Shred. It was Cinco de Mayo and *The NYD* had arranged to have Mexican food catered for a tastefully offensive celebratory "cultural" lunch on the bottom floor. Fern had stood in the middle of the buffet, surrounded by doting coworkers spewing their bullshit. She'd been with the company for about six months and was already an *NYD* favorite. Despite the fact that she was always surrounded by people, I also noticed a sort of vacancy pooling in her eyes. I wondered if she was actually just really fucking lonely. When she left her entourage by the guac and chips and approached me, I felt as if I had been chosen by a celebrity. She casually stood next to me, crossing her arms over her chest, looking out into the mouth-stuffed abyss. I attempted to copy her nonchalance, but instead of staring at the walls, which are all papered in old *The New York Dweller* issues, I looked up at the ceiling. And I accidentally missed what was directly beneath me: little Steph, whom I walked right into, causing her to spill her salsa all over her white overalls and clogs. Even her glasses looked splatter painted. Fern and I laughed so hard that snot leaked out of our noses and onto our chins. The two of us spent the rest of Cinco de Mayo picking tomato chunks out of Steph's curly black hair.

They've been my people ever since.

"Okay, but for real, Rose—are you good?"

Steph's question snaps me out of my nostalgic wormhole and back to the present day. Her gaze is soft and concerned, like a high school guidance counselor's.

Both she and Fern are focused on me, awaiting my reaction. They clearly expect me to flinch.

I take a long sip of my vile Keurig coffee, choking on the aftertaste.

"Me? I'm fine. Swell, really," I say. "Why wouldn't I be?"

"Well, you know." Steph leans forward, huddling close. "Because of the *p*-word of it all?"

"Penis?" Fern whispers.

Steph opens her mouth to say something, then firmly shuts it again. For a twenty-seven-year-old woman who I happen to know owns an entire *closet* worth of vibrators, she really can be quite the wee prude.

Being raised Catholic can do that to you.

"Poppy, you puta," she hisses.

"Estefania!" I cover my mouth, feigning shock. "Language!"

Once our laughter has died down, I answer her question in earnest.

"I'm trying to avoid thinking about it," I admit. "Although work is making it impossible."

"It's almost as if being online twenty-four seven is bad for your mental health," Fern deadpans.

We let out a collective sigh.

One day, when every single person I know is dead and anthropologists are excavating our bones and analyzing our skulls, I truly believe they'll find tiny little holes drilled into our heads where the internet sucked us dry of independent thought.

Like the mark of Cain, but make it a meme.

"Maybe she'll violate parole and get sent back to Albion?"

Steph's tone is hopeful, but she's being naive—there's no way in hell Poppy is going back to prison anytime soon. The media is too enamored with her. *Rolling Stone* would probably consider a first-degree offense a "quirky" personality trait at this point.

"Whatever she does, it's going to be live and in front of an audience," Fern says. "Have you seen her Instagram account?"

"You know I try not to follow that horseshit."

I hate Instagram. I hate filters and juice cleanses and overly whitened teeth. When I joined the Shred, I was encouraged to make an account, and I did, but I never use it. Whenever I'm swept into that vortex, I can feel myself growing dumber by the second.

"For fuck's sake, enough with the 'I'm not like other girls' attitude," Fern says.

"Yeah!" Steph agrees. "It's so trite. You made an account. Use it."

"Bite me." That's all I have to say about that. "Besides, all of Poppy's socials were deleted when she was sentenced."

"Well, I guess we know what her first order of business was when she got released." Steph pauses, pulling out her phone. "'Cause look at this."

I peer over at her screen, and the muscles in my face freeze.

Somehow, Poppy Hastings has managed to amass more than a hundred million motherfucking followers in less than a day.

I knew I should have smuggled Roommate's vodka into my purse. I need a drink.

Stat.

"She's now the twentieth-most-followed person on Instagram." Fern's voice remains flat. "After Katy Perry."

"Gimme that."

I grab the phone out of her hands.

Apparently, Poppy has been posting every hour on the hour—photos of her hotel room, bubble bath, piles and piles of cash, a mysterious head of brown hair lying turned away from her in bed. I wince. She's been giving her new followers a play-by-play of her sparkly life on parole. It's as if she's the producer, director, writer, and star of her own 24-7 reality show.

And she's being heavily rewarded for it. Her comments section is full of people praising her vision and aesthetic.

Realest shit on this app.

Relatable queen.

I'll wire you ten grand for a picture of your feet.

I feel a migraine coming on. Or is it a trauma hangover? I clutch the counter to steady myself, afraid my knees might buckle. Steph and Fern put their arms around my shoulders for support.

I continue scrolling.

Her Instagram Stories are at maximum capacity. Each slide features Poppy, up close and personal, whispering loudly (and erotically) into the camera as if having a tête-à-tête with a close friend. I hesitantly click on the first slide.

"Hello, darlings! How bloody delicious is my new suite at the Plaza? Can you believe I'm paying for this with bounced checks?"

Swipe.

"Aren't my new Jennifer Fisher platinum bangles absolutely divine? I wear them because they remind me of my handcuffs. How does the saying go, dears? You don't know what you've got till it's gone?"

Swipe.

"For lunch, we'll be eating foie gras and Russian caviar off a centuries-old ceramic dish an ex-lover purchased at auction for me. Don't tell his wife. Beats prison food, right, my pets?"

Swipe.

"I might treat myself to foreplay with this scrumptious little busboy who just brought me my afternoon tea. It'll be a first for me—I usually only have sex with men whose wallets are worth snagging while they sleep!"

I can't believe it.

Her jokes, her repartee—it's all built off my exposé, the character *I* crafted her into. She's taking the rhetoric I used against her and making it part of her brand.

If it weren't so eerie, I'd call it brilliant.

I swipe all the way to the very last Story.

"Children, I have the most incredible news," she coos. "I've just signed a *multimillion-dollar* deal with Netflix to turn my life story into a television series. More details to come, but it's all happening, Poppers. I'm finally going to be my very own sugar daddy!"

I spit up my coffee.

The kitchen walls begin to close in.

"Guys, I'm not feeling too well," I blurt out, handing back Fern's phone. "I think I'm going to work from home for the rest of the day. Tell Cat for me?"

Before they can answer, I rush downstairs, collect my things from the middle floor, and dash toward the elevator. It's notably bad form to miss the weekly lineup meeting, but I'm pretty sure that if I don't get out of here, I'm going to pass out, and the blood spilling out of my cracked skull will dirty up the C-suite offices on either side of the floor.

When I reach the pavement, the sky is spinning, which makes the near-midtown skyscrapers flap around me like those tube men at all the Ohio auto dealerships. I already feel drunk, so I figure why not get drunk? I pick up a couple of bottles of wine from a twenty-four-hour liquor store on my way back to Clinton Hill while blasting death metal my mother would call "heathen music." On the subway, I get a few concerned looks. Some folks even swap seats, attempting to position themselves farther away from me.

Smart.

They know a train wreck waiting to happen when they see one.

By the time I reach my apartment, I've already chugged half a bottle of cabernet from a brown paper bag, and Roommate is just waking up. She jumps when I walk through the door, surprised to see me home so early. She's sporting her typical daytime look: her birthday suit with her hair wrapped up on top of her head in a colorful scarf.

She looks me up and down, taking in the stench of fermented grapes.

"You look like shit," she finally says.

"Thanks, I feel like shit, too."

Roommate raises a very thinly tattooed eyebrow but doesn't ask any follow-up questions. The selfless act somehow makes me feel obligated to burden her.

"Poppy Hastings's life is going to be made into a Netflix special." A shred of interest sparks in her eyes. "My life, however, continues to fucking suck."

At that, the spark is replaced with an eye roll. She puts on a pair of large orange headphones and picks up her crochet hook.

"Don't choke on vomit."

I take that as a cue to go to my bedroom and lock the door.

At first, I think I'll journal. I used to look forward to journaling as a kid—scribbling down all of my thoughts without anyone there to judge or edit.

But I'm sick of swimming around in my own messed-up, miserable brain.

I need a break.

No, what I really need is a fucking vacation. My phone keeps buzzing and I know that the Shred most likely didn't buy the sudden-onset-illness excuse I fed Fern and Steph, so I stuff it beneath my pillow and try to pretend I'm in Aruba or Cancun or even goddamn Naples. I try on a few bikinis over my T-shirt and jeans, all the while chugging the rest of my wine straight from the bottle. The bathing suits are tight, left over from the days when Zain would plan these elaborate getaways for us, where we'd go around holding clammy hands and snapping pictures of ourselves in front of landmarks that I couldn't have given less of a fuck about for holiday cards we never sent. Now the strings of the bikini tops dig into the fabric around my armpits, and the weight of being alone crashes into me like the crosstown bus.

I finish my first bottle of wine and twist open the second. The stupid crown moldings on my ceiling are getting blurrier and blurrier, like when you realize the star you were confessing your wishes to was really just a United Airlines plane.

"*Fuck United!*" I yell out to absolutely no one.

The silence feels deafening, so I decide to blast Whitney Houston's greatest hits, which used to be my comfort music. I sway to the beat like a rocking ship, tripping over my own feet and falling face-first onto the hardwood floor. I roll around, a giggling mess, until my chuckles turn into full-body sobs. I take another minute-long sip of my wine, fully aware that this pity party is spiraling into a full-blown breakdown bash but unable to stop in medias res.

One song ends and another begins. The first few notes of Whitney's cover of "I Will Always Love You" blares through my laptop speakers, and my arms and legs fall limp.

This was going to be Zain's and my first dance song. We practiced sidestepping to it in our living room, stepping on each other's toes, Zain dipping me with the dramatic flair of an old Hollywood major motion picture.

Zain and I met in college. Our last names are one letter apart—Aslani and Asani—which meant our packages kept getting delivered to one another by accident. We dated from our sophomore year onward. Being with Zain made sense. Our relationship was practical, like remembering to take your makeup off before bed. He was my first and only boyfriend, and therefore I assumed we'd be together for the rest of our lives. He followed me to New York without asking, taking a job at a pharmaceutical company he hated. We were comfortable together. He knew how many times my alarm would go off each morning. I knew when to pity laugh at his medical puns. When we had sex, I closed my eyes and pretended he was someone else. We named all of our future kids.

I shut my eyes and try to picture Zain's face. His sandy skin, stubble rough against my chin when he leaned down for a kiss.

But the only image my brain can muster is Poppy's smirk.

My eyes fly open.

I try to stand up and promptly fall back down.

Shit.

I really should have digested something today other than two cups of coffee, but how was I to know I'd be drinking myself into an early grave this afternoon? I hoist myself up using my bed frame, taking a seat on my dirty duvet. My Adderall bottle falls out of my purse, and I crack a pill in half before saying "Fuck it" and throwing back the whole dose, then another. I slowly feel my brain start to refocus. Fighting back tears, I reach for my phone, hiding now in the crevice between my mattress and the wall. The last time this happened, I blocked him and erased his contact info. I'm too messed up to remember my own last name, but somehow his number comes back to me like the lyrics of a forgotten song.

The phone rings two times.

No answer yet. I grab the wine opener. In between rings, I twist the cork until it pops.

I frown, staring at my distorted reflection in the bottle.

He picks up after the fifth ring.

"Hello?"

His voice is hushed. I imagine him in his cubicle, seeing my name flash across his screen.

"Do you remember the flowers we said we'd use as centerpieces?"

I've forgotten to say hello, but it's too late to do it now.

"Are you high?"

After everything, there's still a sincerity to his tone.

"No," I mumble. "Well, yes."

"Rose..."

"Answer the question!"

I'm slurring my words, the syllables melting into each other like a day-old frozen cocktail.

"I do," Zain says quietly. "I wanted to forgo centerpieces and place a single long-stemmed rose on every single plate. But you said it was tacky."

I don't remember saying that, but he's probably right. Zain was always listening. I heard everything he said, but I rarely listened.

"Is it too late for me to take it back?" I hear myself say. There's a sharp intake of breath on the other end of the phone. I've caught him off guard. "Is it too late to take it all back?"

He waits a beat before answering. The silence feels like it lasts for centuries.

"Yes, Rose."

I go to take another sip of my wine. The glass clunks loudly against my teeth. I raise one finger to my mouth, checking to see if I've chipped an incisor, then finally allow a tear to escape the corner of my eye.

"Why?"

"Because you never loved me."

"Yes I did."

"Because you never loved me as much as you hated her."

Fuck.

There it is.

I'm wailing, then, bawling with such intensity that I'm afraid Roommate will come barging into my room just to make sure I'm not hurting myself. I cry so hard that I begin choking on my tears, coughing into the phone. I wipe the moisture off with the bikini top I'm still wearing.

"Look, I've got to go." Zain sounds hurried.

I look around for my own excuse to hang up, but I've got nowhere left to be.

"Okay."

"Are you going to be all right?"

"Yes."

"Good," he says. "Oh, and Rose?"

"Yes?"

I love you, I will him to say. I can hear the words in my head. It's a sentence I heard him utter aloud countless times while we were together but never truly appreciated until he left. Unadulterated, no-strings-attached love.

He's right.

I didn't love him then. I don't love him now.

But I'd give anything to hear him say that he loves me just one more time.

"Never call me again."

Then he hangs up.

And everything goes dark.

Chapter Six

The ocean hums, the tide rolling in and out with a steady cadence, the water teasing and tickling the bottoms of my feet. I'm perched on a lawn chair, my legs and arms stretched out in opposite directions, eye-fucking the clear blue sky. It's the kind of day that feels fake, you know? Like a green screen or a Universal Studios set. Then again, beautiful things always have a tendency to feel fake, or too good to be true. I inhale sharply, the smell of the salt water feeding me serotonin through an imaginary IV. My skin sizzles, barbecued by the sun.

I love the feeling of burning to a crisp, searing like a piece of steak. It's simple. I used to go for simple. I'm not sure when everything and everyone became so complicated. The UV rays are streaking my black hair with a lighter brown, and for once in my goddamn life, I feel beautiful. American. Every single one of my senses is alert, awake. And when I reach my hands to my cheeks, I'm shocked to discover that I'm smiling. A genuine, authentic smile.

Without warning, a massive wave rises above my resting place, soaking me. Instead of groaning, I take the new sensation in stride. In fact, I'm laughing, wading around in the water like a child of the tides. I feel like my old self again: the eternal optimist, the positivity police. The rose without thorns. It's almost as if I've never even heard of Poppy Ha—

"Wake UP!"

The idyllic vignette shatters, shards of the heaven I've created flying everywhere all at once, the light sucked out of the sky until I'm trapped in an all-consuming darkness.

I squint at said darkness. "Is this hell?"

"Yes. Clinton Hell."

I open my eyes all the way then and come face-to-face with Roommate. Well, face-to-kneecap. She's hovering above me, staring down at me like a god.

As it turns out, the wet sensation I just experienced wasn't in fact the sweet kiss of an ocean wave. Roommate has been pouring water all over my head.

I give myself a sniff and abruptly dry heave.

Yeah, that wasn't water.

I groan. "What are you doing?"

"Needed to make sure you weren't dead." Roommate shrugs. "You're not. I go now."

"What time is it?" And where is my phone? And why am I on the floor?

"Five a.m. You sleep for twelve hours. Like corpse."

With that, Roommate struts out of my room, but not before turning on the bright lamp by the door, leaving me basking in the stark reality of the artificial light of day. As I writhe around on the floor, blocking out the fluorescence, my bikini top gets stuck to an old chewed piece of gum lodged beneath my bed. That's when I realize that I'm still dressed in the same bathing suit I'd been wearing in my happy-place dream.

What the fuck happened last night?

My head is pounding, and my body aches. I reach around the floor and find one and a half empty wine bottles. And an open container of Adderall, pills scattered all over the floor. There's also a wet spot on my rug that could be one of three things: alcohol, urine, or vomit.

I pray for urine.

Finally, I find my phone under a pile of pillows. Well, what used to be my phone. My screen is cracked down the middle. It's almost as if I threw it against a—

Oh my god.

A wall.

I threw my phone against a wall.

Last night, after I made an ass of myself and drunk dialed Zain.

I tried to booty-call my ex-boyfriend, the man I dated for six years, the one I couldn't bring myself to break up with but also refused to commit to or marry. I think I might even have tried, just an eensy-weensy teeny-tiny bit, to get back together with him.

And I'm pretty sure he basically told me to go fuck myself.

Or rather, he told me never to call him again.

And I made sure I wouldn't by shattering my phone against my innocent eggshell wall.

I know exactly where I am now.

Forget Clinton Hill.

Forget hell.

This is rock bottom.

Okay.

Breathe, Rose.

For the love of god, don't smell yourself, but breathe.

This isn't the end of the world. Unfortunately, this isn't even the end of your life. You can get through this. What's that cliché every pseudojournalist on Instagram is always spouting about rock bottom? That there's nowhere to go but up?

I sit upright, forcing myself to look into the full-length mirror leaning against my closet door, taking in the mess I've made. The woman looking back at me is a total stranger. Jesus Christ, I hardly recognize myself anymore.

No, fuck this.

I refuse to wallow in self-pity. Or, you know, stew in my own urine.

Today is the first day of the rest of my life.

I'm going to change. To become a better person. Starting right now, I'm going to let go of all of this negativity, to stop behaving so selfishly and recklessly. I'll start showing up to things on time—early, even. Every Sunday, I'll call my mother and ask how her week went. The next time Fern suggests going to slam poetry open mic night, I won't even hesitate before saying yes.

I am *reborn*. A new woman, baby. And best of all, I won't waste even a millisecond of time thinking about you-know-who. As far as I'm concerned, she—along with the old Rose—is dead.

A rush of adrenaline overpowers my throbbing head, and I rise to my feet with gusto and stomp over to the shower. After cleansing my body of all my past sins (and my hair of vodka and vomit), I wrap myself in a towel and sit atop my bed. It's really too bad my phone isn't working; I'd love to loop my group chat in on the brand-new me. I make a to-do list instead to ring in this era and email it to them.

Tuesday, April 5
5:37 AM

to Fern Basset, Steph Garcia

Hi guys! I've decided to become an entirely new person. In honor of this development, I've put together an ever-evolving list of commandments that I will be following henceforth. Feel free to add your own to the attached doc.

Rose 2.0:

I will give up my subway seat to people in need, even when I've had a long day and can tell they have a shorter commute.

I will no longer make fun of Steph for casually using words like *abreast* in conversation.

I will stop talking back to Cat when she gives me new assignments, even if I'd rather get torn apart by Canal Street rats than do them.

I will re-up my yoga membership, even though that lady with the boob sweat farted in my face that one time.

I will take up a new hobby like Rollerblading or latte art.

I will redownload Hinge and resist the urge to bully the Chads I match with, even the fiscal conservatives.

I will never again say the name Poppy Hastings out loud. In fact, I won't even think it. In case she appears. Like Bloody Mary.

Looking forward to your thoughts,
(the new and improved) Rose

Satisfied, I press send and lean back onto my duvet. But something catches my eye: a Twitter notification, dressed in blue and sitting all seductively next to my feed.

I reluctantly click it.

It can't hurt, right? Rose 2.0 can handle reminiscing about her wedding centerpieces with her very-much-ex-boyfriend. She can handle anything!

What's one harmless little Twitter notification?

ULYSSES RUTHERFORD REPORTED MISSING BY THIRD WIFE & DAUGHTER

Goddammit.

I've never opened an article faster in my entire life.

Oh god.

It's happening.

Again.

First I scan the piece, picking up just the highlights—the SparkNotes, if you will. Then, once I've gathered the gist, I start over and move through the text with a fine-tooth comb. I look for Easter eggs, for subjectivity and tone, for any bias that could leak from the author's pen onto the page, rendering the work compromised or ludicrous.

Here's the third rule of conspiracy: The devil is most certainly in the details.

And the devil, in this case, is Ulysses Whitney Rutherford III.

Ulysses Whitney Rutherford III is an eighty-four-year-old oil tycoon who, according to this rag, was skiing in Aspen with his latest child bride when he followed an instructor off the beaten path through a patch of trees and never found his way to the bottom of the slope.

The police are investigating his new Mrs., of course. When Rutherford had bedded another Playboy bunny, social media had just assumed she'd said "I do" to the blood linking him to the Mayflower, not, you know, the bald head and shriveled balls. I mean, there's money, and then there's *Rutherford* money: ancient, ever flowing, with the power to restore beauty to the life of anyone who comes into contact with it, much like the fountain of youth. Influential in every circle he decides to favor with his Midas touch, Rutherford has been credited with preventing three stock market crashes, causing two Hollywood divorces, and rigging one pretty horrific election result.

Everyone who knows him owes him.

Everyone who doesn't hates his guts.

I did, too.

Until I met him for a drink at the Carlyle about two years ago.

Rutherford—or Ulysses, as he instructed me to call him—was hiding at a table in the back, munching on peanuts and sipping a dirty martini. It took three rounds of cocktails to get Ulysses talking. He was debonair, holding himself like an aged Cary Grant. He complimented my ankles (?) and told me I had "real spunk." He remained perfectly composed at all times.

Until, that is, I uttered the name Poppy Hastings.

Per Ulysses, the two had met at the Harvard Club, huddled over a game of Texas Hold'em. He'd immediately been impressed by Poppy's poker face and invited her to a dinner party at his property in Greenwich, Connecticut. There, the two had bonded over their mutual affection for Gabriel Ferrier, a lesser-known painter from La Belle Époque. Ferrier had been an overbearing critic of his own work and had burned many of his collections before his death in 1914. In the present day, only eleven Ferrier originals had been authenticated. Five had been purchased by museums.

Three had remained beholden to Ferrier's estate.

Two had been acquired by Ulysses Rutherford.

One belonged to Poppy Hastings.

That night, Poppy had entered the home of Ulysses Rutherford, a stranger. But she had exited as its new owner.

He'd offered her his property as a trade. It had only seemed right. Fair.

So imagine his surprise when an old art historian friend had called months later to share whisperings of a Ferrier making its way back to the market—the exact same piece he had traded Poppy for over dinner.

He hadn't reported the fraud to the authorities because he'd considered his pride to be worth more than one measly house.

Plus, he liked Poppy. She had gumption.

And now, two days after she's been released from prison, Rutherford takes a joyride into the deep, dark forest and becomes a mountain lion's lunch?

You can't tell me that's a coincidence.

I check the time. It's six thirty a.m. If I leave now, I can beat Cat to the office. I can talk her into listening to me before her morning meeting with *The NYD*'s CEO, Gates Silver. She'll see what I see. She did before. She will again.

But something gnaws at me, stopping me in my tracks.

What about Rose 2.0?

What about the list you just sent Fern and Steph?

What about rock bottom?

To which I say: *Bite me, conscience.*

Then I dart out the door.

By the time Cat reaches the office, I'm already waiting. She whistles Joni Mitchell under her breath as she enters the middle floor and walks over to her desk, holding the latest issue of *The New York Dweller*, her fingers separating the third and fourth pages. She's wearing her everyday uniform: a white button-down, black jeans, and Dr. Martens. Strictly business, as always.

When she looks up and sees me sitting in her swivel chair in the dark, she jumps.

"Rose, what the hell are you doing here before nine thirty?"

Ah, so she *does* notice my tardiness!

"And where were you at yesterday's lineup meeting? Your friend Sophie or Stephanie or something mentioned some kind of shellfish poisoning?"

Classic Steph. Always overembellishing when she lies.

"Um, yeah, I ate some bad, uh, crawfish. I'm better now. Anyway, there's no time for that. I'm on to something big. Huge. A story."

A vague spark of interest flashes in Cat's eyes. She takes a seat at the desk adjacent to her own and crosses her legs like she's folding origami.

"I'm listening."

I clear my throat and prepare to launch into my pitch.

"It's about the disappearance of Ulysses Rutherford."

Cat leans forward. "Go on."

"I think there's more to it than meets the eye."

"You think he's dead?"

"I think he hasn't been skiing fucking Buttermilk Mountain for twelve hours."

"And you think the wife did it?"

"Actually..."

"Spit it out."

"I think it was Poppy Hastings."

At the sound of Poppy's name, Cat lets out a small groan and places her head in her hands. I wait a few seconds to see if she'll come up for air before rolling my chair closer to hers and patting her lightly on the back. Her body tenses at my touch, and she sits upright again.

"Rose, are we really doing this all over again?"

"Cat, the circumstances are totally different. Poppy was *just* released from prison."

"We've been over this, Rose. Poppy isn't a murderer. She's a con artist. Another scammer heiress."

"I know for a fact that she and Rutherford were connected. He told me so himself!"

"On the record?"

"Well, no. He told me anonymously. On background."

"So, let's say he resurfaces alive and well. He could claim total ignorance?"

"Technically, but—"

Cat groans loud enough to wake the tech bro neighbors.

"But *nothing*! There's nothing here, Rose. An old billionaire who probably has dementia skied off a cliff, which is tragic, yes. Maybe even a little funny! But it isn't a story. Plus, Poppy is in New York. She's on parole, *and* she's been documenting every second of her day on social media. Screw an alibi; she literally has more than a million witnesses. Which means you're wasting my time. *Again.*"

Cat begins twiddling her thumbs beneath the table, scrunching her Botoxed forehead as far as it'll possibly dent in my direction. It's the face of concern. I can tell she's worried about me. She thinks I've gone off the rails for good.

"Look, Rose. I care about you. And you're a wonderful writer, you really are. But if you go down this path again, I don't know if I'll be able to save you this time. Do you get what I'm saying?"

We lock eyes, and I feel a pang of empathy for her. I can tell she's protecting me.

Or she believes she is, anyway.

"Cat." My voice is barely audible. "Give me some time. Let me prove to you that this isn't all in my head. That it's real. Please."

Cat leans back in her chair so much that she almost falls over. Not that she notices—she's far too busy staring up at the ceiling, mulling over my offer.

"Fine," she finally says. "You can continue pre-reporting. But please keep this quiet. No interviews. No callouts. No writing even a word of this down until I've approved an outline. I want your stream silent and your shit odorless. And this had better not interfere with your daily assignments. Capeesh?"

My pulse quickens. I briefly consider leaning over and kissing her on the forehead, but that might get me fired on the spot.

A smile spreads over every inch of my face.

"Capeesh."

Chapter Seven

"Miss? I'm sure whatever mind-numbing video game you're playing on your phone right now is much more important than all of our precious time, but for heaven's sake, can you please do us all a favor and *pay attention*?"

I'm standing in line at CVS, wedged between an older woman wearing a felt ostrich on her head and a man in a worn-out leather jacket and gold chain spitting angrily in Italian. We're all waiting to use the self-checkout kiosks. There are three bottles of kombucha—a drink that famously tastes like high-quality ass—in my basket. One for me, one for Fern, and one for Steph.

And, surprising absolutely nobody, I'm dangerously close to being late.

I was given the job of grabbing the dirt juice while Fern checks us in at L'évent, a new immersive (culturally appropriative) breathwork studio on Bowery. Run by new-age French monks and designed by Ian Schrager, the studio (which, according to Google Translate, is actually named *the blowhole*) is one part sound bath, one part guided breathing, one part stupidly expensive spa. The owners are staging a soft opening for members of the press and sent the Shred some guest passes, which is the only reason we can afford to check it out. The class promises to cleanse our bodies of toxins and completely open our chakras (which apparently can be closed? No idea what a chakra is).

Yes, I usually detest this kind of Wellness-Industrial Complex bullshit with a hell-fiery passion. But ever since I sent Fern and Steph my Rose 2.0 manifesto in a hungover haze, they've been holding me annoyingly accountable. I briefly considered telling them how quickly I'd relapsed, fallen off the bandwagon. You know, that I'd gone to Cat and practically *begged* her to take my allegations against Poppy seriously. But when I saw them at the office just a few hours after the aforementioned begging, I totally pussied out. It wasn't my fault. They just acted *so fucking proud* of me. And who was I to break their tender little hearts, to burst their bubbles, to smack those looks of respect and admiration off their pretty faces?

So I pranked them instead. I said I'd gotten a great night's sleep. Eight hours! And then I'd come into the office at the break of dawn to "catch up on work" I'd missed the previous day.

Please. As if.

Fern was skeptical at first—nobody in New York has *ever* gotten a "great night's sleep"—but Steph did that tiny fast clapping thing she does. Then we'd group hugged. And you know what? It felt nice.

To hug.

At that moment, I knew without a shadow of a doubt that I was going to go through the process of pre-reporting alone this time. I wasn't going to involve my friends and family, wouldn't strip them of their happy, misguided naivete. I would try acupuncture and drink chlorophyll from one of those gallon water bottles and make manifestation lists. My loved ones could believe I'd been reformed. No one needed to know I was still looking into Poppy Hastings.

Not until I proved what she was capable of, anyway.

You know.

The *m*-word.

As I'm scrolling on my phone, waiting to reach the front of the line, I discover a Twitter account dedicated to Poppy Hastings spottings (not to be confused with Poppy's own account, @TheRealPrisonPoppy). I immediately turn my notifications on. This is perfection! Now I can track Poppy's movements without dressing in camo and stalking her through Manhattan like a fucking psychopath.

I start scrolling.

As it turns out, Poppy moves around *a lot*. Like, an unfathomable amount. I'm starting to think some of the sightings are not actually her but doppelgängers or body doubles. Five minutes ago, Poppy was spotted entering a crowded alleyway in East Harlem. But that can't be right. What would Poppy be doing in East Harlem just twenty minutes after she checked in for a facial in the Meatpacking District?

"Did you hear what I said? Do you have those earbobs in? *Move*."

The woman with the bird on her head is glaring at me.

I look up, alarmed.

While I've been mapping Poppy's supposed whereabouts, the line in front of me has moved up about five feet. As per usual, I appear to be holding everybody back.

"Sorry, sorry," I mumble, rushing toward the open kiosk.

Before paying, I reach over to grab a pack of Extra spearmint gum, and one of the magazines next to the checkout counter catches my eye. In the right-hand corner, there's a small picture of Poppy, dressed in a floor-length mink coat and tiny black sunglasses, waving to the cameras while leaving the Plaza Hotel. But it's the text underneath the photograph that makes my stomach do the goddamn Macarena.

POPPY HASTINGS: AMERICA'S TOP CELEBRITY CRIMINAL RISES TO NEW HEIGHTS

Lord forgive me, but I cannot resist.

I look around to make sure nobody's watching, then add the magazine to my haul, swiping my card so quickly that it takes three attempts for the charge to go through. I practically trip over my feet as I run through the sliding doors, itching to tear open and devour my find.

Once I reach the sidewalk, I rip through the glossy pages until I find exactly what I'm looking for: a write-up of Poppy's exploits.

And there it is in fine print.

Poppy Hastings, blah blah blah, previously locked-up socialite influencer, etc. etc., millions of followers, yada yada yada, to host the next episode of *Saturday Night Live*.

It takes everything in me to resist tearing the magazine to smithereens and laughing maniacally like a madwoman.

I can't believe this.

I mean, I knew she was becoming a Big Deal, but *SNL*?

Poppy's fame is seriously spiraling out of control. A Lorne

Michaels nod of approval is just what she needs to seal the deal on her stardom. In just a week's time, Poppy is going to go from a niche subject of public fascination and vitriol to mainstream, respectable Celebrity-with-a-capital-C.

She's about to be a fucking household name.

My hands start shaking like I'm an addict suffering a bout of withdrawal.

No, Poppy Hastings does *not* get to do this.

She can't faze me right before my chakra cleanse, nor can she add one last-minute ounce of toxicity into my bloodstream. I have to have faith—I can and *will* take her down. But for now? I have to move my ass. Rose 2.0 can't arrive covered in sweat, tardy to L'évent. Rose 2.0 is supposed to show up fifteen minutes early so she can stretch her pelvis and masturbate. Sorry, I mean meditate.

When I arrive at the studio, Fern is smoking a cigarette outside while Steph paces anxiously back and forth by the door. As I breeze toward them, I slap on an unbothered expression. Steph looks up and exhales sharply, then runs to hug me.

"Oh my god, I thought you weren't going to show!"

"I'm here, and I come bearing kombucha." I pull her in, kissing the top of her tiny head. "Fern, doesn't smoking, like, defeat the purpose of what we're doing here?"

Fern frowns, dropping the cig and using the bottom of her steel-toed boot to grind it out.

"Just getting in some last-minute poison," she says, shrugging. "What's the point of doing something good for your body if you don't get to do something bad first?"

I grin, preparing a rebuttal. But Steph speaks first. I can tell she's stressed.

"Sorry, no time for chitchat, Rosie. Get your culo inside and change."

The three of us haul ass into the lemon-scented locker room full of influencers and editors, many of whom have leapt straight off The Shred's explore page and onto the invite list. They all look like swans, their necks elongated, with perfect posture and matching workout sets. Next to these creatures, we don't just look like ugly fucking ducklings. We look like...I don't know. Pigeons, maybe?

"Stop staring," Steph commands. She can be so bossy when there's a time crunch. "Change with your eyes closed if you have to. I want to get a good spot in front."

I strip off my jeans and put on a pair of my mom's old bike shorts from the 80s, which have conveniently come back into style, and a ratty old oversize T-shirt. Once my hair is in a messy bun and my back is loudly cracked (met by dirty looks from the other girls), I'm good to go. I grab my kombucha and phone and attempt to exit the room.

"What do you think you're doing?" An uppity man holding a clipboard and wearing a muscle tank that reads NAMASLAY (ew?) stops me in my tracks. "There are no phones in the Hall of Serenity! *Ever!*"

I swallow a snort.

"Shit, my bad."

He glares at me for cursing.

"What did you say your name was again?"

"Rose Aslani. Sir, yes, sir!"

He glares, then glances down at the list on his clipboard. When he's not looking, I stick my phone up my sports bra and nestle it between my tits, then successfully enter the room.

The lighting in the studio is dim. So dim, in fact, that I can barely see where I'm going. I almost trip over the outstretched legs of an influencer and put us both in the hospital. Picking up a yoga mat by the door, I attempt to orient myself. Steph and Fern are at the very front with Steph lying down, concentrating in Savasana, and Fern sitting upright with her eyes closed. I take the spot directly behind them, trying not to feel too self-conscious about all the other well-tweezed women who will inevitably be staring at my hairy ass as I center myself.

This is, admittedly, one of the stranger parts of working in the industry: Most of the other people at these events are your direct competitors. They're constantly trying to size you up, to figure out if you're actually hot shit or all talk, to decipher whether they have anything to gain from talking to you. Not that I'm exempt or anything. In fact, I'm a total hypocrite. One of the few reasons I actually considered showing up to this sadistic sauna was because I'd heard through the Twittersphere that Jade Aki, the new editor in chief of *Vinyl*, might show. Jade was only twenty-seven when she took the helm of the Shifter Pearce Publishing digital property. I've been dying to meet her and pick her brain, to see if she *actually* lives up to all the hype or if she's just another corporate sellout.

But my intel must be wrong, because the digital prodigy is nowhere to be seen.

Of fucking course.

As I place my kombucha bottle by the front right of my mat and burrow my phone farther down my bosom, I hear someone behind me whisper my name, followed by a snicker. I briefly consider turning around and giving the culprit a good hearty flick but ultimately decide against it.

Steph would never forgive me for causing such a scene.

An instructor wearing prayer beads and a Speedo lights candles in the shape of an eight-pointed star (I thought this studio was run by monks?) and silences the crowd. "Welcome, my friends. Please take the next sixty seconds to enter a meditative space." He perches cross-legged at the center of the room. Music starts blaring from all four corners; it sounds like Megan Thee Stallion, but, like, covered by Enya.

Are we about to be inducted into a cult? Or a pyramid scheme?

Aren't they kind of the same thing?

I stifle another laugh, then hear someone close to me sniffling.

It's Fern. She's doing the same thing.

The next forty minutes are, to put it plainly, fucking bizarre. Our "shaman," Lance, takes us through a breathing exercise to the jolting beat of "Lose My Breath" by Destiny's Child. At some point, I open one eye to find the girl seated next to me fully shaking as if she's having a bad trip or being exorcised or something. I think I even heard Steph spontaneously start to weep. *Weep!* The music keeps getting louder and louder as we move further into our practice, and the lack (or influx?) of oxygen starts to feel like a very expensive microdosing session. I even swear the candles start to flicker, smelling more and more pungent, like ash and sage. The stench rises from the wooden floorboards and fills my nostrils until I'm all smoke and fumes, unable to see what's in front of or behind me.

Goddammit.

Why did I bring kombucha instead of tequila?

Then I fully begin to hallucinate. Lance starts to look a

little bit too much like Zain, flexing his biceps and wiping the perspiration from his forehead, staring at me with his signature look of both pity and affection. I try to get his attention but fall short every time. He hates me! He wants nothing to do with a loser like me. Someone who lies to her friends, obsesses over the past, drinks until she falls asleep. Who refreshes her Twitter feed until her thumbs give out.

I hear a snicker from the back corner of the room, then see a flash of blond hair.

My pulse quickens.

Could it be?

I crane my neck, trying not to attract too much attention. The last thing I need is Lance/Zain coming over to adjust or observe me. But before I have a chance to subtly double-check, I hear a familiar noise.

It's coming from my boobs.

My phone is buzzing.

I casually feel for the device, then slide it up closer to my face. If I'm caught using my phone in the studio, it's game over. I will undoubtedly be publicly shamed and humiliated, hanged in the middle of a metaphorical town square and pelted with rotten tomatoes. I subtly enter my passcode. When I turn my head to the left and peer at the screen, I see an Apple News alert.

This one is from *The Daily Mail.*

**KHALID WARREN HANGS HIMSELF
IN BEVERLY HILLS HOTEL**

Fuckity fuck fuck.

I met Khalid Warren over two years ago when I was invited

to another press event at Soho House on Ludlow Street, a fundraiser sponsored by some up-and-coming prison labor camp fronting as a sustainable underwear company. Fern was supposed to go with me but was asked on a last-minute date by a Portuguese botanist with face tattoos and a clitoris piercing. (They dated on and off for the next five months. It was intense; Fern set a few of her plants on fire.)

So I was on my own and a little bit too tipsy for a networking event, chugging expensive liquor and avoiding making conservation. Then *he* walked into the room: Khalid Warren. Son of self-made billionaire Gustave Warren and super model Aziza Warren. He was a trust fund baby with washboard abs, a Tom Ford suit, and the best jawbone money could buy, infamous for bedding and forgetting Hollywood sweethearts, gambling with Greek princes, and racing and crashing his father's vintage cars (RIP 1963 Ferrari).

The moment Khalid realized I wasn't falling over myself to talk to him, he bypassed all the other women in the room and started chatting me up. When I confessed I was working on a story about Poppy, Khalid stopped sipping his whiskey and began *chugging* it. Apparently, he and Poppy had met a few years back at a dark nightclub in Monaco. They'd ended up hitting it off, venting about their fathers' unfairly high expectations until the bartender yelled last call.

Poppy had suggested they take the festivities back to her hotel room. She'd ordered some party favors, she'd said, but her card had been marked for fraudulent activity and the shipment had been stalled. Khalid had handed over his own black card without a second thought. But when his driver had finally dropped him off at Poppy's suite, he'd been met with 450 grams of cocaine, three expensive European call girls, and a cadre of Monégasque police officers. And while Khalid was busy working out a deal, Poppy was working out his credit line. All the charges were untraceable, of course. But she'd managed to max out the card before he was released from his holding cell.

He and the police had come to an agreement that night: Khalid had paid the coppers an egregious—and most likely illegal—fine, and they'd forgotten about what they'd stumbled upon.

Poppy's name had never been mentioned, and he had refused to let himself think of "that bitch" ever since.

Now Khalid Warren, the unofficial prince of Sunset Boulevard, who has everything and wants for nothing, has hanged himself from his ceiling fan on a Tuesday afternoon. Just a few weeks after Poppy Hastings was released from prison and Rutherford allegedly went missing.

But he died by suicide, Rose, I hear Steph, ever the voice of reason, singing in my head. *He wasn't murdered.*

Poppy has been in New York ever since she was released. Fake Fern is chiming in now. *It's been well documented all over the internet. How could she possibly have murdered someone in California? Or Aspen, for that matter? Right?*

Shut up, I say to the subconscious iterations of my friends. *Shut up, shut up, shut up!*

"Ms. Aslani!" Lance—the real Lance—bellows. "If you're going to insist on being on your cell phone for the remaining five minutes of class, I'm going to insist that you resist the urge to distract your well-meaning peers and take your disruptive behavior *outside*."

Busted.

Every person in the room sits up and turns to look at me.

I gulp, then gather my belongings like the guilty party I am, exiting the studio with my head hanging low. But my mind is racing.

What does it all mean? How could Poppy possibly have pulled this off?

Five minutes later, a string of my sweaty, shaking classmates exits the room. They all take turns shooting me dirty looks. I grin back up at them, daring each and every one to chastise me the same way Lance did. Finally, Fern and Steph make an appearance.

"I can't believe you snuck your phone in!" Steph complains. "Seriously, what am I going to do with you? I can't take you anywhere."

"Oh, stop it." Fern comes rushing to my defense. "That class was twenty percent enlightenment, eighty percent pure horse tranquilizer. I can't believe we still come to these things. I'm so done with the unbearable whiteness of barre-ing."

I nod, trying to neutralize my face. Unfortunately for me, my friends know me too well.

"Hey," Fern says, "what's got you all hot and bothered?"

"Oh, nothing," I say. "Just thinking about eating the rich."

"Is this a prank?" Steph narrows her eyes in suspicion. "Or are you for real?"

"I'm telling the truth," I lie through my teeth. "I'm fine. It's fine. Everything's fine."

Chapter Eight

Everything is** so **not fine.

After learning about Khalid Warren's, er, untimely death, I have snapped. I'm spending an unhealthy amount of time studying Poppy Hastings's movements.

Well, her virtual movements, anyway.

For lack of better words, I'm fucking creeping on her social media accounts.

I'm sitting on my bedroom floor, overanalyzing every caption like a jilted lover. I'm poring over the word choice, the amount of punctuation, each tagged location, every filter, looking for clues. When I get stumped, I even muster up the strength to haul my ass to Roommate's domain and ask her opinion. And nine times out of ten, she just looks at me like I'm deranged and shuts the door in my face.

I know this all sounds a bit stalkerish. But I'm not a stalker, okay?

I'm not. I'm totally not. I promise you, it's all part of the pre-reporting process.

After a year and a half off the case, I'm just refamiliarizing myself with my subject. I need to be prepared, to know Poppy

Hastings's profile like the back of my unmanicured, bitten-nailed, bleeding-cuticled hand. It's crucial that I know everything about this she-demon, from her favorite color (blood orange) to the way she takes her coffee (black with a dash of spice).

Here's the fourth rule of conspiracy: You can never do enough "research."

I stop and take a big swig from the double IPA I picked up on my way home from work, closing my eyes and feeling the cold rush between my ears.

God, if Fern and Steph knew what I was up to, they'd be so fucking disappointed in me. I've been on my best behavior, but hiding the fact that spiraling again has become my second full-time job. Like, I'm spending a fortune on breath mints and eyedrops alone. At work, I participate in brainstorming meetings, pitching ideas and content packages just like I did when I was first hired at the Shred. Whenever Cat gives me an assignment, I smile and thank her for the opportunity. Today I even leapt at the chance to write five hundred words about a brand of cat food popularized by reality stars, which promises to make your feline's shit smell like a Diptyque candle. When I agreed to the story, Cat simply raised a brow. Even *she* is suspicious of Rose 2.0—and she *knows* what I've been up to in my spare time!

Yep. I'm taking pranking to a whole new level.

To get through the daily torture of maintaining my facade, I've developed a series of vices. The first, and the most traditionally questionable, involves doing an afternoon line of Adderall in the bathroom, just to give me a wee three p.m. buzz. I've found that doing so makes me giggle at small inconveniences and renders me far less likely to physically or verbally assault my coworkers.

The second is truly harmless: I've taken to sending our newest interns on wild-goose chases, emailing them essays and features to copyedit, asking them to correct small errors that don't actually exist. While this practice is a bit cruel, I find that their fear of me feeds my ego while also keeping them on their toes. Plus, it's good for entry-level nepotism babies, with their lunch stipends and fancy résumés, to maintain a healthy level of paranoia. They're much more comfortable than I was back in the day. It doesn't hurt to make the newbies sweat every once in a blue moon, bless their flawless pores and perfect skin.

Mostly I just pretend to work at my desk while dissecting Poppy's tweets, TikToks, and Instagram posts like fetal pigs.

Right now, I'm particularly consumed by a square photo on her grid, time-stamped five minutes before Khalid Warren was found swinging with a snapped neck, per the police reports. In the picture, Poppy is standing on an undisclosed rooftop overlooking the New York skyline. The view is practically panoramic—you can see as far uptown as the Empire State Building, as far downtown as the very top of the Freedom Tower. It's a beautiful day; the sky is an azure blue, rich and deceivingly close, as if you could reach out and grab a patch of atmosphere in the palm of your hand. Poppy is wearing heart-shaped sunglasses and a fluffy white bathrobe, which she's holding open right at the bosom. The suggestion is, of course, that she's flashing all of Manhattan. While her back is to the camera, she peers over her right shoulder, her lips curling into a coy smile. The caption reads:

My sociopathy may be chronic, but these tits are iconic.

The caption makes my blood boil, but it's the comments that truly send me over the edge.

Who needs empathy when you've got DDDs?

I'll let u scam away my life savings just to see ur boobs

UR MY HERO!!! How do I grow up 2 be just like u?

I've been staring at the photo for a disturbingly long time. Like, long enough to impact my weekly screen time report. If the government is somehow watching my digital activity through my iPhone, they're definitely convinced that I'm harboring a schoolgirl crush on Poppy. Either that or that I belong in a psych ward.

But my gut tells me there's something wrong with the post.

At first, I think the secret is in the sky—it's too saturated, too pristine for a city as sardonic as New York. I check the weather forecast for that day; it says it was partly cloudy. Ha! Got her. Or have I? I consider celebrating, but then I give myself a reality check. An overcast day is not enough to sway Cat into letting me write this piece for real. All Poppy needed was ten seconds of sun to snap a picture. Or maybe she took it on a different day, then scheduled the post. Even I can admit it's a reach and a half.

Stupid, stupid Rose. Fucking idiot. Get your shit together!

Maybe I'm losing it. I don't sound like I'm losing it, do I?

I take another swig of my beer.

And I stare.

I stare at the picture in the shower and on the toilet and while ordering takeout for dinner. In bed, I conference call Fern and Steph to debrief, laughing at all their jokes and pretending to be interested in how they spent their days as I secretly obsess over the picture. At two in the morning, I give up on sleep altogether. I reach for my phone and continue to stare, praying, asking a god my parents never let me believe in, for a sign, any sign.

I'm this close to throwing my newly repaired screen against the wall for the second time this month when I notice something small in the far left corner of the picture.

I zoom in to confirm my suspicion.

My exhale gets caught in my throat as I choke on my own saliva.

At first glance, it looks like nothing. But if you zoom in really, really close, you can detect a small shadow falling over the buildings beneath the Freedom Tower: two vertical objects, mirroring each other like the reflection in a koi pond. The shadow looks suspiciously like it's being cast by the Twin Towers, but that makes no sense. The Twin Towers haven't been fixtures of lower Manhattan since 2001, and the Freedom Tower has long been in its place.

How could a shadow of the fallen towers linger beneath its successor like a ghost? Could it be an omen of the apocalypse?

There's only one possible answer:

Poppy Hastings Photoshopped the picture.

And poorly, at that.

My heart races so fast I have to place both my palms on top of my chest, deeply concerned it'll run right out of my body. If she Photoshopped the picture, she's hiding something. Right? Right. Right! What else is she hiding? Being a mass murderer? Just kidding. That's ridiculous. A jump. Or is it? I screenshot the photo at least a hundred times, afraid that when I wake up tomorrow and check the post, I'll find the shadow lost to the ether as if I dreamed it or hallucinated its presence. I even email the file to myself with the subject line: EVIDENCE!!!! DO NOT DELETE! EVER!

You're losing it, darling, a British-accented voice whispers to me as I drift off to sleep.

That night, I have sweet, sweet dreams.

Poppy Hastings is ten years into serving a life sentence in a maximum-security prison. Time has rendered her irrelevant, a pop-cultural relic from the 2020s. She is but a footnote in history, while I have gone on to be one of the most influential reporters of all time. I've retired to a remote farm without internet access, where I grow and harvest all of my crops myself. Steph and Fern have neighboring meat and dairy farms. We gather each night and combine the fruits of our labors, preparing lavish meals for our ridiculously hot spouses while our children (who were all born the same month and are the best of friends) play quietly beside us. And there is no mention of Poppy Hastings ever again. She's gone, disappeared, and I am free.

I am finally happy.

The next morning, I wake up with a smile on my face. I immediately check the file to reconfirm my findings. The shadow is sitting there in the screenshot like a loaded gun, ready to be aimed in the direction of my choosing. I breathe a deep sigh of relief.

I take my time getting ready for work. I straighten my unruly hair until it doesn't look half-bad and opt for a button-down dress shirt instead of one of the many T-shirts that live sprawled on the floor at the foot of my bed. I even make time for a luxurious breakfast of hard-boiled eggs and multigrain toast. When Roommate hears the ruckus in the kitchen, she wakes up several hours before her usual call time to see what all the fuss is about.

"Are you sick?" Her expression is one of amusement.

"Quite the opposite," I say. "I've never felt better in my life."

"Your eyes are red." She sniffs me and scrunches her nose. "And you smell like bar."

I ignore her and strut out the fucking door.

When I get to the office, the first thing I do is request fifteen minutes of Cat's time, then reserve a conference room on the top floor so she knows I mean business. I arrive a few minutes before our meeting to set up my proof on the projector, even taking the time to make a brief PowerPoint presentation of my findings.

Five minutes after our agreed-upon time, Cat moseys into the room. At first, she barely looks up from her laptop to take in what I have for her. She continues to type as if in a catatonic state.

"What is it, Rose?" Her voice is static, already bored.

I clear my throat, grabbing her attention. "I have something to show you."

For what feels like five years, I speak a mile a minute. Cat, on the other hand, remains perfectly still. She watches me with an eagle-eyed intensity as I explain my logic—my interaction with Khalid Warren, his connection to Poppy Hastings, the fact that nobody appears to be connecting the dots in the same way I am. Finally, I zoom in on the photo, presenting her with my hidden shadow.

Now, I don't expect to be met with nods of approval or applause. But I do assume Cat will say *something*, anything.

An apology for doubting me.

Words of encouragement.

Most importantly, the go-ahead to start writing my exposé.

Instead, Cat stares blankly out the window.

"Rose," she finally says. "Are you on some kind of medication?"

My stomach drops, leaving a hollow feeling in my gut.

"I don't see how that's relevant—"

"I think you should take some time off."

"To investigate?"

"No. To rest. You're acting manic."

My face falls. I feel the room start to spin a little. Did I snort too much Adderall when I got in?

"Are your pupils dilated?"

Yep. Definitely too much Adderall.

My heart hammers. "Are you suspending me?"

Cat lets out a slow exhale. "No."

"Firing me?!"

"Good god, Rose," Cat says. "I'm suggesting you take a mandatory medical leave."

I clutch the table for support.

"But I'm fine," I whisper.

"No, Rose. You're not. Do you know what you have here?"

"Evidence?"

"A Photoshopped photo, Rose. That's all this is. Do you know a single influencer who *doesn't* Photoshop their photos? I mean, honestly. I'm deeply concerned. I know this isn't PC to say, but you sound certifiably insane."

"But I'm not insane," I can barely hear myself now. "I'm not crazy, Cat. This is real. I'm on to something here. If Poppy is lying about her whereabouts, what else is she lying about?"

"Rose!" This time, Cat yells. The volume of her voice startles me. I sink into my seat. "Listen to yourself. Poppy

Hastings isn't a suspect here. There isn't even a case. Khalid Warren's death was ruled a *suicide*. Ulysses Rutherford has gone *missing*. And Rose Aslani, who was once one of my most reliable reporters, is acting *deranged*."

I open my mouth to defend myself, then immediately close it. Whatever I say now will do nothing to change my circumstances. She's already made up her mind.

"Rose," Cat says again, this time softer. "Take the month. Visit your parents in Idaho or wherever. Go to the spa. Unwind a little bit. This obsession you have…it isn't healthy."

Defeated, I find myself nodding. Then I gather my laptop and notes and get up to leave. I hear Cat sigh behind me.

"Promise me you'll drop this," she says right before I walk out of the room. "You can't write this story, Rose. You never could. You're far too close."

I take a second to consider the request.

"I promise."

Then I slam the conference room door behind me.

At this moment, I only know three things for certain.

I am sure as hell *not* taking a spa day.

There is nothing on this polluted planet that could get me to drop this story.

Cat has no idea just how close I am.

TheRealPoppyHastings ✓ 2d

My sociopathy may be chronic, but these tits are iconic.

PoppersInTheBathroom 2d

Who needs empathy when you've got DDDs?

440 likes **Reply**

— **View replies (31)**

Horny4Hastings 2d

I'll let u scam away my life savings just to see ur boobs

113 likes **Reply**

— **View replies (2)**

PoppinB0ttleZ 2d

UR MY HERO!!! How do I grow up 2 be just like u?

5 likes **Reply** *See translation*

King_exhibitions011 1d

IM PAYING 5 GRAND TO The First 5 People To Message Me "Difficult TIMES" stay blessed y'all _:-D I do logo designs for your brand

Like **Reply**

JohnMayer ✓ 2d

hey sexy

1000 likes **Reply**

— **View replies (210)**

DaliaCutie88 2d

ATTENTION!!!!!! Don't look at my story if you don't want to get excited

Like **Reply**

Truth0vrMattr42 Just now

somebody listen to me before it's too late the illuminati is taking out powerful men first brad zarbos now ulysses rutherford and khalid warren I might be next everyone is on it the president and the royal family and tom cruise please help

Like **Reply**

Chapter Nine

"A vacation?" Steph asks. "You're taking a vacation? I don't understand. You've never taken a vacation. Why are you taking a vacation?"

"She needs a break from your friendship," Fern says, her voice expressionless.

"Not now, Fern!" Steph barks. "This is serious!"

"Guys." I flick a rotten banana peel off my shoulder. "Don't take this wrong way, but can you please calm the fuck down?"

"But I just don't get it," Steph whines. "We never go *anywhere*. We have no lives, remember?"

"Just put Steph out of her misery," Fern groans. This time, I can hear the smirk in her voice. "Admit this is a prank. Where are you?"

I look around me, taking in the stench of days-old deli meat and the slow drip hitting the top of my head. It feels suspiciously like a golden shower.

Not that I'd fucking know what that feels like.

Leave me alone.

"It's, uh, a remote location," I say. "A lot of wafting odors. Temperate with a light drizzle."

"So you're at a resort or something?" Fern asks.

I hear the sound of rats scampering above me.

"Let's just say it's a little crowded for my liking."

"You'd tell us if you were fired, right?" Steph demands. "You've been so good lately, I hate that I even have to ask—"

"Estefania." I resort to using Steph's full name just to get her to be quiet. "As I've already established, I'm at a writer's retreat. Cat put me up for it as a reward for all my hard work as of late."

"But you hate other writers," Fern retorts. "And getting your work critiqued. You've called writing workshops 'pretentious circle jerks for typewriting sadists' before. I remember because I wrote it down to use against you at a later date."

Damn. Having only two friends is really biting me in the ass right about now, huh?

"That's true," I admit. "Writers are the fucking worst. And I stand by that." I pause for a second. "Let's just say...my company is trash."

Just then, the ceiling above me miraculously lifts all the way and an influx of heavenly twilight fills my lair. Before I can appreciate the ability to breathe, someone dumps another garbage bag on top of my head, briefly knocking me down.

This one reeks of freshly spewed vomit.

I dry heave.

"What the *fuck* was that?" Steph screams, "Rose, I repeat, where *are* you?"

"I'm hiding out in a dumpster."

"Be serious!"

"At a writer's retreat, okay? Now, I have to go. I'm being very rude to my fellow creatives. And creativity is next to godliness, as they say."

"Isn't that cleanliness?"

"Bye!"

Before she can protest any further, I hang up the phone and get back to the task at hand: digging through the Rockland Hotel's dumpsters.

Okay. I know what you're thinking.

Rose Aslani, have you completely and utterly lost your mind?

And to that, I say: Would someone without a mind spend her entire day tracking Poppy Hastings's every movement, then rifle through her trash for clues?

Wait. Actually.

Don't answer that.

I've decided to take Cat's advice and use my time off to go on a little trip.

Off the motherfucking deep end.

Armed with my wireless charger and dressed in all black like a bank robber, I've been following Poppy Hastings's movements on socials, determined to catch her in the act.

What act, you ask? I'm not exactly sure. A bad act. A very, very fucking bad act, that's for sure. I'm certain that whatever's coming next won't be good.

My plan is flawless, in theory: watch Poppy's Stories, then trail her around town until she does something notably shady. Wherever she is, I'll be. She'll lead, I'll follow. We'll be attached at the hip like middle school frenemies.

What could possibly go wrong?

Once again, that question is rhetorical.

This morning, Poppy started her day the way she always does: with an unhinged livestream.

"Hello, my darlings," Poppy crooned into the camera, last

night's makeup smudged all over her cheekbones. "I just had the absolute *deepest* sleep. It reminded me of a time not too long ago when I accidentally snorted a little bit too much ketamine with a B-list celebrity in a highly overrated but nonetheless popular band and passed out for eighteen hours straight. The medics said they were surprised I didn't simply pass away that night! Oh, what fun we used to have."

Rolling my eyes, I refocused my attention on the Central Park backdrop of her video. The nearby street sign said Sixty-First Street. I did a quick Google search. There's only one luxury hotel in the area: the Pierre, home to the rich and morally depraved. I'd bet my nonexistent savings account that that's where she's staying.

Gotcha, bitch.

I quickly rushed out the door, mapping out my subway route. I knew that if I took the G to the E, I could be there in forty-five minutes. But by the time I scurried down the steps of the Clinton-Washington Ave. subway station, and swiped my way through to the platform, I was hit with a harsh reality.

The G was experiencing train traffic, because of course it was. I mean, the entire city is falling apart. And go fucking figure, the next train wouldn't arrive for twenty-one minutes.

Why do bad things happen to good people?

Running back up the stairs and onto the sidewalk, I checked the price of an Uber.

One hundred and one American dollars.

Cursing through my teeth, I said to hell with it and called the car. Maybe, just maybe, once my story is finished and Cat is eating her words, I can expense the charge to the Shred.

An hour later, following fifteen unbearable minutes on

the backed-up Manhattan Bridge, I pulled up to the Pierre. A doorman dressed in a purple-and-gold uniform and a funny hat, as if auditioning to be a background actor in Wes Anderson's next hit, opened the door for me. I sprung toward the concierge's desk.

"Is Poppy Hastings staying here?" I huffed, embarrassingly out of breath.

"I'm sorry, miss," the woman said. Her name tag read DARLA. "We can't disclose private information about our guests."

"Please!" I was full-on begging. "She's…my long-lost sister! I need a bone marrow transplant, and she's the only match. I'll *die*."

The concierge just stared at me. I could tell she was weighing the integrity of her position against the fastest possible way to get rid of me.

"Fine," she sighed. "If you're on your deathbed."

I nodded emphatically. She smirked.

"You didn't hear it from me, but Ms. Hastings checked out twenty minutes ago." She scanned my body from head to toe. "Are you her *half* sister?"

"Something like that," I muttered. "Hey, can I get a glass of water?"

"Sure." Darla's voice was saccharine. "Lemon- or cucumber-infused?"

"Lemon, thanks."

"No, you cannot have some water, you street urchin! Water is for guests and guests of guests. Get the hell out of this hotel!"

Some customer service.

Once I was off hotel premises and finally able to catch

my breath, I checked Poppy's social media activity again. Sure enough, she'd updated her Story.

"All my life, I've confused pain and pleasure." Poppy was lying on her stomach, the nook of her cleavage hovering at the level of the camera lens, her hair piled up on top of her head. A man covered in piercings and holding a tattoo gun stood beside her, grinning. "That's why I'm drawn to the work of Sergio, the greatest tattoo artist in the tristate area. Sergio and I, we go way back. He calls my body his Sistine Chapel, covered in hidden messages and forbidden details that give his life meaning and give meaning to divinity. Over the past decade, I've made many trips to Sergio's studio, and he's given me the pleasure and distinct honor of carving his greatness into my flesh. I feel marked by God. I've been a muse to many, yes. I've inspired several works of award-winning art. But it's a much higher honor to *become* the art yourself, no? Now, I know what you're wondering. Where exactly *are* my Sergio originals? That's a secret only my prison wife can tell."

Without warning, Sergio's gun began to buzz, and Poppy let out a little hypersexual moan, then winked at the camera.

I quickly looked up the words *Sergio, tattoo*. The results revealed a studio in a run-down railroad apartment in Ridgewood, Queens—a forty-eight-minute drive away.

How on earth had Poppy made it to Ridgewood so quickly? Could she *teleport*?

I ran to the curb, waving my hand in the air as if I was at a rave. A taxi quickly stopped in front of me, and I hopped in, giving the driver the address. As I sat in the back of the cab, I obsessively refreshed my feed over and over. I vowed not to allow myself to get cockblocked by Poppy's movements again.

If she was done getting tatted, I pledged to be the first to know about it.

After what felt like a lifetime, the car pulled up to the curb.

"We're here," the driver said, stopping the meter.

This couldn't be right.

After paying, I was standing on an abandoned street, Sergio's secret studio nowhere in sight. What I saw in its stead was an empty lot with a FOR SALE sign planted in the concrete and a scary-looking chain-link fence. There was also a bike, paint chipped and wheels slightly deflated, lying next to a wrinkled brown paper bag. In the distance, I heard a dog bark. Loudly. Angrily. For a few seconds, I considered searching the area to see if I'd gotten the location wrong or if the taxi driver had fucked up my directions. But the longer I stood in the same spot, the louder the barking grew.

Sweet baby Jesus.

I was not trying to die today.

Barely thinking, I grabbed the bike, sat on the obscenely low seat, and retraced my steps as fast as humanly possible.

Once I'd biked over to Greenpoint and felt safely surrounded by people, I disembarked from the haunted bike, which squeaked in the same way a little girl screams. I took a seat on the curb, doing my best to ignore the filth. Fighting off frustration, I pulled out my phone and checked Poppy's whereabouts.

Sure enough, she was on the move.

"People always ask me, 'Poppy, what's it like to be you? You're hot, funny, thin, rich, *and* you have a criminal record? You're the full package. Your life seems like a real roller coaster.'" The camera was suspiciously close to her face, focused on her charcoal spider lashes and a single gray-blue eyeball. "Well, my dears, can I tell you a secret? I'm a thrill seeker, it's true. I've dived out of more private jets than most of you have had birthdays. I've gone swimming naked with hammerhead sharks in the Maldives and jumped off the Cliffs of Moher with the father of my deceased lover. But I've never actually been on a roller coaster. In fact, I've always avoided theme parks. Why? All the poor people, of course. Would you expect me to ride Kingda Ka with a bunch of grubby foreigners? Please. I had an image to maintain."

Right then, Poppy flipped her camera, and I let out a gasp.

Poppy Hastings appeared to be seated at the edge of the world. She was flying high above the clouds—or a beach, anyway. From where she was positioned, the ocean looked as small as a reservoir, the people lounging on the shore beneath their colorful umbrellas merely tiny specks of sand. And Poppy Hastings ruled over it all: land and sea, friend and foe. She towered above the world like a fucking Titan, a Greek god at the foot of Mount Olympus.

I wanted her head on a fucking spike.

She licked her cherry-red lips, then let out a bloodcurdling scream.

I knew where she was. But she couldn't be. It was impossible. How could Poppy Hastings have gotten from Ridgewood to the top of Coney Island's iconic coaster, the Cyclone?

For a brief moment, I allowed myself to sulk.

I placed my head in my hands, fighting back tears. My gut told me that the second I arrived at the Coney Island boardwalk and ordered myself a disgusting but delicious Nathan's hot dog, Poppy Hastings would appear on Staten Island. We were playing a game of cat and mouse, she and I. Except, of course, she had no fucking clue we were playing.

Or that I even existed.

I'd been to Coney Island several times, and I absolutely loathed it. The crowds of crying children, the exorbitant ticket prices, the thickness of the air, rich with suntan lotion and blue raspberry colada. But the worst part, above all else, were the hordes of people having fun. There was nothing I fucking hated more than settings in which everyone was having fun but me. They make me feel guilty for not enjoying myself more, like professional buzzkills.

I resolved to go back home and wait for Poppy to make her next move. At least then I could put on a warmer jacket and finally relieve myself of the piss that'd been treating my bladder like a punching bag for the past few hours. I felt annoyed with myself; I hated giving up, feeling like Poppy had bested me. But I had started to realize that this woman possessed otherworldly superpowers. If I was going to catch her, I needed to be better prepared. I needed to be five steps ahead instead of five steps behind.

But as I made my way over to the G, my phone buzzed.

It was a text from an unknown number.

Poppy Hastings will check into the Rockland Hotel tonight.

I called the number back, but it had already been disconnected. Whoever was helping (or misleading?) me must have been using a burner phone. But who could it be? The only person who knew I hadn't dropped this story was Cat. But why would she be assisting me, and anonymously, at that? And how could she have insider intel about Poppy's whereabouts?

Before I had time to talk myself out of it, I decided to move on the information. I could freak out about the source later. Right now, I needed to get to SoHo.

Who needs to pee? Peeing is for losers!

I pulled up the route to Rockland Street, hopped back on my broken bike, and headed straight for the Williamsburg Bridge. I was pedaling like a coked-out traveling salesman, but I didn't care; I was determined to make it to the hotel before Poppy did. I moved with a vengeance, bypassing joggers and pedestrians. I almost collided with a tourist couple and their ten children but swerved around the family at the very last minute.

That was all I needed—to make headlines for maiming twelve innocents. Imagine the spectacle! Cat would off me for fucking sure.

By the time I made it to Houston, I felt like I was floating through downtown Manhattan. I looked up just in time to catch sight of the Calvin Klein billboard, which permanently resided on Mulberry Street.

And I almost went flying off my goddamn bike.

Staring down at me, over ten feet tall, was Poppy Hastings.

In her Calvins, naturally.

This fucking woman.

How could one person be both everywhere and nowhere at once?

I shook off the shock and kept moving forward. When I made it to the hotel, I threw the bicycle to the curb, went inside the restaurant on the first floor, and asked for the table closest to the door. The hostess briefly looked like she was considering turning me away, but then she nodded, leading me to a seating area that was practically hidden behind a waterfall of curtains.

And then it was time to wait.

Sure enough, about ten minutes later, I saw a Range Rover pull up to the Rockland, and Poppy Hastings popped out of the car. I inhaled sharply at the sight of her in person. This was the closest we'd ever been to each other. It was hard to believe that someone who had consumed so much of my headspace over the past few years could be, in all actuality, so petite. God, I hated most short women. So annoying, so dainty, with their high-pitched voices and pocket-size torsos. Like human Polly Pockets. Steph was the only exception. And Poppy was tiny, sure, hovering around five feet, but her presence was ginormous. There was a large fur coat draped over her shoulders, and her signature heart-shaped sunglasses were pushed up the tiny slope of her nose. My heart thumped loudly, an awful techno beat in my chest. I waited for her to walk through the double doors, but instead she walked around the corner toward where I had tossed my bike.

After ten seconds, I got up to follow her. I watched as she looked behind her and from side to side, then took something out of her pocket and threw it in the trash.

I waited another ten seconds, then went outside.

But by the time I made it to the sidewalk, Poppy Hastings had disappeared.

I ran over to the garbage bin, but it was full of sealed white plastic bags. There was nothing lingering on the surface. But this entire day couldn't be for nothing. So I took a deep breath, used what little upper-body strength I had, and hauled myself into the garbage.

Which brings us to the present moment, right here and now.

See? I wasn't lying to Fern and Steph.

I really *am* surrounded by pure trash.

When I return to the office, I'll tell Cat that my mental health vacation was lovely. That I even got to go on a dive. Sure, it was in a dumpster. But what's the difference, really?

Thirty minutes later, I emerge, covered in discarded waste and smelling of raw fish and rotting dairy, victorious. At the very bottom of the pile, I discovered something: a tissue with nothing but a print of Poppy's puckered red lips.

She's fucking toying with me. I can feel it.

I take out my phone and refresh my feed. Sure enough, Poppy Hastings has somehow made it to her suite and updated her Story.

Reluctantly, I click it.

"There's nothing worse than an uneventful evening spent in," Poppy says into the camera, battering her eyelashes. She's surrounded by a fort of pillows, nestled beneath a fluffy duvet. "But tomorrow is a big day full of meetings. I've got a lot in the works, my darlings. And I can't wait to show you what's in store. Now, I hate to sleep alone. But I'm never truly alone, am I? I've got all of you here with me."

She blows a kiss, and the screen goes dark.

And that's the end of that.

Poppy Hastings is tucked away at the Rockland, and I'm covered in someone's actual shit. I desperately need a shower.

I start walking toward the subway station with haste, clutching the tissue I just risked my sanity for between my fingers. But then I hear something, faint and lurking.

There's a quiet clicking behind me. It mimics my gait, slowing as I slow, then picking up to match my quickened pace—the unmistakable staccato of footsteps on concrete.

Someone's tailing me.

My mind races. I don't have a Taser or anything on me. Fuck, why didn't I take that self-defense class my father is always nagging me about?

I look for safe haven signs, but all the shops are closing up.

Hm.

I guess I could always scream?

Adrenaline courses through my veins. Before I lose my nerve, I turn around.

And come face-to-face with the most revoltingly beautiful man I've ever seen.

Chapter Ten

"Who are you, and why are you following me?"

The stranger grunts.

"Who are *you*, and why are you following Ms. Hastings?"

His footsteps echo in the dark. His voice is deep and rough and low with a slight smoker's rasp. It sounds like a slow-burning fire.

"I don't have the faintest clue what you're talking about," I retort. Why didn't I listen to my mother and buy pepper spray when I moved to New York? *Why?* "And I asked you first."

"What is this? Kindergarten?"

"Says the guy following me down a dark alley at night. Why would I tell *you* anything? News flash, asswipe—the victim isn't supposed to make nice with her potential murderer."

Silence.

"Fine," the voice reluctantly huffs.

He steps under a streetlight, and I catch my first clear glimpse of him.

There's a mop of messy black hair on his head, so dark it blends into the night sky behind him. It falls into his face, past his thick, coarse eyelashes. They frame catlike midnight-blue eyes. His gaze is hardened, suspicious, as if he's peering into my mind...which totally isn't focusing on the muscles pressing against his white T-shirt and leather bomber jacket. It doesn't fit him quite right—either a hand-me-down or a gift picked out by an old girlfriend, or perhaps his mother. His dark jeans and shoes tell me that, like me, he's trying to go unseen.

Suspicious.

Then there's that small scar lingering below his left eye, shaped like a tiny constellation.

I gulp, then shake my head, forcing myself to snap the fuck out of it.

Sure, he's super attractive.

But his beauty doesn't outweigh his potential to knock me out, place me in an ice bath, and harvest my organs.

"Look, I didn't mean to freak you out." The stranger avoids my gaze by looking down at his shoes. "I'm just wondering what you were doing swimming through Ms. Hastings's hotel's trash five minutes ago."

I cover my mouth in an attempt to look shocked. "Freak me out? You followed me, you pervert!" I say loudly. The last thing I need is to get caught in the act. But whoever he is, he doesn't look convinced. "And who is Poppy Hastings? I have no idea who that is. Find someone else to badger with your senseless questions."

"Oh yeah?" This time he cracks a smile. When the corners of his mouth turn up, the scar on his cheek sinks deeper into his face, giving him unnaturally sculpted cheekbones. I scowl at them. "Then why do you smell like sour milk and used condoms?"

"That's just my natural musk. Jealous?"

"And how do you know her first name? I never called her Poppy."

Shit.

We stare at each other for a minute longer, each daring the other to speak first. I consider making a run for it but decide against it. At six foot two, this dude could easily catch up and tackle me in a second. Something tells me that the one yoga class I attended in the past month won't make me particularly agile.

"Look," he finally says. "It's complicated. I'm investigating… something."

"So you're, like, a cop?" I frown. "I don't like cops. And they tend to not like people who look like me."

In fact, I have an ACAB dog tag attached to the keys that are wedged between my fingers at this very moment, in the event that I need to clock him in the face.

But no need to mention that.

"No, I'm not a cop." That vicious stare darkens once more.

"A spy?"

"No."

"Good, because no offense, my man, but you'd be, like, the worst spy of all time. I mean, look how quickly I got you to tell me that you're investigating someone."

He grunts, annoyed. Damn, it's easy to get under his skin. "I'm an agent."

"An agent? Like a secret agent?"

"No, like an FBI agent, wiseass."

I look him up and down once more. Between the five-o'clock shadow and the stench of wood chips and pine, this guy seems about as much like an FBI agent as my uncle Ahmad does—which is to say, not at all.

"Then where's your uniform? Why do you look like you're auditioning for an off-Broadway production of *West Side Story*?"

Mr. Night-Stalker-Turned-FBI-Agent winces.

I bite my lip.

"Not that it's any of your business"—he quickly glances over his shoulder—"but I'm undercover."

"As what? An extra in *The Sopranos*?"

"Okay, that's enough out of you," he snaps, but his eyebrows dance. In amusement? Annoyance? I can't tell. Probably a bit of both. "I don't give a fuck if you don't believe me. I only care that you explain to me why you've been tailing Poppy Hastings today."

"Really?" I snort. This dude truly must think I'm an idiot. Either that or that I've never listened to a true crime podcast. "Prove you're an FBI agent."

"You'll just have to trust me," he says.

"Now, why would I do that?"

He sighs, scrunching up his nose. Without breaking eye contact with me, he uses one hand to open up the right side of his jacket and the other to reach inside the inner pocket.

Oh my god. This is really happening.

A gun.

My stalker has a gun.

The next thing I know, the mystery man is huddled on the ground below me in the fetal position. He's flinching in pain, writhing around as if bitten by a snake. My brain belatedly catches up to my actions.

I just used the toe of my combat boot to kick him squarely in the balls.

"What the hell was that for?" he cries.

"You were going to shoot me!" I scream. "You have a gun!"

"What? I'm not carrying a gun! I was taking out my badge!"

"Oh!"

Oops.

I rush to his side and squat down next to him. I fight a strange urge to reach down and peel off his jacket so I can take a peek at what's underneath. But then I remember what I've done. And that he's still a certified stalker who hasn't explained himself. Or at the very least, a dick.

I offer him my hand instead.

He stares at my chewed-off cuticles, grimacing. "You know I could have you arrested for that," he says quietly.

"So you *are* a cop!"

"For the last time, I'm not a cop," he sighs. "Why don't you just call me Simon."

Simon cautiously accepts my hand. I tighten the single muscle in my core, attempting to help lift his body off the ground. He lets out a small yelp, then moans in pain. Even through his jacket, I can make out the hardened ridges of his forearms. Attempting to regain his balance once again, he leans his body weight ever so slightly against me. But when he realizes what he's doing, his back stiffens. He forces himself to stand upright, although I can tell it worsens the pain.

I roll my eyes.

There's nothing lamer than a man afraid of depending on a woman.

"Look, I'm going to need an ice pack and a cup of coffee," Simon says. "There's a diner right down the street. Why don't you join me, and I can ask you a couple of questions? You don't *have* to answer, if it makes you uncomfortable. But I figure you owe me now. You know, for attempting to chop off my dick with the heel of your boot."

I ignore the way his words travel all the way down my body and settle between my legs.

"Actually, it was the toe," I say. "And are agents allowed to use the word *dick*?"

"Only the secret ones."

"So, is this a date?"

"You literally just kicked me in the balls."

I snort, then give his proposal a moment of thought. On the one hand, this man could probably kill me and make it look like an accident. On the other hand, I am admittedly intrigued by his knowledge of Poppy, his sarcasm, and his thunderous biceps.

"Yeah, okay," I say. "But only because I don't want you to curl up and die on the street. I can't have manslaughter weighing on my conscience."

Simon squints at me, trying to figure out if I'm kidding. "You're kind of batshit, you know that?"

"So I've been told." I grin.

The two of us limp around the corner, getting dirty looks from the well-dressed locals meeting up for drinks and the overcompensating tourists posing for pictures. We're clearly not the neighborhood's "aesthetic," but neither of us seems to care very much about appearances. I watch a young woman sitting at an outdoor café wearing baggy cargo pants and a tiny tank top whisper into the ear of a friend, and my pulse quickens.

Could it be that they recognize me?

I know I'm not *famous*-famous, but after my Poppy piece,

people started to know who I was in very niche circles (aka New York media fuckfests). The breakdown that famously followed its release might also have something to do with that.

Calm down, Rose, I tell myself. *You're just being paranoid.*

Somehow, Simon senses my hesitation. He puts his arm around me and guides me away from the group of snickering girls as if shielding me from a crime scene. I follow his lead.

A bell rings as we enter the diner, and I immediately feel at ease. There's a flashing red neon sign on the mint-green building that immediately transports me back to the 80s. The floor is a chestnut-and-white checkerboard tile that flirts with the matching brown leather stools that line the countertop like the Rockettes in formation. The booths are padded, and almost every table holds a tall stack of pancakes (for dinner, naturally), powdered with sugar and drowning in maple syrup. I close my eyes and take in a caloric whiff.

For a brief second, it feels like being back in Ohio.

"Simon! I wasn't expecting you until Sunday." The hostess rushes over to us, greeting my stalker by name. She looks him up and down, taking in the expression of excruciating pain on his face. "Run into a band of thugs, did you?"

Simon's face turns as red as the ketchup bottles lining the counter.

"You should see the other guy," I say sweetly.

He exhales, looking relieved. His cover isn't blown.

Men.

The hostess laughs and begins leading us to the back of the diner.

"Normally, I'd put you in Simon's usual spot at the counter, but that really only works when he's dining alone—which he usually does. Aren't you going to introduce me to your friend, Sweet Cheeks?"

"I—"

"He's not my friend," I interject. He grunts in agreement.

Man, this Simon is really easy to rattle.

"Well, well, well." The hostess grins from ear to ear. "Any nonfriend of Simon's is a nonfriend of mine. Honey, I'm going to grab you a pot of coffee and an ice pack for that groin. I'll be back in a jiff!"

Once we're seated across the table from each other, I burst out laughing. Simon gawks at me. His forehead creases, somewhere between offended and amused.

"What?" he asks.

"Were you born in this booth or something?" I wipe away my tears with the sleeve of my shirt. "What was that routine?"

Simon shakes his head and puffs up his chest, looking down at his menu. Although I'm not sure why he bothers. Something tells me that he knows it by heart.

"Let's just say I'm used to working a lot of late nights," he says. "Maggie is a friend."

There's a tremor in his voice, one that's at odds with his steely expression. A hint of loneliness I immediately recognize.

We sit there for a few minutes, basking in the awkward silence, both studying our menus as if we'll be quizzed on them later in the night.

After a while, I can't take it anymore. I break the silence by popping the question.

"Well, can I see it?"

Simon raises one eyebrow. "What? You expect me to just *whip it out* right here on the table?"

My jaw drops. "Oh my god! Your badge! Not your dick!"

We stare at each other in horror.

Then Simon finally chuckles.

"Gotcha."

I bite my lip, trying to fight a grin of my own. "Not funny."

Simon reaches back into his pocket, this time using the other hand to make a "stop" motion toward me, preemptively warding off any sudden movements. When he's done rummaging inside his jacket, he pulls out a small leather square. Sure enough, there's a gold badge beneath an eagle with its wings spread wide. On it is written FEDERAL BUREAU OF INVESTIGATION, DEPARTMENT OF JUSTICE. There's also a (pretty bad) passport photo of Simon and some text that certifies that this signature and photograph belong to a special agent, by order of the attorney general of the United States.

Fancy.

"Are you even allowed to show me this? Not going to lie, it's kind of weird how forthcoming you're being. Like, you're either lying or you really suck at your job."

He rolls his eyes and snatches it back out of my hands.

"And how do I know this isn't forged?" I prod. "I've seen *White Collar*, you know."

"Well, I work in the white-collar division of the FBI," he says, smirking. "So I'm pretty sure I win that one." He slips his badge into his jacket pocket and turns to face me, his calloused hands clasped together. "Okay. My turn to ask you a couple of questions."

He leans toward me and cocks his head to the right, pushing his hair out of his face. As he pulls off his jacket, the muscles in his arms reactivate.

I suck in my cheeks.

"First and foremost, who are you? I think it's safe to assume that you're not the average run-of-the-mill New York City dumpster diver."

"Correct. I'm an award-winning champion New York City dumpster diver."

"Come on." His eyes widen. "Be serious. I don't even know your name, but you know mine. How is that fair?"

"Fine," I say, giving in. "My name is…Tulip. I live in Clinton Hill, by way of Ohio."

"Amish country?"

"Exactly."

"And what is it that you do, Tulip?"

I consider lying to him to avoid blowing my cover. After all, I'm on a top-secret mission myself. The last thing I need is for this little adventure to get back to Cat by way of a police report.

But Agent Simon has information I need.

He knows something about Poppy Hastings.

And I need to find out what.

So instead, I settle for tweaking the truth.

A harmless prank.

"I'm a writer," I finally say.

"Interesting." The expression on his face tells me that he's surprised. I wonder what he was expecting. "What do you write?"

"Romance novels," I make up on the spot.

"Smut?"

"Why, are you a fan?"

"And you were going through Ms. Hastings's trash because…?"

"Research," I answer. "Inspiration. For a story I'm working on. About...con artists. I've been looking into her whereabouts since she got released from prison."

"Romantic comedy?"

"You won't believe the creative ways my protagonist wields restraints," I deadpan.

Simon bursts out laughing. Then he nods, clearly racking his brain for what to say next. I take advantage of the brief reprieve and take back control of the conversation.

"So, what about you? Why were you following me today, hotshot?"

"Off the record?" he asks.

I nod.

Simon looks both ways, then lowers his voice.

"I wasn't following you. I was following Ms. Hastings. You just happened to show up everyplace she went. Nice performance at the Pierre, by the way. I had no idea you two were so closely related. Stepsisters, was it?"

Now it's my turn to blush.

He saw that? Shoot me. Right fucking now.

I decide to ignore his teasing. "And why are you following Poppy, Agent Cody Banks?"

"Well, what I'm about to say might sound a little, I don't know, out there," he says. "But I'm not entirely convinced her criminal days are behind her."

Before I can stop it, a gasp escapes my mouth, one so loud it could wake up half of Manhattan. I've been waiting *ages* for someone to say that very sentence out loud to me.

I just never imagined it would be my stalker.

Simon studies me, measured, and then his breathing

quickens. He leans even farther forward in his seat. He opens his mouth to speak, but as soon as he does, Maggie returns with our coffee and his ice pack.

We spring apart as if electrocuted.

"Simon, I know you take yours with cream," she sings like she's reciting a nursery rhyme. "And what about you, dear?"

"Black," I cough. "With a bit of spice."

As soon as she's out of earshot, I chug my first cup, then lean forward again.

"Tell me everything you know," I whisper.

"I knew it!" The overexcitement in Simon's voice causes him to wince once again. "You're not just finding inspiration! You're looking into her, too, aren't you?"

"Between you and me, yes, I am." My eyes burrow into his skull. "I believe she may be connected to the disappearance of Ulysses Rutherford and the suicide of Khalid Warren."

"How?"

"How, what?"

"How do you know Poppy Hastings is connected to Ulysses Rutherford and Khalid Warren?"

"That I can't reveal."

He stares back, eyes dark. He's looking at me with such hunger, it's as if I'm a ceiling-high stack of pancakes.

And he's ready to devour me whole.

"I believe you," he says.

"You do?" I feel a warm wetness welling up in my tear ducts. The sensation catches me off guard. I guess I didn't realize how badly I needed to hear those words. "You don't think I'm crazy?"

"Oh, you're definitely crazy," he says, the corners of his

mouth curling upward. "But for suspecting Ms. Hastings is capable of far more than embezzlement and fraud? No, I don't think you're nuts. In fact, I'd say you're seeing things more clearly than most people."

Adrenaline courses through my veins. I bang my fist on the table.

But Simon cuts me off.

"I was actually one of the junior agents assigned to her case a few years back," he says in an urgent whisper. "We'd been investigating her for about two years at that point. A Swiss bank had reported her for credit fraud. One of her checks had bounced. It turned out to be forged, of course. So we'd been slowly putting the pieces together. But the case turned out to be bigger than we were expecting. I mean, at first we thought we were just dealing with wire fraud. A few months in, my superiors believed we'd be able to get her for trafficking, espionage, maybe more. And then Brad Zarbos died."

His expression grows grim.

My heart is speeding down the I-95.

"My team was aware of the fact that Zarbos had had a brief extramarital affair with Ms. Hastings. I was convinced that she'd been involved in his death, especially when it became clear that there were mob ties at play. But then, to our surprise, those bastards confessed—to the murder, to running the gambling ring. To everything! It made no sense. It was too goddamn easy, and these things are never easy. I begged my deputy to hold off on Poppy's arrest, just for a little while, so I could continue investigating the connection between her and Zarbos in case there was some kind of cover-up. But it sounded a little out there, like a conspiracy theory, you know?"

Oh, I know.

He shakes his head, once again looking down at his menu.

"Anyway, they thought I was nuts. Plus, they'd gotten wind of some blog looking to blow the lid off our entire operation. Some shoddy exposé romanticizing con artists and whatnot. We knew if that happened, Ms. Hastings would either run or allow the media to catch her. And honestly, the latter sounded worse. So we ordered the arrest. She went away for a year and a half, but it wasn't enough. My gut told me she deserved to be locked up for life. But there was nothing we could do—the blog post on her came out, and it turned our trial into a spectacle, a complete and utter farce. She became just another viral sensation. Of course, when the review cycle came around, I didn't get the promotion I was up for. Now a murderer most likely is out there on the loose, roaming the streets, and I have to live with that every single day, knowing I could have done something to stop it."

A bead of sweat rolls down my forehead. I clench my fists, digging my fingernails deep into my palms, daring them to bleed. Simon looks up at me, alarmed. From the reflection on my spoon, I can only imagine what I've transformed into.

The face of pure, unadulterated fury.

"What?" He sounds panicked. "I'm sorry, I didn't mean to launch into something so dark. Sometimes I forget that not everyone's day-to-day life involves murder and mayhem. I always take it too far."

He sounds sincerely apologetic, but I don't care.

It's too late for him to take back what he's said.

"I'm familiar with murder and mayhem," I tell him. My throat feels like it's closing up. "Two and a half years ago, I received an anonymous tip about Poppy Hastings. I followed that lead, quietly reporting on her criminal activity for a year—studying her movements and her motivations and her relationships. So when someone close to Poppy was murdered, my antennas went up. I intended to bring Brad Zarbos's killer to justice with my writing. But you know why I couldn't? Because Poppy Hastings's arrest was made prematurely, forcing me to publish my story before it was complete. All to appease the audience of *a little blog*."

Simon's eyebrows shoot up, his entire forehead folding like a sheet of silk. He looks more pained than he did an hour ago when I kicked him in the balls.

"You work for the Shred," he says, his eyes narrowing. "You're Rose Aslani."

"And you're a pompous dickhead," I say matter-of-factly. "You ruined my story *and* fucked up your case. And now you've ruined my evening, too. You had seriously better stay the hell out of my way this time."

"Me?!" There's shock in his voice along with the anger. "You ruined my arrest! Your story turned Poppy's trial into a Hollywood special! She's *famous* because of you. And if you publish *this* 'investigation' before mine is finished, history will repeat itself. And you don't even care."

Now my blood is boiling hotter than the coffee.

I can't believe I ever felt *sorry* for this motherfucker. Clearly I didn't kick this man's balls hard enough. Screw forearms and banter—my first impression of him was spot on. Special Agent Simon is a total creep.

I really need to learn to listen to my gut.

"I know what you're trying to do," I tell him. "But this isn't some revenge fantasy. I *will* be the one to bring Poppy to justice. This is my investigation. *Mine.* You and your black suits and gold badges will do nothing but tip Poppy off. Again. And for the record, you wouldn't know subtlety if it bit you in the ass."

"Subtlety?" He gawks, choking on his coffee. "This from the girl who, I repeat, I found *going through the trash at Ms. Hastings's hotel*?"

"Whatever you do, stay out of my way."

"Fine," he practically snarls. "As long as you stay out of mine."

Simon gets so heated he takes off his jacket and places it next to him in the booth.

Don't look at his biceps, Rose, my head screams. *Focus on his stupid, smug face.*

I stand up abruptly, slamming my hands against the leather of my seat. Simon attempts to do the same but cringes in pain, tumbling back down. Just as I'm about to get in one last snide remark, Maggie walks back toward us with a pad and paper, ready to take our order.

"So, what else can I get you?"

Then she sees the expression on my face.

"Oh dear. Leaving so soon?"

"Thanks for the coffee, Maggie," I say. "But I've got work to do."

Simon growls, anger radiating from his face.

"You don't want to start this, Tulip," he snarls. "It won't end well for you."

"Start it?" I taunt. "Oh, honey. It's already begun."

Then I run out of the diner, slamming the door in my wake.

Chapter Eleven

"You've got to be fucking kidding me."

I look up from where I'm sitting on the sidewalk outside 30 Rockefeller Place, freezing my ass off in the standby line for *Saturday Night Live*. I'm wedged between a couple who literally will not stop making out and a father-daughter duo who flew in from Indiana for the occasion. They're wearing matching PROUD POPPERS T-shirts, which look handmade. I'm trying hard not to vomit all over their craftsmanship.

My plan is simple. After countless attempts to track down Poppy, I finally know precisely where she'll be for, at the very least, a full hour and a half—gracing the *SNL* stage. If I can gain access to the show, I'll pretend to get lost on my way to the bathroom or something and sneak backstage. Once I trick a dumbass NBC page into pointing me in the direction of Poppy's dressing room, I'll tag one of her belongings with a shitty tracking device with a hidden camera in it that I picked up from Best Buy.

One thing's for certain: I'm not letting that minx out of my sight ever again.

The one flaw in my highly calculated scheme is that it's

surprisingly challenging to get into *Saturday Night Live*. The building is guarded like a fucking army reserve, with security at the front and back entrances and metal detectors and turnstiles that require company passes. Getting invited to a show is nearly impossible, unless you're a nepo baby or willing to suck someone off for a seat—which I briefly considered.

But then I remembered that Rose 2.0 is all about integrity.

That traitorous bitch.

So, standby it is! Even if my line neighbors won't stop tongue-fucking each other.

I look up to see a pair of dark blue eyes glaring at me. The heat of their gaze could melt the skin off my face.

Goddammit. I should have known I'd run into Simon here.

Mr. Secret Agent's clothes are casual—a pair of light-wash jeans and a fisherman sweater—but the scowl on his face right now is anything but. He folds his arms over his chest in a way that suggests he's offended by my mere presence. He's standing and I'm sitting, so he's towering over me, clearly looking down on me.

I can't let that slide. I jump to my feet and copy his stance.

"What the fuck are you doing here?" I spit. "I thought I told you to stay out of my way."

I take in the shopping bag in his hand. He appears to have brought a neck pillow, a bottle of Gatorade, trail mix (the most boring snack of all time, go figure), the new Loretta James memoir, and a mysterious folder.

Wait a second.

"Oh my god, are you planning on waiting in this standby line?"

"What does it look like?" Simon grunts, running a hand through his hair.

"It looks like you're about three hours too late, idiot. Everyone knows you have to get here *before* seven if you want a shot at making it inside."

For a split second, I see a glint of concern in his eyes. He clearly didn't do his research. Ha! I'm one step ahead of the FBI agent. The government should pay *me*.

"Can I cut with you?" His voice is so low I can barely hear it.

"What was that?" My lips fight to curl into a smile.

"Can I cut the line and sit with you?" he asks, a little louder this time.

"Un-fucking-believable. He doesn't even say please."

"*Please*, Tulip. Will you *please* do me the honor of sitting next to me in this line and gracing me with your wonderful, upbeat, not-at-all-irritable presence? Because that's all I want to do with my Saturday."

I roll my eyes but size up the Gatorade bottle in his hands. It's half-empty. And yellow. *Fuck*, I really need to pee. I haven't been able to move from this spot in what feels like years.

Then an idea occurs to me.

"Only if I can pee in your Gatorade bottle," I announce with a smirk.

Simon spits out the sip he's just taken. "You can't be serious."

"As a heart attack. And you need to cover me. This line is full of creeps."

He stares at me, trying to figure out whether or not I'm all talk. While he's busy debating the merits of sharing this line with me, I swipe the bottle, squat down, and drop trou, all in one swift movement.

"What the—"

"Ah," I sigh, a ten-pound weight suddenly lifted from my bladder as I pee into the container.

Simon stares at me in horror as I hand back the bottle. The yellow liquid is indecipherable from my urine. He shudders at its warmth against his fingertips.

"You're disgusting, you know that?" He shakes his head. "Are you even human?"

"Takes one alien freak to know one."

"You know I could have you arrested for public urination, right?"

I grab a beer out of my coat pocket, crack it open, then take a long swig. "I thought you weren't a cop."

"And drinking from an open container?"

"Jesus, dude," I snort. "Could you be any more of a fucking narc?"

I sit back down.

This time, Simon reluctantly joins me. He winces as his butt hits the pavement, clearly still in mild pain.

"Do you have arthritis or something, Grandpa?" I prod. Then I wrinkle my nose. "What are you, eighty?"

"No, actually. Some lunatic kicked me in the balls, and I haven't been the same since." He gives me a smug look, then pauses for a second. "And for what it's worth, I'm twenty-nine."

Good age, I think to myself before rapidly suppressing my approval.

"Aw, I didn't realize I'd actually injured you. If there's anything you need, please let me know. I'm here for you."

Simon raises his brows. "Really?" He sounds surprised.

"No, not really!" I snap. "I couldn't give less of a fuck whether you live or die. In fact, why don't you sit a little bit closer to the edge of the sidewalk? Maybe a biker will make this easier on all of us."

"Go to hell," Simon mutters under his breath.

"Believe me, I'm already there."

We sneer at each other in silence for five minutes before mutually opting to ignore each other's presence.

I start scrolling through the Shred's website on my phone and zooming in on the bylines I don't recognize, a neurotic practice I've adopted since starting my mental health leave.

Simon takes out the folder and begins to read. I lean over, curious. He immediately pulls whatever it is he's looking at out of my sight line and glares.

"Why are you sitting out here with me, anyway?" I ask, breaking our silence. Oh well. It was nice while it lasted.

"The same reason as you, I presume." He doesn't look back up. "I'm tailing Poppy Hastings."

"Right, but why sit outside in the cold with the rest of us plebeians?" I gesture to my new friends, who have graduated from kissing to dry humping. "Why not flash your shiny badge and force your way into the building?"

"For someone who has no interest in working with me, you sure do ask a lot of questions," he says. Yikes. I guess I hit a nerve. "And what about you, Tulip? Your little blog couldn't organize a press pass for you?"

I gulp.

Obviously, flaunting my status as a bona fide journo-star to get access would have been preferable. But I can't have Cat or anybody else from the Shred knowing I'm here. Or even that I'm investigating Poppy, for that matter. So my hands are tied.

But that's none of Simon's business.

"Shall we shut the fuck up?" I suggest. "Any more talking, and I'll start to think you actually enjoy my company."

"Can't have that," Simon agrees. "Let's just do this alone, together."

I nod, but just as I look back down at my phone, a nervous-looking kid with frizzy hair wearing a ridiculously long skirt, a fitted blazer, and a bow tie emerges from the door at the front of the line. She's got an earpiece in, and she's holding a clipboard.

Bingo.

Everyone on standby suddenly leaps to their feet, buzzing with anticipation. I jump up and down, attempting to get a better view of the action. Simon struggles to his feet beside me.

"What's going on?" I stand on the very tips of my toes. "I can't see!"

Simon sighs, then leans down and lifts me with ease. My heart thuds at the unexpected contact with his upper arms. I try to steady my breathing as I look out over the crowd.

"You better not pee again," he mutters.

I ignore him. "Look! They're letting people in!" I squeal.

The wait is finally over.

Thank fucking god.

Another minute of arguing with Simon, and I might have done something seriously stupid. The man may be hot, but he's got the personality of a horse turd.

Simon places me gently down, and we slowly start to make our way to the front of the line. My pulse quickens as I think about being in such proximity to Poppy Hastings again. I imagine her picking me out of the crowd during her monologue and looking directly into my eyes, just like she did during her press conference.

Would I blink?

"Tulip, pay attention."

I zone back in just as the father-daughter duo makes it to the page ahead of us, which means we're up next. They're holding hands, squeezing each other tightly. The page smiles at them, then hands them their tickets. The dad then proceeds to hug—I kid you not, *hug*—the poor page while his kid takes a selfie of the three of them.

"This is it," I murmur, taking one last step forward. We're at the front of the line.

But just as I do, the page takes hold of a giant megaphone and turns to face the crowd.

"Standby line is officially closed," she announces. "Better luck next time."

"Fuck!"

Simon curses under his breath, and the couple behind me come up for air long enough to voice their disappointment. The rest of the crowd reluctantly disperses, unsure of what to do with themselves. I start running frantically toward the entrance just as the door shuts in my face.

"Goddammit!" I cry. "What did I do to deserve this? Where is all of this bad karma coming from?"

"Maybe from when you assaulted me?" Simon suggests.

"Or maybe from when I took pity on you and allowed you to cut this line," I snarl. "Line cutters always get what's coming to them. It's the law—which you should know, by the way."

I turn on my heel and start marching around the corner with the speed of a coked-up gazelle. Simon trots behind me, and I pick up the pace, hoping to lose him. When I reach the back entrance and find that it's locked, I let out a loud wail. I start banging my fists on the door just in case.

"Tulip, you need to calm down."

The bastard followed me!

"Don't you have someplace better to be?" I shove him slightly, and he stumbles backward. "Or is stalking me just your favorite activity?"

"Look, it's clear your investigation isn't going too well—"

"I don't know what you're talking about, but *my* investigation is going swimmingly! Swell! All the *s*-words." I'm shouting, but I don't particularly care at the moment. I don't need anyone reminding me how poorly this is going, especially with my entire career on the line. "And what about you, huh? Did the FBI cut its budget or something? Why don't you just get a warrant or whatever? I swear to god, sometimes I think you're not even a real agent."

His eyes grow dark as fury lights his face, somehow making the scar cutting across his cheekbone appear even more prominent. He takes a step forward, and I immediately take one back, but he's too fast for me. We're suddenly standing face-to-face, an inch apart. I can feel his breath on my forehead, hot, heating up my body right down to my core. He looks down for half a second at my lips before meeting my eyes again.

My breath hitches.

"Lovely to see you, Tulip." Sarcasm bleeds from his tongue.

Then he turns to walk away, and I finally let out the breath I didn't realize I was holding.

"You, too—not!" I yell at his back, but it's too late.

He's gone.

Did I really just hit him with a *not*?

My phone pings, alerting me to the fact that *Saturday Night Live* is about to begin. I groan, pulling up the live feed on my screen and zeroing in on Poppy's made-up face. She's dressed in a hot-pink power suit with a fur collar and cuffs, and her lips are painted their signature bloodred. The rest of the cast surrounds her in black-and-white-striped jumpsuits, and I feel my face begin to flush.

A prison sketch.

Their cold open is a prison sketch.

Because of course it is.

It's like the writers have developed a new method of torture just for me.

"Get ready, New York." Her voice is as rich as her marks. "Because tonight? I'm going to kill."

Chapter Twelve

Steph (6:42 p.m.): Hi!!!!!!! We miss you over here on the little isle of Manhattan! Work is seriously SO boring without you. The Shred is going overboard scheduling meetings for next month's issue—which, of course, means I've been doing a big post-mortem analysis of last quarter's issue all by myself, crunching all the numbers for search, social, etc. But will I get any credit for it???? You know I won't. Anyway, enough about me. How are you??? Why aren't you responding to the groupchat? You're not using again are you… sorry sorry I know I promised I'd stop asking you that. I trust you I swear. I just worry, you know? How's your top-secret writer's retreat that Cat shipped you off to? Have you killed your fellow patrons yet? I keep checking for news alerts about the mass slaughter of twenty workshop students, but nothing yet…lol. But seriously, it isn't the same without you. Fern and I have been meeting alone in the kitchen, but it just hits different. We always end up arguing because she takes her pranks too far. Don't tell her I said that. Pls. Lol.

Twitter (7:24 p.m.): No new notifications.

Fern (8:57 p.m.): Okay. So. I know you're, like, sucking Salinger dick in the Amazon or whatever, but you wouldn't happen to have left my spare key in your apartment, would you??? No big deal, but I've gone on three dates with this amazing performance artist who works exclusively with oat milk as a medium... Anyway, things were going great. She was really into all the things I care about—sustainability, Red Scare, neck biting...until I left her alone in my apartment for, I kid you not, TEN MINUTES to go get a six-pack of Three Leaves from the bougie bodega, and the chick goes APESHIT and tears apart my entire place. She found a second toothbrush in my medicine cabinet, which is obviously for you and Steph and not for anyone special, but whatever, and freaks out. So now I'm locked out of my place, I'm not wearing underwear, and I've already drunk half my beers and need to pee. Do you think Roommate would let me crash at yours? Or does she have the key? SOS please answer!!!!!!

Fern (9:03 p.m.): False alarm. Please ignore above text. Was a prank. Hope you're having fun ily

Instagram (10:14 p.m.): Your friend @TheRealPrisonPoppy hasn't posted in a while.

Unknown Number (11:32 p.m.): Looks like the trail's run dry.

Rose (11:33 p.m.): Who is this?

Unknown Number (11:33 p.m.): Who do you think?

Rose (11:34 p.m.): Dad???? Daddy??????

Unknown Number (11:34 p.m.): Very funny. You're hilarious. I can see why you spend your free time dumpster diving.

Rose (11:34 p.m.): And I can see why I kicked you in the balls. Next time, I'll aim for your face.

Unknown Number (11:35 p.m.): Great. Now that we've settled that, what are we going to do about Poppy?

Rose (11:35 p.m.): WE?? There is no we. *I* am going to take a bath, finish my pad thai, masturbate, then go to bed. I have no idea what you're going to do. Probably, like, math or something.

Unknown Number (11:35 p.m.): Math???

Unknown Number (11:36 p.m.): Choosing to ignore that. And we both know you've got jack shit where Poppy's concerned. What do you say, Tulip? Truce?

Rose (11:36 p.m.): Is this a trap? Are you trapping me?

Unknown Number (11:37 p.m.): I'll show you mine if you show me yours.

I put down my phone and let out a loud groan.

God-fucking-damnit.

Just when I thought Poppy Hastings couldn't possibly hurt me more than she already had, she did the one thing worse than overexposing herself, rubbing her fame in my face, and haunting my every day and night. She went dark.

No new posts. No new Stories. No new celebrity sightings or paparazzi photos.

If I didn't know better, I'd think the bitch was dead. But no, death would be too kind, too easy. Besides, Poppy Hastings wouldn't die quietly. She'd die on a livestream with a billion people watching.

How's that for dystopian?

But seriously, this presents me with a giant dilemma. If I'm not tracking or obsessing over Poppy, what the hell am I supposed to do with all this free time? I still have another week left of mental health leave and can't exactly show up at work out of the blue ahead of schedule. Cat will just throw me out onto the street and insist I try acupuncture or something.

The only silver lining to Poppy going dark? If I can no longer see her, Simon is walking blind, too. That fucking asshole, with his know-it-all attitude and misogynistic grunting and absurdly strong arms. He is seriously becoming the bane of my existence.

Well, he certainly got what was coming to him. If I haven't

gleaned any new information in the past few days, odds are he's even more screwed than I am. That'll teach him to call my writing "blogging," to dismiss my investigation as child's play.

To breathe so close to my fucking face.

I sit up in bed, brush the peanut crumbs from my pad thai off the blanket, put away the whiskey I've been nursing, and consider his offer.

On the one hand, Simon is my nemesis, and it's almost midnight.

But on the other hand, I can admit I've reached a total standstill in my investigation. I can't go on as I have, decoding Instagram photos and writing conspiracy porn in my Notes app. I'll take literally any new information I can get, even if it comes from that macho toad.

So many questions left unanswered.

What does he know?

What don't I know?

And why does Simon have a stick up his ass the size of the Statue of Liberty?

Rose (11:42 p.m.): How did you get my number btw?

Unknown number (11:42 p.m.): I work for the FBI, remember?

Rose (11:43 p.m.): Creep.

Unknown number (11:44 p.m.): Crazy.

Rose (11:44 p.m.): Fine. Where should I meet you?

Unknown number (11:45 p.m.): 435 E 13 St. Text me when you arrive.

Rose (11:45 p.m.) Great. Now I know where you live. How are you sure I won't rob you or something?

Unknown number (11:46 p.m.): Tulip, did you really just text an FBI agent that?

I sigh, then hop out of bed and grab my keys, not even bothering to brush my hair or put on proper clothes. I'm dressed in leggings and a baby tee that says MOMMY'S LITTLE NIGHTMARE, which has a gaping hole in the left armpit, but I cover it up with an oversize hoodie. When I open the door to my bedroom, I find Roommate and Boyfriend huddled together on the couch like Russian nesting dolls. She looks up at me, her eyes red and heavy-lidded.

"Oh good, you up," she says, sitting upright. "Have you seen yoni egg?"

"No, I have not seen your yoni egg."

"Too bad."

I turn around and head toward the door, but something inside me stops my feet in their tracks. Could it be a sense of responsibility? I mean, I'm stepping out at midnight to rendezvous with a virtual stranger who basically admitted to running a background check on me just to get my number. What if I turn into an Amber Alert or something?

Locating a pad of Post-its and a pen in a kitchen drawer, I scribble down Simon's address, then peel it off and hand it to Roommate. She looks at me with amusement, biting the inside of her cheek. Boyfriend even raises his head to see what all the fuss is about.

"I am going to this address. If I am not in my bed tomorrow morning, please tell the authorities that I was either kidnapped, trafficked, or murdered by Simon...actually, I don't know his last name. But he works for the FBI and is, like, seven feet tall with dark blue eyes and blackish hair. It shouldn't be too hard to track him down."

"You go on date?" Roommate's eyes are wide with disbelief.

"Did you hear anything I just said? No, it's not a date," I bark, then immediately feel bad. Roommate is harmless. Smelly? Sure. Insane? Probably! But cruel? Not in the least.

"Look, just do it, okay?" I order her, wrinkling my nose. "And maybe shower while you're at it."

This time, I actually make it out the door. "Enjoy!" I hear Boyfriend yell as it slams shut.

I get off the subway at First Avenue and begin my trek toward Thirteenth Street and Avenue A. This part of the city feels cluttered, with drunken, underage college kids hanging all over each other, waiting in line to get into shitty, overcrowded bars. I detest kids. Truly, I think all kids other than my future children (maybe?) should be outlawed. Banned. Put in jail. They're always putting their hands in something sticky and making loud noises and acting needy. Especially when they grow up into adults. Man, I hate adults.

Maybe I just don't like people.

I shove my way past the cretins, though I could very well stroll down the other side of the sidewalk. But I do so with intention—they haven't earned the right to be so carefree, so trusting of the city. New York will betray them eventually, as it betrays us all. It's just taking its sweet-ass time.

"Hey, watch it, lady!" a boy in a baseball cap screams. See, what did I tell you about making loud noises? He can't be much older than eighteen. A baby.

"Yeah, yeah!" I yell back. "Beat it."

"Bitch."

"You got that right."

I arrive at the address Simon gave me and shoot off a quick text to let him know I'm here, and the front door buzzes open.

"Walk up to the fourth floor!"

Simon.

I recognize his voice immediately, deep and raspy, and follow its echo up the stairs. Once I reach the final step, I turn the corner, and there he is, standing in the doorway. He's further ditched the incognito leather look, opting for a pair of light gray drawstring pants and a T-shirt instead. The loose loungewear suits him. He looks more comfortable, less like he's trying to be someone he's not. My eyes trail down his body, stopping right at his waistband before shooting back up to meet his.

Get a grip, Rose 2.0. Eyes up here. This man is not your friend.

Which reminds me of the fifth rule of conspiracy: Keep your friends close but your enemies closer.

How convenient.

I clear my throat.

"Is that a badge in your pocket, or are you just happy to see me?"

"What?!"

"Gotcha."

Simon scowls, but the corners of his mouth pull upward, once again showing off that scar indentation that shaves an inch into his cheekbone. I fight a smile of my own.

"All right," he says. "Come in, Tulip."

"You don't want to stop and frisk me first?"

"Can you stop pissing me off and get in the damn door?"

"I'm just looking for any hidden weapons. Last I checked, we weren't exactly fond of each other."

"Yeah, yeah, fuck you, too. Come in."

We glare at each other for a brief moment, and then I step into his apartment.

To my surprise, the space is nicer than I expected. Though Simon's presumably a straight cis man with anger issues, there's not a single framed football jersey or Coors Light neon sign in sight. The walls are painted a warm hue, and there's a zebra-print rug covering the hardwood floor. His couch is gray, standard—no frills, all business, very Simon. But it's covered in unexpectedly colorful knitted throw pillows and blankets. And yes, there's a La-Z-Boy reclining chair with its own cupholder. But there are also bookcases filled with, like, actual books. I even see a couple of my favorites. James Baldwin. Salman Rushdie. Even Nora Ephron. The lights are appropriately dimmed for this hour, which accidently gives the space a romantic feel. I immediately locate the switch on the wall and brighten the room.

I know there can't be any funny business here tonight. But my hormones appear to be confused. And I need to send a clear message to my hardened nips.

"Is it standard FBI practice to invite your sources over for a drink? Or are you planning to roofie me? With truth serum?"

"Do you think I'm a spy or something?"

"Spy, agent. Same diff."

"Aren't journalists supposed to be all about the details?"

"Well..." I shrug, not wanting to talk about my career. "I'd take a beer if you offered."

Simon rolls his eyes until I can see mostly white, then walks over to the kitchen and pulls two bottles out of his fridge. The opener makes satisfying popping sounds as the caps fly off and the liquid breathes. He hands me one, and I cautiously accept.

"What should we cheers to?" I prod.

He stares at me for a second. Then his eyes light up.

"To white flags." He raises his bottle.

We clink, then drink quietly. I finish my beer in one big swig, then let out a belch loud enough to reach Roommate all the way across the bridge. Simon chokes.

"Jesus Christ, Tulip."

I grin. "What?"

"You downed that kind of quickly." There's accusation in his statement.

"And your point is?"

"You got a problem I don't know about?" His eyes are wide, sympathetic, like he's actually concerned. Except he can't be, because he doesn't know me at all. What, was "out of control" in my file or something?

"Yeah, I've got a problem." I narrow my eyes. "You."

And just like that, the sympathy is replaced with another scowl.

"You know, just because we're working together—"

"*Discussing* working together—"

"—doesn't mean I like you very much."

"The feeling is mutual." I go to take another long, cold sip and find the bottle empty. "And you didn't answer my question. What's with the safe house? Shouldn't we be in a room with, like, two-way mirrors or some shit?"

Simon scrunches up his features, clearly sick of all my cop references.

"I don't know if you checked the time, jackass, but it's a little late for office hours."

"I suppose."

Without being invited to do so, I mosey on over and start going through his bookcases, taking classics off the shelves and leafing through them. I'm surprised to find notes lovingly scribbled in the margins. It appears he dog-ears his pages.

Typical. What a sociopath.

"You can read," I observe.

"More than just cease and desist orders."

I move on from the books and begin sticking my nose into his drawers, but he doesn't try and stop me. It's as if he has nothing to hide, nothing to gain from being secretive or withholding. If I didn't know the male species better, I'd think that Simon is as open as his books.

That's when I notice stacks and stacks of old cassette tapes, CDs, and records, shelved next to a pretty serious-looking old-school stereo setup. It's big and black and looks more like some spy tech than surround-sound equipment. Curious, I turn it on with a big red button and press play on whatever's queued up.

"Wait!" Simon yells from the kitchen. "Don't do that!"

But it's too late; orchestral music starts blaring from all four corners of the room, followed by a familiar beat. At first, I think it's hip-hop—which, you know, catches me off guard in and of itself. But then I hear the bars.

About one of America's founding fathers.

"Oh my god. Were you listening to *Hamilton*?"

"I—"

Gasping, I begin flipping through the rest of his records, each discovery more shocking than the last.

Rodgers and Hammerstein.

The Sound of Music.

South Pacific.

Jersey Boys.

Even the *Mean Girls* musical!

"Holy fucking shit."

"Okay, so I like show tunes," Simon mutters.

"You're. A. Theater. Kid."

"Am not."

"I bet you played Danny in *Grease* in high school."

Silence.

I choke back a laugh.

Simon just narrows his eyes.

"Holy shit. You did."

"Fine. I love musicals, okay?" he concedes, throwing his hands in the air. "So what? I'm from Maryland. When I first got relocated to the city, my parents came to visit me every few months. I'm an only child. They miss me when I'm not around. And we'd go to shows. I find musicals kind of, I don't know...therapeutic. All the extravagant sets and the dance numbers and the music. So I started going alone sometimes. Just when I need to clear my mind a bit."

"Simon, that is just...precious," I admit.

He runs a hand through his mop of dark hair. "Yeah?" A lazy smile curses his lips.

I nod. "But I think it's only fair that you let me write a piece about this in the Shred. You know, as payback for ruining my story."

"You mean ruining *my* investigation."

"And here I thought we were finally getting somewhere."

Simon flares his nostrils and looks away, but I bite my lip in an attempt to hide another grin. This came totally out of left field. I look at Simon, whom I had dismissed as just another product of toxic masculinity, and can't even begin to imagine him swaying his burly body to the beat of Lin-Manuel Miranda's masterpiece, mouthing the words to "Wait For It."

I guess I misjudged his actions. I assumed that the reason he didn't want to lean on me, to appear weak in front of me, was because I am a woman.

This whole time, could it actually have been because of… who I am as a human? You know, my personality? Grating. Cynical. Hypercritical.

Me, Rose?

"My parents never took me to see musicals or plays," I offer. "They were more into sports. The all-American ones, mostly. Football. Baseball. Wherever people bled red, white, and blue. I think it was an immigrant assimilation thing."

Simon takes a seat on the couch, and I follow suit. We maintain a healthy distance of six feet between us, almost the entire length of the sofa.

"My folks never forced me to play sports," he says. "And I was grateful for that."

"But you're in such good shape!" I blurt out, immediately regretting it.

Simon smirks, and I curse myself for feeding his ego.

"Yeah, well, I like to work out, but I never really saw the point in all the meaningless competition. They were pretty surprised when I went into the service. But I was recruited early, in college. I studied psychology, and I was pretty unclear on where and how I'd use it. Mostly, I think they felt relieved that their only kid was going to make something of himself. Serve his country and all that jazz."

"I'm an only child, too," I say. "It can be a lot of pressure."

"Tell me about it," Simon agrees. "Not to mention lonely."

"You must have lots of friends."

Simon grunts.

"Dates?"

Oh my god. Am I…fishing? What the fuck is wrong with me?

"I see women," he says, his voice low. "But I wouldn't call what we do dating."

I feel my face flush a deep crimson.

Is he flirting with me? Am I flirting with him?

No.

Fuck no. I despise this man.

I have to shut this down. Right now.

"Probably because you have the personality of a chewed-up wad of gum."

"At least someone bothered to chew me," he retorts. "You're sitting, expired and unsold, in the back of the bodega."

"Ouch." But I grin so hard my teeth hurt.

We both accidentally lean forward at the same time, and the gap between us shrinks. Simon lifts his arm, and for a split second, I think he's going to place it around my shoulders. Instead, he reaches around me and grabs his beer off the windowsill, taking another sip. I look away quickly, embarrassed.

My hormones are out of control.

"Enough small talk," I say. "You know who else is an only child? Poppy Hastings."

Simon looks up at me. Something flashes in his eyes like a bolt of lightning. What was that? Disappointment?

Not that it matters. We're both here to do a job. We share that understanding.

"I did know that." He brings out that mystery folder and pulls out a file, handing another identical one to me. "She was born to Christine and Oliver Watts in Hastings, England. Her father was a factory worker, and her mother was chronically ill and couldn't work. They cared for her until she was five, when she started exhibiting signs of manic behavior and was institutionalized in—"

"—an orphanage for wayward children," I finish his sentence. "She stayed at Saint Judith's for five years, and during that time, she was separated from the other children for their own safety twice. She had a personal file the size of Texas, from what I hear. Known for starting fights and throwing tantrums. Then, at age ten, she was adopted—"

"—by Georgia and Tom Huxley, who owned a chain of laundromats in London. On paper, anyway. But in reality, they were petty criminals. Their laundromat franchise was a front, used primarily to funnel money."

I stare at Simon long and hard, trying to decipher whether or not he's serious. But there's not an ounce of insincerity in his dark eyes, not a splotch of redness creeping up his neck. My entire body starts to vibrate, my left knee slightly shaking. Simon notices and reaches out one hand to lightly steady it.

"I didn't know that," I finally say. "About her parents, I mean."

"That makes sense," Simon says. His tone is so careful it feels condescending. "The FBI has access to information that regular civilians do not. Not even reporters."

My head is spinning with the implications of what he's just said. Poppy's parents were criminals. Did they raise her to be one, too? All this time, I thought Poppy Hastings had emerged a fully formed psychopath at age twenty.

Was she a product of nurture, not nature?

I look back at Simon. He's already staring at me, his eyes flashing with concern.

"Have you spoken to them?" I ask. "How come they haven't been questioned?"

"Well, that's not my jurisdiction."

"But their daughter is?"

"Poppy became an American citizen a little less than a decade ago. You know that. And it doesn't matter, anyway." His face falls. "Because they're dead."

My stomach sinks. "How?"

"In a fire. Almost three years ago. Gas leak. The entire building burned down."

I take a second to process everything. Poppy's parents were criminals. Maybe she doesn't have antisocial personality disorder. Maybe she was just a victim of circumstance, of a shitty upbringing. I can understand that.

Wait a fucking second.

Am I *empathizing* with Poppy Hastings?

"Well, congratulations, Agent Simon." I swallow. "As it turns out, you're not a completely useless piece of shit after all."

His mouth twitches. "That might be the nicest thing you've

ever said to me," he says. "For the record, I still don't think you should publish that story."

"And I think you should wait to make that arrest," I say.

We lock eyes again, and I feel the skin on my arms pebble. I grab his beer and chug the rest, then chuck the bottle in the bin. Simon watches me as I wipe my mouth with the back of my hand, his eyes never leaving my lips.

"So, what do you say?" He extends his hand. "Partners?"

"And who gets to make the final call? Who gets to bring Poppy down?"

Simon cocks his head and sighs. "I guess we'll cross that bridge when we come to it."

I reach out and shake his hand. It engulfs mine, large and calloused. He squeezes my palm with a strong, firm grip.

"Partners," I say. "Even though I still hate you."

"Yeah, yeah, Tulip." He grins. "I hate you, too."

Only this time, I'm a little less sure either of us means it.

Today—Google Search History

3:21 a.m.

christine and oliver watts - Google Search

www.google.com

3:27 a.m.

saint judiths orphanage - Google Search

www.google.com

3:33 a.m.

georgia and tom huxley - Google Search

www.google.com

3:33 a.m.

georgia and tom huxley dead obituary fire - Google Search

www.google.com

3:41 a.m.

poppy hastings antisocial personality disorder scale test - Google Search

www.google.com

3:45 a.m.

is it normal to hate someone w a burning passion but also want to blow their back out - Google Search

www.google.com

Chapter Thirteen

Here's what we're not going to do on our first day back at the Shred:

1. We're not going to answer any questions about the "writer's retreat" we've been on. Instead, we will smile, nod, and give vague responses.

2. We're not going to give Cat any reason to believe that we've spent the last few weeks doing anything other than taking Himalayan salt baths and microdosing shrooms.

3. We're not going to think, speak, or react to the name Poppy Hastings. As far as we're concerned, Poppy Hastings does not exist.

That bitch is dead.

It's my first day back from my mental health leave (or writer's workshop, depending on who you ask), and I'm feeling as fresh as a newly lasered armpit. A sense of purpose pumps through my fucking arteries. Simon and I have officially joined forces on our investigations, and even though I still think he's a major see-you-next-Tuesday, we're finally making some headway. We're both trying to crack the code on the man currently rotting in a cell in a maximum-security prison in Pennsylvania for the murder of Brad Zarbos. We're even considering taking a little road trip south to Philly.

We have a pretty good system going, Simon and I. We text in code about our case, touching base each night before we go to sleep. Sometimes I ask him what he's wearing just to make him squirm. Other times, he sends inappropriate memes that make me snort with laughter. He never brings up the fact that he wants to make his arrest first, and I never bring up the fact that I plan on breaking my story. We pretend everything is kumbaya and avoid talking about our differences as much as humanly possible. And I ignore the slightly irritating tightening sensation that happens in my chest every time I see his name flash across my screen.

Poppy, on the other hand, reemerged on all social platforms just in time to present an award at the VMAs. She blamed her technology blackout on a phoneless yoga retreat, which, as far as I'm concerned, sounds about as bullshit as my writer's workshop. But she's back in full force—livestreaming her backstage champagne showers, hitting on both Megan Fox and Machine Gun Kelly, flexing an ankle bracelet (monitor) above her strappy stiletto with what is essentially underwear. And her opening remarks weren't subtle, either—they included five references to her time in prison, four mentions of her arrest, three shout-outs to scammers across America, two thinly veiled threats, and one purposeful nip slip. Once again, Poppy managed to go from being a sidenote to a headline. Instead of breaking the news about who'd won, she became the news. It's as if she absorbs all criticism like a loofah—it only makes her stronger, more powerful. The more problematic she grows, the more visible she gets and the more her zealous fans defend her.

Like a motherfucking demigod. Or Satan herself.

But shockingly enough, I'm not allowing any of her good press to get to me. Because I know that Simon and I are making real progress. As far as I'm concerned, she better enjoy her fleeting fame, because it'll last about as long as her first prison sentence.

Sooner or later, we're going to take her down.

On Monday morning, I strut onto the middle floor, laptop under my arm and iced coffee in hand. I feel more like myself than I have in years. Fern and Steph are standing at my desk, ready to welcome me back. I guess they couldn't wait until our noon kitchen date. We lock eyes as I step out of the elevator and rush toward one another, flinging all of our limbs around each other in a massive, messy group hug. Fern grunts, embarrassed by the public display of affection, but I don't fucking care. I squeeze them tightly, juicing them like oranges.

"I've missed you guys," I cry. "I hate everybody but you."

"We missed you, too!" Steph is glowing. "We have so much to talk about. Seriously, I want to hear everything we missed. Where were you, who did you meet, what did you write, how did you sleep, etc. You better not have a new group of best friends. Should we get drinks after work and catch up?"

"I didn't miss you at all," Fern adds. We smirk at each other.

"The retreat was great." I smile and nod as rehearsed. "I'm so glad I went."

"Whoa there," Fern says. "Don't unload on us like that."

I roll my eyes, forever grateful for Fern Basset.

"Wait," Fern gives me a big sniff. "What's that smell?" She and Steph exchange a look.

Shit. I must still smell like I chugged polish remover. Why didn't I remember to douse my clothes in cheap perfume?

"Okay, enough about me." I'm ready to change the subject. "I want to hear about you guys. What's new? What's changed here since I've been gone? Did Queenie stick her head in the shitter when she got assigned that Myers-Briggs piece? I queefed when I saw her byline."

"I'm now editor in chief of *The NYD*," Fern says.

"Classic." I take Fern's prank in stride. "Glad to see you finally got into your apartment and took a shower."

Fern burrows her face into her hands and lets out a long groan.

"Don't ever bring that up again. Ever," she says. "I'm so done dating women. And people. Let's be single together this summer, all three of us."

My heart pangs at the word *single*, and I immediately think of Simon.

Then I hate myself for thinking of Simon.

Stupid, stupid Simon.

You hate him.

Hate.

"And what about you, Steph? How did that big presentation you texted me about go? Sorry I never responded. I've been such a shit friend."

"No worries, I figured you were off the grid," she says. "And actually, the issue meeting is today at one p.m. I assume you'll be at it."

My stomach lurches at the idea of facing Cat again. I'm

worried she'll take one look at me and see right through all my BS. Like a metal detector or something.

"I'm sure I will."

I take the next few hours to catch up on everything that I missed, working quietly at my desk. I'm relieved to discover that not much has changed since I left. The Google algorithm fucked everyone over again, Twitter is still 30 percent Timothée Chalamet memes, and my assignments are still meaningless regurgitations of news that's already been reported and constipated high-end hot takes.

Hey, at least they're consistent.

I check my phone a couple of times, not only to examine Poppy's whereabouts and shitposts but also to see if Simon has texted me with any updates. I hate that he's commanding so much of my brain space lately. I'm not even expecting a message from him until later tonight, but I mentioned having to get to sleep before four a.m. because I had a big day at work. I just didn't explain why.

Simon (11:24 a.m.): Good luck today, Tulip. Don't fuck it up.

I feel my lips start to curl, then immediately frown.

This so isn't like me. I never used to let Zain distract me from my work. Then again, Zain wasn't my archnemesis with biceps the size of my head.

Not that there's anything going on between Simon and me, because ew.

At 12:55, I grab my computer and a notepad and make my way to the top floor. When I walk past the intern table, I hear the same baby bitches as usual whispering about me.

I slow down so I can eavesdrop.

"Did you hear? She was basically forced to take a month off."

"I heard she was hospitalized, hooked up to an IV and everything."

"No way! I thought it was a psych ward."

Unable to take it anymore, I turn around and face the little turds.

"For the record, it was a *writer's retreat* and it was *great* and I'm *so glad I went*!"

The girls all stare back at me, their mouths agape, expressions frightened, as if they weren't expecting to ever hear me speak or to have a voice at all. They look like teenagers at a slumber party who unintentionally awakened a vengeful spirit during their amateur séance. They didn't expect their Ouija board to actually work. It was all supposed to be a harmless joke.

"That's all."

I turn on my heel and walk away.

Then I look at the time on my phone.

Oh. Shit.

Teaching those punks a lesson actually cost me several seconds of my precious time. I'm running late to my first meeting back in the office, which is so last season's Rose. I sprint up the stairs, almost tripping over my boots a couple of times and falling flat on my face, but I make it. I reach the door and burst into the conference room, heaving from all the unexpected cardio.

The room is packed, and the presentation has already begun. As I enter, all eyes turn to look at me, and Cat goes silent. I lift one hand in an awkward wave, my middle finger twitching.

Steph shakes her head, and Fern swallows a giggle.

"Rose." Cat's voice is flat. "I didn't realize you'd be back today."

"Oh." I clear my throat. This is uncomfortable. "Yeah."

I take a seat in the back, farther away from my friends than I would like. A few people move away from me as if I'm the carrier of some sort of contagious, deadly virus. I frown and sniff my armpits.

It must be my catching unpopularity.

"As I was saying," Cat continues, "our next cover is going to be controversial, but it'll be a conversation starter. A true mark of our times. The team and I wanted to pick someone who could spark a real debate on the internet, who our commentators would go crazy over. And after this weekend's awards ceremony, I think we can all agree that there's no one who better defines this cultural moment or the shifting trend landscape. It's been a logistical nightmare to plan, as she's so in demand."

Cat stares directly at me, and we lock eyes. I think I even detect a lump in her throat.

"But I'm so proud to share that our next cover star will be none other than"—she sounds hesitant, apologetic—"*the* Poppy Hastings."

My jaw drops to the floor.

The room erupts into roaring applause and excited whispers just as my vision starts to blur. Black spots speckle the ceiling, the windows, the floor. I press my back against the wall, attempting to steady myself. In the corner of my diminishing field of vision, I vaguely see Fern and Steph darting their eyes toward me, alarmed expressions on their faces.

I raise one hand to my chest to make sure all my parts are still intact.

"No."

I hear the word before I even register that it was me who said it. But once it's out in the ether, I can't very well take it back. Everyone is watching me, waiting for me to speak. I feel like I'm in *The Hunger Games*. With the help of some random woman in sales, I stand up on my own two feet and turn to face Cat.

"Excuse me?"

"I said no," I repeat, doubling down on my position. "The Shred can't feature Poppy Hastings on its cover. We're the publication that helped put her in prison. Am I the only person who understands how ludicrous that is? How hypocritical it makes us look?"

"Rose..." Cat warns me with her eyes.

"And what about Poppy, huh?" I go on, ignoring her. "Why would she even want to be on the cover of the Shred? Of the publication responsible for such a scathing exposé?"

"According to her team, she's a big fan," Cat replies. "I think the words they used were *eternally grateful for the exposure*."

I physically recoil.

Has Cat been playing me this entire fucking time? Cover shoots don't happen overnight. In fact, this has probably been in the works since the day Poppy was released. The pre-reporting approval, the medical leave...Cat was just finding new and innovative ways to keep me busy, distracted, and complacent.

She didn't even want me in the office when she made the announcement.

I hear a gasp and recognize it as Steph's. She understands what those words mean as well as I do.

And she's anticipating what I'm about to do.

"No. I have worked too hard and undergone too much at this company for you to put me through this. I will always be grateful to you, Cat, for putting my name on the map."

Fern reaches out to Steph and grabs her hand.

"But if you put Poppy Hastings on the cover of the next issue of the Shred, I'll fucking quit."

Cat narrows her eyes.

"Let me save you the trouble," she says. "Please clean out your desk, return your laptop to HR, and hand over the passwords to your VPN by the end of the day."

I feel my left knee start to shake.

"What are you saying?"

I already know the answer.

"You're fired, Rose. Effective immediately, you no longer work for the Shred."

Chapter Fourteen

"Are you sure you're okay?" Steph asks for the zillionth fuck-ing time. "I know you hate when we ask you that, but considering the Poppy of it all, and after what happened the last time work went sideways, we just want to make sure you're not, you know, back on another bender or holed up in your bathroom or—"

I'm three-way FaceTiming with her and Fern from the car, which means my camerawork is shoddy at best. My hand keeps shaking, and every time we hit a bump in the road, I drop the phone. Not to mention that Simon has been blasting god-awful show tunes (kill me) nonstop, so I have to pause and turn down the volume every five minutes, to no avail—he just smirks and turns it back up.

He's determined to make my ears bleed.

That motherfucker.

It's sixty-two and partly sunny, and we're driving with the windows down. There's a light breeze slapping me in the face, sending my curly hair flying in all directions. I cough, spitting out a chunk of split ends, then catch a glimpse of myself in the side mirror.

Yikes.

I look like Medusa. On a bad day.

The trees are decorated in bright green hues, as well as the occasional cherry blossom, the true taste arbiter of spring. They release a perfume that swirls through the thick humidity like a droplet of food coloring. All in all, the world feels somewhat peaceful from the vantage point of the highway.

You'd never know, for example, that just yesterday, I blew up my life like an atomic bomb and left my guts splattered all over Gramercy.

I readjust my headphones, pushing them tighter over my ears just in case Simon can hear what my friends are saying. He's looking particularly broody today in all black—jeans, T-shirt, and his leather jacket. From this close up, I keep getting whiffs of his scent, a mix of burning wood and something I can't quite put my finger on.

Lemon?

No, something sweeter, headier.

Blood?

"I'm fine," I reassure Steph, but also myself. "Better than fine, actually. I haven't felt this great in years!"

I'm selective with the language I use, careful not to tip off my road trip companion to the fact that something is wrong. I don't want Simon to know that I'm officially no longer working with the weight of a nationally recognized organization behind me. I'm afraid it'll mean he'll no longer want to partner with me.

Or worse, that he'll take it as a sign that he's won and Poppy is his.

Deep down—like, way, way beneath my skin and blood and guts and shit—there's also a tiny piece of me that's ashamed to have been fired. Maybe it's a first-generation immigrant guilt thing. If my parents knew what I had done, the scene I had caused, they would be so fucking disappointed in me. And I don't want Simon to think of less of me.

I already think less of myself.

"Where are you even going?" Fern whines. "You're really only going to give us 'I'm going on a road trip with one of my workshop people'? You're not running away, are you?"

"Yeah!" Steph agrees. I see her emphatic nodding. "I told you that you weren't allowed to make any new friends, remember?"

I sigh.

Lying to Steph and Fern is getting harder and harder. At this point, I should probably just fess up and tell them the truth. But then I would have to admit to leading them astray for a whole-ass month, for relapsing into chaos, for abandoning Rose 2.0 before she even got off the ground. And something tells me that convincing my friends this was just a long-game prank isn't going to cut it.

"Hey, inspirational speaker, you should probably think about shutting the hell up and hanging up soon." Simon nudges me. "We're almost there."

At the sound of Simon's deep, husky voice, my two best friends shriek into their headphones, almost blowing smoke through my eardrums.

"Rose Aslani," Steph singsongs, "are you with a *b-o-y*?"

"Gotta go, bye!" I shout as quickly as possible, hanging up before I get bullied into answering any questions.

I look up just in time to catch my first peek at a colony of long horizontal brick buildings, set behind barbed wire fences and guarded by several men with machine guns. There's a yard of patchy grass and a basketball court that's severely lacking in baskets. Most notably, the structures have nearly no windows, nothing to let the sunlight seep in.

It feels like a social experiment, a child's rendering of Area 51.

"Nervous?" Simon's voice is softer now, almost gentle.

I shake my head. "I don't get nervous."

But I doubt he buys it. His eyes briefly flicker to mine, then back to the road ahead. He clears his throat, the scar on his cheek creating that indentation I love.

"Well, Tulip, welcome to Clearfield Super Max, Pennsylvania's favorite maximum-security prison."

After Cat publicly humiliated me by firing me in front of all of my coworkers and higher-ups, everyone expected me to break. Steph and Fern followed me home and refused to leave, afraid I'd do something drastic, like set fire to the *NYD* offices or kidnap Cat's dog and drive it to New Jersey.

Honestly? I didn't blame them. Psychotic episodes were not off the table, given what happened after my Poppy exposé was published. But for some reason, I feel eerily calm. It's like I'm drifting at sea. I know the end is coming, that I'll eventually starve or develop scurvy or whatever. But as of now, I'm just watching the waves break, listening to the rush of the current.

After I was fired, I anticipated a meltdown, too. But I just remained quiet and introspective. After listening to us argue for hours—and to some semihysterical crying from not me—Roommate kicked them out. But she continued to spy on me closely from the kitchen, as if I was on suicide watch or something. So when Simon texted me and asked how I felt about going down to the prison for a face-to-face with Dimitri, the man who had confessed to Brad Zarbos's murder—fresh out of solitary confinement for biting a guard—I'd immediately grabbed my keys and muttered to Roommate that I had a date with a prison cell.

If I didn't know better, I'd say she was worried about me. But I do know better. Plus, she'd promptly asked my permission to throw an orgy in the apartment while I was gone.

For what it's worth, I said no.

At the time, a visit to a penitentiary sounded like a welcome distraction. Not, you know, a field trip to a museum of this country's most dangerous criminals.

But now we're here, and there's no turning back.

Simon and I step out of the car and lock the doors. Clearfield looms over us like a tidal wave or some other natural disaster. And in a way, that's exactly what it is. I'm struck by how noiseless the area is, so empty it almost feels abandoned. Like it could have lived a thousand lives before we stumbled upon it, collecting dust and stories. But these structures are home to chaos. To cracking bones, to stolen lives. To regret that ages poorly and perspective that ripens every year.

I suddenly realize that I'm terrified to enter. To see a place that gathers discarded items like a lost and found, that reflects back the imperfections you're too afraid to face in the mirror.

I swallow hard. "I don't know if I can go in there."

Simon hesitantly reaches out his hand, then flinches, instead opting to pat me on the head. Like a dog.

"Come on, Tulip," he says. "I didn't peg you for a pussy."

I frown.

I'm not. That's true.

"You're not afraid of anything. Remember? Besides, you'll be with me the entire time. I won't leave your side."

Simon offers me his arm. I reluctantly take it, which feels oddly infantile, yet intimate. He leads the way toward the entrance of Clearfield, and I slowly follow.

I expect him to flash his badge upon arrival, to let the guards know he's in a position of authority. Instead, he chooses to fly below the radar. We both check in at the guard station, providing our names and contact information and filling out a form. I decide to give a fake ID left over from college and phone number, just in case someone decides to look into who's been visiting Dimitri. Before I can lean over and check whether Simon has done the same, he pulls away his clipboard.

"Hey, Joe Goldberg," he grunts, wagging a finger. "No creeping!"

Damn.

Next, we go through a series of metal detectors and get patted down by officers. They go through the canvas bag I've brought with me, which reads VICTIM OF THE IRS, and discard my granola bar, much to my chagrin. Once they've verified that we won't be a threat to ourselves, the guards, or the inmates, we're escorted to the visitation room. What television shows aren't able to capture is how fucking cold it is—freezing, sterile. There's a series of stools and plastic dividers, a set of pseudo phone booths. A sheet of thick bulletproof glass cuts the room in half. Armed men and women skulk in the corners, watching us with eagle eyes.

I gulp.

"Follow me." Simon struts over to the middle booth with confidence, taking a seat as if he's done this before.

Then I realize he probably has.

"What should I say?" My mouth suddenly feels dry.

"Nothing," Simon growls. "Just follow my lead, okay?"

We wait for about five minutes, and then Dimitri is escorted into the room. His hair has been shaved into a buzz cut, and he has a tattoo of what I think is the outline of a bear on his forehead, the lines shaky and indecisive. One of his eyes is gray and the other is blue. They look solid, heavy as marbles. The guard uncuffs him, and he takes a seat across from us. We're a table's distance from each other, and I consider what could have been had circumstances been different.

Would fate still have led us here?

Fuck it, I should have taken an Adderall in the parking lot.

Dimitri takes the phone off the hook and raises it to his ear. We do the same.

"You're not my lawyer," he observes.

"That is correct," I say, ignoring Simon's advice. "Mr. Dimitri, my name is Tulip, and I am a journalist. This is—"

"A friend," Simon cuts me off. His nostrils flare as he glares at me, and a rush of adrenaline shoots down my spine.

Dimitri frowns, his marbles rolling into the back of his head. "You are not my friend."

"But we share a common enemy," Simon says, the indentation in his cheek deepening.

"And who might that be?"

"Poppy Hastings."

At the sound of Poppy's name, a vein in Dimitri's forehead pops. He looks back up at the guard and barks something in Russian. The guard shakes his head. When Dimitri turns back to face us, his skin is drained of color.

"I don't know who that is." He crosses his arms in front of his chest.

My cheeks flush. "You're lying!" I point and yell, unable to help myself.

Simon puts one hand on my knee, signaling for me to stop.

My skin burns beneath my jeans at the point of contact.

"Please, don't go," Simon says. "We only require a minute more of your time. My partner and I, we have reason to believe that you, sir, are innocent and don't deserve to be rotting away in here for the rest of your life. If you work with us, tell us what you know about Ms. Hastings and why you're covering for her, we can protect you. I promise."

I wince at the word *promise.*

Why is Simon making a promise we don't yet know we can keep?

"There's no point to all of this. I did it. I confessed."

"We know that."

"So then why are you here, filling my head with this nonsense?"

"Don't you want to go home, to smell the salt air in the Rockaways?" Simon interrupts.

"Please, stop."

"You have a son, right? Sergey? You must know that his wife is five months pregnant."

"I said stop."

"Wouldn't you like to meet your grandchild, to help raise him, to watch him grow up?"

"She'll hurt them!" Dimitri murmurs under his breath. "Don't you see? I can't. I can't escape her. Them. Nobody can."

"Who will hurt them?" I jump in. "Are you saying Poppy will hurt your family?"

Silence.

"Hurt them how?" I'm panicking now. "Torture?"

"Not torture," Dimitri whispers. Even from behind the glass, I can tell he's blinking back tears. "Kill. Just like Georgie. Tommy. Dead. All dead."

"What?" Simon sits up straight, alarmed.

"I can't say anything more," Dimitri says. "In fact, I've probably said too much. If she finds out I was talking to you, I'll be dead by morning. Dunamis sees all. Don't you see? They're everywhere. They're out there with you. They're in here with me. They are me. They're probably you, too. I'm already dead."

"Please, one more minute."

"Guards!"

Dimitri starts to shriek like a motherfucking banshee, and my pulse skyrockets as I try to control my uneven breathing. The guard who escorted him into the room rushes in and places handcuffs back onto Dimitri's wrists, then quickly shoves him out of visitation. As he's dragged away, his screaming turns to laughter.

Haunting, explosive laughter.

Simon and I sit there, stewing in stunned silence.

After a few minutes, he stands up and quietly walks out of the room, his head hanging low, pensive. We collect our things at the guard station, Simon fills out a few more forms, then we walk back to Simon's car.

As I take my place in the passenger seat and Simon turns on the ignition, I open my mouth to say something, then quickly shut it again, unsure of where to begin. We back out of the parking lot and start driving away. Clearfield starts to look smaller and smaller, like a tiny speck of dirt on the horizon.

Almost as if it never existed at all.

We drive in silence, processing everything that just

happened. Dimitri's demented break, his confession. The fear flaring behind his dead eyes like muted wildfire.

Simon runs a hand through his hair and grunts. I peer over at him, my eyes narrowing.

"I told you to stay quiet and let me handle it," he finally says. "Do you ever do what you're told?"

I roll my eyes. "Not really, Mom."

He mutters under his breath and blinks a couple of times in protest. I fiddle with my seat belt. I keep waiting for Simon to turn on the radio, to blast those dreadful show tunes he loves so much—I'd even be okay with *Next to Normal*, which he insists on belting at the top of his lungs—but he stays contemplative. We hit the highway, finally putting enough distance between ourselves, that madman, and the maximum-security prison fever dream.

"Georgie and Tommy," I mutter. There's a noise in my ear, buzzing and incessant. "Those names sound familiar. Where have I heard them before?"

"Georgia and Tom Huxley." Simon's eyes remain on the road. "Poppy's adoptive parents."

My heart slows to a stop. I suck in my breath.

But I thought...

"Poppy's parents are dead," I whisper.

"Burned to death in a fire," Simon confirms. Then his voice wobbles. "Or so we thought."

A heavy silence follows. Simon shifts uncomfortably in his seat.

"You think they're alive?"

He shakes his head.

"You think Poppy killed her parents?"

"I don't know. Maybe. He's scared of her."

"Why would she kill her parents?"

"I don't know."

"What does that have to do with Brad Zarbos?"

"I don't know."

"And why would—"

"I don't fucking know, okay, Tulip?" His voice booms, and my breath catches in my throat. "I don't fucking know how to connect the dots. But Dimitri's scared of her. Clearly. She has something on him. That must be why he confessed."

More deafening silence flows between us. I stare out the car window, surprised to find myself blinking back tears.

"Look, I'm sorry, I shouldn't have yelled," he says quietly. "Sometimes I just get so angry at myself. For not seeing the bigger picture. For not being good enough at this shit to beat her at her own game. And that man in there? He's dangerous. If he had said something, done something to you..." He trails off, unable to finish his sentence. "Anyway. I shouldn't have taken it out on you."

My pulse escalates as Simon looks over at me. His eyes lock with mine, deep blue and pooling with regret. And something in my gut flutters. I blink, and in a split second, the sensation is gone. But I'm left with a disturbing urge to lean over and run my tongue down that indentation in his cheek. When I meet his gaze again, I find his eyes slightly hooded, and I swallow hard. He takes one hand off the steering wheel and places it on my upper left thigh. The skin beneath his fingers begins to pebble, and I bite my lip, waiting for—

A car suddenly honks. Simon curses under his breath, his attention returning to the road. The spell between us is broken.

We both sit in stunned silence, the lingering tension growing uncomfortably heavy.

I roll down a window just as Simon opens his mouth to speak.

"What the hell is Dunamis?" I ask.

"What is this, *Jeopardy*?" he tries to joke. His mouth curves upward just a millimeter.

"Come on, don't play dumb," I say. "Dimitri. He said, and I quote, 'Dunamis sees all.'"

My brain rewinds to the visitation room. Dimitri lost it so suddenly that it drowned out a lot of what he'd said. But my mind is snagged on that word. *Dunamis.* Or is it a name?

"I've never heard it before," I admit.

"Neither have I."

Simon begins to whistle a familiar tune, and I look over at him in surprise. Color has returned to his cheeks, giving his features a rather boyish flare. I admire him for a brief moment before he notices me checking him out and smirks. I glare into the rearview mirror, annoyed.

"What's got you all peppy?" I ask. "*Legally Blonde: The Musical* ask you to audition for Elle?"

"Not quite, Tulip."

He offers me a true smile, and my chest tightens.

"Do you smell that?"

I sniff the air, finding only gasoline and a whole lot of nothing. My nose wrinkles.

"Smell what?"

The bastard only grins wider.

"We've got ourselves a lead."

Chapter Fifteen

A few days later, I'm keeping myself busy searching the name *Poppy Hastings* on Crazy Days and Nights, a celebrity blind item site famously run by a bigwig Hollywood entertainment lawyer, when my phone rings.

I look down at the caller ID and bite back a grin.

"Who the hell calls anyone anymore?" I greet Simon, my voice mockingly cheerful.

"What are you doing right now?" he asks, ignoring my taunt.

I look down at my laptop. So far, I've decrypted three blind items that I think might be about Poppy. One accuses her of yachting, which I've gathered is essentially prostitution for rich people and takes places exclusively on yachts (and usually involves at least one Pussycat Doll? Unclear). The second seems to suggest that she's currently sleeping with Leonardo DiCaprio, but I've vetoed that as conjecture. I mean, at twenty-eight, she's way, way too old for him. Finally, the third confirms that she's taken to selling her used underwear online, which I obviously already knew.

I've been bidding on her listings for, like, ever.

Duh.

God, I really need to get a fucking life.

"Um." I do another line of the Adderall I crushed up earlier to help me focus. "Research."

"On Dunamis?" He sounds excited.

It's almost cute.

Almost.

"Uh, yeah. Sure. Let's go with that."

"Same. Do you want to go first, or should I?"

I exhale a quick sigh of relief. "Go for it."

"Okay, so." Simon takes a deep breath, and I can practically hear him running his hand through his dark hair. "I did a primary search on the web, as I'm sure you did, and came up with nothing. I mean, it was eerie. Besides some biblical stuff—it also means *power* in ancient Greek—there was no record of that word ever being used in any sort of modern context. So I dug a little deeper."

"Deeper?"

"Yeah. On the dark web. You know, rare artifacts, extinct species, sex trafficking, illegal substances, cults? Anyway, it was pretty quiet on there, too. I thought maybe I had the spelling wrong or that we misheard him or something. But just when I was about to give up, I found some conspiracy theorist thread on a shady apocalyptic subdomain, and there was a comment from a user named Zeus that mentioned he had a personal grievance with an organization called Dunamis. He made it sound like some sort of crime syndicate."

"Wow," I say, taking it all in. Simon's been doing actual casework while I've been obsessing over Poppy Hastings like some schoolgirl with a crush. Cool. "So how do we find Zeus?"

"One step ahead of you, Tulip," Simon says, a smile caught between his tongue and his teeth. "I sent him a message pretending to be a fellow nutjob with questions about this paper he wrote about the moon landing being fake. We're meeting up with him at some swanky restaurant in midtown tonight. I assume you don't have plans?"

My cheeks flush because he's right. I don't.

"What if he's dangerous?" I ask. "If he's mixed up with Poppy and this crime syndicate or whatever, he could be bad news. What if he pulls a weapon or threatens us or something?"

Simon pauses, considering. "We'll size him up beforehand. Go undercover. It'll be fun."

"Fun," I echo. "Undercover as what?"

"A couple?" The words come out as a question. "We can pretend to be on a date. It's a nice restaurant. He'll never suspect a thing. Once we know it's safe, all will be revealed."

A date.

A fake date.

With Simon, my archnemesis.

What the fuck is this, a rom-com? I thought it was a thriller.

The author of my life better get their genres straight before I end up the butt of the joke.

"All right," I agree, "but I'm not paying for a fucking thing."

He snorts. "Don't worry your pretty little head, Tulip. We'll have a nice loud fake breakup afterward. You can even kick me in the balls again if you'd like."

"I would," I say. "And I'm ordering desserts. Plural."

I hear the muffled sound of Simon's laughter on the other end of the line, like he's trying to conceal his amusement.

"Is that what it's like to date you? You're already a handful."

"Both hands."

There's a moment of awkward silence before Simon clears his throat.

"So, I'll pick you up in a couple of hours, then?"

"This isn't a real date, dickhead," I remind him. "I'll meet you there."

"And thank god for that," he says. But there's a lack of conviction in his voice. "By the way, what did you find?"

"Um, same as you."

Then I hang up before he can ask any questions.

I finish off what's left of my wine, then peer around my hurricane of a bedroom, prepared to get ready for my fake date with a little bit of a buzz. Blasting a bit of angry feminist pop from my iPhone speaker, I check the only fashion newsletter I subscribe to, *NoorYorkCity*, for outfit inspiration. Normally, I can't be arsed to care about consumerism, but this site is actually pretty smart—*and* run by another Iranian American. And there are so few of us Middle Eastern women in media that I feel like I have no choice but to stan. (Ew. But that's literally how she talks.)

After consulting Noora, the writer behind the stack, I pull a slip dress out of the back of my closet and tug it on. It's simple and black with a finger-width of lace lining the hem. I haven't had any use for it since Zain left, so I buried it deep behind the rest of my wardrobe. After weeks of barely leaving my bed, it fits a little snugly, hugging my curves. But it'll do for the occasion. I run to the bathroom and throw on a little bit of mascara and a pinch of blush, actually taking the time to spritz some product into the chaotic mop on top of my head.

When I look in the full-length mirror, I'm pleasantly

surprised. I look half-decent. Less like a miserable shrew and more like someone with their shit together.

Would you look at that! It's Rose 2.0.

I grab my keys and head for the door, pausing only briefly to take in Roommate and Boyfriend playing a heated game of naked Twister on the kitchen floor. She looks at me from beneath his armpit, her head between her legs and her hair falling in her face, and simply sucks in her cheeks.

"I'm going on a top-secret undercover mission to catch a conspiracy theorist," I mutter, knowing she'll assume I'm joking.

"Mm-hm."

Hey, everyone already thinks I'm crazy.

I might as well act the part.

I book it to the restaurant, not wanting to deal with Simon's bitching if I'm even a minute late. Melchior is located in a corporate area of Manhattan, populated by bankers and businessmen wearing double-breasted suits and smoking cigars. Upon arrival, I'm greeted by glass double doors and a maître d' wearing tiny white gloves, sporting a mustache that curls up at the ends. I give him Simon's name, and he informs me that the other member of my party has already been seated. He leads me through the sea of white tablecloths and patrons seated beneath chandeliers that cost more than my parents' mortgage until I spot Simon nestled in the very corner of the room.

And my heart drops.

His dark hair has been combed back, exposing the scruff on his chiseled jawbone and the scar indenting his cheek that I've grown so fond of. He's dressed in a sharp navy suit that hugs his muscular physique in all the right places. His head is down as he stares at the watch on his wrist with a frown, and then he looks up suddenly and sees me. My heart thuds loudly as his eyes widen with something like astonishment. He runs his eyes up and down my body slowly, drinking me in. His gaze burns a hole through my skull, and my leg muscles clench.

Great. This is just what I need.

An uncontrollable physical reaction to Agent Asshole's unfair hotness.

"You're early." I take the seat across from him.

Simon blinks as if waking from a trance, and I smirk. It's nice seeing him off his game like this. He's usually such a control freak.

"I wanted to arrive before Zeus so I could bug his table," he explains, subtly pointing toward his ear. I lean in and notice a small listening device I hadn't spotted before. "I tipped the maître d' twenty dollars to point me in the direction of his table. Then I pretended to trip on my way to the bathroom. Knocked right into a poor busboy carrying a pitcher of water. While he was cleaning up broken glass, I stuck the mic up under that tablecloth. All in a day's work. Anyway, he's seated right behind you. Don't turn around."

I turn around.

Zeus is a tiny man in his late forties with long chestnut hair that he wears braided down his back like a horse. He's wearing round spectacles and an argyle sweater-vest, the sleeves of the button-down underneath evenly rolled up to his elbows. I notice that he's taken the time to rearrange all the items atop the table to his liking, from the cutlery to the candle to his water glass. He taps his fingers on the table three times before looking at the door.

"That's him?" Zeus uses his pointer finger to attack a booger, then looks around before subtly wiping it on the underside of the table. Ew. "He doesn't look evil to me."

When I glance back over my shoulder at Simon, he isn't watching Zeus.

He's staring at me.

"I thought I told you not to turn around."

His mouth twitches, and mine dries out.

"When are you going to learn?" I retort. "I don't like being told what to do."

He frowns at me, but I maintain eye contact, refusing to back down. Then his gaze turns from annoyed to something else. The deep blue of his eyes flickers, and he licks his lips. I bite mine, fighting a hunger that I'm pretty sure has nothing to do with the ridiculously small entrées that they definitely serve here.

"What?" I ask, trying to shake the tension.

"You look..."

"Ridiculous, stupid, cringey?"

"Beautiful."

Simon looks away, and I drop my eyes to my menu, trying to slow the organ doing fucking parkour in my chest. The hairs on my arms have risen in surprise, and I hide them behind my back lest they betray me.

I can't explain the effect Simon has on my body. I really can't. Maybe I just need to get laid. It really has been a while. Too long. An embarrassingly fucking long time.

The waiter brings Zeus a steak, precut into tiny little pieces, and a glass of milk before strutting over to us and taking our order.

"I'll have your most expensive appetizer," I announce. "And a glass of wine. Oh, and a cocktail! A martini. Please."

The waiter raises a brow. "Celebrating?" he asks, the question dripping in judgment.

"Yup," I say with a grin. "It's our anniversary. How many years has it been, sugar lips?"

Simon shifts in his seat, visibly uncomfortable.

"Um. Five. Snookums."

I burst out laughing.

"I think he's going to propose tonight," I whisper loud enough for Simon to hear. His face turns beet red, and he begins to cough. The waiter pours him a glass of water, then winks at me. I wink back, and he scurries off.

Simon chokes, spitting out his water. "What the hell was that?"

"I was improvising!" I say with glee. "You were right—going undercover *is* fun. For someone who does this for living, you sure suck at it. So, what's your budget for the ring? Forty K? Fifty?"

"Shut it," he says just as the waiter returns with my beverages. He narrows his eyes as I double-fist my cocktail and wine. "Drinking on the job, huh?"

"Mind your business, Sweet Cheeks." I take a big gulp of my martini. "Arguing about my substance abuse is *so* year three. We almost broke up over it, remember?"

He grimaces at the words *substance abuse*.

I do, too. I'm not sure why I said them.

They just sort of slipped out.

"So, what do we do now?" I ask, nibbling on my olives. Simon's eyes immediately fall to my lips, and I swallow. Hard. "Want to play two truths and a lie?"

"Not really," he says.

I ignore him, tapping my fingers on my chin.

"I'll go first. I've never seen *Fleabag*. I'm banned from Venmo. And I'm legally unable to enter any Benihana location in the United States or Canada."

Simon's jaw drops, but his eyes dance.

"Why the hell would you be banned from using Venmo?"

"Wrong!" I cry. "I can quote *Fleabag* from beginning to end. Your turn!"

"And Benihana?"

"That's a restraining order story for another time. Come on, don't stall."

Simon's forehead scrunches as he thinks. I giggle at the seriousness of his expression.

"Okay," he says. "I have a tattoo. I lost my virginity at age fifteen. And I once crashed my parents' Camaro because I was singing along to the radio too passionately."

"Oh my god, this is too hard. Because, on the one hand, you're probably still a virgin. You've probably never been able to get a girl—or a guy, I won't assume—into your bed, and even if you did, you'd scare them away with your lack of conversation skills. But on the other hand, there's no way a tight-ass like you would have a tattoo. So I'm torn."

Simon chuckles. "I'm an excellent driver, Tulip. And when I have a woman in my bed, there isn't much time for conversation."

He leans in, his voice low.

"She's usually too busy screaming my name."

My breath hitches.

Against my better judgment, I find myself wondering just

what it would be like if I were that girl, pressed beneath the heat of Simon's body.

And my vagina grows a fucking pulse.

"Where's the tattoo?" My voice comes out strained.

He opens his mouth to answer just as the waiter reappears with my food.

We boomerang away from each other as if shocked by a faulty electrical outlet.

"The most expensive appetizer on the menu." The waiter smiles smugly before leaving.

I turn to look back at Simon, but whatever heat I felt seconds ago is gone. His attention is now wholly fixed on Zeus.

"What is it?" I ask.

"He's on the phone," Simon murmurs. "Be quiet, I'm trying to listen."

I pout. "I want to hear!"

"Lean in, then," he says. "Press your ear against mine."

"Won't that look, like, super fucking suspicious?"

Simon scowls, then leans in and steals the fucking breath out of my lungs by kissing me lightly on the cheek. His lips are soft against my skin.

I shiver.

"What the fuck are you doing?" I hiss.

"Just listen, wiseass."

I muster all my strength and focus on seeing through my lust-filled fog just in time to catch the tail end of Zeus's phone conversation.

"Yes, yes. I know, Lionel. Sunday at eight. No, I won't forget the dancing clogs. Enough about the damn clogs!" He snaps. "Now, I've got to go. There are two nincompoops snooping on me at the next table. Yes, through a listening device. Yes, they can hear me right now. Yes, I'll tell them you say hi. Lionel says hi."

Then he looks directly fucking at us.

"Shit." I release a breath I didn't realize I was holding. "What do we do now?"

"I think we go over there," Simon says slowly.

"Is it safe?"

"Just stay behind me." He uses that bossy tone I've come to like and loathe in equal measure.

I roll my eyes and stand up abruptly, then strut over to Zeus's table. Simon runs after me, cursing under his breath.

I reach the table and take the seat next to Zeus. "You rang?"

"Good, you decided not to waste any more of my time." He adjusts the napkin he's wearing as a bib. "I assume you're the reason I'm here?"

"We had to check you out and make sure you weren't a serial killer." I shrug. Simon curses quietly to himself.

"And?" Zeus wiggles his brows.

"Jury's still out."

Zeus nods approvingly, gesturing for Simon, who's hovering above us like a creep, to take a seat. He obliges, and we watch in awe as Zeus takes each piece of steak and chews it precisely three times before swallowing.

"Now, what's this about?"

"We're here to ask you about one of your theories," Simon says.

"I have many theories, boy," Zeus scoffs, taking a swig of his milk. "You'll have to be more specific. Are you a flat-earther? Or is election rigging more your speed?"

"Actually, we're curious about Dunamis."

Zeus drops his fork, which makes a loud clang against his plate before falling to the floor. The waiter hurries to pick it up before bringing over a fresh set of cutlery. Zeus watches him with hawk eyes, waiting for him to be out of earshot before lowering his voice to a whisper.

"Are you with the organization?"

"No?"

"No? Who do you work for?"

I blush. "Um. I'm a writer of sorts."

He barks out a laugh. "Then do us both a favor and don't dare to say that name in my presence ever again," he says with a sincerity that stops me dead in my tracks. "I like my life, thank you very much. I have no interest in ending it early."

"Please, Zeus. Just tell us what you know, and we'll be on our way."

He snorts, a little milk coming up his nose and trickling down to his lips.

"Zeus. I've never heard someone call me by that name in person before."

"What's your real name?" I ask, already knowing he won't tell me.

"So many questions from a young woman with so few answers." He places his hands in his lap and sighs. "Fine. I'll talk, but then I am going to walk away from this table and you are never going to contact me again. And no mention of the *d*-word. Do we have an understanding?"

Simon and I both nod, and Zeus reaches down and pulls out the bug Simon planted underneath his table, crushing it in his hand.

"Very well," he says. "That which you seek is a centuries-old secret society. Although it's more like a cult, the biggest in the world. It's multilevel and made up of people from every corner of humanity, from the unfathomably rich to the unspeakably poor. Any of the patrons in this establishment could be a member, but so could our waiter or the busboy out back."

"Dude, that makes no fucking sense," I interrupt. "A group like that could never exist without people knowing about it."

"If you'll allow me to finish, *dude.* Although I've never been able to discern how members are selected, once they are tapped, they have to offer up a piece of life-altering collateral to ensure their place in the system. A terrible secret or a humiliating truth—something concrete. Blackmail, you see. The only way to rise through the ranks is by doing tasks for the organization, no questions asked. As you rise up in *the* society, you rise up in *our* society. They're interconnected, the positive and negative space that make up the same picture."

"So, the fucking illuminati, then?" I spit.

"Do you always use such colorful language, young lady?" Zeus shakes his head with distaste.

"Ignore her," Simon urges. "Please, go on. What is the organization's primary goal?"

Zeus turns his attention back to Simon, his face twisted into a smirk. "On the surface? To court power and buy influence in every pocket of the universe. But beneath that? I've never known. Their true aim remains a mystery to me. All I'm certain of is that they'll protect their secret with their lives. And ours."

We stew in the horror of that statement, too stunned to blink or even let out our breath.

I decide to break the silence.

"Does anyone else think this sounds like a load of fucking bull?"

Zeus untucks his bib and folds it into a perfect square before placing it on the table.

"Watch your tongue, girl. I've already told you too much. The universe isn't ruled by one god but many men. And we are powerless to stop them. The best we can hope to do is stay out of their way."

"Call me girl one more time and I'll shove this fork into your neck," I say sweetly. "And how do you know so much about this? Why should we believe you?"

Zeus's eyes glaze over for a split second, but he blinks twice and gets back to business.

"There was a man I cared about very much. He disappeared some years ago, barely left a trace. I let myself into his apartment and rifled through his things. All I found were a few phone numbers and addresses and a single name—a name I never allow to leave my lips in public. My research took off from there. Plus, I enjoy exposing the hidden truths of this dark world we inhabit. I could tell you a thing or two about UFOs that would shake you to your core."

"Lunatic," I pretend to sneeze.

Simon kicks me under the table.

"As for the question of belief, I suppose you and your lover will have to determine that for yourselves."

Simon's eyes narrow, and we immediately begin speaking over one another like a broken tape recorder.

"He's not my—"

"She's not—"

"We're not together," I manage to get out.

"No, that's not right." Zeus frowns, looking confused. "Your bodies have been turned twenty degrees toward one another since you took your respective seats. Whenever you look at each other, your eyes dilate and your pulses exceed the average beats per minute. And I scent the unique air of arousal. You're attracted to each other at the very least."

Simon's mouth hangs wide open, while I begin stuttering in response.

"I—I—"

"Well, I really should be going," Zeus says, standing abruptly. The waiter rushes over with his coat, helping him into each arm, dusting off the shoulders. He turns back to face us and offers an apologetic smile. "I look forward to never doing this again."

Then he walks out, leaving us with absolutely fucking gobsmacked expressions on our faces and one expensive-ass bill.

"Holy fucking shit," I murmur. "Did that man just say he could scent my—"

"Do you get what this means, Tulip?"

"That the FBI is going to stop letting you expense meals?" I force out a joke, my hand getting clammy with nerves.

"Poppy could be a member."

Oh.

Oh.

"That would explain how she's been able to get away with the murders thus far. I mean, she could have ordered lower-level recruits to take out her marks and make it look like there was no foul play. All while she hides in plain sight, in the public eye."

Simon's eyes blaze with excitement, and I know the same fire is reflected in my own.

"Then maybe she blackmails others to take the fall because they think they'll rise in the syndicate? It's a pretty far-out theory. But it makes more sense than anything else we've got, right?"

"Right," I say hesitantly. "Or maybe we're fucking clinical. I mean, this is all escalating a tad quickly, isn't it? Aren't conspiracy theories meant to stay...theories?"

"We just might be, Tulip. But we're going to take these fuckers down. Once Poppy falls, they'll all fall."

For the first time in my life, I have nothing left to say, so I simply nod.

Here's the sixth rule of conspiracy: If something seems too good to be true, it probably is.

We signal to the waiter. He returns with our check and two glasses of champagne.

"Compliments of our staff," he says. "Congratulations to you both."

Simon smiles, taking his glass and raising it to his chin.

"Happy anniversary, baby," he says. "This was the best one yet."

And I swallow the liquid, the taste dangerous and the sensation sharp in my gut, liking the sound of those words on his lips a little bit too much.

Chapter Sixteen

"What did you do?"

I wake up to see Roommate's face upside down, folded over my body like a cashmere sweater. Not just her face—her arms, her collarbones, her nipples. She's wagging her abnormally long pointer finger directly at my eye socket.

"What? Nothing," I say. "What are you even talking about?"

"There's person banging on door."

That's when I hear it.

The *thud*, *thud*, *thud*.

My heart accelerates. I sit upright, hiding beneath my comforter, my brain producing and absorbing all the worst-case scenarios like a goddamn maxi pad.

Could it be Dunamis? Do they know about our little excursion to visit Dimitri? Our dinner with Zeus? How did they find me so quickly? Don't pseudonyms mean anything in this town anymore?!

"*Rose!*" someone on the other side of the door yells. "Open up!"

Oh.

It's just Simon.

I jump out of bed and throw an oversize sweatshirt in Roommate's direction. She catches it and looks down at the fabric, confused.

"Cover up," I say. "We've got company."

"Boo," Roommate says, reluctantly pulling the garment over her head.

I glance in the mirror.

There are bags under my eyes the size of pigeon shit. I smudge concealer over them like it's a Magic Eraser, then pull my hair out of its ponytail. Better. After I gargle with mouthwash (no time to brush my teeth), spritz myself with my only bottle of perfume (or use deodorant), and throw on my favorite I FUCKED YOUR DAD T-shirt, I'm satisfied.

Out of the corner of my eye, I watch Roommate watching me get ready.

"You care what person thinks," she observes. "How strange."

"Kindly shut the fuck up," I say before opening the door to find him standing there, freshly shaven, a duffel bag over his shoulder.

Simon, of course, looks as if he's been up for hours. His dark hair is in its regular messy state, yes, but his eyes are alert, latching on to me like Velcro. He's wearing a green Henley, blue jeans, and his favorite poorly fitting leather jacket.

I think I even detect a hint of cologne.

"How did you get my address?" I raise my eyebrows in accusation.

"FBI, Tulip. Remember?"

He pushes past me, entering the apartment before I have a chance to invite him in. My anxiety spikes as he takes in the tiny living space, the cracked paint, and the pile of dirty dishes in the sink. Compared with his bachelor pad, our Clinton Hell haven looks like the "before" picture on a home makeover show.

"So, this is where you live." Simon looks around. "Neat freak, huh?"

"Sorry, my sugar daddy was a little late to make his deposit this month," I snap, feeling uncomfortably off my game. "And you are here because..."

Simon lifts an eyebrow. "Someone didn't read the news this morning."

"Someone decided to drop by unannounced before I've had my fucking coffee."

"Well, you'll have to grab your fix on the go," Simon says. "Pack a bag, Tulip. We're heading to D.C."

"D.C.?!" My jaw drops. "As in, the District of Columbia?"

"No, as in Detective Comics. Yes, the District of Columbia, smartass." He rolls his eyes, picking up a stray bra hanging from a pan hook in the kitchen. "Ollie Pierce died in a drunk driving accident last night."

Oh.

Shit.

You've probably heard of Ollie Pierce. I mean, everyone has—he's one of the hottest actors in Hollywood right now. Or *was*, I guess. The child of a famous old-school director and a B-list actress, nepotism cherry-picked Ollie right out of the womb and gave him a career. He's a product of the Broadway-debut-to-Disney-Channel child star pipeline. But as an adult, he struggled to land roles at first, to be taken seriously as an actor and not just as a former teen celebrity.

When I met Ollie, he had just been cast in *Summer Swingers*, a three-hour art-house film, by Mortie Williams, an infamously neurotic conceptual producer, and was exiting a year-long funk. He drank heavily and excused himself twice to do cocaine in the bathroom. (He even offered me some. He was *such* a gentleman.) He had an old-Hollywood charm to him—the chiseled jawline, the piercing (ha) blue eyes.

Believe it or not, Ollie actually reached out to *me* about Poppy. Apparently, he had heard rumbling around town that someone had plans to take her down and wanted in. But his agent had insisted that he speak to me exclusively on background, which sucked. He hated to do anything anonymously.

What was the point of performing without an audience?

Ollie had met Poppy Hastings at the *Vanity Fair* Oscars after party. They'd spent the night flirting on the dance floor, discussing Ollie's career prospects. She'd commiserated with him, sworn she saw potential in his broken career, and, most importantly, promised him that he was special. And like a fool, he'd believed her. Poppy was developing a project, she'd said. A feature film based on her life. She thought there might be a role in it for him—a big, fat, juicy leading role with the type of material they play at awards shows before cutting to the actors in the front row. The only problem was, she was having a tiny financing issue.

What Poppy needed was a partner.

The next morning, Ollie Pierce woke up alone. When he checked his bank account, he was short $500,000. Apparently, in his inebriated state, he had written Poppy Hastings a check—one she'd been quick to cash. The move had practically bankrupted Ollie, who was on his last legs after getting cut off by his parents over a very public DUI.

But when I next met him, that was all in the past; Ollie Pierce had bounced back. *Summer Swingers* was a sleeper hit, an instant cult classic. And after two stints in rehab, the man was proudly sober and speaking openly about his past struggles with addiction and substance abuse.

So what the flying fuck was Ollie doing driving under the influence with a suspended license at the peak of his career?

"I'm guessing he wasn't the one driving his car that night," Simon says. "But the authorities—and his family, for that matter—don't seem to care much about finding the truth. Not with his track record."

"But that doesn't explain why we're going to D.C.," I whine.

I've barely recovered from our last fun little road trip to prison. Plus, something tells me that five hours locked in a small vehicle with Simon isn't the best of ideas. I might have spent a night or two this week getting off to the memory of his breath on my ear and the sound of "baby" on his lips. And I maybe had a teensy-weensy harmless wet dream about him hate-fucking me into oblivion. All in all, it was no big deal. Just hormones.

But that isn't making it any easier to look him in the eye right now.

"Isn't it obvious?" Simon's excitement is palpable. He's practically frothing at the mouth. "This confirms that Poppy's working through your list of sources. And yesterday, you told me there were only two men you spoke to who hadn't been targeted yet. One was Ollie Pierce. The other will be her final mark, our last chance to catch her in the act. She's going after—"

"—Representative Mark Ford."

Roommate mutters something in another language and leaves the room.

I give in and start packing a bag.

There's no traffic at six a.m. on a Thursday, so Simon and I make it to D.C. in record time—just under four hours. I make a real call to Fern and Steph to let them know I'm going out of town for the weekend (although they both assume it's a prank), then a fake call to the office to inform them that I'm following a lead.

You know, just to keep up appearances for Simon's sake.

On the drive down, it finally dawns on me why he's so eager to take this trip (besides the obvious excuse to annoy me with show tunes for another 240 minutes): Simon is from the DMV area. His family lives in Maryland.

For Simon, going to D.C. means going home.

I catch him up on Representative Ford on the way there. Ford is a Republican representative from the great state of Montana. In his late sixties and married with two adult daughters, Mark Ford is the poster child for traditional Christian values. He's very vocally for abstinence-only sex education, removing evolution from science curricula, and federally funding Sunday schools. And unsurprisingly, he's against funding women's health organizations. He thinks divorce is crass.

And don't even get him fucking *started* on sex work.

Mark Ford is a man who is used to getting what he wants when he wants it. When he met a well-dressed woman in the lobby of the Watergate Hotel who didn't work on the Hill and appeared to be drinking martinis alone, he assumed she was a prostitute. He paid her bar tab for the rest of the evening, then quietly booked a room. He never imagined that the seemingly well-behaved woman from across the pond was secretly recording him with her iPhone as he solicited her for sex.

But then again, he didn't yet know that he was dealing with Poppy Hastings.

He did, however, set up monthly payments to his blackmailer, a small price to pay for keeping his reputation intact. Not to mention his marriage.

Yep, here's the seventh rule of conspiracy: All politicians actually are scum.

Believe the hype.

Mark Ford was one of the few men I spoke to for my article whom I despised from the moment I shook his hand. His white hair was coiffed, his button-down starched, and his god complex radiated from every orifice of his body. He spoke to me as if I were a silly, naive little girl even as he detailed his exploits and asked for my help. Of all my sources, he's perhaps the one who least deserves to be saved.

But I can't very well let Poppy have her way with him.

That's not justice.

It's vengeance.

As we drive into the D.C., I'm struck by how spread out the city is. There's so much open space, so many green pastures. For a swamp, it's oddly...open concept? The neighborhoods feel smaller, with shorter buildings and homes and storefronts, each painted a cheerful color. Trees pepper the sidewalks, shading pedestrians and oxygenating the air. We drive across a bridge, and I look out over the Potomac—from afar, I can see the National Mall. The Lincoln Memorial looms large over picnickers and tourists, the very top of the Washington Monument tipping its hat with playful phallic undertones.

Seeing these structures in person feels oddly familiar, like spying a celebrity on the street and recognizing them from DeuxMoi or some shit.

I've visited D.C. only once, as a child. My parents brought me here over Thanksgiving week, and we did so much sightseeing in one day that my ankles melted into the concrete. We took a White House tour, got lost at the Spy Museum, and even waited in line at Thomas Sweet in Georgetown to try their government-sanctioned ice cream. My family dressed in outrageously patriotic garb—American flag–embroidered hats and I HEART D.C. T-shirts. I remember feeling embarrassed, wishing they'd tone down their loyalism. Mostly, I was hyperaware of the fact that a family of brown people in Americana gear looked suspicious to some people, like an anomaly. My parents' blatant attempts to fit in only made us stand out. That feeling underscored the whole trip for me and left me with a distaste for the city. But perhaps that resentment was unfounded, a product of my isolationism.

Seeing this place through Simon's eyes, however, is an entirely different experience. He narrates our drive, pointing out his favorite museum (the National Air and Space Museum, known for its impressive collection of planes and rockets); the first bar he went to when he turned twenty-one (an unassuming underground college bar called the Tombs, where the bartender stamps your head on your birthday and you get free drinks all night long); his go-to spot to take a date when he wanted to impress her (the Tidal Basin, a man-made reservoir that's famous for its cherry blossom festival, which we apparently missed by a week). He laughs, recalling a time he and his buddies were caught smoking weed at two a.m. on the steps of the Thomas Jefferson Memorial by a security guard and he ripped his pants hopping a fence. Panicked, he'd called his mother, and she'd had to drive forty-five minutes into the city to pick him up. The stunt had gotten him grounded with no phone privileges for two months.

As he gives me his hometown tour, a new side of Simon emerges. His serious disposition and mission-driven machismo melt away, and what's left is so much goofier. Every time he geeks out over a particularly charming cobblestone street or Victorian-era town house, his grin grows wider than the Cheshire Cat's, and his scar burrows into his cheek. As he drives and speaks, he flaps his free hand around wildly, emphatically acting out his stories like a little kid.

The weather is hotter than in New York because we're farther south, so he rolls down the window. The wind blows his tousled dark hair into his eyes, and I laugh as he gathers the front strands in his hand, creating a makeshift ponytail above his forehead so he can see where he's going. We're having such a lovely time that I almost forget we're here to catch a serial killer in the act. And that we're competing for the catch. Oh, and that he's a pretentious douche.

"So." He pulls over on a quiet street in the trendy, quickly gentrifying neighborhood of Shaw, filled with biergartens and overpriced coffee shops. "I figure we can follow Ford to work tomorrow and then tail him over the weekend. I booked us a room at the Holiday Inn closest to Capitol Hill. Separate beds, of course. That cool?"

"What, the FBI couldn't shell out for a swankier setup?" I kid, but only slightly.

Simon stiffens. "That's taxpayer money you're joking

about," he says, reverting back to his stoic self. "But if you're willing to spend the Shred's money on the Ritz…"

"Yeah, yeah." I shrug. "Sounds perfect. Should we go check in?"

"Actually, our room isn't going to be ready for another few hours." He scratches his head. "I wasn't expecting the drive to be so quick. Want to do something in the meantime?"

"What, like, together?" I ask. "You and me, right now?"

"You don't have to be so weird about it." His shoulders bunch by his ears. "I've got plenty of high school friends I could catch up with instead. I'd just feel weird ditching you in the middle of the nation's capital with, you know, a murderer on the loose. My bad."

"Right, right," I say, sensing his nerves. "I guess we could, like, hang out or whatever. What did you have in mind? Hot dogs at a Nationals game? Oh wait, no, I've got it—*Porgy and Bess* at the Kennedy Center. Oh shit. That's it. I'm right, aren't I? You can tell me, I won't shove it in your face."

Simon rolls his eyes and starts backing up the car.

"You ask too many questions," he says. "At some point, you're going to have to learn to just trust me."

We drive in silence for the next fifteen minutes, Simon humming a song from *Les Mis* under his breath. I watch as the city turns from a Yuppie paradise where young professionals in yoga pants drink iced coffee on the go to an underfunded urban landscape with homeless encampments set up under every bridge and inside every tunnel. It's clear to me that people in this city live in two separate worlds…and that the urban planners have intentionally done as much as possible to keep the two isolated from one another.

I swallow hard, looking up at Simon to see if he notices, too. There's a forlorn expression on his face.

"The government isn't perfect," he says. "But I tell myself it's better to try to change it from the inside than to stand on the outside, judging it and doing nothing. Also, we're here."

I look out the window but see nothing.

Simon parks the car in an empty lot next to the highway and gets out.

I follow him, looking around, a bit put off by the lack of foot traffic.

"Did you take me here to kill me?" I ask. "Because if so, well done."

Ignoring my wisecrack, Simon locks the car, then starts walking uphill. When we finally reach the top, we're staring at a large stretch of green grass. But unlike the National Mall, it's entirely abandoned—there isn't a single person tanning or a children's game of flag football. It's eerily quiet, so much so that you can hear the whistle of the wind passing softly over the Potomac.

Simon turns to me and spreads his arms out wide.

"Welcome to Gravelly Point," he says, smiling. "My favorite place in all of the DMV."

I look around, trying to figure out what's so special about this particular patch of turf. As I do, Simon begins his trek to the center of the field. He's running at full speed, and I struggle to keep up with him.

By the time we reach his desired location, I'm completely out of fucking breath. Simon lies down in the grass on his back as if playing dead. I join him, and we both stare up at the sky, watching the clouds pass overhead.

"It's...tranquil?" I try, still unsure of what to say.

Simon is quiet for a moment, introspective. Then he lets out a shallow breath.

"When I was growing up, I'd come here after school sometimes just to avoid going home," Simon says. "Not that there was anything wrong with Easton. It's just so...I don't know. *Ordinary* is the word I'm looking for, I guess. People who grow up there usually love it so much that they stay. Marry their high school sweethearts, take over their family's businesses. It's the way of the land. Even back then, I knew that wasn't for me. I wanted something more. Maybe not, you know, stalking newly released criminals. But more."

"I hear you," I tell him. "I used to think that way. I actually believed moving to New York would solve all of my problems. Can you fucking believe that? In actuality, it just made them worse. Putting distance between my parents and me didn't kill my resentment. Living with my boyfriend—sorry, ex-boyfriend—didn't force me to fall in love with him. And being in a city that romanticizes the grind didn't make me a better reporter. It just meant I became obsessive about my work. It became my entire personality."

"Ex-boyfriend?"

"Wow, that's all you got from that?" I shake my head. "Jealous much?"

I feel his eyes on me without having to look.

"Maybe if I had stayed in Ohio, I could have just been Rose," I add.

"Maybe." Simon thinks for a second. "Or maybe you'd just be somebody's daughter. Or wife."

I turn over to stare into his dark eyes. But he remains laser-focused on the clouds above.

"I've got one question for you," I say. "If you craved excitement, why did you go looking for it in an empty park?"

The corners of Simon's mouth curve upward.

Then he points at the sky.

"Wait for it, Tulip."

Then I hear a sound, a rumbling of some kind.

At first, I think we're experiencing an earthquake or a volcanic eruption, but I know that makes no sense. It's violently loud, like a broken engine or a singer clearing their throat into a microphone. I crane my neck to see if there's a motorcycle or some other vehicle headed toward us, desperate to locate the source of the noise.

Out of nowhere, a plane flies directly over us, so low to the ground that it feels as if I can reach up and graze it with my fingertips.

Oh my god.

I scream, but the plane is so loud that my voice is swallowed by the sound. Adrenaline pumps through my veins, and my entire body hums like a chamber choir.

Holy catharsis.

Almost like it's a reflex, Simon reaches out and grabs my hand, squeezing it. His hand feels big and all-encompassing, his skin rough and calloused against mine. I fight the urge to imagine the way they'd feel on other body parts and squeeze back, shutting my eyes. I feel his breath against my forehead.

He leans over, his lips brushing my temple, then the corner of my mouth.

As quickly as the plane arrived, it's gone, gliding over our bodies like a tidal wave and taking off into the blue abyss.

Simon lets go of my hand. Every hair on my body is standing up straight.

"That was fucking insane!" I scream. "Where did that even come from?"

Simon laughs, running his hand through his hair nonchalantly, unfazed by our near-death experience.

"We're right next to Reagan Airport. Amazing, huh?"

"I don't have the words," I say truthfully. "Thank you. For taking me here. That really did put things in perspective."

Simon sits up, looking down at me, and I suddenly feel self-conscious. I'm still wearing the T-shirt I grabbed in a hurry this morning, and the concealer I smudged over my face has surely rubbed off. I'm a mess, grass stains all over my jeans, drool dripping down one side of my face. I use the back of my hand to wipe at the corner of my lip, but he grabs my wrist.

We lock eyes, and I feel the heat of his gaze melting a hole through my skull.

My heart flips, and I pull back, the trance broken.

He frowns, then looks back down at the grass.

"Look, I have to get dinner with my parents tonight," he says, red creeping up his neck. "I can't come to town and not see them. That would be treason."

"Oh, yeah." I'm immediately disappointed by the idea of parting ways, but I don't want him to know that. I don't know what I'm feeling. Or why. "That makes sense."

"Do you want to go?"

"Go where?"

"To dinner, obviously." Simon raises a brow. "With my parents. Keep up, Tulip."

"Oh," I say. My body feels hot as I attempt to keep my face neutral. "Do you often invite your sworn enemies to meet the 'rents?"

"Only after near-death experiences," he laughs. I join in, awkward at best.

"Yeah, I guess I could. As long as it's not, like, our second fake date or anything."

The red claims new territory on the rest of Simon's face. He immediately looks away, trying to mask the color. But it's too late.

I see him clearly.

"Strictly business," he chokes.

MELCHIOR'S WEDNESDAY NIGHT DINNER REPORT

BY ZSA ZSA

What a busy night! We did more than six hundred covers today, including quite a few last-minute reservations, celebrity walk-ins, and an order sanctioned by an FBI agent! The weather was exceptionally warm, so we were able to seat more patrons outside. Bustling indoor environment, which lasted all night long. Regardless of the hectic pace, the energy was high and the night went smoothly overall.

A staffer called out sick at the last minute, so server Anna was kind enough to stay on for a double. There were multiple birthdays, including that of the Croatian ambassador and the head of Interscope Records, who was seated with an emerging artist who signed a copy of her new album right there at the table and gifted it to the staff at the end of her meal. Notably, many appeared impressed by the appearance of a "canceled" old-school Hollywood director and his wife and three kids. We had to confiscate five phones. Another party shared that it was their first time dining with us at Melchior and they couldn't have loved it more!

We had a bit of a...how should I put this...snafu in the evening. A man, dressed in a sharply tailored suit and acting rather erratically, charged in and claimed to be the FBI agent who had contacted us earlier. He demanded that we show him the reservations manifest. When he refused to show his badge, I politely declined. The man excused himself to the bathroom but ran right into our busboy, Marcus. A crystal water jug was shattered, and several patrons, including a pro pickleball player, were splashed with lemon water. I apologized profusely, but one of the victims in the splash zone threatened to write to the *Post.* So keep your eyes peeled for that article.

I later discovered that the man resorted to tipping our maître d', Gustave, an Andrew Jackson in exchange for a peek at the reservations—an oddly small amount of money for a bribe. Gustave was reprimanded immediately for accepting it. Guest reserved table under a false name but will not be welcomed back to Melchior.

Returns:

- Kitchen sent a duck canard by accident instead of a duck l'Orange. Guest decided to try it and ended up loving it.
- Promo dessert provided.
- Return on espresso martini. Asked for decaf instead.
- Return on caviar. Too fishy. Did not like.

Thank you, and see you tomorrow!
Z

Chapter Seventeen

"So, tell me about Simon as a kid. And please, don't hold back."

I tuck a loose strand of hair behind my ear and lick the rest of the tomato soup off my spoon. Simon's mother throws back her head and laughs, her entire body shaking. Then she takes another bite of her bruschetta and answers with her mouth half-full .

"Where to begin, huh, Artie?" She laughs again, nudging her husband. "Well, let's see. There was that one time when the little guy threatened to run away from home but instead just camped out on the roof for twenty-four hours."

"Oh my, I forgot about that!" Artie grins. "We had the whole neighborhood looking for him. Police. Firemen. The Boy Scouts. You name it. We patrolled the town from dusk till dawn, put posters up, the whole nine yards. Finally, one of our neighbors spotted this troublemaker hiding behind the chimney of our own house, all wrapped up in a sleeping bag. Dang well near gave us a heart attack."

I look over at Simon, who has all but melted into a puddle under the table, and try to picture that little kid, scared out of his mind, hiding from the rest of the world just feet from his own twin bed.

"Why'd you run away?" I ask Simon.

He runs a hand through his hair. "I don't remember," he says, shaking his head, fighting a smile.

"Nonsense!" His mother pinches his cheek like he's a toddler. "Simon was having a tough go of it. He was a sweet boy, real empathetic. Understood people, but people didn't understand him, you know? When he was in elementary school, before he started commuting into the city, he got picked on real bad by his peers. They'd beat on him and stuff. Mostly because he was always crying in public. I told him he ought to do it at home, where it was safer!"

"Mom!" Simon all but yells, but the corners of his mouth continue to turn upward. "You want to tell her the names of all the girls who rejected me next?"

"Oh, hush, honey," she says. "You bring your girl home to meet your mama, but you won't tell her why you're famous this side of the Potomac? Please."

"I'm not his girl," I say quickly.

"She's not my girl," I hear Simon say in tandem.

Simon's mother glances at us, shifting her attention from one to the other, then raises an eyebrow exactly like Simon does. She's got the same thick, dark hair, too, though hers is graying, and the same freckled skin. He looks much more like her than his father.

"Well, all righty, then," she says. "My apologies for misunderstanding the situation. It's not like Mr. Hotshot over here ever tells us details about his personal life in the Big Apple. Or his work."

"I work for the government." Simon shakes his head. "You know I can't talk about my cases. They're classified."

"Yeah, yeah." She shoos the words away like a fly. "You're not James Bond, doll."

"So, uh..." I turn toward Simon and think quickly on my feet, trying to change the subject for his sake. "Why were you always crying? Dog ate your homework? Got an A-minus on a test?"

"Oh, he's been like that ever since his old man passed."

"Mother!"

This time, Simon's not smiling. Not even a little bit.

We all sit silently for a second.

Simon stares at his plate.

His mother widens her eyes like a puppy.

I twitch nervously in my seat.

"I didn't know," I whisper. Then I turn to Artie, the man seated next to his mother. "So, you're not—"

"Oh, no, no," Artie says. "I married into the family when Simon was seven. Love him like a son, though. Raised him to be a man."

Simon reaches out and pats Artie on the shoulder, giving him an affectionate squeeze.

"So, how did he...your dad...actually, I'm sorry. That's inappropriate. Fuck." I say. "Shit, I'm sorry for saying fuck. I shouldn't ask that. I'm bad at this. And you don't have to answer."

The truth is, I get weird around death.

No one close to me has ever passed before. The closest thing I've ever felt to grief has been over Poppy's victims.

Brad Zarbos.

And honestly, Poppy herself.

"No, it's okay." Simon's normally rough voice is softer around the edges. He glances at me. "I'm good to talk about it. He had stage-four lung cancer. It was surprising—he never smoked or anything. I was really little."

I see a small tear form in the corner of his eye, but he quickly blinks it away and clears his throat. Unable to contain herself a moment longer, his mother gets up out of her seat and pulls him into a hug. He laughs, reluctantly accepting her embrace.

Soon we're all laughing, too. It feels good, like slowly releasing the air out of a tire.

"Great, Mom," he mutters. "Now Rose has rolled around in all our dirty laundry."

"Is Rose your American or Arabic name?" his mother asks me.

"Um, just my name. In both English and Farsi. My family is Iranian."

"Oh, you'll have to forgive me." she bites her lip. "So much for my Southern charm."

"You're Southern?"

I frown at Simon. How much don't I know about this man I've been spending nearly every damn day with?

"Virginia, Tulip," he says, smirking. "You can quit holding your breath. We moved to Maryland after Mom and Artie remarried."

Simon's mother stares at us, her eyes twinkling as she registers our rapport.

"Why do you call her Tulip, sweet pea?"

"It's a long story," he says, shutting down the topic. "No time to get into it now. Anyway, I've got to use the restroom. Will you please excuse me?"

He stands up and walks toward the little boys' room just as the waiter arrives with our pizzas. Behind me, I hear a table singing happy birthday to a woman in her eighties. The walls have been signed by patrons through the years underneath a large mural of the founders holding hands, an older couple from Sicily. There are paper lanterns on every table, and the menus are coated in plastic.

I like that Simon's family chose a pizza parlor for dinner, a casual Italian restaurant. It's warm and unpretentious, just like them. I shut my eyes and try to imagine my parents in a place like this and cringe. Mispronouncing the menu items, bickering about who gets to pay the check.

They'd stick out like a sore thumb.

Simon's mother puts her arm around her husband, and he kisses her on the top of her head. She takes a long swig of his beer, handing it back to him nearly empty. He laughs, wagging his finger at her. I can see his undershirt peeking out from under the flannel he's wearing tucked into his jeans, his balding head shining under the fluorescent lights.

They did a good job with him, with Simon. Their family may be fractured, but it's so obviously full of love. And now that I think about it, it makes sense that Simon had a painful childhood, one full of loss and grief. Only someone who experienced real fucking hurt at a young age would go looking for meaning in the mundane and end up stumbling upon murder and mayhem. Only someone who grew up in a life full of uncertainty could be forever drawn to chaos. Someone like me.

"My son likes you," Simon's mother says as soon as he's out of earshot.

"Don't tell him, but I kind of like him, too," I smile.

"Although he's annoying as hell sometimes. And stubborn. And rude. Plus his love of *Rent*...seriously, for someone who can't carry a tune to save his life, that man sure does a shit ton of singing."

"No, I mean he fancies you," she says. "You know. Boy meets girl. Girl meets boy. They fall in love."

"More like boy meets girl, girl kicks boy in the balls." I roll my eyes.

I wait for Simon's mother to wince at the word *balls*, but she doesn't flinch. She continues to look at me, her eyes peeling back layers like an MRI, while Artie pretends to be busy on his phone.

"A mother knows."

"It's not like that." I gulp, looking around anxiously. "We're just working together."

"So, you're coworkers, then?" Artie asks. "At the bureau?"

"Well, no, not exactly..."

"Good." Simon's mother sips her wine. "At the very least, he has a friend. He deserves one after what those Feds put him through."

Wait a damn minute.

"What who put him through? What are you talking abou—"

"Rose!"

Simon comes charging toward our table from the bathroom, toilet paper stuck to his shoe. He looks like the Terminator, only surrounded by loads of children, grannies, and families.

I giggle.

"You've got to see this!"

He hands me his phone, which is open to Instagram. (Simon has an Instagram account? Great! More things I don't know about him.) At first I'm not sure what I'm looking at. Then I see what he's referring to.

Poppy Hastings has just updated her Story.

I nervously click it.

"Hello, my lovelies! I know the media likes to paint me as a villain because I stole a few measly millions from a handful of rich old white men, but a little-known fact about me is that I'm actually quite charitable. I've sat on the board of organizations, thrown fundraisers, and have never missed a nonprofit gala in my life. Plus, in prison, I used to flirt with the simpleminded guards and hand out the spoils of my labors to my fellow inmates to promote peace and harmony within our walls. So when the president of the United States invited me to livestream the annual white-tie dinner at the White House, I couldn't exactly pass up the chance to show off my more philanthropic side—or to hit on his gorgeous wife. What can I say? I'm addicted to power. As for my parole officer, do you really think Bill from Wichita would say no to a request from the commander in chief? Please. You're killing me, darling!"

She takes a drag from a cigarette, blows a ring into the camera. Behind her, I can see the 365 steps, one for every day in a year, that lead to the dome of the Capitol Building…the very same building where Representative Mark Ford works. Someone standing next to her casts a shadow, slicing her face in half.

She's not alone.

She winks at the camera, then turns off her phone.

I do the same, handing it back to Simon.

We lock eyes.

In my periphery, I see his mother suggestively waggle her eyebrows at Artie.

"You know what this means, don't you?" Simon asks.

I nod.

"Poppy Hastings is in D.C.," I say. "She's here to finish the job herself."

"Not if we have any say in it." He cups his hand around his mouth, shielding his words from his glowing parents.

"What are you saying?"

"Let's catch the bitch in the act."

Chapter Eighteen

After saying a quick goodbye to Simon's parents, we double back to Capitol Hill and stake out the White House, waiting for Poppy to exit her dinner with the president (proof that we're truly living in a simulation). We're joined by a couple of evangelicals who have been sleeping on the lawn in a tent, attempting to convince politicians that the apocalypse is fast approaching and that we should be using all our resources to prepare.

Honestly, they've convinced me. Judging by the signs, they're on the fucking money.

Around eleven p.m., we watch from afar as Poppy leaves the building, flanked by security, and walks toward a black town car. We get into Simon's beat-up Honda Civic and tail them all the way to the Commodore Hotel. Upon arrival, she opens the door to her car, looks both ways, and then enters through the revolving door. Five minutes later, Simon parks his car on the street (a surefire way to get a ticket) and follows her.

"Wait!" I shout. "What about the Holiday Inn?"

"Fuck the Holiday Inn." Simon grins. "We're getting a room at the Commodore."

He offers his arm, and I smile, taking it and slinging my overnight bag over my shoulder. We strut into the lobby like supermodels even though we're dressed like hitchhikers. (Okay, fine, just me.) The space is filled with politicians surrounded by government aides, wealthy Georgetown kids looking to give daddy's AmEx a workout, and businessmen pretending to take phone calls while they look for young, impressionable women to dine on and dash. I bet this hotel is crawling with goddamn criminals. Even if we don't end up catching Poppy Hastings, we might end up accidentally walking in on some other international scandal.

Simon approaches the concierge's desk and rings the bell. I wait for him to flash his badge, but he doesn't. Instead, he leans over the desk and flutters his eyelashes, pushing up the sleeves of his shirt to expose his forearms.

At the sight of his taut skin and muscles, my insides immediately melt like butter.

The concierge? Not so much.

"ID and credit card, please."

There's a flash of discomfort on Simon's face, but the line between his eyebrows is gone before I have time to react. He reaches into his back pocket and takes out his wallet, forking over what looks like his personal credit card and driver's license.

I guess he'll just have to expense the room later. Does the FBI even do expense reports?

"Excuse me, ma'am." He flashes that indented smile. "My boss just checked in, and I'm going to need the room right next to hers. She's extremely demanding, known for making outlandish requests at all hours of the night. If I'm not able to get to her within seconds when it occurs to her that she can't live without a pair of slippers made from the hide of miniature horses or can't sleep on a pillowcase that isn't covered in dried male crocodile tears, she'll lose her mind and take to social media."

He gives the concierge a wink that has my vagina fluttering.

But she just frowns.

"I'm sorry, sir, but I can't guarantee we have a room available at all this last-minute, let alone the one next to your boss," she says. "We book up six months in advance here at the Commodore."

I suck in my cheeks, but Simon doesn't miss a beat.

"Please, I'm begging you. My boss is difficult, and if I don't get upstairs as soon as possible, she'll have my head. And I quite like my head. I've been told my pretty face is my best asset." He runs his tongue over his lower lip, calling attention to just how pretty that face is.

"I don't know."

Damn. This woman's got a libido of steel.

So Simon switches tactics.

"She'll make my life a nightmare. Our lives. Because, well, she'll most likely complain about her experience at this hotel. She might even mention you by name. And I'm sure that's not the kind of publicity the Commodore is looking for, now is it?"

"Your boss is Poppy Hastings?" she asks, narrowing her eyes.

Simon is an idiot.

Poppy is the blueprint, one of the most famous people in the world right now.

Of course the staff knows who she is.

I look up at him, panic in my eyes.

But he doesn't even blink.

"That's right," he says. "And if you think she's crazy, you should see her fans. Believe me, they're worse. Always taking things a little too far. Let me ask you a question: Have you ever been doxed"—he glances down at her name tag—"Janet? Not so fun, I can tell you. Do you live alone?"

Janet gulps and turns a little green.

"Well, let me just call up to Ms. Hastings's room and confirm your story—"

She reaches for the phone, but Simon gently places his hand over hers. Her entire body jolts at the contact.

I guess no one is immune to Simon's charms after all.

"Please, Janet. She just texted me that the wallpaper is moving. If I'm not there to give her a cranial massage in minutes, there's no telling what she'll do to me."

He's full-on flirting with her now, stroking his thumb over the back of her hand.

"Well, we wouldn't want that," she says, her voice shaky. "Here is the key to room five-oh-four. She's in five-oh-five. Please, go now, before it's too late."

"Thank you very much." Simon nods, his face serious. "And if I see this online tomorrow, I'll know who tipped off the press. Remember that. By the way, has anyone ever told you that you look like a young Elizabeth Taylor?"

Her *entire body* blushes.

Simon grabs the key, throws his shoulders back, and stalks toward the elevator. I quickly follow after him.

Once we're safely inside, I break into an uncontrollable fit of laughter.

"Where the hell did that come from?" I ask, wiping away a tear.

"I'm an FBI agent, remember?" he says, sheepish. "Plus maybe I've seen one too many dramatic musicals. All that Broadway finally paid off, baby. My acting chops have kicked in."

"Well, bravo," I say, smirking. "You had me fooled."

The elevator opens on the fifth floor, and we follow the arrows toward our room. We stop outside of Poppy's, and I place my ear against the door, quieting my breathing.

"I can't believe she's in there," Simon whispers.

"So close, and yet so far," I say, thinking back to the Rockland.

Simon sighs. "Come on, let's go set up shop."

He places the card over the key reader until the light turns green, and Simon and I enter the room. The space is small but ornately decorated with a breathtaking view of the National Mall and the Washington Monument. The room has white marble walls that look cold to the touch, two fluffy robes I can't wait to collapse into, and...

One queen-size bed.

We both stare at it for a moment, horrified.

"Of course." Simon curses under his breath. "I didn't specify that I needed two beds. I'm sorry, Tulip. This is my fault. I'll sleep on the floor."

"Are you sure?" My voice comes out strained. Not entirely my own. "That would probably be for the best..."

But Simon is already throwing pillows off the bed and creating a makeshift mattress for himself on the carpet, moving robotically around the room.

"Yup, it's fine."

He doesn't even look up to meet my eyes.

"Fine," I echo.

Whatever.

If he doesn't care, why should I?

I chuck my duffel on the bed and kick off my sneakers by the door. God, I smell like a New York sewer after Saint Patrick's Day. As in, completely fucking vile. There's only one thing I want to do right now.

"I'm taking a shower," I announce to Simon's back. "I reek of road trip. Plus my clothes are covered in grass stains, thanks to *your* happy place."

"Oh, please." Simon looks up then, unable to resist a raised brow. "You loved it."

I blush but refuse to grant him the satisfaction. Instead, I grab one of those snow-white robes and strut toward the bathroom.

Once inside, I remove my T-shirt and jeans and throw them into a messy pile on the floor. Simon made us leave so quickly this morning that I didn't even have time to put on a bra, which is fine by me. I hate bras anyway—they're patriarchally restrictive, like fucking garter belts. With my hair piled on top of my head, I turn the water toward hot until it's boiling, scalding, then climb into the shower. I let the water soak through my skin, washing off the day, if not the past few years.

Without meaning to, I think about Poppy on her bed on the opposite side of the wall. What's she doing right now? Flirting with a room service waiter? Watching Netflix and daydreaming about her own made-for-TV movie? Speaking to millions of Instagram followers while sitting completely and utterly alone, not a friend left in the world?

I feel a pang of loneliness in my gut.

Or maybe it's just shampoo getting in my eyes.

Either way, it stings.

After cleansing every inch of myself thoroughly, being sure to take full advantage of the expensive bath products that high-end hotels provide free of charge, I dry myself off, then help myself to the fluffy robe. I crack the bathroom door open, and I can feel Simon's body heat on the other side, an invisible current. Uncharacteristically self-conscious, I tie the robe tight around my waist before walking out of the bathroom. I head toward my duffel, grab my brush, and run it through my hair. The bristles get caught in the large knots in my unruly curls, the remaining water from the shower pooling at my shoulders.

Simon is occupying himself in the corner of the room. He's unpacking all of his things even though we're only staying the night, like a total freak—dividing his underwear from his undershirts, putting them all into separate drawers. He hangs his jacket in the coat closet, almost like he's trying to keep himself busy in a desperate attempt to avoid talking to me.

"What's that?" I gesture to the bulky black equipment he hauls from the bottom of his bag and begins setting up against the bedroom wall.

"A listening device," he explains, "so we can check in on Poppy. I brought it with me just in case. This way, we'll know the second she sneaks out of her room or lets someone in."

"Smart."

I briefly consider annoying him further, then decide against it. We've been getting along so well on this trip. I may even consider abandoning my pledged vendetta against him in favor of a slightly bemused affection. Why ruin a good thing?

Especially when we could drink instead.

I head over to the minibar and survey the goods. A handful of nips ranging from subpar vodka to expensive whiskey, a few bags of nuts, the odd candy bar. After a few seconds of debate, I grab the tiny bottle of tequila, pop it open, and prepare to down it like a shot.

"Tulip, what the hell are you doing?" The urgency in Simon's voice startles me. "We have to pay for that!"

"So?" I step back and settle into a defensive stance. "It's on the FBI, isn't it? I'm a taxpayer. This is how I choose to spend my taxpayer funds."

Simon watches incredulously as I down the entire bottle in one gulp.

"They upcharge like crazy for those things." He shakes his head in disbelief. "It'll be so expensive."

"And once again, why should I care?" I ask, getting annoyed.

"Because."

"Because why?"

"Because the FBI isn't fucking paying for it!" he finally huffs. "I am, okay? For all of it."

He sits down on the bed and rests his head in his hands, breathing heavily for a second. When he looks back up, his face is red and twisted with pain. His body shakes slightly as he opens his mouth, then closes it again, unsure of where to begin.

"I don't understand."

It's all I can say.

I can't find any other words.

"The FBI doesn't know I'm looking into Poppy," Simon sighs, unable to meet my eyes. "When Ulysses Rutherford went missing right after Poppy was released, I brought it up with my supervisor because I knew they were connected. And he immediately told me to drop it, that Poppy was no longer a suspect. Now that I know about Dunamis, it all makes sense. I bet he's dirty, a turncoat. But I refused to comply. Remember how I told you I was pressured into making the arrest early? The truth is, they made the arrest without me. And I wasn't just denied a promotion. I was demoted. To fucking desk duty. That's why I haven't been using department resources and have been reluctant to flash my badge. That's why I haven't been carrying—they took my gun from me. I can't even protect you, Tulip. And the best part? Nobody knows what I'm doing here. They think I'm on vacation."

His nostrils flare as the desperation in his expression turns to sheer, unadulterated rage.

"Now do you get it? This is personal for me, Tulip. She ruined my career. Taunted me. Took everything from me. I have to be the one to put her away again. It's my only chance to save my reputation and get my old job back."

My hands grow clammy.

Part of me wants to chew him out for misleading me. To call him a bastard, to smack him hard across the face.

But the other part knows that this might be my only chance to reveal my own secret. It's my one shot from the universe to come clean about everything.

No lies. No pranks. No pretense.

Just Simon and me in a tiny room in a fancy hotel, being completely and terrifyingly honest with each other.

He finally cranes his neck to look at me, and I stare into those dark blue eyes. I see something familiar: obligation. A desire to earn back respect. To prove your own sanity.

And to question whether you're still sane at all.

"Please don't hate me." His voice catches, causing my heart to hiccup. "I never wanted you to get swept up in this, I swear.

But when Poppy went dark and the trail went dry, you were the only person I knew who was invested enough to help me. I couldn't tell anyone else in my life. Not my colleagues. Not my family. No one. I've been so alone in this."

I shut my eyes tightly, internalizing the moment.

When I open them, the words pour out of me like the tequila from that tiny bottle.

"The thing is, I haven't been really, totally, one hundred percent up-front with you either."

Simon cocks his head in confusion, frowning.

I take it as a sign to continue.

"So, uh. Don't freak out or anything. But I was fired from the Shred. My editor, Cat? Well, she knew I was pre-reporting at first. I had her sign off on it, I swear. I didn't lie about that. But then, I…well, I went a little off the deep end. I made this presentation about Poppy's Instagram and Photoshop—"

"The Twin Towers thing?" Simon interrupts. "God, that drove me crazy!"

"Yes!" Wow. Maybe we really are cut from the same cloth. "Anyway, after that, she thought I'd lost it. Not, you know, totally ideal. She made me go on mental health leave, which I was actually taking when I, uh, ran into you in that alley. Remember? Your balls. My boot. Anyway, my plan was to prove to her that my theory was right, that I wasn't fucking crazy. But more broadly, to prove to the world that Poppy wasn't worthy of her celebrity. That she should be behind bars. That she fucking sucks. To make up for all the harm I caused with my first article, you know? I mean, you said it yourself—I'm the reason she's famous. But the day I got back, I found out that the Shred is planning on featuring her on the cover of their next issue. So, yeah. I went berserk and threatened to quit. But Cat beat me to the punch. Anyway. Simon?"

I look up from my rant to find Simon's forehead creased, his eyes scrunched. I shift forward, concerned he's gone into cardiac arrest. But he springs back from me, a fire burning bright in his eyes.

"You lied to me, Tulip."

There's a dangerous edge to his voice, the accusation hanging heavy over my head.

So I do what I do best.

I go on the offensive.

"And you lied to me, jackass. Don't be a fucking hypocrite."

He inches toward me like a predator, his gaze darkening with feral delight.

There's a hunger beneath them, a flicker of something primal. Almost animal.

"You want to play that game? I'm fighting to keep a job. You already lost yours. I'm not sure you have a leg to stand on."

"I'd rather be crawling on my hands and knees than throwing a hissy fit like a little bitch," I retort.

"Your hands and knees, huh?" There's that edge again. Playful. Menacing. "You just have to go there, don't you? Always have to fight back, to do the opposite of what I say, to throw me off my game."

"What game?" I'm seething, seeing nothing but red. "You were on the sidelines until you met me. I made you a valuable player."

The douchebag has the nerve to laugh at that. A deep, raspy snicker that gets caught in his throat.

"And here you had me thinking you were a threat. Promising

to ruin my investigation by tipping Poppy off with your little story again. But you have nowhere to take your story, do you, Tulip?"

He leans in so close that his breath tickles my ear.

My breathing grows shallow.

"I'll answer that for you. You have no publisher. You have no editor. Your story is as good as dead. You're completely at my mercy."

"Never," I practically choke. "Your boss won't believe you, and neither do I. This is a draw. I'll never let you win."

"Is that so?"

Simon's grin turns wicked. He uses the rough pad of his index finger to paint a line across my collarbone. I shiver at his touch, and he clicks his tongue in approval, the sound sending a signal loud and clear. Informing me that he is well aware of the involuntary, extraordinary, completely fucking senseless way my body responds to him.

"You know what, Tulip?"

Simon's hand lingers where the two sides of my robe come together.

For a second, I think he's going to pull it open.

Even more concerning?

I would let him.

"What?" I practically whimper.

"I think you're tired of fighting back. And I think you're so fucking sick of people expecting you to have your shit together. I know your secret. What you really want. What you *crave*."

"Oh yeah?" I manage to look up from where his finger is trailing down the damp material covering my torso and give him a challenging, defiant look. "And what's that?"

His teeth graze the corner of my earlobe.
Nipping.
And against my better judgment, I let out a small noise.
"To lose control."
And then Agent Simon leans in and kisses me.

Chapter Nineteen

It's not just any kiss.

Simon kisses me so hard that I lose my center of gravity, knocking all the air out of my lungs. His lips are punishing, bruising against mine. He bites so hard that he draws blood, the taste metallic against the insides of my cheeks. The intensity of his kiss resurrects my entire body, bringing me to life. His stubble grazes my chin once, twice, and my limbs turn to liquid as I unravel beneath him. Then his tongue slips in, inquisitive at first, then with the confidence and brute force of a man starved. He explores the roof of my mouth before intertwining his tongue with my own, the sensation leading us both to groan.

Simon breaks away from our kiss suddenly, and I'm left panting.

"Tulip." His voice is restrained. Desperate. "Do you still hate me?"

"I don't know."

My thoughts are racing, staggering. All I can think about, obsess about, is the absence of his skin against mine. Our eyes lock, and the heat of his gaze burrows into the pit of my stomach until I'm forced to rub my thighs together to numb the ache. He takes notice, a vein popping faintly in the center of his forehead.

"Fine. You can still hate me. But do you trust me?"

I can't focus.

Can't speak.

His words are drowned out by the thumping in my chest, matched only by the growing thrumming between my legs.

"Wha-what?"

"I need you to tell me you trust me, Rose," he says. "Is this okay?"

At that moment, I know I'm totally and utterly screwed.

Because he didn't call me Tulip.

Nope. Not this time.

That fucker had to go and call me Rose.

I nod.

Mouth the word *yes*.

And he lunges for me.

He grabs my head between his hands, so big that they engulf my entire face. I run my nails down the back of his neck, finally allowing them to explore that thick head of dark hair. But it's not enough. I want to feel more of him, to see all of him. Need consumes me, and I begin clawing at his shirt, tugging at the hem. He pulls away from me, looking down and smirking, shaking his head.

So entitled.

"Looks like someone needs a lesson in giving up control."

"Shut your damn—"

Before I know what's happening, Simon picks me up and throws me onto the mattress before covering me with his own body, caging me in. He runs his tongue down the side of my neck, focusing on a sensitive spot right above my shoulder. I shudder beneath him, and he chuckles darkly. His chest presses me down, trapping me beneath him, as his hands grab my wrists, holding them captive above my head.

I hear the clang of metal and gasp when I feel something cold constrict my movements, followed by the click of a lock. I wriggle on the bed, but my range of motion is limited.

The asshole has handcuffed me to the headboard.

"I thought you weren't a fucking cop," I hiss.

"I'm not a cop." He leans down and kisses my temple. "And I'm no longer a field agent." He meanders down to the corner of my mouth, leaving tiny pecks in his wake. "Hell, tonight, I'm barely even a man." Simon is now towering above me, all broad muscles and chiseled definition. I picture what lies beneath his clothes, and my mouth waters. Without thinking, I suck my bottom lip between my teeth. Simon growls in response.

"Do you know what I am, Tulip?"

"A pain in my ass?"

Simon reaches down and lightly smacks the space between my thighs that's now barely covered by the robe hitching up my legs. My body practically convulses in shock.

"Wrong answer, baby." His voice is cutting, like gravel. "Such a wiseass. Always has to mouth off. I can't wait to feel that mouth when it's wrapped around my cock."

My jaw drops at his filthy words.

Is this the same man who wouldn't stop singing "I Dreamed a Dream" on the car ride down to D.C.?

Before I have time to process, his hands have moved down my torso, hoisting up my waist and gripping my ass. He takes a handful in each palm and squeezes. I buck my hips in response.

And that small, reflexive motion causes something in Simon to snap.

He tears open my robe, unwrapping me without care, letting out a strangled exhalation at what he finds underneath.

"Fuck, Rose." His words vibrate against my quickly hardening nipples.

He takes my left breast into his mouth, running the pad of his tongue over one bud before sucking it into his mouth. He uses his hand to fondle the right before switching his attention to the other side. My body writhes beneath him, as I struggle against my restraints.

"You're so fucking beautiful," he says, nuzzling the ridge between my breasts. "That wild look in your eyes when you're fighting with me. Flirting with me. Fucking me. So goddamn perfect."

He shifts his weight back over me so that we're face-to-face. With a charged look, he grinds into me, the zipper of his jeans creating delicious friction against the spot that aches the most. I gasp as I feel his length rubbing against me.

Once.

Twice.

"Do you feel me, baby?" He pushes his hips against mine, and I tremble. "Do you see how crazy you make me? How hard?"

"Simon," I gasp. Because it feels good. Too good. "Shirt. Off. Please."

"What was that?" His smile belongs to the devil. "Funny, I don't think I've ever heard you use that word before."

I narrow my eyes, about to respond. But he thrusts forward again, this time shifting between the apex of my thighs, momentarily blinding me. When I regain my sight, his gaze is boring into me, cocky and full of lust. His eyes don't break away from mine as he lifts his shirt over his head and throws it across the room. I try my hardest not to gawk at the sweat rolling down his chest from his pecs to the hard ridges of his abs, at the happy trail above the deep V that points down his pants like a poisoned arrow. There's a large tattoo on his shoulder, a black circular pattern with four distorted rings, two open and two closed. In the middle lies a couple of dots, one larger than the other, like a pair of eyes, always watching. I try to lean forward and lick the space between them, but my neck won't reach far enough.

I grunt in frustration.

Simon chuckles at my annoyance, and his laughter reverberates down my spine.

"It's funny," he murmurs. "You say you hate me. You're not sure you even trust me. But if I were to reach between your thighs—" He slips a finger inside my entrance, and I let out a yelp. "Yep. Just as I expected. You're so wet for me. Fucking soaked."

His finger begins moving in and out of me at a slow, punishing pace. Studying my sounds and facial expressions as I react to his touch, he adds a second finger. We watch together as his hand pumps into me, working us both into a frenzy, and then he lowers his head to join his fingers. As if he can't resist giving in to temptation, he uses his other hand to part my lips, giving me a slow, lazy lick.

My entire body jolts at the touch of his tongue, and he shakes his head, holding my body down, locked beneath him like my wrists in the cuffs. "I can't tell if you actually taste this good," he mutters to himself, "or if I've just wanted this for too damn long."

Before I can demand to know exactly what the fuck that means, his tongue reaches my clit, circling it slowly, while his fingers quicken their torturous pace. I let out a broken moan. Simon's tongue barely grazes my most sensitive spot, refusing to press down, to give me the pressure I need. My legs start to shake in anticipation, and his lips finally wrap around me just as his fingers brush against a spot deep inside of me that Zain could never quite find.

"Simon," I cry. I'm close, but a part of me doesn't want to let go. To give in. To be completely vulnerable in front of him. With him. "I can't."

"You can," he commands.

He lifts his head and removes his fingers, and my body immediately mourns the lack of contact. But then I feel him close in again, his breath hot against my entrance.

"Go on, then," he says. "You want a semblance of control? Take what you need."

I begin moving. Jolting my hips, chasing my pleasure while riding Simon's mouth. I feel him everywhere—in the pique of my breasts, the spot beneath my stomach, the curl of my toes. And I lose myself to that feeling. Of him all over me, within me. Having me. Owning me.

"Oh god," I breathe. "Oh god. I'm going to—"

"Go on," he encourages. "I want to feel you come against my tongue."

And those dirty words are my undoing. I let out a sob, then fall apart, quaking uncontrollably, the tension of the past few weeks, the past few years, evaporating from my body.

When I regain consciousness, I find Simon hovering above me, unbuckling his jeans and dragging them down his legs. His lips are gleaming—from me, I realize. My face flushes, and he quirks a brow before licking his fingers, as if he wants to savor every last drop. I stare, unable to move, as he drops his underwear. When he stands back up, I'm at eye level with his length.

My mouth goes dry.

For the first time since meeting Agent Simon, I'm actually fucking speechless.

"Let me grab a condom." He turns to get his duffel.

"Wait," I say. "I'm on birth control."

His eyes search mine. "I'm clean."

"Then…" I widen my legs, a silent invitation.

"How do you want it, Rose?" His words are tight, like it's taking all his effort not to explode.

I just continue to stare.

"Don't hold out on me now," he warns, the head of his cock easing against my entrance, teasing me. The movement sends a wave of awareness through my body, waking me up from my post-orgasm daze. My head snaps up at him, and I roll my eyes. He nods. "There she is. There's my girl."

"Rough," I tell him. "I want you to take me rough."

Simon curses under his breath, then slams into me. I open my mouth for a second, feeling him fill me entirely, to the hilt. Then his hands reach up to grasp my cuffed ones, and I feel myself squeeze around him. Groaning, he sets his slick forehead against mine, our noses grazing almost tenderly against one another.

Then he starts to move.

He's tentative at first, but soon his hips begin to buck at a relentless speed. I wrap my legs around his waist, pulling him in closer, and he reaches down to tilt my body at an angle that somehow forces me to take him deeper, harder. My pulse quickens, blood coursing so loudly through my veins that I'm sure I've popped an artery.

"Look at me." Simon's pupils dilate as he watches the place where we're joined together. "Look at how beautifully you take me."

The slap of our bodies.

The heat of his words.

It's all too much.

My moans escalate, growing louder as my jaw clenches, my muscles contracting. Simon reaches down between us and begins to stroke that spot between my thighs, and I cry out, alarmed by how readily I'm giving up my power, allowing him to have authority over me. Over my body. My pleasure.

"That's it," he coaxes. "Scream for me, baby. Come for me, Rose."

And I do.

Simon follows me over the edge, and we fall together violently, so uncontrollably that every atom in my body disintegrates and regenerates, every inch of my flesh on fire, every joint spasming until I am one quivering, defeated mess.

Not Rose 2.0.

No posturing, no facades.

Just me, stripped and exposed for Simon to see.

He uncuffs my wrists and pulls my body into his, sweetly kissing the top of my head. I melt into his chest, limp and sated, breathing unevenly.

My eyes flutter closed for just a brief moment.

"Good girl," he murmurs.

"I win," I whisper.

"You win," he says. "You were right. I never stood a chance against you."

Chapter Twenty

I'm in the kitchen on the top floor with Fern and Steph, covered in coffee stains, doing a bad John Oliver impression. Fern keeps telling me that I've never looked better, a blatant, obvious prank. Low-hanging fruit, so to speak. The coffee seeps down my T-shirt until it drips onto the sticky floor. Steph is dabbing at the white fabric with a paper towel, chastising me in Spanish, reminding me to be careful around hot beverages. Cat walks past the spectacle and gives us a suspicious look. Then she announces that she'll see us in the lineup meeting in five minutes. We all do our best to hold it together and nod until she's out of sight, and then we fucking lose it, breaking into fits of laughter. Fern cackles so hard that coffee comes up her nose. Steph keeps snorting, then gasping in horror at the noise she's making. Then we link arms, little Steph in the middle, and make our way to the conference room together. Fern is telling us about a girl she has started seeing who likes to spit in her mouth. She thinks this could be the one. Steph calculates the actual odds of that being true, pulling numbers out of a goddamn hat like the tiny magician she is.

Someone comes up behind us, dancing in our shadow. I can't see them, but I can sense them. A warm body. Cold exterior, but hot to the touch. They begin walking in step with our group. Without warning, the shadow reaches out and links arms with me. I jerk away and abruptly turn to my left, only to discover that it's Poppy. But it's also not Poppy. It's a different, more subdued version of the woman I've come to despise and depend on in equal measure. She's dressed in blue jeans and a ribbed tank top, an understated outfit that makes her look mundane. Average. Just like everybody else. She listens to Fern's story like it's the most natural thing in the world, giggling at all the right moments, as if on cue. I wait for someone, anyone, to react to the fact that she's here. To cause a scene in the middle of the open-plan office. But nothing happens. Steph and Fern hardly blink, engaging her with banter and giggling at her outrageous puns.

Guys, do you see this? I scream silently in my head. *Poppy is here with us.*

What do you mean? Fern can read my mind, as always. *She's been here all along.*

With you, Steph chimes in. *She's always with you, Rose. You carry her everywhere you go.*

A soft light filters in through the floor-to-ceiling windows of the Commodore, speckling the ceiling. My eyes slowly flutter open. The first thing I notice is a soreness in my body, hidden between my legs. The second? The mattress below me is rising and falling like the tide, a meditative pulse.

Then the events of last night flood back, and I look beneath me.

That's no mattress.

I'm nestled into the crooks and crannies of Simon's chest.

I allow myself a peek up at his face, and my heart drops. He's fucking beautiful as he sleeps. Peaceful. There's no hint of his usual frown burrowed into those chiseled cheeks, and his dark hair tangles loosely over his eyelashes. A fallen angel. He breathes deeply, the curly hair on his chest playing pirates on the sand of his skin. He smiles in his sleep like a little boy on Christmas Eve. He looks so earnest, sincere. Innocent.

But then I remember the dirty words that fell from those lips, and my face flushes.

A tingle sprints down my spine as I relive flashes of memory—his hand cupping my face, his facial hair brushing against my abdomen.

The handcuffs restricting my wrists.

I look down at my hands.

Sure enough, red raised marks line my skin, branding me as his.

I gulp.

"What are you doing up?" he murmurs, his eyes still closed. "Go back to sleep."

"It's light out." That voice is too high-pitched to belong to me.

"So?" His voice reverberates against my body, collecting in my core. "Close your eyes, and you won't be able to see the light any longer. Problem solved."

I turn onto my side, resting my chin in the palm of my hand, but Simon acts quickly, wrapping his arms around my back and pulling me close once more. Our torsos are perfectly aligned, and his breathing sends tiny air currents onto my neck, tickling my collarbones. I take his advice and shut my eyes tightly for a second, trying to savor this moment.

After everything that happened with Zain, I had just accepted that a part of me was broken. That after my nervous breakdown, there was a small piece of the person I was before that I'd never regain. That I was capable of love but incapable of being *in* love. But maybe the problem wasn't me. Maybe it was just the person I was with. Who would have guessed that it would take *another* nervous breakdown, hitting rock bottom, and getting fired to see myself clearly again? How was I to know that the single greatest gift Poppy Hastings would give me would be—

Wait.

Wait a damn minute.

Fuck.

"Simon." I tear away from his embrace, and his body jolts in surprise. "Simon, wake up."

"Mm-hm," he moans.

"Seriously." This time, I smack the back of his head, and he growls. "Get up."

"What the hell, Tulip?"

I see we're back to Tulip now.

"Poppy. We forgot about Poppy."

"Oh. Fuck."

"Yep. My thought exactly."

He pushes himself upright, using the same biceps that flipped me on my back like a fried egg just hours before. I look away, embarrassed by my own indecent thoughts, which is unlike me. I've notoriously never been one for ladylike behavior. But after everything we did last night, I feel different around Simon in the light of day. Something unspoken has changed between us. Shifted.

He's seen me naked, both literally and figuratively.

I was vulnerable with him in a way that I usually reserve for...well. No one.

Simon rubs his eyes. He stands up, cracking his back as he stretches, then walks over to the listening device he set up inside the closet. He puts on the headphones, picks up a piece of black equipment, and moves it around the wall like he's looking for an unborn baby's heartbeat. I stare at his back, noticing how the freckles snake their way from his neck down his shoulder blades like a scatterplot.

Then I hear him gasp.

When he turns back to face me, there's panic in his eyes.

"She's gone," he croaks. "Poppy Hastings is gone, Tulip. We lost her."

My stomach lurches.

I begin feeling around on the floor for my phone, but I find only Simon's belt. When I finally locate it on the bathroom sink, where I put it when I took my shower, I have dozens of messages. I ignore the texts, missed calls, and voicemails, immediately heading for Twitter.

When I see what's trending, I hold my breath and will myself to pass out.

Representative Mark Ford dies of a heart attack at age 45.

"No, no, no, no! Fucking hell!"

I hear Simon yelling across the room, and I know he's seen it, too.

Then I hear a loud bang.

When I reenter the bedroom, I find Simon throwing open the drawers in a fit of rage, tossing his clothes back into his bag like they owe him money.

If I were a stranger, I'd find this to be a fucking comical sight: a white man, face splotched bright red, prancing around in front of a window fully nude, angry packing. But the way he's shaking his head and muttering under his breath lets me know that now is not the time to make a hilarious joke.

Then I notice his bleeding knuckles, the cracked wallpaper, and the dent in the wall.

"What the—"

I rush over, checking out the damage.

Shit.

A hotel like the Commodore is going to charge Simon a fortune for these repairs. Considering he was freaking out last night about the cost of the fucking minibar, there's no way he's thinking with even an iota of his brain. I stand back, in awe of his raging temper.

He's clearly losing his shit.

My hand hovers above his back, and he flinches.

I cringe. Historically, I'm not great at comforting people.

He rolls his shoulder, brushing me off.

Sighing, I shelve my own disappointment about Poppy's escape and focus all my attention onto calming down this grown-ass man.

"Look, dude. I know you're upset. I'm fucking pissed, too. Trust me. This isn't ideal. I mean, obviously Representative Ford didn't have a heart attack. Poppy must have slipped out of her room and spiked his drink or something. Or ordered a member of Dunamis to do it. But throwing a tantrum and trashing a hotel room like some punk kid isn't going to undo any of that. So let's channel our rage, okay? What we need to do is get back to New York and regroup. Figure out a new approach. It's going to be okay."

Simon turns to face me, an incredulous look on his face.

"*Going to be okay?*" he practically spits. "We just lost our one lead, Tulip. *Our only lead.* Ford was the last source on Poppy's hit list, and we missed our chance to catch her red-handed and find Dunamis. Who knows when or if she'll strike again? Not to mention that *a man fucking died.* Don't you get it? We have zilch. The FBI isn't backing me. The Shred fired you. And I spent a gazillion dollars I don't have on this swanky hotel room for nothing. So tell me, how exactly is everything going to be *okay*?"

My chest constricts, the severity of Simon's tone slapping me in the face.

He's hurt, I tell myself. *He's acting out of hurt.*

"I wouldn't say you booked this room for nothing." I'm trying but failing to disguise the pain in my voice. But it's coating my tongue, lining every word. "What about last night?"

"Last night? You mean when you seduced me into letting our suspect slip through the cracks?"

What the fuck? I think.

"What the fuck?" I say.

"I'm such an idiot. I bet that was your plan all along, wasn't it? Get me to trust you. To tell you everything. God, to introduce you to my *mother.* Then distract me with sex, let Poppy escape, and go write your story all by yourself. Right?"

"Seriously, I repeat: *What the fuck?*"

"God, I must be the stupidest man on the planet."

"Simon."

"I'm just a big joke to you, huh?"

"Will you please shut the fuck up for a second and let me think!"

By now I'm screaming, too—so loudly, so forcefully that my lungs threaten to give out. Janet is going to break down the door and tell us to lower our voices.

"First of all, *I* distracted *you*? Fuck you, Simon! I seem to recall *you* kissing *me* last night. *You* touching *me*. *You* fucking *me*, jackass. You cuffed me to the bed, remember? Begged me to give in to you? Don't kid yourself. You seduced me, Simon. Good luck sleeping soundly in your overpriced bed in your fucking government-sanctioned apartment, asshole. Because this is your fault. You're the reason Poppy got away with this."

"Stop."

"Representative Mark Ford's blood is on your hands."

"I asked you to stop, Tulip. Please."

Simon is pacing back and forth so quickly that I'm worried he's going to ram a body-size hole through the wall. I'm suddenly hyperaware of my size—barely five foot three, and I still haven't gotten around to buying that pepper spray. If Simon gets heated enough, he could pummel me with a single fingertip.

But what scares me most is that part of me wants to let him.

"And how do I know this wasn't *your* plan all along, huh?" My own temper is taking over, overwhelming my common sense. "I told you things, too, didn't I? For all I know, you exploited me, slept with me, and are now planning to blackmail me by bringing what you know to the Shred and getting me tangled up in some kind of lawsuit. Typical. I should have known better than to trust a glorified fucking cop."

"That's bullshit, and you know it."

"Do I? You know what I always say, Simon? Fuck me once, shame on you. Fuck me twice, shame on *me*."

Simon finally stops raging around the room and stands perfectly still. He looks contemplative, like he's trying to select his words as carefully as possible. His face is drained of color, and his shoulders sag. I can tell he's tired of fighting.

He's close to submitting.

Even in his state of exhaustion, I admire how handsome he is, flaws and all. But then I remember everything he's just accused me of, and I spiral into a pit of conflicted emotions that only my ex-therapist could dig me out of.

I never knew it was possible to despise and desire someone in equal measure.

Simon looks at the ground, unable to meet my eyes.

"I think this was a mistake."

"What was?" I ask, mortification roaring in my ears. "Working with me or screwing me?"

"Both."

Hot tears form in the corners of my eyes, but I blink them back.

I don't want him to see me break. Then he'll know he's won.

That he has a true hold over me, over my emotions.

I can't believe that for a single fucking moment, I allowed myself to hope. Screw that. Once you taste optimism, the cynical truth sits heavy and bitter on your tongue. I'd rather swallow this one alone, in private.

"Good. You took the words right out my mouth." I cross my arms. "I couldn't agree more."

We stare at each other, the tension filling the room like a gas leak.

I can't help myself. My self-destructive tendencies flare. And I strike one final blow.

"The only reason I touched you is because I pity you, Simon. What a sad man, full of broken dreams and wasted potential."

He swallows. I see the bob of his Adam's apple.

And I know I've actually landed my punch.

Then he hits back even harder.

"Better a man facing a sobering reality than a delusional addict who can't tell fact from fiction. You really have lost your mind."

My face pales, and his voice immediately softens.

"Shit, Rose. I'm sorry. I shouldn't have said that."

But it's too late.

I walk over to my barely opened duffel bag in the corner and quickly put on my change of clothes, then scoop up my laundry from the bathroom floor. I throw my hair into an I-don't-give-a-fuck ponytail, the beauty equivalent of giving someone the finger, turn on my heel, and head out of the room.

"Where do you think you're going?" Simon calls after me. "I drove us here, remember?"

"I'll take the train," I huff.

"Rose, I—"

I hear him begin to say something, but before I change my mind, I slam the door.

Here's the eighth rule of conspiracy, kids:

Trust *no one.*

FIRE DEPARTMENT — DISTRICT OF COLUMBIA

Public Records Unit / ACR Section

9 MetroTech Center, Washington, D.C. 11201-3857 • (718) 923-1995

Ambulance Call Report/Prehospital Care Report Request Form

SECTION A CUSTOMER INFORMATION

Name Mark Ford Telephone Number (1) 202-666-8072

Address 1326 N ST NW State D.C. Zip Code 20005

Note: Please make sure you complete this form and attach all required documents. Enclose a check or money order made payable to the **NYC Fire Department and a stamped self-addressed envelope (with postage).** Mail checks or money orders directly to the address and unit listed above. Only money orders or checks will be accepted for Requests (no exceptions). **DO NOT MAIL CASH.**

SECTION B PATIENT INFORMATION

Name of Patient: Representative Mark Ford

Date: 03 / 15 / 24 Time: 3 : 55 AM [X] PM [ ]

Location: 1326 N St NW Washington, DC 20005

Incident: Myocardial infarction (MI), traces of methylmercury found in blood

Hospital taken to: Medstar Georgetown University Hospital

Is the patient a minor? Yes [ ] No [X]

Date of Birth: 01 / 25 /1979

Last 4 digits of Social Security Number: 9844

If available, please provide ACR/PCR number: N/A

What is the requester's relationship to the patient? Spouse

CUSTOMER – PLEASE READ AND SUBMIT THE REQUIRED ITEM(S) BELOW

- An original notarized letter from the patient authorizing the release of this information.
- Proof of parental status or guardianship, if the patient is a minor. Acceptable proof is a copy of the patient's birth certificate or a court document showing custody / guardianship.
- Proof that a court has appointed you executor or administrator of the patient's estate, if the patient is deceased (Letters testamentary or letters of administration).
- Payment in the form of a check or money order in the amount of $1.50 for each report.

Chapter Twenty-One

In movies, whenever a heroine is spiraling out of control, she slinks around in lingerie and smudged mascara, drinking dirty martinis and blasting jazz. According to the old white men who run Hollywood, there's something inherently sexy about a woman unraveling; poor mental health is just about indulging in vices and flirting with hysteria. Plus, those women are almost always white. Why let them have all the fun?

I, on the other hand, go the complete fucking opposite route.

You know, burrowing in my depression room, not showering for days at a time, sustaining myself exclusively on microwave meals because I lack the energy to get out of bed and walk anywhere farther than the bathroom or kitchenette. Watching Netflix even feels like too much work. Instead I just lie on my back, staring up at the ceiling, occasionally scrolling on TikTok or refreshing Instagram, waiting for Poppy to update her Stories.

It's been two weeks since D.C. Fourteen days since we let her slip through our fingers.

Simon was right. With my last source gone, I'm totally

unable to predict Poppy's next move. I'm right back at square one, none the wiser. And Simon hasn't so much as sent me an angry text or left me a drunken voicemail since our fight at the Commodore. I flip-flop between resenting him for assuming the worst and empathizing with him, knowing that he's probably feeling as shitty and hopeless as I am right now. Part of me believes we should be wallowing together, passing a bottle of cheap vodka back and forth on his couch, imagining what could and should have been. The other part of me can't get over the accusations he made about the person I am on the inside so shortly after *being* inside of me. He made me feel so small, and for that, I don't know if I can forgive him.

And I certainly can't fucking forget.

I kill time by doing lines of Adderall and spending every last dollar I earned at the Shred ordering liquor from apps that will deliver bottles to my door. I replay conversations in my head and chastise myself for having them the wrong way, then beat myself up equally for the ones I never had at all.

Whenever I shut my eyes, I'm haunted by my past mistakes, small moments from my childhood that I've suppressed and compartmentalized. My mind now chooses to dangle them in front of me like an all-expenses-paid vacation from hell.

Like the time my English teacher, Mr. Collins, mispronounced my last name in front of the entire class, and when I corrected him, he accused me of being aggressive and talking back. I was sent to the principal's office, my predominantly white peers snickering behind my back. *They're still thinking about it*, my brain sneers. *Everyone is laughing at you.*

I wail into my pillow like a scream queen until it starts to feel so soft against my skin that I begin to fall asleep. I tell myself I'll just take a quick nap. Then I sleep until nightfall, wasting the entire day. But you can't waste time you never had in the first place. Now I'm merely existing, the hours bleeding together to create one meaningless pit of coasting.

God, I fucking hate myself.

My one hobby is calling my parents, then hanging up. Mostly to seek comfort in the familiar—to hear Maman's voice, her thick accent stroking her throat as she coughs "Hello?" into the phone. Other times, it's out of frustration. I fantasize about yelling at my parents, calling them out for my inherited trauma, chastising them for raising me as a citizen of an in-between state, relegating me to the role of an observer instead of a participant.

In my dreams, I confess to my exhaustion, to my desire to belong somewhere and believe in something other than myself. To let go of my self-deprecating humor and defensive rhetoric and vulgar mouth and just let myself be. To cry in front of others, to be present with the people I care about, to love and be loved in return.

But the second I hear ringing on the other side of the line, I freeze.

My parents and I have always maintained a great relationship by accepting that our connection is conditional. They tell me they're proud of me, and I tell them I'm okay. That's the genesis of my affinity for "pranks"—lying about my sanity is the one I've always done best. I keep them at arm's length, never letting them get to know the real me. And in turn, they embrace the fake me. It's a system that works and one I've always been hesitant to poke holes in.

Especially not when I'm messed up and depressed.

Having not left the house in a dangerous number of days (I'm sure the lack of fresh oxygen to my brain will have some sort of effect in years to come), the only human being I've been seeing regularly is Roommate. She's been spending slightly less time with Boyfriend and slightly more time bringing me leftover goulash she's trying to get rid of and barging into my bedroom to ask what I think of her outfits, most of which involve even fewer clothes than usual now that we're nearing summer. I even cried to her about everything that went down in D.C., although she seemed pretty fucking bored by my antics...until I brought up Simon's kinks. That perked her right up. If I didn't know better, I'd think she was trying to check up on me.

That she's worried about what I might do if I'm left alone.

I've stopped answering Fern and Steph's texts altogether, unable to expend the energy required to keep up the ruse that everything's normal. Without their constant prodding, the consistent structure of the workweek, or a lead in my investigation, I've virtually cut off all ties to the outside world.

The only person left in my life is Poppy Hastings. Poppy. My Poppy. The person I loathe more than anything on the planet, who wouldn't even recognize me on the street. I spend all my time with this concept of a woman, this enigma, thinking about her every move and obsessing over her thoughts and motives. Wondering what she's doing right this moment, how she faked Representative Ford's heart attack.

Waiting for her next move, if she has one at all.

I start to ask myself, could Simon be right?

Could I actually be losing my mind?

If Poppy really was punishing the men who turned on her

by speaking to me, maybe this final act of vengeance will be her last. Maybe she'll close the curtains on this chapter and focus instead on counting her money while the rest of Dunamis watches. But my gut is telling me that simply isn't true. Poppy has a taste for violence, one that has surely developed into a compulsive craving.

The ninth rule of conspiracy? Don't overthink it.

Where there's smoke, there's usually a little English orphan who has set her own house on fire.

On a Tuesday night in late May, I'm half a bottle of Scotch deep and recording videos of myself lip-syncing to a track of Poppy's voice when I hear a knock on my door.

"Go away!" I immediately quit the video app.

There isn't an answer, just more loud banging.

"Simon?"

Silence.

Then there's the sound of someone wrestling with the doorknob, turning it back and forth with what could be a screwdriver in an obvious attempt to pick the lock.

"Whoever you are, just know that I have a gun!" I scream at the intruder.

Somehow, the idea of being murdered in my bed isn't enough to motivate me to actually get up and fight. Instead, I resign myself to my fate, creating a fort with my sheets and hiding beneath the covers.

"Hi-yah!" shouts a high-pitched voice.

Someone kicks the door open and comes barging into the room. From beneath my blankets, I see the shadow of a small figure.

My assailant's voice sounds oddly familiar.

"Steph?"

I peer across enemy lines with one eye.

"Rose? Do you really have a fucking gun?"

Steph scrunches up her nose, then pinches it shut with her fingers.

My fortress must reek.

"Um, no," I say. "I just thought you were coming in here to kill me."

"We were worried you had killed *yourself*," says a lower voice from outside the room. I don't need to crane my neck to know who it belongs to. "Nice to see you're alive, by the way. Thanks for responding to all our texts. You're a really good friend, you know that?"

"I'm going through some stuff."

Steph is already walking around my room with a trash bag, collecting empty pill bottles and takeout boxes, preparing to fumigate the space.

"Did I miss something? Have you been running a speakeasy out of your apartment or something? Because it smells like a dive bar in here."

"Did I miss something? When did you become the Karate Kid?" I shoot back.

Steph crosses her arms over her chest and exchanges a look with Fern.

"Steph has been taking self-defense classes after work once a month," Fern says. "Something you might actually know if you spent more time listening to us and a little less time talking about yourself."

Ouch.

That one really hits me right where it hurts.

"I listen." I reach for a bottle that Steph immediately pulls out of my reach. "I listen to you, Steph, when you freak out about work for the billionth time. And I listen to you, Fern, when you rant about your relationship exploits for hours on end. If anything, you guys don't listen to me. Ever since Poppy was released—"

"Jesus Christ, Rose," Steph says. "Watch what you're saying. Fern is right. This is a problem that *way* predates Poppy. You don't listen to us. You might hear what we say, sure. But you don't actually register any of it. You're too self-involved, and frankly, you obviously still don't trust us completely. Instead, you keep yourself heavily medicated and lie to us about anything you're worried will scare us off. But that's not what friendship actually is, is it?"

Steph takes a deep breath, then comes and sits beside me, braving the odor to place a hand on my back.

"Look, we're worried about you," she says. "We know something is seriously wrong this time. Losing your job, running away—these aren't pranks, Rose. They're real problems. But we can't help you with them if you aren't honest with us about everything."

Fern walks over to us and sits down on the other side of my feeble body. She pats the top of my head once, a sign of deep affection coming from her.

"We're still here for you, dude," she says. "You've been a crazy bitch, sure. But you're *our* crazy bitch. And we're not going to let you waste away in this deathtrap, smelling like old Cheetos and throwing back uppers like an Upper East Side mom with a philandering husband."

I blink back tears as I slowly peel off my sheets and blankets.

Fern and Steph stare at me—the oil solidifying in my hair, the flakiness of my hibernation-shocked skin.

"You guys won't think of me the same way if I'm honest with you." My entire body is shaking. "You two are the closest I've ever felt to anyone, ever. I don't want to lose the only group I've ever really belonged to."

"We're not going anywhere." Steph's voice is quiet. "But how can we truly be close if we don't even get to know the real you?"

So I count to five, say a Hail Mary, and start at the very beginning.

"When Poppy Hastings was released from prison, I had another meltdown. I got fucked up and called Zain and hit on him, and it was the fucking worst, you guys. All that Rose 2.0 stuff I emailed you? It was a lie. Not even a prank—a lie. I just didn't want you guys to know I was bottoming out because I knew you'd try to stop me."

"Stop you from what?" Fern rubs her temples.

"From investigating Poppy."

Both Fern and Steph moan, and I raise a hand to stop them.

"I know, I know," I say. "Wait, please let me finish."

I tell them. I tell them the whole ugly, rat-infested story from beginning to end. I tell them about investigating Rutherford's death and being put on mental health leave, which led to the boardroom brawl that ended my journalism career. I tell them about meeting Simon in that alley, learning about Poppy's parents, our trip to the prison, and the subsequent revelation about Dunamis. I tell them about Poppy targeting the men who had turned on her by talking to me, about my trip to D.C. with Simon to shadow Representative Ford before it was too late.

Finally, I tell them about sleeping with Simon, about essentially blowing up the last remnants of my life.

I shut my eyes, banishing the memory. "By the time we were done, so was Poppy. Mark Ford was dead, Poppy was gone, and we were right back to square one. We got into this giant fight, and I said some things I shouldn't have said, and he called me a junkie, which I'm pretty sure I actually am. Now I've lost Simon, my lead, my job. I've got nothing but this insane hunch that she isn't done. She's going to hurt someone again. Only this time, I've got no way to predict her next move. I have no idea how I can prove she's even doing any of this. Maybe Cat and Simon are right and I really am just insane."

"Rose." Steph unexpectedly pulls me into her arms, using one hand to stroke my hair and the other to rub my back. "You're not insane. Obsessed, maybe. But insane? I don't think so."

"Dude, the woman you wrote an exposé about turned around and started murdering your sources, all while simultaneously becoming this gigantic celebrity, and you couldn't tell anyone why you suspected her?" Fern says. "It's out of pocket, sure. But I'm pretty confident that would send anyone off the deep end."

"I'm sorry I didn't tell you guys sooner." I'm weeping, relief pouring out of me. "At first I didn't want to betray my sources. But then I think I was just scared. If you believed me, it meant I really was responsible for the death of all these people. If you didn't believe me, I was just a whack job with a fixation on a problematic celebrity. I thought I was in this alone."

"You're never in it alone, idiot." Fern hugs me. "No matter

how unhinged you get, you're stuck with us. Just think of this as a really great prank."

We all laugh then. A much-needed belly laugh that leaves my abdomen in stitches and the room spinning.

I missed this, I realize. A part of me needed this more than I was ready to admit. Needed to depend on people, to be a true part of something.

Maybe I'm no longer an outsider, and that's okay.

Because I've got my group chat.

"Okay, I have a million questions," Steph says. "But my first is, what's our next move?"

I collapse back onto my bed. "*Our* next move?"

"I mean, after we give this room a deep clean or incinerate it altogether, put you through a car wash, chop off all your hair, find you a new therapist, and detox your body from all the liquor and speed."

"Don't forget pay rent," Roommate yells from the hall.

I realize then that she must have called my friends and told them to come. Someone had to let them in. I smile, grateful for the act of kindness.

"Oh yeah, and find you some kind of job," Steph says. "But after all of that, what's our next move?"

"I don't want you guys involved in this," I say, sincerely. "I mean, did you hear that bit about the global crime organization? These people are dangerous, Steph."

"Petty criminals? Please," Steph says, sticking out her chest. "You think I'm scared of Dunamis? Ridiculous. What do you think all that self-defense was for? I'm pretty kick-ass now."

I giggle, imagining all five feet of Steph taking on a large hit man.

These people don't know what's coming.

The three of us are like the Powerpuff Girls. But, you know, broke and busted.

"Well, I don't really have anything to go on without Simon," I admit, a sad tinge to my voice.

"You really like him," Fern observes. "Good. I was starting to think you were celibate."

I roll my eyes. "It doesn't matter. Simon and I are done. I don't want to talk about him, especially now that I've got my ladies back. We don't need him. We need to learn everything there is to know about this secret society. Who's in it, how it works. And its connection to Poppy."

"I can access the *New York Dweller* database, easy." Steph nods. "I'll do it when I'm back in the office.

"As for stalking her social media," Fern says, "I can't believe you didn't come straight to the source."

Goddammit.

I hate everyone but my friends.

"We can meet tomorrow after you guys finish work," I tell them, getting excited. "That should give me enough time to Marie Kondo the shit out of my life. And maybe look into NA."

"Here comes Rose 3.0," Fern says, cackling.

"To Rose 3.0," Steph says, taking one of the empty bottles out of her trash bag and raising it high.

"To Rose 3.0," I echo.

And this time, I think I might even mean it.

Chapter Twenty-Two

I tell Steph and Fern to meet me at the same diner Simon took me to the first night we met. Partially because I want to reclaim the space, to enter the restaurant without thinking of Simon limping his way to the back booth, of the way his gaze devoured my body and snagged on my eyes like a fishhook. But also because I sort of want to see Maggie again. I really do like her.

That much wasn't a lie.

Not to mention that spending weeks eating the bare minimum has made me ravenously hungry for pancakes. Lots and lots of pancakes.

When I walk into the diner, I feel changed. Born anew. Freshly shaven, doused in lotion, and wearing a pair of overalls that has been buried deep in my closet since the late 90s. But that's not all that's different about me—I haven't had any alcohol or abused any of my medications since Fern and Steph's intervention. And while my head hurts like a motherfucker, I also haven't thought this clearly in days. Weeks. Maybe even months. It's like every neuron is suddenly on high alert, like a tripped alarm system.

Immediately, I find myself overwhelmed by the smells and sounds of the diner. Eggs cracking against a frying pan and sizzling on the stove. Oranges being squeezed, the juice separated from the pulp. The joy of the iron skillet, the hand-whipped dough quickly rising, filling in the gaps between metal and the margins. All of the tension in my muscles releases at once.

I can hear everything—the servers in the back shouting orders between table runs, booths full of old friends trading snippets of ethically sourced gossip, fighting families shouting obscenities before passing the butter. It's an orchestral masterpiece that awakens every nerve ending in my body and grounds me in the present moment.

Wow. Do people know about sobriety? They should really teach this in schools.

The truth is, I was in isolation for far too fucking long. And not just after my trip to D.C. The narrative I've been feeding myself about the way I fit into the world—as a keen observer, witnessing everything but belonging to nothing—hasn't attuned me to my current reality. If anything, it has dissociated me from it. But Fern and Steph reminded me yesterday that I have a choice to make. I can *choose* to involve myself in the world, to be active instead of passive.

To be a character in my own story instead of just the scribe.

Instead of walking to the same booth I shared with Simon and risk hormonal flashbacks, I grab a barstool and take a seat at the counter. After a few minutes of people watching, Maggie comes around with a plastic-covered menu and a water glass. When I turn around to greet her, she yelps in surprise.

Then, without asking, she pulls me into a hug.

A big fucking bear hug.

It's very confusing. I mean, the last time I came by the diner, I was there for all of twenty minutes, and my visit culminated in a shouting match and the slamming of her front door. It's not like we have some special connection. Why the hell would she be excited for the sequel?

Still, I shock myself by embracing her back.

"I didn't think we'd see you again, Sweet Cheeks." Her mouth is stretched into a smile so wide it takes up her entire face. She fills my glass to the very brim. "Last I heard, our Simon had scared you off with his bad behavior. Don't think I didn't yell at him for talking to you like that, by the way. No manners, these men. He can be a little bit of a hothead, you know?"

"I've figured that out." I attempt to mask the bitterness in my voice but fail miserably. "But really, I owe you an apology for last time. And I need to try that coffee I didn't get around to enjoying."

She chuckles. "One pot, coming right up."

But instead of heading back into the kitchen, Maggie lingers for a moment.

"I know it's not my place, but give him a chance, would you?" Her eyes plead with me, widening like a sinkhole. "I know he can be a little hard to read, but you should hear the way he talks about you. Waxes poetic like a total sap. We all make him fun of him for it, but secretly I think it's sweet. He's been through a lot and has trouble showing people that he cares. But I think he really does. Care, that is. About you."

Wait a minute. Simon has been talking to the staff of his favorite diner about me?

Was this before or after our fight?

Before. Definitely before.

I shake my head. "I'm not so sure about that, Maggie."

She just glows back at me, a light so bright it outshines the fluorescents of the diner.

"Well, I'm not always right"—she winks—"but I've also never been wrong."

With that, she disappears into the kitchen. I sit slumped over on my stool, my slack jaw reaching the floor, overthinking her words. What did Simon say to her? Is he waiting to hear from me? Should I call him?

What would I even say without the influence of amphetamines?

I'm seconds away from taking out my phone and sending him a cryptic text when I feel someone throw their arms around me, embracing me from behind and placing their hands over my eyes.

"Who is it?" I stifle a giggle.

"Your mom," Fern deadpans.

"Stop, that's too far!" I exclaim. "I would literally rather be mugged."

"Oh my god, are you crazy? Don't manifest that!" Steph chirps, and we all laugh.

I turn around to greet my friends, and they grab seats on the barstools on either side of me. Steph takes out her phone and immediately looks up the menu while Fern starts researching the most popular food items via geotag.

The gang really is back together.

"How was work today?" I ask, perhaps a little too nonchalantly.

My friends exchange a quick glance before responding. I fucking hate that they're uncomfortable talking about the

Shred in front of me. They're probably worried it will trigger me to spiral again.

Or something.

"Seriously, guys. We need to be able to chat about this stuff. I can handle it. Just tell me!"

Fern lets out a whistle, then grabs my water glass and takes a big sip without asking.

"In that case, it was complete and utter shite," she says. "Cat is seriously up my ass over these deliverables for the Pop—well, the *she who will not be named* shoot. And of course the queen bitch herself has been impossible to coordinate with. Her publicist told me, and I quote, 'Poppy likes to go off book.' *Off fucking book*. And that was in response to a *B-roll* request. Imagine how rogue she's about to go in this interview."

I think of all the things Poppy might say and gulp.

Her reach is no longer just an annoying and creative method of taunting me. It's a full-on threat. She could actually mobilize her depraved fan base to do something reckless. Not to mention Dunamis.

Speaking of which.

"Steph, any luck looking into, um, you-know-what in *The New York Dweller*'s database?"

I peer around the room, eyeing the other patrons with newfound suspicion. If Zeus was actually telling the truth, anyone in here could technically be a Dunamis recruit.

Even Maggie.

Shudder.

Fern snorts, pulling a vape pen out of her pocket and taking a sneaky hit. "*You-know-what?* Jesus, you guys. We're, like, the worst spies of all time. Can we come up with better code words?"

"Fine," I agree, lacking the energy to put up a fight. "Steph, did you have any luck finding information about…*Jumanji*?"

Both of my friends stare at me.

"Jumanji? How is that any better?" Steph bites her lip to keep from laughing.

"I don't know, it kind of sounds similar?" I shrug. "I don't see you coming up with any brilliant ideas, Estefania!"

Fern starts to slow-clap, building up to a thunderous round of applause.

"Ah, feisty! There's the Rose we all know and love."

And I smile.

Because she's right.

"If you two are about finished…" Steph slips on her glasses, which act as her proverbial talking stick. "It took me three all-nighters and five of those bottled espresso drinks, and it required me to cross several company lines that could very well get me fired—and rightfully so—but I finally did it. I got into the system and sifted through hundreds of pages of *The NYD*'s backlog. Not just every article published over the last century, either. I'm talking about archival records. Emails, even deleted ones. Letters and transcripts and pages and pages of interviews. I think my eyes are still bleeding."

I feel a sob catch in my throat. "That's…that's amazing, Steph."

Steph's job at the Shred means *everything* to her. The fact that she would put so much on the line without even asking is a testament to how much she cares. How strong our little found family is.

And I'd do the same for either of them in a fucking heartbeat.

"Let's cut all the emotional crap and skip ahead to the good part," Fern says. I swallow said emotion and roll my eyes. "What did you find? Anonymous confessions? Stories without enough credentials to be published? Proof obtained illegally that had to be classified?"

Steph's eyes flash with something violent.

We all lean in.

"Something even crazier."

I hold my breath.

"Nothing."

"*Nothing?*" Fern says.

"Nothing?" I repeat, in shock. "But *The New York Dweller* has been around for almost two hundred years. We—sorry, they—have two thousand reporters spread out over a hundred and seventy countries. And you're telling me no one *ever* wrote or recorded a mention of D...Jumanji?"

Steph's tiny face turns red. She begins bouncing around on her stool.

"Well, there was one tiny, measly weird thing I wanted to flag," she says. "There was one mention of a *d-u-e*-namis. You know, Jumanji, but misspelled with an extra *e*? It was an anecdote in a story about JFK's assassination. Apparently, a young child kept crying out the word shortly after the incident but couldn't explain why. I looked up their name, and there's no record of what happened to them. It was almost like someone tried to scrub the whole incident but missed this one document because of the typo. But that gave me an idea: researching other misspellings that could have slipped under the radar. And I found several reports of a *d-o-o*-namis, and *d-u-n-o*-mis, and a spelling with an extra *s* on the end. All of the mentions were about witnesses of historical events muttering or mumbling the word. Watergate. The market crash. Even Britney Spears's conservatorship and the *La La Land* mix-up at the Oscars. But everyone who says it seems to evaporate into thin air like a ghost."

That comment knocks the air straight out of my blackened lungs.

"But that would mean…" My body is overheating like a laptop. "Are you actually saying…are you suggesting…"

"You think it's an inside job?" Fern gets straight to the point. "That Jumanji somehow infiltrated *The NYD*?"

Steph nods with conviction.

I slump down onto the counter, contemplating this revelation.

If *The NYD* is compromised, that means the organization tapped someone high up, someone with influence. Or multiple someones. But to do what?

Or maybe the better question is, what *couldn't* they do?

"Fuck. Am I just experiencing detox-induced clarity for the first time in months, or is this a little too far-fetched? Are we seriously supposed to believe that every catastrophic event over the last couple of centuries can be attributed to a secret society addicted to power? What are we, the stars of a shitty A24 movie with no plot? What's next? Politicians drinking the blood of children to stay young forever? Give me a break. Like, realistically, this can't be true, right?"

I'm vaguely aware that I've begun to hyperventilate, but it's a distant, detached sort of awareness, as if I've exited my corporeal form and am now hovering in the air, watching myself have a menty b.

"Okay, let's not spiral," Steph says, ever the voice of reason.

"Let's review the facts one more time. You're a reporter, remember? You've done your research. Prepared for this. There's something we're missing here. If we go over the story enough times, we'll crack it. Let's go back to the drawing board."

I allow the strength and stability of Steph's voice to pull me out of my existential dread.

"Okay." I exhale, attempting to get a grip on reality. "So, here's what we know. A few years ago, Poppy Hastings was a socialite living in New York City with suspected ties to the English aristocracy. I received an anonymous tip encouraging me to look into her, and I did. I interviewed five people, all anonymously, all on background. The first was Brad Zarbos, who all but admitted to having an extramarital affair with her. A month later, he was found suffocated in his bed. Three months after that, Poppy was arrested by the FBI for fraud and embezzlement. My story was published a week later. By the time she was sentenced, she was a viral sensation.

"She remained that way, locked up behind bars, until a few weeks ago, when she was released early for good behavior. Shortly after that, my second source, Ulysses Rutherford, went missing, but his body was never found. A week later, my third source, Khalid Warren, hanged himself in his hotel room, and then Ollie Pearce, my fourth source, died in a drunk driving accident. All influential men, all dead before their time. Meanwhile, Poppy's influence grew and grew. She landed the Netflix deal, hosted *SNL*, attended awards shows, all in plain sight. Until she was invited to an event at the White House the same night my last source, Representative Ford, died of a heart attack."

I pause to catch my breath.

"Yeah. That's about it."

I haven't included anything about Jumanji, because that's all conjecture. Reported. Alleged. And a good journalist never goes on the record without confirming her information first.

"So, did you guys pick up on anything?"

I look up to find Fern gripping the sides of her seat and Steph with her manicured hands clapped over her mouth. They're both fidgeting.

I burst out laughing. They look like they're going to explode.

"All right, then, kids. Who wants to go first?"

Steph opens her mouth, but Fern cuts her off before she gets the chance to speak.

"Did you ever find out who tipped you off?" she asks. "The first time, I mean? About Poppy?"

I frown, racking my brain. I never thought too much about who sent in the tip. Poppy hurt so many people, I always just assumed it was one of her victims. Her marks.

Could that have been an oversight?

"No," I admit. "And that wasn't the last time it happened, either. When I was tracking her, I received another anonymous tip. A text that time, from an untraceable number. Must have been a burner. It told me where I could find her. I don't know why I never looked into it. It's like I have a guardian angel."

"Right." Fern nods. "Or a devil."

A wave of nausea hits me. What does she mean by that?

"My turn!" Steph sings. She's already got a smug look spreading across her face, and her jutted-out chin tells me she thinks she's found something big. "I think I spotted a crack. And I can't believe you two losers missed it."

We both turn to her, waiting.

She puffs out her chest, enjoying the attention.

"Well? Are you going to tell us, or is this like that game, Plenty Questions?" Fern complains.

"It's called *Twenty* Questions, you buffoon!" Steph huffs, correcting Fern like I knew she would. "And fine, I'll tell you. But you're no fun. It's Zarbos."

She crosses her arms, swelling with pride.

I squint at her. "What about Zarbos?"

"He's the key," she says, waiting for me to get it. But I don't.

She sighs. "You said it yourself—he basically told you that he and Poppy were involved. I mean, his confession is the reason you suspected Poppy in the first place. And Simon confirmed that they were having an affair. But think about the murders in reverse order for a minute. Ford? Heart attack. Pierce? Vehicular manslaughter. Warren? Suicide. Hayes? Missing. But Zarbos? Brad fucking Zarbos?!" She's bobbing up and down like a Pez pen. "He was *suffocated*. Violently. In his own bed. Do you see now? One of these things is not like the others."

"Oh my god," Fern murmurs. "What if she didn't mean to kill him? What if it was a crime of passion? Maybe she was, like, actually in love with Zarbos."

I scrunch my forehead, confused.

And then it fucking clicks for me, too.

"You mean she lost control of her temper? She didn't plan it? His death was…an accident?"

Steph gives me two thumbs up, a gesture so juvenile it provokes a strangled giggle.

"If she had planned to kill him, wouldn't she have covered it up better?" she says.

I suck in my cheeks.

She has a point.

"My guess? Once she got out of prison, she ordered Jumanji to execute the others to send a message and cover it up. But Zarbos? Her first kill? I bet that was all her. Maybe she murdered her lover in a fit of passion. And do you know what that means?"

I'm almost afraid to ask.

Luckily, I don't have to.

Because a familiar deep, gravelly voice answers the question for me.

"That everyone has a weakness," says Simon, appearing from behind me. "A weakness can be exploited. And Poppy Hastings's is Brad Zarbos."

Chapter Twenty-Three

I blink at Simon three times, waiting for him to elaborate.

He just looks back at me, staring me down.

He looks good. Better than good.

Fucking fantastic.

He's trimmed his mop of messy dark hair into a clean cut, and he's wearing a black tie and matching slacks, his tailored white button-down hugging his arms in all the right places. There's a navy-blue nylon jacket draped over his shoulders that says FBI in yellow block letters. For the first time since we met, he looks like an actual agent.

His mouth curves upward, causing that tiny scar on his cheek to indent like a dimple.

My stomach does jazz hands.

"Rose, are you aware that there's a cop staring at you?"

Fern's words barely register as he looks me up and down. The tension between us is pulsing through the diner—his left eye twitches to avoid breaking my gaze, and my lips purse as I fight the desire to lick away my anxiety. It's a visual standoff, allowing me ample time to take in the changes in him, to drink him in like a cup of Maggie's coffee.

"Are you guys going to eye-fuck all day?" Fern butts in again. "Or is someone going to explain what the hell is going on?"

Simon composes himself quickly, taking a step back and turning to face the girls.

"I'm so sorry, how rude of me." He grins, stretching out his hand. "I'm Simon."

My brows rise to my hairline. Who is this chivalrous stranger? And what has he done with the real Simon?

Steph stares at his hand. "We know all about you." She glares, as if she could burn through to the bone with her retinas. "Rose came clean and told us everything."

"Shut up, Steph," I hiss under my breath.

Simon cocks his head. "Really?" I start breathing through my mouth instead of my nose in order to control my heartbeat. "I thought you were more of a go-it-alone kind of girl?"

"Yeah, well, that was the old me," I tell him. "You're talking to Rose 3.0."

At that, Simon's smirk finally falters.

He raises a brow, waiting for me to make a wisecrack.

But I resist.

"Nice to meet you, Rose 3.0," he says. And I can't help but grin.

But then I remember D.C., and the warm feeling flooding my face freezes.

"What are you doing here?"

The severity of my tone cuts Simon's expression like glass. His forehead wrinkles.

"I came to warn you."

"Warn me? How did you even find me?"

"FBI, remember?" He waggles his brows.

Steph lets out a strangled noise. I scowl in her direction.

"And what have you come to warn me about? The dangers of consuming too much caffeine?"

"Cute." He crosses his arms over his chest. "It's Poppy. I'm worried she's going to come after you."

All the blood rushes out of my face as I fight to remain calm, to regain the upper hand.

"What? How could you possibly know that?" I demand.

Simon grabs the stool on the other side of Fern. She squints at him, and I can see her trying to decide whether she admires his gall or detests his arrogance. I crack up as I watch these two opposite-yet-oddly-alike people in such proximity.

He takes out his laptop. It's a bulky piece of hardware with five extra layers of security baked in. I watch as he enters code after code, as well as a retinal scan, to access his files. But then he's in, and we're staring at an encrypted document written in some kind of language I can't understand.

"What am I looking at?" I ask, impatient and slightly annoyed that he's managed to make me feel dim-witted within five minutes of seeing me again.

"Answers," he says. "So, after our, uh, excursion to Washington a few weeks ago, I was feeling really down about losing our final lead. Plus, working alone after getting to bounce ideas off of you wasn't exactly paradise. I missed having a partner. I missed you, Tulip."

"Tulip?" Steph mouths.

I just shake my head.

Simon *missed* me. He may have turned on me, but he regretted it. Does that make it any better? I'm not sure. No, not really. But it's a comfort to know that all that time I was thinking about him, he was thinking about me, too. Our consciousnesses were mingling in some parallel dimension, trying desperately to get back to each other before our physical selves were ready to commit.

"So you decided to come here and scare me into working with you again?" I prod.

We sit there, eyes locked.

Something unspoken passes between us that feels miles deep and centuries old.

Then Maggie comes out of the kitchen, ready to take our order.

"What in the devil's name are you doing here?" she says to Simon, pinching his cheek. I giggle. "You're not stalking this poor girl, are you?"

"Not now, Mags!" he says. "I'm devising a master plan."

Maggie throws back her head like a kraken and releases a thunderous, full-body laugh.

"Well, well, well," she says, throwing me a wink. "Don't let me stop you, Mr. Bond."

As she walks past the bar and toward a group that's just arrived, I see Simon's neck turning red with embarrassment.

Unfortunately, my friends do, too.

"Oh my god, your neck!" Steph shrieks, not even trying to hide her amusement. "What is that?"

"He must have syphilis," Fern deadpans, nodding knowingly.

Simon raises his brows. He gawks at Fern, trying to figure out if she's kidding. After a brief moment of introspection, he starts to crack up. Relief washes over me as I watch the two of them laugh together, a bond forming before my eyes.

"I get why you all are friends," he says. "You're crazy, too."

All at once, I hate Simon. Loathe him. Resent him so much for making me want to forgive him by showing me what my life could be like with him in it. For getting along so well with my friends and laughing at my jokes and looking so damn good in a button-down. It feels unfair that someone could be so cruel with one breath, then break through my pretension and connect with the very innards of my being the next.

I want to spit in the same face I'm dying to reach over and kiss.

"So." I try to sound bored and take a sip of my coffee. "Me? Poppy? You were saying?"

"Right." He lets out a tight breath. "I went over it a million times, and it just didn't make sense. Why would Poppy go to the trouble of hiring Dunam—"

"Jumanji," we all say at the same time.

"Um, okay. Jumanji," Simon corrects himself. "Why would Poppy go to the trouble of assigning low-level Jumanji recruits to take out your sources as a warning when she could just cut the snake's head off, so to speak, by taking *you* out? Wouldn't that send a clearer message?"

I tremble, imagining that it would.

"Unless, of course, she knows what she's doing—playing a game, toying with you. Taking out insects in a web you spun yourself, knowing you're the only person making the connections. You've said it feels like she's taunting you. What if you're not paranoid? What if she's drawing this out, making it as painful as possible for you, until..."

Now my entire body is shaking.

If what Simon is saying is true, it means that Poppy Hastings isn't just a murderer.

She's an evil mastermind.

And what's worse? She's been one step ahead of us this entire time.

Of Simon.

Of me.

"Oh my fucking god. She's going to kill me," I say weakly. "She's having her fun with me first. But then she's going to get rid of me. I don't know how, and I don't know when. Maybe she'll make it look like an accident or an illness or a natural disaster. A house will drop on my head or someone will push me onto the subway tracks. But you're totally right. She's going to get me. It's only a matter of time."

"She'll have to get through us first," Fern says. Steph squeezes my shoulder.

At the very moment I need it most, I'm reminded that I'm not alone in this.

I'm not going to stand back and watch as my story comes to an end.

Instead, I'm going to flip the script and rewrite the narrative like a real reporter.

The tenth rule of conspiracy? There's strength in numbers.

"How am I the final girl right now?" I complain. "The final girl is *never* brown. Everybody knows that!"

Maybe a few weeks ago, being the target of the most famous secret serial killer in the world would have felt more feasible. Obvious, even. But now that everything is a little less cloudy, even I'm having trouble believing this latest twist.

"What a minute," Fern says, turning to Simon, fists clenched. "Why did you come all the way here? To bid her farewell? Give her a parting gift? Break her heart a second time?"

Blood rushes to my cheeks. I silently thank Fern for the reminder that Poppy isn't the only one who has hurt me recently.

"Of course not." The inflection in Simon's voice causes me to pause. "I thought once you knew what was happening, we could work together to find something on her. A dirty secret, a vice. An outstanding fucking parking ticket! Anything we can use to trap her. I mean, the one thing we've got going for us is that she doesn't know that we know that she knows. You know?"

Steph lets out a whistle. "Well, I'll be damned." She looks between Simon and me. "There are two of them."

There sure are.

"Look, Tulip," Simon continues, ignoring her comment, "if what your friend said is true and Poppy actually cared for Zarbos enough to regret his death, we can find a way to use it to our advantage."

I make the mistake of glancing at his midnight-blue eyes, and my stomach sinks.

"How?"

Simon opens his mouth, but Steph interrupts.

"Wait, secret agent dude," she says. Simon groans at his new nickname. "Hold that thought. You must have access to the police report, right?"

He nods.

I squint at her, confused.

"Can you pull up a list of everything found at the crime scene on that wack, archaic computer of yours?"

He rolls his eyes, then begins typing furiously. I peer over his shoulder, transfixed by the speed with which he decrypts the files, then selects the right one. He turns to Steph, triumphant.

"Good. Now read it aloud."

Simon obliges.

"One goose-feather comforter, king-size. Four pillows with silk pillowcases. One crystal glass containing two fingers of whiskey. A pair of Tod's loafers, size eleven. Two candles from Le Labo. An alarm clock. An Alexa. Cartier cuff links. Shaving cream from—"

"Whoa, whoa, whoa," Steph says. "Back up a second. Did you say an Alexa?"

He nods, and Steph's face lights up.

Once again, I'm lost.

"Does the FBI have that in evidence?" Another nod. "Can you get it for me?"

Simon clears his throat several times, deep in thought. "It won't be easy," he finally says. "But yes, I probably can."

They make eye contact, sharing a sudden understanding.

Fern begins to nod.

I stare off into space, hoping for clarity, but come up with absolutely fucking zilch.

"Am I the only one who's really confused right now?" I ask.

"Rose, I think I have a plan," Steph says, biting the inside of her cheek. "But you're not going to like it."

Chapter Twenty-Four

You know it's about to be summer in New York City when the air starts smelling like straight piss. It's thick and repugnant and perfectly complements the mountains of trash on every sidewalk and behind every building. Manhattan, especially, starts to feel like a Legoland of sweat and urine and tears as strangers smash their mouths together on street corners, perspiration crawling down their backs, their saliva mixing with melted mascara. It's a beautiful backdrop for anyone who's ever thrived on chaos. People like me.

And I don't even like this fucking city all that much.

"Are you sure you're okay?"

Simon pokes his head out of the diner and finds me frantically pacing on the sidewalk. I excused myself to get some air after being faced with the idea of being offed by Poppy Hastings and her weird-ass pseudocult. Then Fern and Steph peeled off to prepare for the challenging days ahead. Now it's just Simon, me, and the giant fucking elephant in the room that is our failed attempt at a nonrelationship. We have only a few days to lay a trap for Poppy, and there are so many moving parts that I feel like the ringmaster of a traveling circus or something. But we only have two choices: move forward, or intentionally let ourselves fall back.

And honestly? Steph's plan is so batshit crazy that it just might work.

Simon glances down at me nervously, tugging at the collar of his jacket.

"Are you going to come back inside?" he asks. "You know, you could very well be mugged at this time of night."

I purse my lips. "In all my years of living in the city, I've literally never seen a mugger," I scoff. "A gun on the subway? Sure, once or twice. A fistfight between two people waiting for the light to turn? Definitely. But a mugging?"

"It's rare, but it's not impossible."

"As rare as a celebrity who knows how to apologize."

Simon bursts out laughing, and my insides turn to khoresht at the rough, musical sound. Fuck. I hate that he still has this impact on me after stomping all over my stupid heart. When will that dumbass organ link up with my brain and develop some common sense?

"What's with the chivalry?" I resist the urge to run my eyes up his torso, keeping them locked on the ground. "I haven't heard from you in, what? Two or three weeks? For someone so concerned about my safety, it's not like you tried to reach out after...well, you know."

"Yeah. I know."

There's an awkward seven-beat silence. I'm about to take the L and sulk home when Simon opens his mouth.

"Look, come back inside. Let's have another cup of coffee and talk. You're vulnerable out here. What if Poppy has a member of Dunamis watching you as we speak? Remember what Zeus said? It could be anyone."

I make eye contact with a man taking a shit across the street and shudder. Make no fucking mistake, I can defend myself. Let's not forget that the first time I met Simon, I kicked him in the balls. But taking on my nemesis *and* an entire secret society?

Even I can admit that I may need a bit more muscle.

"Okay, fine," I say, strutting past him without a second look.

If I make eye contact with Simon, it might lead to an actual conversation.

Or worse.

Like, you know...*kissing*.

Vom.

He follows close behind me, speaking to my back. Careful, trepidatious. So unlike the Simon I know—knew—who took pleasure in teasing me and messing with me.

"I'm sorry for barging in on you guys like that," he says. "I know you probably had it handled. But I couldn't stand the thought of you walking into an ambush. Not when I could do something to stop it."

"Mm-hm."

But what I'm really thinking is: *What the fuck are you doing here, Simon? What do you want from me? Did you really have to go and screw everything up by blaming me for Poppy's actions? Did you have to call me insane? I mean, you were kind of right. But still! Rude! Are we back to working together now? Or are you just trying to protect me, you fucking idiot? And did you get new cologne or something? You smell amazing.*

Instead, I just slosh my tongue around in my mouth as if I'm chewing gum.

"Look."

Simon suddenly walks around and stops right in front of me, planting himself firmly between my body and the diner's double doors. I allow myself to look up at him briefly, blinking more times than is probably healthy for your average human woman.

I imagine I look possessed.

"You have every right to hate me, Rose," he says.

The sound of my name on his tongue makes my muscles tighten.

"It's Rose again, is it?" I say curtly. "And yes, I do."

"Good." He smiles at me. I barely avoid looking at the indentation in his cheek. "Then at least we agree on something. But truly, the way I spoke to you in D.C.? It was not okay. I shouldn't have lashed out. I overreacted."

"Overreacted?"

You know what? Fuck this.

I begin to walk again, this time in the opposite direction. Away from the diner, from all of it. I'm desperate to put some distance between myself and Simon and his deep voice and his earthy scent that makes my head dizzy and my palms sweaty. I can't think clearly around this asshole.

And that's what I need to remember—he's an asshole.

"You *overreacted*? Overreacting is crying when your favorite character on a shitty TV show dies. Overreacting is throwing your pasta at the wall every time your mother makes a comment about your 'healthy appetite.' What you did was not an overreaction. It was cruelty, plain and simple, and if you had bothered to apologize sooner, maybe I would have—"

Only I don't get to finish my sentence, because I'm so busy

screaming at Simon in the middle of an empty street on a weekday that I accidentally walk straight into an MTA utility pole.

A few seconds later, I'm flat on my back staring up at three Simons, three strands of dark hair hanging over six eyes. I hear what sounds like an ice cream truck playing its jingle in the background. My brain is throbbing, but I blink twice and my vision clears, steadying itself. I raise one hand to my forehead and discover a bump the size of a Bop It.

I cringe.

"We've got to stop meeting like this."

Only this time, our roles are reversed. Simon extends his hand toward me. I reluctantly grab it, and he pulls me to my feet. Suddenly, I'm inches away from his face, leaning my weight on his shoulder, clutching the toned muscle bulging beneath his sleeve.

Simon holds his breath for a second.

I lean slightly forward.

He tilts his head.

We stare at each other.

Then I pull away at the last moment.

Simon practically groans. "That's it. I'm taking you back to the diner. I need to look at your head and make sure you're not concussed."

"I'm fine. Don't overreact. It's overbearing."

"Don't be so nonchalant about your health!"

"Then take me to a hospital," I say. "Or did you forget that *agent* isn't synonymous with *doctor*?"

"I was trained as an emergency responder at Quantico," Simon says, rolling his eyes—but only a little.

"I didn't know you went to Quantico."

"There's a lot you still don't know about me."

Well, that's the understatement of the fucking millennium.

Without warning, Simon puts an arm around me. For a moment, I think he's about to push me into incoming traffic. Instead, he begins to walk toward Maggie's. My brain experiences a hostile cold rush as city lights flood my peripheral vision like a fairground. And although I feel the pain in my head dulling by the second, I lean my head back against his shoulder and briefly rest my eyes.

"Hey! Wake up!"

Simon is yelling.

My eyelids flutter open. I'm now perched on top of the closed toilet lid in what must be the diner's bathroom. Simon's rough hands are on my shoulders, and he's shaking me. Aggressively. His grip is so tight that I can feel my skin bruising.

"Ouch!" I yelp. "Watch your hands."

"That's all you have to say? Watch your eyes!"

"Don't you know that *assholes* aren't allowed in the ladies' room?" My attempt at a retort is weak at best. I'd hoped to add a bit of fire to my delivery, but I'm still a little out of it.

"Don't *you* know you're not supposed to fall asleep when you have a concussion?" he asks, his eyes wide with panic. "What if you had died in my arms? How would I explain that to your friends, huh? How would I live with myself?"

"Well, a) I'm clearly not concussed, as evidenced by the fact that I'm still, in fact, alive," I say, cracking a smile. "And b) you could have just said you smacked me across the head with a garden shovel and been done with it. Think about how mad Poppy would have been when she found out you beat her to the kill!"

At the sound of Poppy's name, Simon goes from furious to sullen. He pauses to gather himself.

"Seriously, Rose," he finally says. "I won't lose you. I refuse. This matters to me." He takes a deep breath and makes a sweeping gesture with his hands. "*You* matter to me."

I fake a sneeze, trying to make it less obvious that I'm blinking back tears. At least I can blame my emotions on a traumatic brain injury.

"Well, you have a funny way of showing it."

Simon winces.

"You're right. I was cruel that morning. I never should have called you names, and I should not have blamed you for what happened. This isn't an excuse, but my outburst was about me, not you. I just felt so defeated, insecure about the fact that I'd lost so much to Poppy and couldn't make it right. My job, my friends—my sanity, to some extent. Having her so close and letting her slip away...I felt like a failure. I let myself believe I was nothing, that I had nothing left. But I was wrong. I had you. I had you, and I fucking blew it. And I may never forgive myself for that."

I sit up straight so I can finally face him. He's taken off his jacket and unbuttoned his dress shirt, revealing a tiny glimpse of that swirling black tattoo on his shoulder. The pain in his eyes is visceral, like he's stared at a screen for too long and is starting to get vertigo.

I clear my throat.

"You think I'm mad because you freaked out? Everyone freaks out, Simon. Me probably most of all. I'm upset because I was *real* with you. Honest with you. Vulnerable in front of you about the fresh hell the past few years have been for me, and you didn't hesitate to use that against me. I met your parents, and you took me to your private place, and we showed each other parts of ourselves that I thought were reserved only for us. That night, I opened up to you in a way I never had with anyone, ever. It felt raw. And little by little, I felt myself starting to heal. You know why? Because I thought I could trust you. Which, by the way, is so cliché and stupid and *lame*. And that's your fucking fault! You turned me into a cliché, and I fucking hate you for that."

When I come up for air, Simon's dark blue eyes are welling. His jaw tightens, and then he opens his mouth to speak.

His voice breaks.

"I'm so, so sorry." He fights back tears as my own hesitantly make their way down my cheeks. "You're right, and I'm sorry, Rose. I shouldn't have hit you where I knew it would hurt. And I sure as hell shouldn't have let you leave that room. I should have fought with you instead of against you. Giving in just felt a hell of a lot like giving up."

"Well." I bite back some of my vitriol. "Maybe I didn't need to be so quick to accuse you right back. Or call you names. I guess we never fully trusted each other, huh? Mostly because you suck."

"Are you just going to insult me all over again now?"

"And you're desperately impatient. Not to mention annoying. A pain in my ass."

"I'm walking away in three, two…"

"I suppose what I'm getting is, I'm sorry, too."

Simon widens his eyes. A glimmer of hope returns to his face.

"You are?"

I shrug, trying to reconcile the words coming out my mouth with the flurry of thoughts in my brain. If I'm honest—which I'm trying to be—a part of me already knew that Simon was operating from a place of insecurity that day. That he was acting out of anger. I was just embarrassed by his sharp tongue, humiliated by his willingness to point a finger. But resenting Simon is so draining and takes up so much energy. Rose 3.0 wouldn't force herself to be angry with someone for the sole purpose of maintaining a silly grudge. She would admit how she actually fucking feels.

She would be brave.

"I just felt like an idiot. For believing, you know...that you felt it, too."

Simon takes my face in his hands, and I immediately shut my eyes to avoid looking into his. He plants soft kisses on my eyelids. They tickle. I involuntarily let out a small sound.

"Rose, I need you to listen to me."

"I am listening—"

"And not interrupt, please, for once in your life."

I shut my mouth.

"Everything you felt that night? I felt it, too. Right down to the thing about the inner monologue I never let anyone hear. Before I met you, I kept everything close to my chest. I had to after what Poppy's case did to me. Even my parents, my friends? They barely knew anything about my life. They couldn't name the song I listen to when I'm sad or my favorite feel-good bad movie. And it wasn't their fault; I didn't let them know me. And now I've met you, and you're crazy, but you're fascinating, and it feels like I no longer know when to shut up. So I run my mouth until it gets me into trouble."

There's a sudden and disturbing fluttering in my chest.

"I'm trouble," I murmur.

"I know."

"No, you don't. You don't want trouble like me."

"You're the trouble I need, Tulip. Not want. *Need.*"

The rough pads of his fingers brace my chin and angle my head up toward his. His breath ghosts across my mouth, and my gut clenches. I get frustrated waiting for him to make a move, so I lean in and brush my lips against his. Very slowly, he draws my lower lip between his teeth, then sucks lightly to soothe the sting. I reach for him, drawing him toward me. And he chuckles darkly against my lips, his voice vibrating down my body, before he swallows me whole. My tongue paints the roof of his mouth, and I groan against the heat.

It's too much and not enough all at once. My pulse accelerates.

"Maybe it's better if we just remain partners," I say as I move my lips gently down his neck, nibbling on the stubble beneath his chin. In a totally nonsexual way. "You know, platonic partners in crime. Professionals. Things are just simpler that way. We can still be friends."

I feel Simon still, his breathing heavy.

He takes my hand and lowers it down to his crotch. My mouth turns dry as he presses it against the hardness between his thighs, beneath his suit pants.

"Rose," he whispers, his breath hot against my ear.

"Yeah?"

"Does it feel like I want to be your friend?"

I exhale headily, then shut my eyes and let myself touch him with abandon. He grows harder beneath my fingers, and

I squeeze slightly. Simon's eyes narrow. He removes my hand, brushing a strand of curly black hair out of my eyes and tucking it behind my ear.

I look up and catch him staring at me, observing me with wonder.

Like he can't believe I'm real.

"I'm actually becoming a new person this time," I mutter. "I'm changing everything about myself. I'm going to be a different woman."

"Now, why would you go and do that?" He raises my hand to his lips, kissing the back before taking my pointer finger into his mouth. "You're perfect exactly the way you are."

I remove my hand and crush my lips against his. He meets my intensity, his tongue matching mine stroke for stroke. I'm about to hand myself over, to lose myself in him, when something occurs to me.

I pull back and stare at him, his lips red and bruised.

"Why aren't you touching me?" I demand.

He raises a brow. "Sorry, did I dream the last five minutes? Pretty sure that's exactly what I've been doing."

"Don't be a smartass," I tell him. "You've been letting me touch you. There's a difference. And as much as I like having your balls in my court, so to speak, it's not like you to let me take the lead."

"Fine," Simon says. "Maybe I don't want to take advantage of you when you're fragile. What if you regret it after a cold compress and a glass of water?"

I roll my eyes, but inside my chest, my traitorous bitch of a heart squeezes at his concern.

"Simon?"

"Tulip?"

"I'm not actually concussed."

"Okay."

"I was just being dramatic."

"Naturally."

"Seriously, I'm fine."

"Sure."

"Touch me."

"No can do."

"Oh, come on," I complain. "Don't make me beg."

"As much as I like the sound of that—and believe me, I do—the answer is still no. Not when I brought you here to nurse you back to health. I don't want to lose control."

My eyes light up in fiery defiance.

A challenge.

"Is that so?"

Simon nods, but his gaze doesn't leave mine. He watches intently as I grab the hem of my T-shirt and wrestle it over my head, leaving me bare-chested and perched atop the toilet seat. His eyes narrow as my nipples sharpen into twin peaks from the exposure. I caress my left breast before turning my attention to the right. A breathy moan escapes my lips as I apply just the right amount of pressure and imagine my own hands are Simon's.

"How about now?"

I look up at him with hooded eyes and watch him swallow. Hard.

Encouraged, I slowly move my hands down my torso toward my hips. Lower. I undo the buttons of my jeans, then slide my hand beneath my panties, inhaling sharply when I make contact. My fingers graze a sensitive spot, and my breath hitches. I begin to draw lazy, tortuous circles, then travel farther down to collect a bit of the moisture that's pooled at my entrance. Surprised, I curse quietly, then insert two fingers.

When I glance back at Simon, his expression has turned feral.

"You think we're playing another game, don't you? You think you're winning by refusing to touch me. But when I close my eyes"—I squeeze my lids shut and add a third finger—"and do this"—I withdraw, then slip them back inside, and my hips buck at my own touch—"I feel your hands on me. I pretend it's *you* fucking me with your fingers."

I hear a loud clang against the wall and realize Simon has thrown aside his belt. In one swift movement, his pants and briefs are on the ground by his ankles, and his length is at eye level.

"Touch yourself," I whisper.

This time, he listens without putting up a fight, wrapping a large hand around himself, taking his time stroking from base to tip, his eyes never once leaving mine. I whimper and quicken the pace of my own hand, mimicking his accelerated rough strokes.

"What else am I doing to you?" he growls. "Tulip?"

"Licking me." The tension in my core grows unbearable. "Eating me. Feasting on me." I shut my eyes and imagine Simon's tongue between my legs, at the apex of my thighs, at my entrance. My body begins to tremble uncontrollably. "Oh god, I'm going to come."

But before I give in to the release, Simon's control snaps. I hear an animalistic sound, then feel strong hands lift me off the toilet and set me on the edge of the sink.

"Always have to prove me wrong, don't you?" he murmurs, his face flushed. "You never take no for an answer. You need to push back even when I'm doing the right thing."

My jeans are ripped down my legs like a Band-Aid as the proof of Simon's arousal pokes me in the stomach. He spreads my legs farther, and I bear myself to him completely. I watch as he stares at my wetness, now dripping down my thighs, and I swear his eyes turn from blue to black.

"Simon," I plead.

God, this man.

I can't believe we wasted so much time hating each other.

But maybe I got it all wrong. I don't think I ever actually hated Simon at all, not really.

I only hated the parts of Simon that reminded me of myself.

"So, Rose Aslani," Simon hums into my ear, licking the shell and nibbling on my lobe. "Rumor has it that you might die this week. How do you want to spend your last hours on Earth?"

I laugh, then reach out and press against the brick wall of his abs.

I ponder the question. How *would* I want to spend my last moments on this godforsaken planet? As I took my very last breaths, what would I want to know I'd done right?

I look back up at him. I have my answer.

His smile lets me know that he does, too.

Simon leans down and presses a kiss to my forehead.

"Hold on to the sink."

CRIME SCENE REPORT		
1. Collecting Officer's Name: CATHY	2. File Number: #1710011550IHK	3. Date of Collection: 03/28/2023
4. Location of Offense: 325 N Maple Dr Unit 11021		
5. Nature of Offense (including name(s) of victim(s); attach additional pages or reports if necessary) The expired, BRADLEY ZARBOS, age 37, was found in bed, at his CA home. Cause of death: asphyxiation. Ruled: homicide.		

6. EVIDENCE COLLECTED

a. Evidence Tag Number	b. Description of Item	c. Location at Crime Scene
425	goose-feather comforter, Bergdorf Goodman	floor, left side of bed
426	silk pillow, Frette	foot of bed
427	silk pillow, Frette	left side of bed
428	silk pillow, Frette	right side of bed
429	silk pillow, Frette	head of bed
430	crystal tumbler, Baccarat	bedside table
431	suede loafers, size 11, Todd's	floor, right side of bed
432	santal 26 candle, Le Labo	bedside table
433	Palo Santo 14 candle, Le Labo	vanity
434	alarm clock, MoMA Design Store	bedside table
435	Amazon Alexa	vanity
436	luxury lubricant, Uberlube	inside bed
437	tissues, Kleenex	inside bed
438	dream journal, Smythson	vanity
439	ballpoint pen, Montblanc	vanity
440	taxidermy ostrich	righthand corner, by window
441	"It is our choices that show what we truly are." Dumbledore quote. Framed.	Hung above headboard
442	paper mâché mold of own hand	displayed in glass box, center
443	Infinite Jest, David Foster Wallace	unread, book shelf

Chapter Twenty-Five

Have you ever woken up convinced you were going to die?

It's a beautiful Sunday, the kind that rarely happens in the depraved fog of a late Brooklyn spring. It's sunny, about seventy-five degrees. Bright but not blinding. Warm but not humid. The light speckles the sidewalk in a distinct way that makes it look bejeweled, like a biblical crown dug out of the earth. There are kids selling lemonade on the corner and people gathered on their stoops all down the block. It feels like an infomercial, a semigentrified piece of propaganda to get people to move to the city without revealing how much they'll struggle once they arrive. The trees are lined up like ladies-in-waiting, swaying gently in the wind, indicating a breeze that's too good to be true.

I've woken up earlier than I usually do, so it's quiet.

Almost too fucking quiet.

But just quiet enough.

When I have too much time to think, my mind wanders to the Sundays of my youth. The busy Sundays, more sad than scary, when my mother would sit at the kitchen table, quizzing me on American history. *You have five minutes to name the capital of every U.S. state. Tell me the first and last name of every American president in reverse order.* She'd time me with a stopwatch, staring me down with hawkeyed intensity. It felt like a ritualistic practice—it was as if I was running track drills, running in order to survive.

When it was bright out, I rarely went outside. I was lazy as shit and scared of everything and everyone. When I did venture beyond my comfort zone, I did so in solitude. I'd go to the mall and observe the typical teenage girls in their natural habitats. Flocks of followers, all dressed the same, worshipping their leader. Gathering for meals, then taking a single bite from a morsel of food and forgoing their supper. Laughing at the fuckheads who broke their hearts, begging them to offer even a crumb of affection for the ladies to communally taste. Pulling off price tags and stuffing merchandise into their backpacks. Insulting one another with a smile, then wrapping their arms around each other's shoulders, just inches from their throats.

Is this what it's like to be young in America? I remember thinking.

Is this what my parents want me to become? Is this all I'm missing?

The nights would come on like that one song you can't escape, the one that plays in every store, spins on a loop at the radio station. My father would put on the television and yell at an endless field in a glutinous, stubby accent about a game he couldn't quite understand. He'd chastise me for my lack of enthusiasm, forcing my mother to feign smiles and cheers, as if we were captives in a stronghold, puppets in his prison of Americana.

I dreaded those nights and would count down the minutes. It wasn't that I thought my parents didn't love me. I knew they did. They just loved the idea of passing more. But they were blind to a reality I saw all too clearly. It slapped me across the face like a scorned lover, winked at me in the dark folds of night as I tossed and turned in my bed, unable to fall asleep. No matter how convinced my father was that we were starting to become one with our country, America kept chewing us up and projectile vomiting us out like a vegan who had accidentally ingested a small chunk of lamb.

We would never be one with them, and I knew that the sooner we accepted that, the sooner we could escape the constant disappointment of trying and failing to fit in. I just wish I had learned how to embrace what made me different without becoming so cynical, self-deprecating, and suspicious of others. In my dreams, I saw it as a choice, not a piece of trauma from my past that I had to heal from, to overcome. Something I'd done versus something done to me. But few have that luxury.

So many have the privilege of learning to forget.

I remember the first time I was mocked by my classmates. I was at a school event, maybe a bookfair? A welcome assembly for new students? The details have become fuzzy. I was in charge of greeting people, shaking their hands, like an usher. My public school loved putting me in high-profile positions like these. They adored showcasing their diversity, pitting me against my peers. My administration's pride and joy was selecting me for positions I was neither interested in nor qualified for, for the sole purpose of showing off the fact that I wasn't a fifth-generation attendee.

Naturally, my peers resented me for it. My parents told me not to pay that any heed. They were proud of me for becoming part of the community. My family lived to watch me excel, as long as it was on their terms.

Anyway, where was I?

Oh, yes, the slight.

Once all the students were lined up in rows like ducks, the headmaster—or principal, rather—instructed me to go sit with my friends. The only issue was, I had very few friends. Acquaintances aplenty, sure. There was no one who was outwardly rude to me or would offhandedly wish me dead if they, say, came face-to-face with a powerful sorceress looking to cast a curse. But no true friends. No one who smiled up at me from the pews and waved me over to their section or wanted me by their side when the bell rang.

My classmates turned their noses up and pretended I didn't exist. They talked about me while I sat behind them, which is, I believe, much worse than talking behind my back. Their behavior implied that they didn't care if I could hear them; I was someone who was deserving of pain. They were ambivalent about hurting my feelings. I was as discardable as an old notebook that had been filled up to the margins—replaceable and forgettable.

But I never fucking forgot.

These are the moments that pieced me together, that made me half a person.

Today, I prove that I am whole.

Today's the day we take down Poppy once and for all.

I wake up to texts from Steph and Fern letting me know that everything is in position. We run through the plan one last time, double-checking to make sure we're solid, that we've examined the risks from every possible angle.

Simon nuzzles my neck, filling my body with a pure warmth that transcends my physical senses. He rolls over on his back and extends his arm. I burrow into him, pressing my face to his chest and wrapping my legs around his knees. He puts one hand on the small of back, sleepily moving it in circles. I close my eyes and let myself be present in this moment.

It might be one of the very last in which I feel safe.

Simon starts to hum something under his breath. The tune sounds familiar, like a jingle you might hear in an infomercial as a child. It lies dormant in your brain until one day, you hear it again, and that latent memory activates like charcoal, longing to feel that same excitement of innocence again. I think back to sitting in my kitchen in Ohio, eating sugary cereal and watching cartoons. When I really focus, I can hear the sound of my father's car backing out of the driveway, of my mother turning on the shower before walking me to school. The house was quiet in the mornings, but the kind of silence that comforts you rather than unsettling you. There was a soft lull coming from the radiator that sounded like an intruder making their way through the back door. Above the living room couch was an American flag taped to the wall.

When I look back at Simon sleeping peacefully, even knowing what's to come, I feel both proud and envious. He's so confident that we'll make it out of this alive.

Me? I'm not so sure.

Are a healing journalist, a disgraced FBI agent, a brilliant software engineer, and the Shakespeare of social media a match for a sociopathic socialite and her band of thieves?

I think maybe we've got a shot.

But why do we have to do this *now*, when I've got Simon lying in the fetal position on my overripe mattress, singing in his sleep, smiling to himself?

I slip out of bed and creep toward the shared bathroom, careful not to make too much noise as I pull the bedroom door closed. There's a box from Lucali on the floor, filled with only crusts, and two wine glasses, stained burgundy at the very bottom, sitting atop our makeshift coffee table. A pair of Simon's boxers—worn and faded with tiny Disney characters stitched across the crotch—are wedged between the cushions of the secondhand couch.

It's a tableau from the night before, our last hoorah before our grand finale, when the curtain will be drawn with Poppy and me on either side of it.

When I step into the shower, I turn the knob all the way counterclockwise until it's scalding hot. The temperature shocks me, and I feel my scalp start to burn, my skin turning tender and red, like an uncooked chicken breast. I exfoliate my body from the whitehead on my nose to the pores on my back, sloughing off my past.

Today, I'm ready to be born anew. I may be playing fucking dirty, my morality tainted and muddled, but at least I'll be physically clean.

I throw on jeans and a tank top, then run a brush through the knots in my hair. Simon wrinkles his nose in his sleep, his nostrils flaring as he dreams. I watch him in a daze, wondering whether he ever does the same to me—wakes up with a full bladder in the dead of night, relieves himself, then sneaks back to bed while watching my chest rhythmically rise and fall. I want to kiss him goodbye, to leave an imprint on his forehead, but I'm too afraid to wake him. And if he wakes up, he'll realize that I'm doing this without him. That I'm making my move, following through on my promise. So instead, I just linger a little bit longer than usual before rushing out the door. I work extra hard to commit all the details of Simon to memory—the precision of his jawline, the tiny slope of his nose, even the spring of drool flowing from the corner of his lips. I want to download every feature onto the hard drive of my brain so I can replay them later once we're apart. But something tells me that no amount of recapping will cut it.

Nothing beats the real thing, live and in person.

Simon will be pissed when he wakes up and finds me gone. But it was always meant to end like this. Just Poppy and me in an old-fashioned showdown. We'll each get in our final blows, then the score will be settled once and for all.

Will our plan be enough to beat her? I know better than to underestimate Poppy Hastings. Say what you want about our socialite grifter, but the woman is a genius.

An evil genius, sure.

But a genius all the same.

Do you know the eleventh rule of conspiracy? The more you lose the plot, the closer you're getting to the truth.

When I reach the front door, I hear a noise behind me.

I turn around to find a startled Roommate exiting her room, Boyfriend sitting up in bed behind her. Her hair is piled on top of her head like a bird's nest, and she has glitter freckled across her face and a penis drawn on her cheek with what appears to be black eyeliner.

"Where you go so early?" she asks.

I zero in on her, startled by the cadence of her voice.

She sounds like she cares.

"Nowhere. A work thing."

I start to turn around, then stop short.

"You know, you're not a half-bad roommate. I don't know if I ever told you that. Thank you. For putting up with me."

She narrows her eyes. "What the fuck are you about to do?"

I smile to myself, then raise my finger to my lips and shush her before walking out the door.

There's a buzz on the street. Storefronts are just starting to open, the proprietors lifting the chain-link grills guarding the fortresses of their front doors. I can hear old men yelling to each other from corner to corner. Early risers stop at magazine stands to buy reading material and cigarettes, leafing through the glossy pages while sipping their shitty bodega coffee—black and bitter, just the way we like it. Just like us, like me. I see a woman pushing a grocery cart down Fulton, filled to the brim with colorful hats. She's humming loudly to herself, a tune I don't recognize. There's a beat to the way she's tapping her feet, vivacious and catchy, much like her smile. As she passes me, she gives me a little wave.

"Beautiful day to be alive, isn't it, child?"

Once she's in my periphery, I feel a weight settle heavily on my chest. It's as if I've swallowed a golf ball. As if, you know, I've ever played golf in my fucking life.

But I know what I need to do next.

I feel around for my phone in my canvas bag, pulling it out without looking, without breaking my stride. Then I dial the number by heart and listen to the ringing on the other end, my heart racing.

I'm about to hang up when I hear his voice.

"Aslani residence, who speaks, I may ask?"

My father's English is as broken as the day we moved.

"You don't need to ask that anymore, Baba," I remind him. "We have caller ID, remember?"

"Rosie?"

I hear him calling for my mother.

"Benny! Come quick! Rose is on the line."

She picks up the other phone in the kitchen. "Rose?" I picture her sitting at the table, crossing and uncrossing her legs with the indecision of a toddler. "How are you? Are you eating? You look thin in your photos."

"I'm eating." I roll my eyes. "Wait, what photos?"

"Your author photo," my father says. "The one on your blog."

Despite the fact that my parents still think the Shred is a blog, a smile spreads across my face.

"You guys have been reading my work?"

I'm surprised. We never talk about my writing. They usually just ask me how Zain is, where Zain is, whether I think Zain and I will ever get back together, get married, and have a million babies.

"Of course," my mother says. "We read every article. Your latest is taped up right now, on the fridge. 'Gwyneth Paltrow Could Sell Me Her Period Blood and I'd Rub It on My Pores.' Very creative title."

I let out a grateful snort, still in shock that my parents keep up with my writing career. But my laughter stops when I remember why I've called. It's time to finally start being honest with them for the first time in my entire life.

It's what Rose 3.0 would do.

"The truth is, I don't work for the Shred anymore." I take a deep breath. "I was fired a few weeks ago for pursuing a story my editor wanted me to drop."

There's a moment of silence on the other end of the line. I bite my tongue.

"Good," my father says. "I didn't raise you to be a quitter. We never liked that website anyway. Why don't you go work for the *New York Times*? I read their newspaper much more anyway. It's good. You should call them!"

"Yes, Rosie!" My mother's voice is chipper, high-pitched. "Why don't you email the *New York Times* and ask them for a job?"

I let out a sigh of relief. My parents aren't disappointed by the news that their only daughter is pushing thirty and unemployed.

"I'm a bit surprised, if I'm being honest," I admit. "I thought you guys were all about the American dream. Pulling yourself up by your bootstraps and working hard to make something out of nothing. Fitting in with your neighbors, being true Americans."

"Oh, honey," my father says. "We only did that because we thought it would be easier for you if you had a sense of belonging."

"You weren't ashamed of who we are or where we come from?"

"Of course not!" My mother sounds appalled. "We were only thinking of your happiness."

All this time, I've been blaming my parents for raising me with a foot in each world, resenting them for stripping me of my culture and forcing me to assimilate into a world that didn't want me. But I guess they were only trying to protect me from the hardship they endured.

Maybe the only person I needed protecting from was myself.

I look up and realize I've arrived at my destination.

Somehow, my first open conversation with my family has carried me all the way here. My pulse quickens in anticipation.

This is really happening.

My entire life is about to change.

"Guys, I have to go," I say. "But if anything were to happen to me, I want you to know how much I love you. Both of you. And how grateful I am for this life you sacrificed so much to give me. I know I don't say it enough. But thank you."

"Why are you talking like this?" my mother demands to know. "Did you total your car? Did you not get those articles I emailed you about the texting and the driving?"

"Oh, hush, Benny," my father laughs. "She lives in the big city, remember? She doesn't have a car."

"Right, right," she says. "Well, you can ignore my emails, then. We love you too, azizam."

"Very much," he adds.

With a deep breath, I hang up the phone.

The white paint on the walls is peeling, and there's graffiti dribbling down the stairwell. A faraway speaker blasts old-school hip-hop, and the sound of a metronome clicking echoes through the hall, reverberating off my bones and through my bloodstream. I wait at the top of the stairs for a second, willing myself to go in, worried that I'm unprepared.

Before I have a chance to make up my mind, the door flies open, inches from slamming into my face.

"What the fuck are you doing here?" Cat asks.

Chapter Twenty-Six

Cat's eyes narrow, her white-coverall-clad body shifting to create a barrier between the door and me. I watch as she drinks me in, from the lack of circles beneath my eyes to what I'm sure is a sated afterglow.

For the first time in years, I actually look healthy.

I wiggle my eyebrows. She stares back at me, her face furrowing with suspicion. I take a step forward, and she folds her arms, protecting her territory.

"You were fired, Rose. *Fired.*" She shakes her head furiously. "Are you really going to do this to me? To the company? Do I actually have to call security on you?"

I sigh.

A few months ago, there was nothing I wouldn't have done to try and gain Cat's respect, to get her to see me as a peer rather than an apprentice.

But now?

Quite frankly, I couldn't give less of a fuck.

As far as I'm concerned, Cat is simply the person standing in the doorway, keeping me from ending this once and for all.

"Cat, I'm not sure how to say this." I tighten my ponytail,

preparing for battle. "But if you don't move aside by the time I count down from five, I am going to have to physically remove you. Are you picking up what I'm putting down?"

Her jaw drops at my threat, hanging loose and slack.

"Five, four..."

She mutters under her breath and shifts an inch to the left.

Thank fuck.

Triumphant, I give her a wink.

Then I throw back my shoulders, take a deep breath, and open the door.

The first thing I notice is the music blaring loudly from the overhead speakers, the kick of the bass vibrating through the unpolished floorboards. Then I hear applause reverberating off the exposed brick walls, roaring like a fire from the front of the space. Light leaks through the floor-to-ceiling windows, bright and bold, matching the skylights and the disco ball polka-dotting the room with little white spots. Assistants wearing headpieces scurry around, mumbling into their microphones and taking mile-a-minute notes on their phones. I pass a giant craft services table full of decadent desserts: a tower of French macarons, strawberry shortcake with dollops of fresh cream, crepes covered in powdered sugar. The delicacies are accompanied by bottles of sparkling water and rosé champagne, but nothing in between.

There's a station set up by the far right wall for the glam team with a brightly lit vanity covered in products donated by Crème de la Mer, Dr. Barbara Sturm, and Il Mikiage. A stylist fusses with a cotton-candy-colored wig that appears to be made of human hair, curling it with an iron the cost of a small dowry. There are racks and racks of designer clothing—sequins and full tulle skirts and hand-stitched embroidery—lining the wall on the far right. Beneath the fabric sit red-bottomed high heels and studded strappy sandals from the finest shops in Europe.

Spider Order, celebrity stylist, gushes over the craftsmanship of a leather belt with a buckle that resembles a pair of overdrawn red lips smoking a cigarette. Camp, he calls it. (What is camp? I still don't know.) But the rest of the room is mesmerized by the main attraction, crowded by a creative director named Craig and Bryan McGillan, world-class photographer and winner of the 2013 Pulitzer. When they move back a bit, I can finally see a sliver of the pie, of the person everyone's fussing over.

The person we're all here for.

Poppy Hastings is much smaller up close than she is in pictures.

She's wearing a poofy white ball gown with a fitted bodice, the word JAILBAIT spray-painted across the bust, and her silky blond locks have been woven into a braided crown around her head. Her ears are dripping with diamond chandelier earrings, and her lips are lined in crimson. She's lying down in an antique claw-foot bathtub, which someone has filled with red petals.

Rose petals.

If you squint and blur your vision, it looks like she's bathing in a pool of blood.

Poppy stares seductively up into the camera lens, her ample cleavage the closest thing to her photographer. "Criminally divine," he says as Poppy lifts a single petal and places it between her teeth, licking the flower. All eyes are on her lips as she suckles, magnetically drawing all the room's energy into her vortex.

"You're a natural, gorgeous," Bryan coos. "Those tits must have been sculpted by god himself."

Poppy stops eye-fucking the camera to study him, biting her lip.

Bryan's arms are covered in tattoos, and his tapered pants are slim fit, snaking their way around his bulge. Based on her expression, he isn't her first choice, but he'll do nicely.

"Would you like to see them up close and personal?" she purrs. "Perhaps later tonight?"

Bryan turns bright red, his face contorting into an apologetic smile.

"I'm flattered, sweetheart, but I've got a boyfriend at home."

"So?" She flutters her eyelashes. "I don't mind sharing, darling. Bring him along as well."

I clear my throat.

Everyone turns to face me.

Poppy breaks eye contact with Bryan, visibly annoyed by the disturbance, and looks for the cause. When her eyes land on me, they widen, brightening with something that almost looks like...excitement? No, that can't be right. The room is dead silent. Not a single camera snap, text ding, or screen tap. I swear not one person breathes for a solid twenty seconds. My face almost turns blue from holding my breath. But then Poppy suddenly sits up straight and begins clapping her claws together with glee. Amusement.

I refuse to look away.

"Hello, Poppy," I hear myself say.

She lifts herself out of the tub with toned arms. She takes a step forward, leaving a trail of rose petals in her wake. Then she smiles at me, so wide she bares her canines.

"Hello, Rose."

My stomach flip-flops.

"You know who I am."

She smirks, and everybody else in the room suddenly evaporates.

It's as if we're the only two people who exist.

In this studio.

On this planet.

"Don't be ridiculous, dear. Of course I know who you are. You're the entire reason I'm here." She gestures around the space. "But you know, my darling, if you wanted to get me alone, it only would have taken a bottle of Veuve Clicquot and a strategically placed strap of lace." She throws her head back and laughs. "I'm much easier to please than you might think."

Her eyes are dancing.

It occurs to me that she's very much enjoying this.

But I'm not going to give her the satisfaction of playing her game.

I'm in control here. We're doing this my way.

"Don't bullshit a bullshitter." I take my time hitting each consonant, rolling my eyes. "I'm here for only one thing: your confession."

In the corner of my eye, I see Fern filming the entire encounter on her phone. She's been shooting B-roll for social since the start of the shoot, before I walked in, just like I knew she would be.

Just like we planned.

"My confession? Fine, I'll confess!" Poppy licks her lips in anticipation. "Confession: I'm mildly aroused right now. I might even need to take five for a wank. Anyone else?"

Someone in the back of the room giggles.

"Come on, Pop," I goad, using a nickname I know she despises. "Everyone here already knows how brilliant you are, how cleverly you committed your crimes. Why stop there, limit the spread of your genius? Especially when you've secured *such* epic bragging rights."

Poppy's mouth twitches, and I know she's tempted.

To take credit. To spill the beans.

But before she can say anything, Cat interrupts.

"Ms. Hastings, I cannot apologize enough for this. You see, Ms. Aslani is ill. She's a very troubled girl. In fact, her employment was recently terminated—"

"Let her finish," Poppy barks. She flicks her wrist, shooing Cat away.

Cat's jaw drops in disbelief.

"As I was saying," I continue, taking my moment back from Cat, "you *will* confess to the murders of Ulysses Rutherford, Khalid Warren, Ollie Pierce, and Representative Mark Ford. Right now. On camera."

Fern smiles and waves.

Cat screams but is silenced by a PA.

Poppy *tsk*s, shaking her head with a Cheshire Cat grin. "Oh, Rose. That's ridiculous. You're as crazy as those bitches in the clink. You have no proof."

"Perhaps not. But I do have proof that you killed Brad Zarbos. And if you don't do as I say, said proof will be released to the press within the hour."

Poppy's grin fades away, and her mask drops, but only for a second. "You're bluffing." She purses her lips. "Brad was a friend of mine. I was just *gutted* when he died. His security cameras never showed the culprit."

"That's true," I concede. "But tell me: *Did the police ever think to check the Alexa?*"

For a moment, Poppy looks confused.

Then her face suddenly drains of color.

"Funny thing about Alexas—in order to catch your commands, they're always listening. Always *recording*. And if you're lucky enough to have a tech genius as a best friend"—this time, it's Steph's turn to wave—"someone who can hack into the system? Well, then you might be able to hear past conversations. Sounds. *Screams*."

Poppy bites her lip and lets out a forced cackle. "You're lying."

"Am I?"

I exchange glances with Fern and Steph. The former zooms in on Poppy's pale face. We've totally got her.

"Feel free to call my bluff."

I wait for Poppy to bend to my will. She looks at my friends, then back at me, before clasping her hands together tightly, twiddling her thumbs. She's weighing her options. Never once does she drop her smile, that veneer of confidence.

Her ego will be her undoing.

"Oh, fine—to hell with it!"

She throws up her hands, then hikes up her skirt and settles back into the bathtub, kicking her heels up onto the rim.

"F-fine?" My voice is shaking. I didn't expect her to give in so easily. Is she actually going to just...confess? I've always hated villain monologues in fiction. They feel too convenient. Unrealistic.

Is *this* camp?

"You want to hear a story, dearest Rose?" She uses one finger to beckon me closer. "And none of that absolute garbage this sad excuse for a paper publishes. A real story. Juicy. Full of twists. Suspense."

Poppy whistles, high-pitched and shrill.

I look around the room at my old colleagues.

Is everyone hearing this?

"I knew you would, dear Rose. People like us, we've always got one ear out for a good fairy tale, don't we? Since you're a reporter and I know you have an appreciation for the facts, I'll do you a favor and start right at the very beginning: me. This story starts and ends with me, darling. I am the focal point, the protagonist, the prize. Although my parents didn't see it that way. Yes, the rumors are true—I was orphaned. Abandoned. Which at the time was truly dreadful and unfortunate. But I now understand that the trauma was a *pivotal* part of my origin story. Every hero must confront challenges, hardships, and overcome them. Triumph! This is true of me as well."

"Is that how you see yourself?" I raise a brow. "As a hero?"

Poppy clucks her tongue. "Not just a hero, darling. *The* hero. In everyone's story."

I clench my hands so tightly into fists that I feel my skin break, my nails draw blood.

This narcissistic sociopath actually fucking believes that?

That she's the universal main character?

"But the adversity didn't last long, I presume, seeing as you were adopted," I point out. "By Georgia and Tom Huxley. Criminals."

"Pfft, if you can call them that," Poppy huffs. "Truly an embarrassment. They couldn't even launder money correctly. Can you believe that? But their skills were enough to get them noticed, I suppose, as low-level as they were. Enough to get me tapped, too."

"Tapped?" I lower my voice. "Tapped by who?"

I suck in my cheeks.

"Why, by Dunamis, of course!"

My heart practically stops beating. I look over at Fern, panicked, to make sure she heard Poppy, too. That she's still recording. Her creased forehead matches my own. We share a look of disbelief.

Is Poppy actually going to reveal information about Dunamis on camera?

I hear the crowd starting to murmur, although they don't dare to look up and meet our eyes. Confusion spreads across the studio like wildfire, engulfing the faces of my peers and burning their guards to the ground until there's nothing left but ash and fear.

Just as Poppy intended.

"My adoptive parents were entry-level Dunamis recruits but could never rise above their station. Underachievers, that's what they were. They messed up every one of their tasks. Every flipping one! It was, quite frankly, humiliating to be associated with them. Especially since I felt in my gut from a young age that I had true potential. I could make a difference, become anyone I wanted. I was born a star. They were just...debris."

"So you surpassed your parents in rank?"

"Surpassed? I *decimated* those fools. Dunamis noted my beauty—my blond ringlets, golden skin, trim figure—when I entered my teens. They knew as well as I did that my body would become a weapon I could wield. So they invested in me. They gave me the resources and training to infiltrate high society. Taught me to fit in with the most posh circles, the upper-crust elite. But I did much more than blend in. I dominated. I quickly discovered that there is nothing on God's green earth that is easier or more rewarding than manipulating powerful men. The rich are so feeble, so malleable, with their empty lives and fat pockets. They see someone beautiful and young and simply yearn to possess her. But one sincere compliment, one true conversation, sends them reeling. They almost always lack affection, be it their mothers' love or their fathers' approval. And they understand that it's the one comfort they can't buy. So I give it to them, free of charge. And they become putty in my hands."

"Nothing is truly free of charge," I point out. "What did they give you in return?"

I think of poor Khalid and Ollie. Swindled. Preyed upon because of their insecurities and vices.

"Everything."

Poppy lets out a thunderous laugh, then takes a handful of rose petals and throws them into the air, closing her eyes as each velvet piece falls down upon her cheeks like stray tears.

"So you were sent to assassinate rich men? Why?" I still don't get it.

"Of course not." Poppy wrinkles her nose. "How gauche! No, Dunamis simply gave me marks and asked me to dig up their secrets and pass on information, which was simple enough. A man will say just about anything when he's crying on your shoulder. Or doing lines off of your natural breasts. Or dining on meringue cake at the Cipriani. Or when his cock is in your mouth." She points at a random assistant. Their face turns bright red, still facing the ground. "Remember that, dear."

She turns back to me, her eyes sparkling with mischief.

"But I became too comfortable. Accustomed to the

lifestyle. I found that I actually enjoyed doing GPG—that's a grand per gram, darling—or going out to eat and ordering one of everything on the menu. Flying private suited me well, and cheap fabrics truly began to give me a rash. I no longer desired a life that was simply adjacent to wealth and prosperity. I wanted that life for myself. So I left London to start over in New York. I was an anonymous chameleon, turning into whoever men needed me to be at any given time. I was like a golem, shaped in the image of their ultimate desires. They trusted me because I was a member of the one percent, just like them—a descendant of the aristocracy, of old money. That meant that they could take off their masks around me and show me the ugly truth. The women they'd killed in drunken rages. The money they'd stolen using insider tips from their hedge funds. The developing countries they'd sunk by extending their influences. The working class they'd exploited in order to get their products manufactured at low cost while they pocketed billions.

"I learned by working the circuit that all rich men are the same. They only want one thing, and that's power. Their egos are like inflatable pool toys, and their morals are like mood rings—they can change any time. Gallerists in New York City, producers in Hollywood, royalty in London, businessmen in Paris, sheikhs in Dubai—it didn't matter. I had them all under my thumb. I transformed myself into the perfect woman for every man I met. I absorbed all of their interests—cricket, gambling, fine art—and learned the jargon required to be taken seriously. I washed all my money and opened up new banks account in different names. I made sure to treat the clientele the first time I met them so they didn't think I was using them for their trust funds. Pay first, steal later, you know? You've got to spend money to make money. Dunamis was furious, of course. As were my parents. But they continued to give me assignments, rewarding me for each successful mission. It wasn't enough, though. I wanted more. I wanted it *all*."

Poppy turns sharply and looks me dead in the eye, her voice grating against my ears.

"So I stopped waiting for someone to give me the life I longed for. I reached out, and I took it."

Something clicks into place.

"That's when you began stealing from your marks. Dunamis never asked you to grift. You did that for yourself."

She snaps her fingers. "Now you're getting it!"

I consider everything I know about the secret organization. They don't seem like they'd take too kindly to someone disobeying orders.

"Weren't you worried they'd take you out?" I ask. "Punish you?"

Poppy rolls her eyes. "They just scolded me, if anything. I knew I was too valuable to kill. But my parents weren't so sure. The next time I returned home, they confronted me. Can you believe that? *They*, the failed petty criminals they were, had the nerve to chastise *me*! Those poor dirty commoners! My parents had the gall to suggest that my new extracurriculars were drawing unwanted attention from both Dunamis and the FBI. There had been whispers. They were concerned that the American police—what a joke—were building a case. They begged me to stop. But I didn't take them seriously. After all, I'd been rewarded with status. With respect. What did they have? Nothing. They were vermin."

Poppy spits on the floor, shaking her head.

"But then they threatened him"—her voice catches—"and I had no choice but to take action. I watched that house burn to the ground. I smiled as I lit the match. Dunamis was so impressed by my ruthlessness that they promoted me. My parents would have been so proud."

Holy shit.

Poppy actually did it.

She murdered her parents in cold blood.

I gape at the outright confession but collect myself in time to ask, "Him?"

For the first time since our conversation started, Poppy's face actually falls. She glances down at her hands, and for just a millisecond, I think I see her lower lip tremble. When she looks back up at me, my stomach sinks.

She looks crestfallen.

"Him," she whispers.

My gut tells me I already know the answer.

"Brad Zarbos?" I try. "You were in love with Brad Zarbos?"

Poppy snorts, her face cold. "Love is *so* proletariat. What I felt was much more poignant, poetic. Dignified, even. I was attracted to who he was, but also what he was. Brilliant. Powerful. But yes. As much as I was capable of loving someone, I loved Bradford."

"But..." My voice trails off as I subtly look at Fern's camera. "You still killed him."

"That"—her voice is razor-edged, cutting—"was an error in judgment. When I learned that Bradford had spoken to you, I felt blindsided. Utterly devastated. Betrayed. I confronted him, and when he admitted to it, something in me snapped. I did what I never, ever do, my dear—I broke my own rules and lost control. I mean, *murder*? It's all so grotesque. At the very least, I could have staged it to look like a suicide, you know? But I was a bit upset and sloppy, so I suffocated him to death just a teensy little bit. Gah! Is that my fault? Give a girl a break! I'd had a bad day. It was just an accident. One I intend to hold *you* accountable for, missy."

When I look down at my hands, I realize that they're shaking uncontrollably.

I hide them behind my back.

"So you're planning on killing me, then?"

Poppy gawks, incredulous. She chokes on a laugh, which turns into a cough. I stare back at her, confused by her reaction. Looking around the room, she clasps her arms behind her head and leans back, relaxed.

"Rose. My darling. You are a riot." Her lips curl into a smile. "If I wanted you dead, you'd already be dead. It's really that simple."

My stomach churns with uncertainty as my brain struggles to remind me that we have the upper hand. Poppy is surrounded by Shred employees and contractors. Fern has her entire confession on camera. Steph's hacked recording might not be enough to convict her for murder, but it's definitely going to raise suspicions enough to reopen the investigation.

For Poppy, there's no way out.

So why is she looking at me with pity?

"That doesn't make any sense," I whisper.

"Stop overthinking, darling. Not everything *has* to make sense," she says. "All you need for something to become real is for enough people to believe that it is. A theory can take on a life of its own and ultimately turn into the truth."

Poppy's voice rings through the air and stops me in my tracks.

"γνῶθι σεαυτόν."

I watch in horror as every single person in the room looks up.

All at the same time.

In complete synchronicity.

The personal assistants cowering by the entrance. The camera crew surrounding the set. The glam squad packing up their equipment. They all stop what they're doing and turn to face Poppy, wearing the same robotic, wicked grins.

Bryan McGillan takes out his camera's memory card and steps on it.

Spider Order pulls a gun out of his pocket and turns it on Steph.

Cat grabs Fern's phone out of her hands. She smashes it on the ground.

Then she looks up at me and smiles.

Poppy pulls a loose piece of hair out of her crown and wraps it around her finger.

"Now do you see, my sweet?" she croons. "I am the only truth that matters."

Chapter Twenty-Seven

"Tighter!" Poppy cries.

An intern—the same one who gawked at me by the water fountain mere weeks ago—complies, tightening the rope around Fern's wrists. She's seated on the floor next to Steph, who has already been bound and gagged and is vigorously fighting against her restraints. Another mouthful of bile makes its way up my throat, and I fight the urge to gag up the contents of my stomach.

I was a fool to think we could ever beat Poppy.

Beat *them*.

Every single person in this studio other than Fern, Steph, and me is a member of Dunamis. And they're laughing at us. They have us completely surrounded.

Stupid. That's what we are.

Fucking naive idiots with a death wish.

Poppy slips out of her dress. She's wearing nothing but a lacy white thong and pasties underneath, but she doesn't appear to care who sees her naked body. When she's done undressing, she saunters back over to the tub and sits on the edge. Then she gestures for me to join her.

I open my mouth to protest but then feel the cold barrel of a gun pressed against my temple.

"No need for the fucking theatrics," I mutter before begrudgingly trotting over to her side. She pulls me into her lap and wraps her arms around me, giving my abdomen a squeeze.

"Well, that was fun, wasn't it?" Another squeeze, this time harder. "It's so nice to spend time together like this, isn't it?"

I struggle to breathe. She loosens her grip, but only a smidge.

"I don't understand," I force out, gasping for air.

She sighs, then begins running the tips of her fingers up and down my arms. Her touch is feather light and leaves raised skin in its wake.

"It turned out my daft parents were right for the first time in their bloody lives. All my activity tipped off the Feds. They were looking a little too closely into my affairs, and Dunamis grew concerned. I'd left too many fingerprints all over the white-collar crimes to avoid being arrested altogether, so I made a decision to play the martyr. Everyone loves a martyr, don't they? Such an effortlessly chic role. Timeless! I was willing to take the fall for fraud, do time for a year or so to keep attention off Dunamis. Of course, the organization could have dealt with it—we have eyes all over the government, the prison system, the police force. But it would have been *such* a hassle to cover it all up, you know? So I decided to be a good little girl and pay for my mistakes, at least on paper. I knew that if I served myself up on a silver platter for their benefit, those at the top of the organization would be indebted to me once I got out. Then I'd be unstoppable—able to do what I wanted when I wanted. The most powerful people in the world would *owe* me one. And I intended to collect."

"With the lives of the people you couldn't trust?"

"Precisely!" She applauds around my waist. "But if I was inevitably headed to prison, I wanted to do my arrest right, on my own terms. I wanted to go down in history! To become a household name. You see, in order to carry out my work up to that point, I'd had to be infamous in important circles but nonexistent outside of society. I'd had to be a ghost, untraceable. The mystery intrigued the men I targeted. But no one outside of the crowds I ran in knew who I was. I had power. I had influence. But I'd never had fame. I wanted to experience notoriety. I wanted to be the one to tell my story. And that's where you came in."

"Me?" I'm unable to mask the surprise in my voice. "I didn't know your arrest was imminent. I had nothing to do with this fucked-up ego trip."

"Oh, please." She suppresses a giggle. "Don't play innocent. Who do you think tipped you off in the first place?"

My hand flies over my mouth.

The floor of the studio is suddenly on the ceiling, and a blinding light pours through my head and adds to the ringing sensation in my ears. I feel like I'm on a cruise ship being pummeled by waves, the sea rocking me nauseatingly back and forth.

No.

It's not fucking possible.

No way.

Then the past few years begin to play like a carousel in my mind, a montage of me staying up until two in the morning, face covered in a five-o'clock shadow of Dorito dust, scouring the details of Poppy's case. Ignoring Zain as he told me about his day or tried to bring up issues in our relationship. Saying *no thanks* to invitations to go out on the weekends with Fern so I could go over Poppy's testimony with a highlighter again. The breakdowns and panicked calls to my parents. The therapists who told me they couldn't help me after just one session. The Twitter trolls who flooded the comments of my articles with vitriol. My coworkers with sympathetic faces who quickly began to gossip about me whenever I left a room. I'd lost so much, given up so much, to pursue this story that I'd become its puppet.

It had just never occurred to me that Poppy Hastings was the one pulling my fucking strings all along.

"But why?" I blurt out. "I wrote you as a villain. I called you callous. Cruel. Deceptive."

"Pfft." She buzzes her lips. "The whole world ate it up, didn't they? I don't understand why anyone would ever want to be depicted as the good guy. Society puts too much of an emphasis of being perfect, and you know what? We feel stifled by it. That's why your readers choose to worship 'bad' people like me. Don't you see? I am nothing but a mirror reflecting the worst versions of themselves. And if I can get away with murder and still be beloved, there's hope for them yet."

I think about the person I became during this investigation. Selfish. Flaky.

Was my obsession with Poppy Hastings just me staring into the mirror? Did proving to the world that she was evil actually have more to do with proving to myself that I was good?

"Why pick me?" I ask. "I barely had a byline."

"True, you were a nobody. I considered going with a more seasoned, successful journalist. Someone with credentials and a major platform. But the truth is, I'm a huge fan. Really, Rose. Massive! I've read all your pieces about your upbringing—how you feel like an outsider, an infinite observer with one foot in one world and one foot in another. What can I say, my dear? Your writing resonated with me. I, too, feel like I belong everywhere and nowhere all at once. Like I am of myself and myself alone."

"I'm not like that anymore," I push back. "I've changed."

"Is that right?" Poppy turns to me and pouts. "Well, that's too bad. I liked you just as you were. We're not so different, you and I. We're both underdogs. We understand what it's like to be overlooked and misunderstood. We understand each other. That's why I trusted you to tell my story, to paint me the way I wanted to be depicted. Because, my darling, it's exactly what you would have wanted. It's how your story should have been told."

"How fucking dare you?" I shout, pulling away from her body as hard as I can, fighting against the restraints of her arms. "Acting like you know me? The truth of it is, you ruined my life. You took everything from me. You think I'm *like* you? I *despise* you. You are everything I stand against. You killed those men! Or had them killed by low-level Dunamis members. *My* sources. To punish them for turning on you for a story you wanted written! You're a monster."

Poppy spins her head and narrows her eyes but holds on tight.

"So you would have had me show weakness, then? Had me act differently? Please. Darling, let me clue you in to something." She swishes her tongue around, against the inside of her cheeks. "There's no such thing as an innocent billionaire.

Anyone who has that much money didn't get it legally. They're either exploiting their workers or sleeping with their partners' wives or scamming their investors. What I was doing was simple: stealing from criminals and keeping money out of their hands. I was a humanitarian."

"But the only person you ever helped was yourself."

"That's not true." She pulls my head toward her face and kisses me squarely on my forehead. Her lips leave a red lipstick mark against my skin, branding me. It stings. "I gave you a career. I helped you. And face it, Rose—I didn't give myself life. The public did. *You* did. I wasn't born Poppy Hastings; I was created. You made me into a myth."

"I'm not like you," I repeat, mostly to myself. "Maybe I created you. But I can destroy you, too."

"My dear, poppies might be deadly. But roses have thorns. Don't get it twisted—we're both beautiful, yes, but we're dangerous all the same."

Without warning, she releases me and throws me to the ground. I look over at my friends, who are struggling against their captors, their faces wet and eyes red.

I grit my teeth and fight back tears of my own.

It wasn't supposed to end this way.

It can't.

"I'll tell the authorities," I growl. "You might as well kill me, because if you leave me here alive, I'll tell everyone who will listen who you are. What you did. If you're lucky, you'll get away from the FBI. But you'll never escape Dunamis, right?"

Poppy slips off the edge of the tub and struts toward me, her porcelain skin glistening beneath the spotlight above us. She uses the back of her hand to wipe her face so that her makeup spreads from cheek to cheek, staining her skin and teeth. The lower half of her face is red and violent, an image from a nightmare.

But it's the way her eyes slice through my skull that will haunt me for eternity.

"Best of luck with that, my dear. I've been hiding in plain sight. Who do you think the public will believe? The most famous person in the world? Or a clinically insane, unemployed stalker and her friends?"

Cat grunts from the sidelines. And I know without a shadow of a doubt that every time she stalled my story, misdirected me, or led me to believe I was crazy, she was acting in the best interests of Dunamis. I should have seen this coming. But I was so far gone that I stopped trusting my gut, started questioning my sanity, and struggled to see what was right in front me.

"Well, this has truly been a blast." Poppy nods at Spider Order, and he hurries over with a trench coat, slipping it onto her shoulders and tying it tight at the waist. The makeup artist I spotted earlier brings over a wet wipe and begins meticulously dabbing at her face. The rest of the room begins packing up equipment, cleaning the room, wiping down surfaces until there's barely any sign that anyone was ever here. All that remains is the claw-foot tub full of rose petals and my friends, bound and gagged against the wall.

"I think we got the shot, don't you?" Poppy says. "Bryan is *such* a talent. I can't wait to see the story! Anyhoo, we really should be going. But please be in touch, my darling. And if you ever decide you want to live up to your truest potential, do let me know. The organization would have so much fun with you."

My head throbs. Partially from the withdrawal, but also

from the pure chaos of being part of a QAnon thread come to life. This is the threat, I realize. Making the wrong people famous. Giving terrible people power. Allowing them to grow omnipotent. Society will feed the machine until it turns them into monsters.

If only it wasn't too late to do it all differently.

She turns to leave, and for the very last time, I memorize the black magic that is Poppy Hastings. The power in her gait. The sway of her hips as she walks toward the door. The way she releases her hair from its braided crown and lets it fall down her spine until it reaches the small of her back. All purpose.

All power.

What will my life look like without Poppy in it? I've spent nearly every waking moment since I learned of her existence thinking about her, looking for her, trying to get inside her head. I think back to the night in D.C. when I could feel her presence radiating through the thin wall that divided us, simultaneously drawing me in and pushing me away. I remember Pennsylvania, saying her name in front of Dimitri for the first time and watching him quake with terror, in awe of her authority. I recall following in her footsteps all over New York City, from the Upper East Side to Coney Island, until my feet were numb and my confidence crushed. That was the fateful day that led me to Simon after I rolled around in a garbage bin at the Rockland—

Wait a second.

"There's just one thing I don't understand."

Poppy pauses but doesn't turn around.

The rest of her posse looks around, murmuring quietly to one another, confused by the interruption.

She's listening.

"I get why you sent me the anonymous tip. You wanted to be famous. And you got your wish." She turns to look over her shoulder. We lock eyes. "But why clue me in the second time? When you were checking into that hotel?"

Poppy's forehead creases into thin lines. Her smile falters slightly.

"I didn't contact you a second time," she scoffs.

A voice echoes from the stairwell behind Poppy.

"I did."

And then the windows shatter.

Chapter Twenty-Eight

I cradle my head in my hands as glass hails down from the sky. My ears ring from the thunder of the explosion and the shouts of the Dunamis members scampering about the room, ducking for cover. Once the debris settles, I glance up and spy men wearing black bulletproof vests, helmets, and goggles pouring through the front door and scaling the side of the building. They're holding rifles the size of both of my arms put together and shouting to one another in some kind of code I can't understand.

A red laser beam sweeps across the wall until it locates its target: the center of Poppy's forehead. She raises her hands over her head, licks the leftover makeup smeared over her lips, and offers up a bloody smile.

I follow her gaze to the door, waiting to see who will emerge and take credit for making Poppy's head into a bull's-eye, for texting the anonymous tip that led me to the Rockland Hotel.

Footsteps sound on the staircase.

Heavy breathing, followed by familiar muttering in a foreign accent.

Another SWAT team member struts inside, their body smaller and more nimble than that of their colleagues.

A woman.

"Don't move a fucking inch," the agent shouts at Poppy before turning her attention to me. "Hello, Rose. A work thing, huh?"

Shocked, I stagger backward, my mouth forming an O.

I can't fucking believe it.

"...Roommate?"

She cackles, her thick Eastern European accent caught deep in her throat.

"Actually, it's Annie. Short for Antanova. Agent Antanova, CIA. But you can keep calling me Roommate, since you obviously never bothered to learn the fake name I gave you, you conceited little shit."

My face burns at her accusation.

Mostly because she's right.

Another agent runs in behind her, catching their breath, winded from the stairs. Roommate glares at him.

"Did I miss it?" he wheezes.

Roommate rolls her eyes, and my jaw once again goes slack.

"Boyfriend?!"

"Oh, hi, Rose!" he says, his voice cheerful. I gawk. This might be the first time I've ever seen him fully dressed. He turns to Roommate, his hands on his hips. "Did you already tell her I'm Interpol?"

"You're *what*?"

"Oh, come on, Rose." Roommate—sorry, *Annie*—taps her army-grade boots impatiently. "Catch up. Think about it. Wasn't the timing of when I moved in suspicious? The fact that I was always home, always listening to you and your yappy little friends drone on and on about Poppy this, Poppy that?"

"I thought you barely spoke English!" I practically cry.

"Ridiculous girl!" she snaps, but her lips are fighting to keep from curling at the corners. "The CIA and Interpol have been working together for *years* to track down information on Poppy Hastings. Do you know how many crimes she's committed? Can you even begin to imagine the international waters she's crossed to escape the authorities? We've been investigating Poppy's connection to Dunamis, building our case, for *years*. But I moved in to keep an eye on you after Poppy's arrest once we caught wind of her rather unorthodox attachment to you. It became clear that you were the right one to corner her, to get her to confess. It was only a matter of a time."

She looks between us, taking in the red lip print on my forehead that matches the smudged paint all over Poppy's face.

"And it looks like I was right."

I look between Roommate and Boyfriend, both towering over me in their black protective gear, trying to process how this is possible. How I missed something this big. Roommate, who once gave me an edible before work and forgot to tell me. Boyfriend, who has repeatedly asked me to pose nude for his life drawing class.

Roommate and Boyfriend.

Undercover agents.

"But...you two are freaks!"

Boyfriend chuckles. "I'm flattered, Rose. I can't speak for Annie, but I'll miss you, too."

"Hello!"

Poppy's shrill voice pulls me out of my stupor, and I look around the room once again. All of the crew members, the turncoats, are lying on the floor facedown, their hands behind their backs as armed agents work to handcuff them. A circle of gunmen surround Cat, who is scowling miserably while attempting to mask the shaking of her left leg, the fear in her eyes. Against the wall, another agent is making quick work of untying Steph and Fern's restraints. The latter howls the second she's free, giving Poppy a look that says *I'm going to fucking end you.*

But I have a feeling someone is about to beat her to the punch.

Poppy interrupts once again, batting her eyelashes at Roommate.

"If we're all done catching up like old friends, can you please do me the honor of pointing that *thing* away from my face and explaining this misunderstanding, my dear?" She looks at the gun with disgust. "Truly, there's no need for weapons. They're so tacky, don't you agree?"

"Not as tacky as a prison jumpsuit," Roommate snorts.

Boyfriend high-fives her and makes a zinging sound.

I smile.

So it wasn't all a lie. They're still the same people.

"As much as I'm looking forward to interrogating you, I won't be the one to put you in handcuffs," Roommate says, shrugging.

"How kinky, my dear," Poppy slurs. "And who, dare I ask, will be afforded this pleasure?"

Then Simon walks through the door, and my heart falls to my feet.

His chiseled jaw is clean-shaven and his dark hair combed

straight back, and I take a sharp breath. He's wearing a finely tailored suit, which hugs all the delicately carved curves and ridges of his body, and when he stops in front of me and reaches out his hand, I take it. He pulls me to my feet, then wipes away the lipstick mark on my forehead, leaving no trace of Poppy behind. Then he winks at me and pulls something out of his pocket. I stifle a laugh.

It's his FBI badge.

"I *knew* you were a cop," I tease.

He kisses the top of my head. "Secret agent."

Poppy looks up at him, her breathing suddenly growing uneven. There's a glimmer of confusion in her eyes, followed by disbelief. Then she nods as if accepting her fate.

"You," she whispers. But her intonation lifts at the end, making it sound like a question.

He takes a step forward. "Me."

Poppy shakes her head slightly. I catch her eye and give her a triumphant look.

Game over, bitch.

She actually smiles back.

"Brilliant," she mouths.

My smile drops.

"Poppy Hastings," Simon says. "You have no idea how long I've waited to say this. You're under arrest for the murders of Brad Zarbos, Ulysses Rutherford, Khalid Warren, Ollie Pierce, and Mark Ford."

Fern (3:20 p.m.): Where the fuck is everyone??? Can we please reconvene outside? Idk if it's the severe trauma I've endured today or if I'm just starting my period but I'm seconds away from asking the hot FBI agent with the killer fade to read me my Miranda rights…help

Maman: (3:41 p.m.): Eshgeh delam you are on TV right now I did not know you were doing acting in New York but you are very good on this show I am so proud!

Maman (3:42 p.m.): Your father says it is not an episode of CSI? Call me?

Steph (3:55 p.m.): Does u guys think that wrapped up a little too neatly? Like, Poppy confesses and we all live happily ever after?! Like, am I the only one waiting for the other shoe to drop or have I listened to too many true crime podcasts lol

Baba (4:01 p.m.): Please call your mother. She is very confused. We are worried.

Maman (4:02 p.m.): Are you answering your father and not me? Call me.

Fern (4:07 p.m.): Update I came on too strong to the sexy agent lady and she fled the scene. Does anyone want to get a drink? Or maybe some nachos?

Steph (4:08 p.m.): How can you think about food at a

time like this? Rose can you answer or are you still talking to the police

Fern (4:08 p.m.): Estefania, she obv can't answer that q if she's being interrogated lmao

DO NOT CALL THIS NUMBER EVER (4:15 p.m.): Hey Rose. I know it's been a long time. Just wanted to say that I saw on CNN that you finally nailed Poppy. I'm glad. I hope you can finally feel peace now. Wishing you the best. –Z

Therapist Julee (4:20 p.m.): Hi, Ms. Aslani. Perhaps I was a bit hasty in suggesting we terminate our sessions. Feel free to call me to schedule something next week.

Chapter Twenty-Nine

"I don't care if she stole the crown jewels from the king of fucking England. That bitch broke my iPhone camera, and she owes me five hundred dollars," Fern complains, leaning her head on Steph's shoulder.

The three of us are huddled on a Brooklyn brownstone stoop, covered in an itchy blanket that a paramedic lent us out of the kindness of their heart. Our arms are around each other, and there's a bruise beneath Fern's eye and a cut on Steph's lip. I'm still shaking slightly from Poppy's arrest.

But we're here.

Alive.

Together.

"What about when she gave me the kiss of death?" I chime in, pointing to my forehead, where the imprint of Poppy's lips once sat. "When she had me in that tub, I swear to god I was *this* close to shitting my pants."

I shudder, thinking about the wet, warm sensation of Poppy's mouth against my skin. Fern squeezes my shoulder, and Steph reaches out and holds my hand. We're all interconnected like one living, breathing organism. Giving and taking.

"Well, I for one was never scared," Steph says, puffing up her chest. "Not even for a second."

"Bullshit," Fern snorts. "I totally thought we were goners."

"Fern!" Steph and I chide in unison.

"I'm sorry, but it's true. I seriously thought we were going to die there in that studio. The second Cat went psycho, I thought to myself, *Fern, prepare to die*. And then do you know what my brain showed me? You two fuckers. And I realized I'd never be able to tell you guys how much I love you. Or, you know, prank you again."

We both stare at Fern, gobsmacked by the display of emotion.

"Fern, you absolute sap!" Steph cries, pulling her into an uncomfortably tight embrace. Fern mutters something about boundaries under her breath. "Work on Monday is going to be *so* weird now that I know you're a total softie at heart."

"Not to mention that we work with at least a dozen people in a global secret society," Fern adds.

"Shit. I guess we'll have to put in our notice, huh?"

I frown at that comment. "What do you mean? You think all those people will still be employed and not rotting in cells come next week?"

Someone behind us clears his throat.

"Well, considering that they're all denying any involvement, swearing they've never heard of Dunamis, and are claiming they were coerced by Poppy, I'd say it's likely."

We all turn around to face Simon.

His suit is slightly wrinkled, and his combed-back hair is rumpled, most likely by the hand he loves to run through it when he's thinking. When his eyes meet mine, he gives me a cocky grin, one that exposes that indentation in his left cheek. My heart beats just a little bit faster.

"Since Dunamis destroyed your phones, and the rest of the group got rid of any evidence tying today's event to the organization, it's basically your word against theirs. All we heard through that door was Poppy's confession, which, paired with that spotty recording Steph was able to find on the Alexa, will be enough to put Poppy away for a long, long time. But the rest of them? They'll get interrogated but probably won't turn. Dunamis has trained them well. Maybe Cat and the other one will get fined for taking up illegal arms, but that's about it."

"How is that possible?" I demand, my hands clenched into fists. "They had us cornered. They threatened us. They hurt Fern and Steph!"

"And I believe you. But a jury won't. Not without any evidence."

"They touched things!"

"They were working in there all morning at the shoot. Come on, you three. You know I'm right."

"You're rarely right," I retort.

Simon's dark blue eyes glimmer in challenge. "Is now a good time to bring up how my alarm didn't go off this morning?"

Steph clears her throat, and Fern's mouth curls into a mischievous grin.

"We'll give you two some privacy to do...whatever this is."

I nod, grateful for their discretion. "Hate everyone but you two."

"Hate everybody but you, too," Steph says before dragging Fern away.

Simon takes a seat next to me on the stoop, and I

immediately fall into that crevice in his chest, the one that's perfectly carved to fit my body. He wraps his arms around me and exhales softly.

"So, is now a bad time for me to scold you for sneaking out?" Simon teases. "Imagine my surprise when a woman shook me awake, telling me it was time to go, and I opened my eyes and came face-to-face with your roommate and not you."

I chuckle, thinking about all the times Roommate has rudely woken me up.

Then I swallow.

"That's actually Agent Annie to you," I say.

He nods, then looks off into the distance, pensive. "When she explained who she was, I was shocked. After everything that had happened, I still somehow didn't see that coming."

"Me neither," I agree. "But it makes sense. Even for New York, she was a shit roommate."

Simon chuckles against me, and the sensation vibrates all the way down my body.

"I'm sorry I left you behind," I tell him softly. "I won't do it again."

"Good," he says, kissing my cheek. "Because you're stuck with me. I think I'm going to keep you, Rose Aslani."

A chill runs down my spine at his words.

So assertive. So possessive.

So Simon.

"What do you think Dunamis will have to say about that?" I murmur. "How are we going to bring them down, Simon, when they could be anybody, anywhere, anytime? What are they even planning?"

"Whoa, there." He pulls up my chin with the rough pads

of his fingers so that my face is tilted toward his. "I plan on speaking with every single person in that studio. We'll get our answers, don't you worry. But let's take it one arrest and one day at a time. Today, we took down Poppy Hastings. After years of playing her game, we finally won. Tomorrow, we'll deal with the rest."

I beam, understanding what this means for him.

For us.

"I'm glad you made the arrest," I whisper.

"Thank you," he says. "And it gets better: I'm going to be promoted. The chief just told me. No more desk duty. What will happen to your story?"

I take a moment to consider.

Come to think of it, for a second there, when my life was actually at risk, I forgot about exacting my revenge via byline.

Huh.

"I'm not sure," I confess. "You'll have to give me something headline-worthy from your interrogations to include. Maybe an exclusive with the agent who made the arrest? A lawsuit? Or a missing persons case?"

"Rose Aslani, are you condoning a murderer?"

"Me? Never. That was your basic bartering. I'm Iranian! Plus, I simply support women's empowerment."

Simon moves his hand from my chin to my hair, tugging on my ponytail.

"Is that so?" he says, his eyes dancing. "I guess you'll just have to frisk me for information."

"As Poppy once said, everything has a price." I bite my lip.

Simon kisses that sensitive spot behind my ear, and my toes curl in my sneakers.

"Also, looks like I'm in need of a new roommate," I whimper as he works his way toward my jaw. "Any leads, asshole?"

Then he reaches my lips and kisses me deeply, tentative at first, but then with so much longing that my body melts underneath him, a pool of exhaustion and pure want. Relief. He cradles my face in his hands and looks at me as if I'm his.

And you know what? I think I just might be.

The twelfth rule of conspiracy?

Sometimes you've got to accept that you'll never have it all figured out.

You just have to let go and enjoy the ride.

"Come on, Tulip," he says. "Let's go home."

Epilogue

Ten months later

"Stop touching your face or you're going to ruin your nails!" the nail technician screams at me for the umpteenth time.

I look up from my phone, startled.

"I'm not touching my face," I say, defensive. "Why? Is there something on my face?"

To check, I touch my face.

"Fuck! I just touched my face!"

The nail technician—HELGA, her name tag reads—gives me a glare that could kill a man in less than five seconds. She grabs the hand I'm now using to shield myself from her and examines her work.

She grunts. "You ruined your nails," she says flatly.

"No I didn't!" I pull back my hand hard enough that my fingers slip through hers, smudging the nails completely. "Shit, I ruined my nails!"

Helga shakes her head. "You need to watch your—"

"Language," I interrupt, rolling my eyes. "I know, I know."

Some things never change.

But a lot of others fucking have.

For one, I moved in with Agent Simon in his Alphabet City no-longer-a-bachelor pad. He makes me pancakes on Sunday mornings while singing show tunes from *Heathers: the Musical*, and I haven't yet burned him with my straightening iron in his sleep.

In other words, I think it's going quite well.

When Simon asked me to move in with him, I said absolutely fucking not. It wasn't that I wanted to stay in Clinton Hell, where the man on my street corner started to sound less senile and more like a young Sophocles after midnight. It was just too soon, too sudden, too under the wrong circumstances. I mean, Simon and I were trauma bonded. We had been through some *shit* together. But so had my dentist and me. And you don't see me moving in with Dr. Moscovitz, now do you?

I eventually said yes, of course. The pros just began to outweigh the cons. The way the nape of Simon's neck smells after he showers, for example—like soap and lemon zest. The rush of warmth I get, against my better judgment, when I wake up to the sound of him humming as he slips into one of his tailored suits. The fact that his cabinets hold eight plates and eight bowls and eight glasses, like he's constantly on the verge of hosting an impromptu dinner party. The way he kisses my forehead gently, just the faintest press of his lips, when he thinks I've fallen asleep before him and I feel like letting him.

Fuck it.

I'm in love with Special Agent Simon.

Make fun of me if you want, you stupid whores! I no longer care. I don't know when I became this way. Part of me hates how happy he makes me. What will happen to my edge if I'm dumb and in love? But then I remember that Rose 3.0 doesn't care about her edge. She just wants to live in the moment with Simon and his Broadway recordings and his butterfly kisses and his pocket boners in our little apartment until he shoots me with a tranquilizer gun and forces me to move to the suburbs and raise chickens. Or whatever.

I love seeing Rose 3.0 through his eyes. She's confident and cocky and, above all else, comfortable as hell being who she is. She's not Middle Eastern or American or a Brooklynite or a New Yorker. She's not even a journalist or a conspiracy theorist.

She's just Rose Aslani.

And somehow, that's enough for both of us.

When I first had the revelation that Simon loved me, unequivocally and wholeheartedly, for exactly who I was, I called Fern and Steph in a panic. Steph picked up on the first ring. Fern picked up on the third. I told them I was thinking of letting my asshole hair grow out again. Steph was appalled but respected my choice. Fern didn't really get what the big deal was. She'd never waxed her asshole, she explained to me. The hair wasn't even long enough to braid.

My friends both left the Shred after the incident. They decided that going back would be too difficult. Nothing like being bound and gagged by your coworkers to create a hostile office environment, you know? Steph decided that after years of being afraid to take time off or look over her shoulder, she was ready to be her own boss. She's working as a freelance software engineer and graphic designer. She pays her rent by upcharging rich Upper East Side twits for websites using Squarespace and WordPress templates, which literally take her half an hour to make. Then she spends the rest of her time on her dream project: coding an app called Bathroom Confessionals, which allows women who met wasted in bar bathrooms and didn't exchange contact info to find each other and become real-life friends. It's like missed connections for the drunkest girls at the party. I couldn't love her more.

Fern, on the other hand, accepted a bigwig job at HBO, running the social channels for all their queer content. She won't tell me how much money they're paying her, but she did move into her very own apartment in Greenpoint, and it has a private terrace, so I'm guessing a lot. I'm not surprised, though—Fern was always the most famous person at the Shred, the girl everyone wanted to be friends with despite no one understanding that her sardonic sense of humor meant she didn't actually like them back. I've always felt special knowing that she chose Steph and me. I guess we all chose each other. She's been single for about six months—perhaps her longest dry spell ever—and she's been teaching herself how to play the upright bass on her nights in. The other day, she even made an earnest, kind remark about the sweater-vest someone was wearing at brunch. I choked. There wasn't a wisp of sarcasm wafting anywhere near her. Her pranking days are behind her.

The last project she worked on at The Shred was Poppy Hastings's cover.

For a few months after Poppy's arrest, I had nightmares. Visceral ones, the kind where you wake up shaking and covered in sweat and smelling like a dumpster. I pictured Poppy face-to-face with me, threatening me with her words and taunting me with her eyes. I heard Brad Zarbos's last words, desperate and fleeting, as the life drained from his lips. I could even hear the sirens of the police cars Simon arrived with, which whisked her away to the precinct where she awaited trial.

But the trauma of her arrest began to melt away, like all hard things do, with time. The summer heat grew sullen and turned into a light fog, then into a harsh, cold winter. I remained inside and eventually stopped hearing footsteps behind me, following me wherever I went. Simon and I played old-fashioned board games like Monopoly and Candy Land and Scrabble, games I had sworn off because they reminded me of my childhood. My father always tried so desperately to get us to play, my mother mumbling in confusion but pretending to understand the rules so the night wouldn't end in another squabble.

And when winter finally drew its last breath, we visited them, Simon and me, in Ohio. My father took him out for a burger and asked him what his intentions were, as my mother confessed to me while we drank gimlets and watched *Legally Blonde*. I giggled to myself, imagining Simon's bright red face in the dimly lit tavern, choking on beer as my father asked if he planned to make an honest woman out of me. That weekend was the best time I'd spent with my parents in a long while. When I told them I'd started taking Farsi classes in an effort to connect to my heritage, they didn't get defensive or throw a fit. They didn't ask me about my five-year plan, and I didn't lose my temper when my mother begged me to let her take me to her salon so they could try something new with my hair. I had a feeling it would end in a wax, and I didn't feel like telling my mother I'd decided to "let myself go."

When we got home after that trip, I slept through the night for the first time without waking up to check my phone for an anonymous text.

Then and there, I knew I'd be okay.

Watching the internet turn on Poppy didn't hurt, either. First there was the hashtag #PoppyHastingsIsOverParty, followed by the think pieces, of course. None of them could trump my feature story for the Shred, though: photos taken the day of Poppy's arrest, accompanied by the headline AMERICA'S CELEBRITY SERIAL KILLER. The piece was a literal bloody revelation, detailing all of Poppy's criminal offenses now that they were part of the public record. It was also a cat-and-mouse tale about a writer and her subject and the ways in which they had taunted and played with each other until they'd both cracked wide open.

The lucky thirteenth (and final) rule of conspiracy? When all else fails, fall back on what you know.

The truth.

Following my article's publication, all the companies who had signed Poppy dropped their brand deals overnight. A bunch of them published statements about the dangers of giving the wrong people power, about glamorizing people who do criminally bad things, about the ways in which theorizing on the internet can lead to a slippery slope of madness. You name it, someone wrote it. Netflix ripped up her hundred-million-dollar contract and instead reached out to buy the film and TV rights to my story, which I happily sold. I'm living off the advance as we speak.

The best part of all? Poppy Hastings's murder trial wasn't even televised, thanks to a personal plea from my FBI connection. Nope, Poppy was quietly convicted and transferred to a supermax prison to serve three back-to-back life sentences. Her social media accounts were all disabled. YouTube took down her vlogs. Hulu even deleted her episode of *SNL.*

When it was announced that the princess of Denmark was secretly running orgies out of her summer palace and Twitter ate it up like a vegan corn dog, I knew it was game over. The people had forgotten Poppy Hastings. The cultural zeitgeist had moved on.

She had been sentenced to the most tragic fate of all: irrelevance.

And I was stuck in the rubble of her demise, left to figure out who I was without her.

I'm still learning how to be okay with being just me, Rose Aslani—1.0, 2.0, 3.0, infinity. It doesn't matter. I am who I fucking am. I haven't completely changed my personality. I've just evolved into a slightly superior human being. My flaws, my mistakes, my instincts—they all inform the person I am today. But I'm back in weekly therapy, regularly attending NA and AA meetings, and I've cut out the people who dismissed my concerns as a "meltdown" and consistently made me feel "crazy." I wouldn't be who I am if I hadn't written that article, drunk dialed Zain, dived through that dumpster, or kicked Simon in the balls. And how much fun would that be? No fucking fun at all, if I may say so myself.

Living in the present isn't easy, but I'm working on it. It's like flexing a muscle that has been in a cast for months. You have to start slow, with tiny subtle movements, until you build up your strength. I like to pay attention to my surroundings and report certain observations to myself out loud. It's like I Spy, except I only play with myself. I suppose that's a good thing—I need something new to amuse me now that my friends and I have put our pranks (okay, fine, lies) to rest.

Like, right now, as I walk through the East Village and toward Simon's (my! our!) apartment, I strut by a group of teenagers passing around a pack of cigarettes. One of them lights the wrong end and sticks it in his mouth, confused about why it's not working when he inhales. His friends howl at him, recording the entire event on their phones.

"Losers," I say out loud, making an observation.

"Kids," I correct myself a moment later.

I pass a thrift shop with a rainbow assortment of worn-in Hawaiian button-downs in the window for thirty dollars a pop. "Overpriced," I say to myself. Then I see a man taking a shit on the steps of a church. "Hilarious," I observe. I FaceTime Simon to show him, but he doesn't pick up. I try calling, but it goes straight to voicemail. He must be on the subway. I settle for snapping a quick picture and continue walking.

I pass a new-age matcha bar painted head-to-toe in mint green with a line of young girls out the door and around the corner. "Tourists."

There's a couple having a violently loud fight on the street corner. He grabs at her pocket and pulls out her phone. She screams at the top of her lungs and hits him over the head with her purse. He staggers backward, then runs away. "Badass."

Cherry blossoms from a nearby tree on Avenue A float above my forehead, hailing down on my shoulders. Instead of flicking off the flower petals with my signature Rose cynicism, I actively accept the smile spreading across my face. I place one behind my ear, then catch my reflection in a Greek appliance store window. My cheeks look flushed, and my hair flows behind me, an unruly mess in the wind. I look happy.

"Progress."

There's a sports bar, the kind with outdoor picnic tables and umbrellas and groups of men in jerseys holding pints and melting barley, shouting over each other and fighting for the best view of the wide-screen. One television in the center of the outdoor setup is showing a Yankees game. Men with real New York accents, black stubble, and gold chains bang their fists on the tables and slobber all over their chest hair.

I approach our block, then use my own set of keys to let myself into the building. The four flights of stairs take it out of me, and I'm panting by the time I make it to our floor. When I reach our door, I collapse, pouring all my weight onto the handle. But it's open, and I accidentally fall inside, catching myself at the very last second.

"You forgot to lock the door again!" I call out to Simon.

Silence echoes back through the apartment.

I take a step inside and immediately feel my stomach churn.

Our apartment looks ransacked.

The books and records are splayed all over the floor, the hardwood scuffed. Mugs are shattered, photos from Simon's childhood torn out of albums. The space now looks like it belongs to a squatter.

Were we robbed?

I take a deep breath and enter the bedroom. The bathroom was hit, too—there are products all over the floor, my toothbrush is in the toilet, and Simon's wash kit has been plucked from the medicine cabinet.

When I enter the bedroom, my heart drops.

All of Simon's clothes are gone.

I double-check, then triple-check. Not a single thing of mine is out of place. My jeans are folded neatly on the storage shelves. My T-shirts sit crumpled in the hamper. Every sneaker, every sweatshirt is there. Even my one good blazer for boring networking events is swinging from a hanger. But nothing of Simon's remains. Just the lingering smell of lemon zest and the faint hum of a show tune.

Did Simon leave me?

He wouldn't do this to me.

Would he?

He loves me.

Doesn't he?

That's when I find the note sitting squarely on my pillow like a hotel mint. There's a red lipstick print on the bottom. I touch it, and a tiny bit of red pigment comes off on my finger. It's fresh. A shiver runs through my body until every inch of me is shaking. Fern and Steph will have to come over to comfort me. To figure out what the hell we're going to do. If I have a panic attack, if I die of a goddamn broken heart, they'll find me here and piece me back together. It's what we do.

I take a deep breath and read.

You know where to find me.

We'll be waiting for you.

My knees feel weak, like mashed potatoes. I crumple to the floor and swallow my sob. The first thought that comes to me is so bleak that I can barely process it.

Dunamis has kidnapped Simon.

But then I flip over the card, and what I see guts me like a fish.

There, printed on the back, is a symbol.

Thick, black. Four distorted circles, two open and two closed.

A pair of eyes, always watching.

The mark of Dunamis.

And the very symbol that Simon has tattooed on his shoulder.

Beneath it, a tiny inscription:

That third act reversal? I never saw it coming.

Genius, darling.

NEXT FROM

Iman Hariri-Kia

Coming Fall 2025

Chapter One

"So, let me get this straight: You're breaking up with me to be with someone who *doesn't exist*?"

A dribble of Busch Light trickles its way down Job's chin like a loose tear. Sighing, I pick up my napkin and dab. "Not to be with," I explain for the zillionth time. "Because of."

The line cook calls out an order from the back of the house. A baby emphatically flaps his arms, knocking over a large Sprite. Job tugs at the bottom of his "The Spice Must Flow!" T-shirt, a nervous tick I almost immediately picked up on after meeting him. At first, I found it kind of endearing. I mean, *I make him uncomfortable! That must mean he* really *likes me, right?* But after a couple of weeks, I came to the unfortunate conclusion that it's just another coping mechanism, one that allows him to avoid confrontation (and eye contact) for as long as humanly possible.

In total, Job and I spent about three months dating, but so little of that time was quality that it might as well have been three minutes—which is, coincidentally, about how long he lasts in bed.

If I'm being generous.

"I don't get it," he whines. "That's make believe. This is reality. You do know he's not going to come to life, right?"

"Yes, I know he's not going to come to life," I snap. "And quite frankly, the implication that I, a woman, can't discern fact from fiction manages to be both misogynistic and idiotic. So, congratulations. You're not only a sexist. You're a tool, too."

Job pulls at his wheat-like hair, his face flushing tomato red. "If you know that he's not real, then why are you leaving me?"

I roll my eyes.

"*Because I am looking for a great love. One that could bring the gods to their knees and spin the earth off its axis*," I recite from heart. "And Ryke has taught me that I don't need to settle for less than I'm worth. That there are men out there that will put in the work, the time, and the effort, to get to know the real me. To be there for me. To really fall in love with me."

Job snivels in his seat, and I fight the urge to cringe.

Honestly? I can't believe I once believed that Job "Space Travel Is The Next Frontier" Pesce could possibly be my one true love. Sure, when I came across his dating app profile last fall, I found him to be mildly attractive. Between his wisps of yellow hair, pale complexion, and five-foot-ten (five-foot-nine, I'd come to discover; predictably, he lied about his height in his bio) stature, he looked nothing like Ryke. But he had a niche Jonas Brothers' lyric in his prompts and a sort of mysterious, closed-mouth smile in his photographs, one that compelled me to swipe right.

That smirk screamed danger. I wanted to know all of his secrets.

On our first date, he took me to the planetarium, where I immediately began stacking red flags like pancakes. He didn't hold the door open for me. Red flag. When I was telling him what I studied in college, he cut me off before I could finish. Red flag. I asked him his favorite Taylor Swift song, and he said, "Shake it off." Red fucking flag. But then the lights shut off, the ceiling lit up, and Neil DeGrasse Tyson's voice boomed from the speaker system. Hundreds of constellations glittered overhead. The earth spun in hypnotic motion. And as we watched a detailed recreation of the Big Bang, an event that literally expanded the universe and created the world as we know it, Job put his arm around me and leaned down to whisper in my ear. "You remind me of a star," he said. "You shine so bright."

I mean, first of all, cringe.

Still, my breath hitched. Despite the extreme levels of corniness, the sentiment reminded me *exactly* of something Ryke might have said.

Suddenly, the red flags I'd noticed before started to look really pink.

Before I could overthink it, I leaned over and kissed him. He opened his eyes in surprise as I crashed our lips together. For several seconds, nothing happened. I held my breath and waited. For the room to spin and time to stop. For my heart to explode out of my chest and my vagina to grow a pulse. To feel something.

Anything.

But all I felt was his semi-hard boner pressing up against my leg.

The relationship should have ended then and there. And it would have, had I not promised my brother, Tey, that I'd give the next guy I dated a serious chance. So, I stuck it out for a few months, hoping the tide would turn, that I'd sense that "aha" moment, when everything clicks into place. But the bond never solidified. I got tired of laughing at his borderline offensive jokes and faking orgasms when I could have been at home. Reading. Writing. Spending quality time with Ryke.

Now tears, actual tears, well in his eyes. I exhale, preparing myself for what will inevitably come next. All of them do this when I break up with them. Every single goddamn time. They cry. They scream. They call me names. I usually just have to wait it out, like you would a petulant toddler throwing a tantrum. They're reeling from the familiar sting of rejection. But the funny thing is, they don't actually want me either. Not the real me, anyway. It's companionship that they're after.

What really tickles my fucking pickle? Not a single one of these men ever expects to be dumped! Isn't that absolutely baffling? Even when they've done literally nothing to deserve being in a relationship. They're not looking for a partner, but someone to make them feel special. A woman who is willing to thank them for doing the bare minimum—with a smile to boot. And that's not me.

Not anymore.

"But I treat you like a queen," he complains.

Now I really have to laugh. "Job. Be fucking for real. You never text me first. Whenever we go out, I have to take the initiative and make a plan. Your background is a picture of you and your mother—that your ex took. Oh, and you never go down on me."

"I'm Italian!" He cries.

I shake my head sadly. "No, Job," I say. "You're a pussy."

"You bitch!" Angry now, he slams his fists on the table and stands up suddenly, inadvertently causing a scene. The rest of the room turns around, taking note of us. Him, sweat circles lining his armpits and steam coming out of his nostrils. Me, legs crossed and hands intertwined on the table. I'm the picture of composure, which only serves to underline and escalate his hysteria.

The line cook pauses to listen in.

That baby sucks its thumb.

Job's forehead vein begins to throb.

"Those dumb romance books you read have given you unrealistic expectations. And it's not like you ever had time for me anyway. Always writing your dumb flipflops—"

"Fanfics," I correct him.

Very popular fanfics, at that.

"Whatever."

We're in the final stretch now. I can feel it. He's about to cut his losses and go home. Later, he'll call his mother to cry and complain. If his friends ask, he'll tell them he ended things because he realized that he's out of my league. I'm not hot enough. He can do *so* much better. Etcetera.

Good.

I'm fucking starving.

The sooner he settles on this course of action, the sooner I get to eat.

Job takes one last swig of his beer, then attempts to look me dead in the face. Unfortunately, he's pissed, so it comes out a bit cross-eyed. I choke on another laugh.

"Face it, Joonie. There were always three people in this relationship: You, me, and Ryke."

"No, Job," I stand up and pat him gently on the head, like a wounded animal. "There was only ever me and Ryke."

That about does it.

Job blinks once.

Twice.

The crowd returns to their own personal crises, bored with our antics. My phone buzzes in the palm of my other hand. I think about the laundry I left unfolded on my bed, how many episodes of *Love Island* I need to watch before I'm caught up. Job gives me one last desperate, pleading look.

I shake my head.

And he walks out the door.

Relieved, I sit back down and open up a menu. Minutes later, I flag down the waiter.

"Can I please put in an order of fries and a carafe of wine?"

He nods, scribbling away quickly on his notepad. "That was quite the show."

"Sorry about that," I wince. "Some guys just don't know when to take a hint, you know?"

The waiter smiles. I know exactly what he's thinking.

I'm in on this joke. I am not like other guys. I am the exception to the rule.

I drink him in. The lean lines of his torso straining his apron. The dimple indenting his left cheek. The sandy curl of his hair. He's cute, don't get me wrong. First love interest material.

But he's no Ryke.

"Dining alone then, miss?" He asks.

I smile and shake my head.

"I've got company."

The waiter walks away, confused. His brows furrowed and his head hung low.

And I take out my book and begin to read.

Reading Group Guide

1. *The Most Famous Girl in the World* satirizes several literary genres, holding a mirror to the art of fiction and finding humor in the common tropes and archetypes throughout modern literature. What tools or techniques does the author use to create satire? What genres and tropes are reflected in this satire?

2. If Poppy Hastings were a real person, how do you think the media would treat her? Would she become a household name? Would she be condemned as a criminal? Celebrated as a scammer icon?

3. Be honest, would you be a fan (or a follower) of Poppy Hastings in the real world?

4. Both the protagonist and antagonist in this novel—Rose and Poppy, respectively—share their names with flowers, and at one point, Rose uses the name Tulip as an alias. Do you see any symbolism in this connection? What does this say about the characters in the novel?

5. What was your initial impression of Simon? Did you trust him? Were you suspicious of his motives or standing with the FBI?

6. What does "camp" mean to you, and how did you see it at work in this novel?

7. This novel examines some of the most nuanced and bizarre aspects of modern society, but one question stands above all: How do we choose who to make famous, and *why* do we turn people into celebrities?

A Conversation with the Author

What inspired you to write *The Most Famous Girl in the World*?

I first had the idea for this novel back in 2021. My friends, fiancé, and I were at dinner discussing the rumor that Trump had allegedly promised to pardon "Tiger King," who was serving time for attempted murder-for-hire. My partner, Matthew, turned to me and asked, "Can you imagine if the most famous person in the world was an actual *murderer* and people just didn't care?" The wheels in my brain immediately started turning. I called my agent with the synopsis two days later.

In the years since I began working on this novel, the question that inspired the text has only grown more relevant. Anna Delvey has her own house-arrest reality show and a Netflix adaptation. Elizabeth Holmes was given a redemptive *New York Times* profile and has rebranded as "Liz." More than ever, America seems fascinated by antiheroes, women's wrongs, and the conspiracy and lore behind people's ill decisions and power plays. How far would a charming celebrity con have to go to turn the public against them? That's what Rose, myself, and this campy satire of a story would love to unpack.

Your debut novel, *A Hundred Other Girls*, was published two years prior to the release of *The Most Famous Girl in the World*. How has your writing process changed since your first book? Do you have any advice for debut authors?

So much of my process—and life!—has changed since I first sat down to write *A Hundred Other Girls*. At the time, I was working both a full-time editorial and a part-time freelance writing job. My debut novel was the first project that I had complete creative control over, from ideation to creation. I truly allowed my imagination to run rampant, to write the kind of coming-of-age story that I'd always wanted to read as a new adult. My dream was to one day pay my rent with my words.

By the time I sat down to work on revisions for *The Most Famous Girl in the World*, I was living my dream come true: I am officially a full-time writer and author! I was also no longer creating experientially, but for consumption—writing and editing with an audience in mind and attempting to cater to my readers. This proved to be a challenge in its own right, as my brain became slightly overcrowded by the voices and opinions of others. But you can't write a perfect book for everyone, and learning that was a true lesson in patience and self-trust.

My biggest piece of advice to debut authors remains the same: Finish! That! Draft! So often, aspiring writers talk themselves out of finishing their manuscripts because they lose interest in the idea, feel overwhelmed by plot holes, or want to alter the character development. But if you force yourself to finish that first draft, you can go back and address those issues in the revision stage. Remember: you can't edit a book that doesn't exist and sometimes, a messy manuscript is better than a perfect first paragraph. And I want to read your story.

***The Most Famous Girl in the World* takes place in the same universe as your debut novel, and the protagonist Rose even mentions a few characters from *A Hundred Other Girls* by name. Why did you choose to intertwine these worlds?**

Thank you for noticing! *The Most Famous Girl in the World* and *A Hundred Other Girls* coexist in the same universe for several different reasons. The first, of course, is fan-service: I wanted to create Easter eggs for devoted readers. I'm a huge fandom girlie and absolutely love any and all opportunities to look for connections between stand-alones by the same author. So being given the chance to create that excitement in my own works of fiction is thrilling.

The second boils down to three little words: New York City. I've always been fascinated by novelists who are able to cast their backdrops as characters. As someone born and based in New York, I wanted to world-build a version of the city that felt almost fantastical, that would be experienced differently based on the borough, neighborhood, or local. Noora and Rose both have very different relationships to New York City, but I love the idea that at any point in time, they could both be sitting across from each other on the subway and be none the wiser.

Finally, the third reason has to do with my favorite topic of conversation: representation versus tokenization. Both of my novels center around Middle Eastern American female protagonists, but their experiences as first-generation citizens have been vastly different. By acknowledging their awareness of each other, I hope to underline that Middle Eastern women do not exist in a monolith: their stories are varied, their personalities are unique, and the way they interact with their identity depends entirely on the individual.

This novel is full of unique and larger-than-life characters—like Roommate and Poppy, to name a few. Which character was your favorite to write?

I love this question! In case it wasn't abundantly clear from my backlist, I'm obsessed with writing messy, complicated, and, at times, unlikable marginalized characters.

While I absolutely adore Rose and Poppy (and need to further explore their relationship to each other on page at a later date), my favorite characters in *The Most Famous Girl in the World* are Steph and Fern. Not only are they hilarious and utterly relatable, they're also such *good* friends. They hold each other accountable and love unconditionally. And I believe that the people we meet and trauma-bond with in toxic work environments like the Shred and *Vinyl* will be our people for life.

Hence: *I hate everybody but you.*

Separately, I need Leila from *A Hundred Other Girls* and Fern to meet more than my next breath.

What was the most challenging aspect of writing this manuscript?

Although there was a lot of humor and inside baseball in *A Hundred Other Girls*, this was my first time writing satire. *The Most Famous Girl in the World* tells a story of one extremely exaggerated worst-case scenario, and the biggest challenge when writing and revising was letting the reader know that the novel is self-aware, without overtly telling them. The line between wink and nod, and screaming, "THIS IS CAMP," felt impossibly thin at times. But by messing around with meta narratives, formatting, and breaking the fourth wall, I think we accomplished what felt like a particularly demanding feat.

Additionally, while *A Hundred Other Girls* was primarily focused on identity exploitation, *The Most Famous Girl in the World* navigates mental illness and substance use disorder. It was very important to me that Rose be allowed to unravel and hit the dark depths of rock bottom that are messy to write and not very pretty to read about, while also being afforded the levity to poke fun at herself and her situation. I think that women of color in fiction are still, more often than not, rarely given the grace and space to be complex and unpleasant on page in the same way as their white counterparts. With the help of my editors and sensitivity readers, I am proud that Rose is being given the opportunity to make peace with all of the past, present, and future iterations of herself.

What message or feeling do you hope readers take away from this novel?

Well, after that ending, I hope their tummies hurt from laughing and their throats are sore from screaming!

In all seriousness, I love that *The Most Famous Girl in the World* is both a super fun but also surprisingly insightful read. It is my hope that readers will leave with a greater understanding of why we, as a society, choose to make certain people famous, as well as the psychological reason that we tend to hyperfixate on people who are so bad that they make us feel good about ourselves.

It is also my intention that this novel lead to a larger meditation on mass hysteria, online conspiracy, and how a thought so small can spiral into movement that feels larger than life—especially as we head into an election year.

Finally, I hope that Rose's relationship to her Middle Eastern American identity and experience as a fractured, first-generation observer will serve as a reminder that marginalized people contain multitudes and do not have a one-size-fits-all, easily packaged understanding of their personhood. Most of us are just trying to figure it out, little by little, day by day.

I see bits and pieces of myself in both Rose and Noora's journeys, and I hope you do, too.

Acknowledgments

The Most Famous Girl in the World is a true labor of love, and one that could not exist without the following people, my people.

This novel would not have happened without the support of my incredible agent, Taylor Haggerty, who I called in April 2021 and excitedly word-vomited the entire plot. Thank you, Taylor, for championing all of my ideas, even the unhinged ones. I don't know what I would do without you in my corner. And thank you to the entire Root Literary team, especially Jasmine Brown, for convincing me that this was a story I could share with readers after safeguarding it in my head for so long.

To my editor, Kate Roddy, who not only understands, but loves my characters as if they were her own: Thank you for your patience as we nailed the tone, pacing, and precision of this story. Thank you for cheering on Rose throughout every step of her journey. And thank you for dealing with my neuroses—I was so nervous to write a follow-up, and you alleviated so much of that fear through trust and empathy. I am very grateful.

A big thank-you to my marketer extraordinaire, Cristina Arreola, and brilliant publicist, Kathleen Carter, for always getting it right. I swear to god, sometimes it feels like you two are in my head or something. Thank you for all of the hard work that you pour into these projects and for giving *The Most Famous Girl* the best chance of success. Y'all really are the dream team.

To the rest of the Sourcebooks family: Thank you so much for believing in me and my ideas. You make me feel so cared for and appreciated. To the design team, Brittany Vibbert and Kelly Lawler, thank you for seeing this book's potential and your determination to nail this cover. To my beautiful cover designer, Emily Mahon, thank you for bringing my dreams to life. You are a magician. And to Jessica Thelander, Thea Voutiritsas, and Dee Hudson, thank you for your copy edits, sensitivity feedback, and ensuring that every single reader feels seen, heard, and cared for throughout the pages of this book. Thank you for taking their safety seriously.

Addison Duffy, you are simply the best. Thank you for fangirling over everything that I write. Nobody does it quite like you.

To my parents, Gisue Hariri and Bahman Kia: Thank you for the unconditional love and support. Please do not read the spicy scenes in this book. To my sister, Ava Hariri-Kia: Thank you for being my favorite person. I want to grow up to be just like you. To my aunt, Mojgan Hariri: Thank you for being my number one cheerleader. And to my grandfather, Karim Hariri: At 98, thank you for waiting so patiently over the past two years for this novel to hit shelves.

Ariel Matluck and Simone Rivera, thank you for listening to all of the voice notes and always being there to drink a BOW and talk it out. I love you both very much. Willa Bennett and Melanie Mignucci, thank you for all of the coffee runs, smoothie walks, and phone booth cry sessions. You two are never getting rid of me. Ashlie Williams, thank you for always being so excited on my behalf. Cassidy Sachs, thank you for answering all of my questions, always. Alexandra Falkner, thank you for my beautiful website makeover. Audrey Ellen and Ivor Jackson, thank you for attending the dinner that sparked the idea for this book. (Simone—yes, you were there, too. But I already acknowledged you.)

Dr. J, thank you for teaching me that all of the success in the world means nothing if you're not physically and mentally well enough to appreciate it. Writing a sophomore novel turned out to be much scarier than I anticipated, and there were times when my impostor syndrome felt paralyzing and my self-doubt felt crippling. Thank you for helping me acknowledge and celebrate the small wins. I would not have been able to go through this process again without you.

To all of the booktokers, bookstagrammers, booktubers, and book bloggers who screamed from the rooftops about *A Hundred Other Girls*: Thank you for making every single one of my dreams come true. I am so grateful for each and every one of you. To my readers, my Cherry Pickers, my community members who have been here since the beginning: Thank you for being the most kind, considerate, thoughtful space on the internet. Thank you for interacting with everything that I write with curiosity and in good faith. I couldn't do this without you. I feel incredibly privileged to have you all in my life.

And finally: to the love of my life, my husband to be, the first person who reads everything that I write, Matthew Falkner. Thank you for always asking, "What if?" I love you.

About the Author

© Louisiana Mei Gelpi

Iman Hariri-Kia is a writer, editor, and author born and based in New York City. An award-winning journalist, she covers sex, relationships, identity, and adolescence. Her work has appeared in *Vogue*, *New York Magazine*'s The Cut, *Harper's Bazaar*, *Cosmopolitan*, *Teen Vogue*, and more. Her debut novel, *A Hundred Other Girls*, was published in July 2022 to critical acclaim. You can often find her writing about her personal life on the internet, much to her parents' dismay.